THE MEANING OF NAMES

THE MEANING OF NAMES

a novel

KAREN   GETTERT   SHOEMAKER

 RED HEN PRESS | *Pasadena, CA*

Book design and layout by Mark E. Cull
Cover design by Nicholas Smith

Library of Congress Cataloging-in-Publication Data

Shoemaker, Karen Gettert, 1957–
  The meaning of names : a novel / Karen Gettert Shoemaker.—First edition.
    pages cm
  ISBN 978-1-59709-959-2 (alk. paper)
  1. German American women—Fiction. 2. World War, 1914–1918—United States—Fiction. 3. German Americans—Violence against—Fiction. 4. Familes—Fiction. 5. Influenza Epidemic, 1918–1919—Fiction. 6. Nebraska—Fiction. 7. Domestic fiction.
  I. Title.
  PS3619.H64M43 2014
  813'.6—dc23
                    2013031148

The Los Angeles County Arts Commission, the National Endowment for the Arts, the Pasadena Arts & Cultural Commission and the City of Pasadena Cultural Affairs Division, Sony Pictures Entertainment, the Los Angeles Department of Cultural Affairs, and the Dwight Stuart Youth Fund partially support Red Hen Press.

First Edition
Published by Red Hen Press
www.redhen.org

ACKNOWLEDGMENTS

The list of people to whom I am grateful begins and ends, as all such lists do, with my parents, Floyd and Christine Gettert, and with my siblings, Linda Kallhoff, Joan Gilbreth, Sandra Bates, Duane Gettert, Larry Gettert, and Barbara Waterman. It expands to include my extended (and extensive) family of beloved aunts, uncles, cousins, nieces, nephews, in-laws, and a few outlaws. We are a family rich in storytellers and listeners. The world needs both kinds.

I am also grateful to Pam Barger, Marge Saiser, Mary Pipher, Twyla Hansen, Kelly Madigan, and a host of other writers who have supported and encouraged me over the years, including my fellow faculty at the University of Nebraska MFA in Writing Program.

I am deeply grateful for the time and monetary support afforded me through the Nebraska Arts Council, the Kimmel Harding Nelson Center, and Brush Creek Foundation for the Arts.

And finally I want to thank my husband Dave Shoemaker and my children, Ryan and Raina. They are at the heart of all my stories, all my life.

In embryonic life, a baby girl's ovaries are endowed with a fixed number of ova and at birth they will contain all the eggs her body will ever produce. In organs no bigger than the very tip of her mother's little finger are nestled the seeds of the next generation.

"We are nesting boxes," our mother told us,
"the future always within us."

THE MEANING OF NAMES

CHAPTER ONE

When Gerda was five, her older sister came home to die. No, not to die, to give birth, but dying is what she did. She had married one of the Ernesti boys, one of the boys their father approved of—Gerda could see that even then. At the age of five she knew how to read what her father wanted, what her father believed—that certain people were chosen, that worldly success marked God's favor. When Phillip asked for her sister's hand in marriage, it was as if Papa Drueke fell in love with her as well. Her value, uncertain before, became suddenly apparent. Papa knew of whom God would approve, and that wealthy Ernesti boy was one of them. He paraded the news of the engagement as if the young man was a prize he himself had won. When the Uncles stopped over, he bragged about him like he'd never bragged about his own. His chest puffed up like a prairie grouse whenever he said his name—"my son-in-law, Phillip Chiles Ernesti," as if his older brothers, those men in whose presence he had been so often silenced, wouldn't know who he was talking about if he didn't say the whole name.

Elizabeth was fourteen years older than Gerda. She had long fingers, blunt at the ends as if she had been born for scrabbling and working. She had a scar on the fleshy pad at the base of her thumb where a rooster had caught her with its sharp beak the day Gerda was born. She had been sent outside, away from their mother's labor bed when that feathered beast came at her all wings and shrieks. She should have been scared, she told Gerda years later, but when she saw the bloody, jagged *S* on her hand she knew the baby they had waited for would be born alive, and a girl.

"*S* is for *sister*," she used to whisper to Gerda as they curled their bodies together before sleep. "*S* is for *shelter*." She traced the shape of the letter on her hand. "Gerda means *shelter*. Remember that." Gerda learned to write by recalling the shape of the scar. Beginning with *S* she moved outward to all letters, all language.

Gerda can see her hands and that scar even now, though she can no longer recall the details of her face. She no longer knows if her Elizabeth's eyes were gray like Papa's or brown like her own. Her hair was dark and thick and curled easily into the chignon she always wore. When she stood, the top of her head was even with the wardrobe in the room they shared and she seemed big as all heaven to Gerda. But her face, Gerda can't remember her face, only her hands.

Mama and the women who came to help didn't see Gerda when the screaming started. She slipped from the doorway to the narrow space beneath the bed while they held her sister down. She stayed there all day and half the night, and nobody went looking for her. Elizabeth's cries filled the house, so no one noticed Gerda's absence. Under the bed she could watch the weight of her sister buckle and roll with the pains that wracked her, Gerda's face so close to the thin bed slats. Women's feet moved sometimes fast sometimes slow past the arc of her vision. Only inches from Gerda, they could have been miles away.

When Gerda heard someone say, "It's almost over," she pressed her hands against the rough burlap underside of the mattress, right where she thought the baby would be and she prayed. "Oh most gracious Virgin Mary . . ." Her voice caught in her throat. She couldn't remember the words that Elizabeth had taught her. She tried desperately to recall the Memorare. She mixed it up with what she could remember from the Hail Mary, "Holy Mary, Mother of God, pray for us sinners, now and at the hour of our death—" but the word *death* frightened her even more than Lizzie's screams, and she forgot the words of even that simple prayer. "Oh most gracious Virgin Mary," she whispered again, turning it into a chant. "Oh most gracious Virgin Mary oh most gracious Virgin Mary oh most gracious . . ." She repeated the phrase until silence settled hard into the room.

Her right hand, when her fight had ended, hung over the edge of the bed just inches from Gerda's face. Gerda reached out slowly. With the tip of her finger she traced the scar at the base of Elizabeth's thumb until someone pulled her hand away to fold it across her chest.

They buried her on a rise out back of St. Michael's. Phillip Chiles Ernesti named the baby Marie and put her in the same pine box. He kept the cash Elizabeth had brought to the marriage bed and never darkened the Drueke threshold again.

Mama's face took on the solid paleness of the tombstone that day and the woman who had been their mother never gazed again from the darkness of her eyes. And Papa—Papa walked away alone from that mound of dirt. Gerda can still see his black funeral coat receding ahead of them. When a cold, gray wind whipped dried leaves into a fury around Gerda and her mother, he disappeared from sight. Gerda clutched the coarse wool of her mother's skirt, afraid she too would be spun away by the wind, and called, "Papa! Wait!" until someone shushed her.

She thought it was Elizabeth's voice and, God forgive her, she hid her face from her sister as she would from a beast of wings and shrieks. Gerda ran after her father. Crying, she left her sister behind on that rise back of St. Michael's. How could she know another scar was forming even as she ran? The beginning of a language she could not bear to speak.

JANUARY, 1918

"I know you, Fritz Vogel," Gerda whispered. "You just want me to miss my train."

He feigned sleep, snoring softly and rhythmically into the small dish formed at the back of her neck. Wisps of her heavy hair swayed in response to his breath. His arms wrapped around her, his big hands cupped her soft belly, and his legs entwined with hers. Under cover of quilts and darkness she was completely trapped. To free herself she turned not away but toward him and closed her eyes. She trailed her lips along his collarbone, pausing at the hollow at the base of his throat, then fanned her hands around his ribs— that cage of his heart—and pulled him toward her. The weight of his desire settled into her and time slipped skin on skin toward morning.

She held him even as one small part of her rose from the bed and prepared to leave. Her mind checked the list she had made the day before when the telegram came. Her sister's terse message gave her scant time to respond in any way but with movement, and she began immediately to get ready to travel to her aunt's funeral. She had no time to consider her welcome at the other end or Fritz's response to her leaving. She mentally counted out the clothes she had packed for the three boys she would bring with her and rethought the instructions she had written out for her daughter, who would stay with Fritz. Breathing in the musky scent of him, she held the image of the train tickets in her satchel alongside the image of the food she had prepared for Katie—canned beef and corn, salt pork—easy choices an eight-year-old could handle. The boys she had bathed the night before, the trunk they would share already packed and loaded into the wagon. Sighing at the trill of pleasure that came with Fritz's lips beneath her earlobes, she remembered the lunch that still needed to be packed for the trip, the chickens that still needed to be fed, the items needed to occupy those rambunctious boys for the long hours ahead.

She had moved quickly after she read the wire. Sorting out the cleanest clothes and ironing while Katie and the two oldest boys took turns cranking the agitator on the washing machine, pushing each shirt and pair of trousers one by one through the wringer.

"Work fast," she had said to Frank and Ray, "but don't get your hands caught in the wringer." She showed them the lever to pop if the clothes or, God forbid, one of their hands got caught between the rollers. Everyday dangers offered a new chance and a new way for her to teach them to save themselves. "I can't be everywhere," she told them.

Ray, her clown, rolled his eyes at that. "Seems like it to me," he muttered.

The house was steamy with wash and ironing smells and warm from the oven where bread browned into crusty loaves when Fritz came in from the barn. He'd not seen the neighbor arrive with the wire and so had no warning of the plans Gerda had set into motion. He stood inside the back door watching with astonishment the turmoil before him. Gerda's struggle brought her halfway down the stairs with the black travel trunk thump-thumping behind her before he saw her. He rushed to help before she hurt herself and before—and this was Gerda's plan—before he had a chance to say no, to argue with her about her decision to go back to eastern Nebraska to her aunt's funeral. He was a man of action, and though she wouldn't admit such calculations even to herself, she knew if she kept him moving he would do for her anything she asked. If he stopped and considered the magnitude of what she was doing, he would plant his feet and become not the mountain she counted on, but the mountain she would have to move or cross, and that mountain she knew to be formidable. When they got the trunk down the steps and set up out of the way of the chaos in the kitchen, she reached out and touched the inside of his wrist with the tips of her fingers.

"I called for you when this came, Fritz. I called and called, but you didn't answer." She held the telegram out to him. "Fritz—" she said. She stopped moving for a moment and leaned into him, her cheek against his neck, the palm of her hand over his heart space.

He put his arms around her and held the telegram out at arm's length, reading through squinted eyes over her shoulder.

"That's your mom's sister, isn't it?"

"Yes." She began moving again, directing first one child then another, and the whirlwind of activity pulled Fritz toward her. He followed her from room to room, task to task, listing the reasons why she should not go, but he was off center, moving at her rhythm, and she countered him at every turn. Yes, it had been years since she'd last seen her aunt, all the more reason to go and see the others who were still living. No, her father had not changed, probably never would, but this trip would be for her mother, for their children, that old anger needed to be put to rest. Yes, there is a war going on, but that is over there, in Europe, and we are here, in Nebraska, miles from danger. No, she'd not been on a train since they'd moved to Stuart, but she was a grown woman and she knew how to handle her own children, did she not? All this stated calmly, over her shoulder as she worked. There was, in the end, only one reasonable thing to do, and Gerda was doing it.

They worked together then, Gerda and Fritz and the three oldest children—even the baby Leo cooperated by entertaining himself—until past midnight, and when they all lay down on their beds they closed their eyes and slept soundly and immediately, while outside, a barn owl's soft call was the only sound for miles and a heavy fog moved through in the night. It crackled each surface with hoarfrost that turned white the world and everything in it, edges blurred by the minute spikes of ice.

When dawn came Fritz tried once again to change her mind, but they both knew Gerda's plan was underway and Fritz had only the choice to hold her this way for this small amount of time.

"You will come home again, won't you?" he whispered this into the thick of her hair, as if he didn't want her to hear the question he could not stop from asking.

"Of course." She tipped her head back to look at him, so surprised by his question she laughed. "I'm not leaving *you*. I'm just going to a funeral. I'll only be gone a few days." I promise, she thought to add, but the words seemed at that moment both foolish and unnecessary. "Why would you ask such a thing?" The idea of her not coming home to her husband so preposterous it had no roots in her mind.

Fritz turned onto his back and stared unseeing at the ceiling.

"Fritz? Why would you ask such a thing?"

"What are you going to say when your father tells you to stay?"

Gerda shook her head. "He won't ask me to stay. That's—nonsense."

"Is it?" Fritz turned toward her. He had such fierce eyes at times. "Is it?"

She kissed him then, long and slow. "I'm a grown woman now, Fritz. Have you not noticed?"

He noticed. Abruptly he pulled her to him with such fervency she couldn't catch her breath. "You come back," he said, his lips close to her ear. "You come back."

In a blink, he was lifting her trunk onto the train and waving goodbye, the lump in his throat too big to swallow.

The plume of steam from the train hung in the cold, still air over the tracks as it left the station, backlit by sunrise. A heartbreakingly beautiful sight it was, the black train snaking through a world white with frost under a soft pink dawn, but Fritz turned away unseeing and led Katie back to the wagon and then back to the empty house. Katie patted his arm, mirroring her mother, before he headed out to the barn to finish chores. Katie stood at the window and watched the great wall of his back move away from her. His breath rose in sharp, white puffs.

Gerda would be halfway to Atkinson by now, he thought, and in that way he followed her east, each depot flashing in his own mind (*farther from home, farther from home*). Though it made no sense at all, the sun seemed to follow her eastward as well. The day slipped from silver to gray before settling too soon into wintry darkness.

He spent the day in the barn among the animals and tools where he could ignore Gerda's absence, though even there the weight of it would not let him breathe freely. For his supper she had left the spicy sausage he loved, and it refused to settle, sitting instead like a hot ball at the base of his chest. "I bit into that supper you give me and it bit back all night," he imagined telling her, but when he remembered she wasn't there to tell, the ball seemed to grow until finally he couldn't catch a deep breath at all. He walked outside into the frigid cold and stood looking up at the night sky. A thumbnail moon peeked out between fast moving clouds.

He heard the wagon coming up from the main road before he saw it. The clear air carried the rattle and jangling sounds easily. Fritz waited to see it pass by the road east of the barn, but when he saw the horses turn in at the end of his lane he walked down to meet it.

In the sway of the wagon's light he saw his neighbor, Aloys Baum, and his hired hand. Despite the cold, Aloys was hatless, his hair stood in shifting spikes in the breeze and Fritz imagined Gerda's voice saying it was too long for a civilized man. The horses sensed him before Aloys saw him and their heads came up and they stumbled lightly to the side. When Fritz came abreast of the team he called them Boss and patted the withers of the one nearest to him. He could feel the grit of a long day on the big horse, and he knew Aloys was coming home from somewhere farther than the close town of Stuart.

"I was hoping you'd be up, Fritz." Aloys set the brake on the wagon. "I saw your light."

Fritz glanced toward the house where he saw the lamp in the kitchen window, a brightness that darkened the rest of the house. Even from here he could feel the emptiness.

"Yeah," he said in answer. "Just doing some cleaning up down in the barn, getting things ready. Won't be winter forever." He lifted his cap and set it back again. "I'm guessing."

Aloys twisted and folded the leather reins in his hands and didn't say anything for a bit.

"You're out late." Fritz was not willing to ask questions but felt curious all the same.

"Went to O'Neill." Aloys didn't look up. "The boy here," he tipped his head toward the young man beside him, "turned twenty-one last month."

He didn't have to explain. Fritz knew then they'd gone to register for the draft. Registration was held every three months in the county courthouse, had been since June of last year, just after America entered that war over in Europe.

"Long drive for one day," he commented.

"Ja." Aloys sat up straighter, arching his back to stretch the muscles. "Stopped in Atkinson on the way back." His words came out with a clipped articulation, as if he was practicing a newly learned language and wanted to get the accent right. "Stopped at the café there at the edge a town."

Fritz knew Aloys hadn't stopped to tell him where they'd eaten and he felt a twinge of impatience. "I know the place."

Aloys spit suddenly, a golden arc of tobacco juice that landed expertly between the two horses.

"They quit serving sauerkraut." For the first time he looked directly at Fritz when he spoke. "And hamburgers."

Fritz felt a tightening in his chest again; that ball of air seemed to grow.

"'Liberty cabbage' and 'ground beef sandwiches' is what they got on the menu now."

The two men looked at each other but neither seemed to know what else to say.

"There's a lot of Germans living around here," the boy spoke up. "More Germans than anything else."

Aloys didn't look at him when he answered. "*Ja*, but there's getting less all the time." He looked at Fritz again. "And ain't nobody movin' away."

"It's just words." The boy slouched in the seat in a way that would have given an older man a backache. "We could a still ate there."

With either too much or nothing left to say, Aloys slapped reins to the horses' backs and headed out onto the road. Fritz stood in the yard and looked around as if the dark had suddenly come alive. He walked toward the barn first, thinking crazily he should saddle up one of the horses and go after Gerda, but when he got to the barn he heard Katie open the kitchen door. She didn't call to him. She just stood in the rectangle of light, her thin arms hugging her shoulders, small child looking out into the darkness, and the sight of her made Fritz want to cry out, "Run!"

Run where, he thought, from what?

Of course, he had known they weren't isolated from the war out here. Rumors of hostility against Germans were present like a tickle at the back of the throat in every conversation, no matter the topic. Men he'd known since he'd moved to Stuart eight years back seemed to have become shortsighted, not seeing his greetings until and unless they were too close to ignore him. Still, the reports of discrimination against Germans had seemed like news from distant lands. A young German lynched in the streets of St. Louis, another in Wyoming. In Iowa, men were jailed for speaking German in public.

But not in Nebraska, Fritz thought. It wouldn't happen here. Like the boy said, there were so many Germans living here. They wouldn't turn on each other. He'd stake his own life on that belief. A thought pressed suddenly up against his rib cage and he felt again that he couldn't catch a deep breath. Would he stake Gerda's life on that belief? Had he already?

ट

Gerda knew enough about the superstitions of leave-taking to not let the Stuart station dip from sight while they watched—if you watch it disappear you'll never live to see it reappear—so she kept the children busy to be sure they didn't press noses to the window and watch Stuart as they rounded the bend. She didn't want them tempting Fate to keep them from returning, as surely it would if she didn't appease it with ritual and care. She directed the children to set out the blankets and arrange the basket of their things under the seat. However, when the train rounded the far curve east of Stuart she looked up without meaning to and saw the Stuart station disappear from sight. Slivers of fear clung to her like cat hairs she couldn't brush away. *Bless me, Father, for I have sinned. I fell prey to superstition and allowed it to guide my actions and the actions of my children.* No way to win, she thought, and she rubbed her eyes with the heels of hands trying to erase the image. Her attention diverted, the boys clambered to the window, too excited to notice her worry.

She placed her hands one atop the other in her lap and waited for her breathing to slow. She noticed the frayed cuffs of her coat. It had been beautiful once, she thought, brushing the tiny loose threads with a wetted finger. Suddenly she could see her father's calloused fingers pulling at the warp and weave of the deep green wool, checking the tightness of it as if he could foresee the winds that would assail her and only he knew the exact pattern and thickness that would protect her.

It *is* a beautiful coat. Chiding herself for her own first thoughts took up a great deal of her time, it seemed. That she and Fritz could not afford new coats was no reason to hang her head in front of her father.

"Look for hawks and ducks along the river." She sat up straighter and turned her attention again to the boys. Like their father, they needed a job to do to keep them happy. "In fact, Frankie, you're the oldest and you have the sharpest eyes. I'm putting you in charge of spotting birds between here and Grandma's house."

"What about me?" Ray asked. "I have sharp eyes too."

"And you'll need them, young man. I'm putting you in charge of spotting the cattle. I want both of you to help Leo keep track of the cows."

"What about horses?" Frank asked. He pointed at a wagon on the road that ran parallel to the train tracks. "There're two now."

"An automobile! An automobile!" Ray called excitedly. "There's an automobile on the road!" That brought them all to the window; even other passengers turned to look. The driver shot a gloved hand out the window and the boys waved wildly as if the greeting had been directed at them alone.

Gerda studied the excited faces of her children as they watched the car on the road. She seemed to have so little time to really study them, to know their changing faces, their growing bodies. The two older boys looked like miniature versions of their father, blond waves threatening to curl when they got too long, and blue eyes in round, open faces. Only Leo had the high brow and long face of the men on her side of the family. When she looked at him, she saw her father. Even his hands, emerging from the soft and pudgy shape of a baby's fist, had tapered fingers and were elongating into what her mother had once called piano hands. She watched those hands now, splayed against the glass, and thought that when her mother and father saw those hands, surely they would . . . they would what? What did she think they would do when they saw those hands? Forgive her? Is that why she wanted to go home? For forgiveness? The very thought brought with it the taste of metal, and to dispel it she pulled the picture book out of her bag to be ready for the boys when the spotting and counting lost their novelty.

She had thought about her mother and father every day since she and Fritz had moved away from West Point. Her daughter, Katie, had been the toddler whose nose pressed to the glass then when they headed west, and Frank was yet to be born. How had the years passed so quickly?

I was once a child too, she thought. *I have awoken to the smell of bacon already frying and coffee brewing, to the deep voices of men just in from chores, the cold stiffening their greatcoats, the clatter of dishes and the baritone words forming a comforting song.*

How could any child recognize the gift of that time before becoming a part of the stomp and shuffle of the new day? It was once Now. She had lived it, breathed that bright air, and then it was gone. When she thinks of her life in her mother's house, images rush through her mind in a blur. In that Now, Gerda is a little girl walking home from her sister's funeral, her fist clutching the harsh wool of her mother's skirt. In another Now, Gerda washes the muslin rags red-stained with womanhood. Now she waves goodbye through a train window, her father on the platform with his hat pulled low over his ears, hands dug deep in his coat pockets. Mama beside him staring at the train wheels set into motion on the track heading west.

"Look up at me, Mama," she whispered against the train window, her breath fogging upward in twin paths from either side of her nose. "Look at me and tell me you love me."

Ah, little girl, I want to shake you. Hold you.

Gerda had known before she saw the signature on the telegram that it had not come from her father: too many words. Yes, it had been years since she'd seen him, but she was sure her father was still a man more concerned with economy than clarity. She took the folded buff-colored paper out of her satchel and looked at it again.

"Cancer took Aunt Elsa this morning stop Burial on Tuesday stop Mama needs you stop and I too stop Love Katherine stop"

Katherine. She had been a flighty little girl when Gerda moved away, but now she wrote messages such as this. "Mama needs you." The words warmed a cold place somewhere inside Gerda, and she read it again.

Outside the window, the plains sprawled devoid of color and contrast. Morning looked like noon and the whole day could have been evening. The horizon, that line where sky touches earth, disappeared and there was no distinction between near and far. Shapes were merely large or small if they appeared at all outside the frosty train windows. Mostly there was only whiteness.

As is the case on such days, the world shrank to what was immediate to each soul. When earth and sky are one, the only reference point is the self. Most of the train's occupants fell into a kind trance of silence between each station stop. The January wind blew across the treeless plains, grabbing gusts of icy snow that rattled the windows, and the train car itself shivered against it at times. To keep warm, people huddled beneath coats, blankets, and buffalo robes. The hypnotic motion of the train soothed the rush of Gerda's heart that had been set pounding the day before when she first read the wire. Feeling surer of herself, she kept the children busy with finger games and puzzles until the rhythmic motion of the train lulled them to sleep, and for a long while she simply watched the world go by.

Across the aisle from her sat the only other woman who had gotten on at the Stuart station. In the flurry of departure Gerda had paid her little attention and now the woman had dozed off as had most of the other passengers. In the silence Gerda studied the cut of her dress and saw that it was rich and looked sewn by a tailor, not a farm wife. She noticed things like that, the way the cuffs were tightly machine-stitched, not merely hand-basted and pressed. She checked the pleating on her own sleeve in comparison. The traveling bag the woman carried was a deep burgundy tapestry with leather handles and brass fittings. At first glance Gerda didn't notice the wear on the edge of the bag, the tear in the seam that had been poorly mended, but once she did, she saw, too, the ragged hem of the tailored dress, the shine at the elbows of her coat. She studied the woman a little closer. She looked tired to the bone; even with her face slack in sleep she looked as though all she wanted was to rest. When the blanket she had wrapped around her legs slipped to the floor, she didn't stir. Gerda reached across the aisle and pulled it up, tucked it in between the woman's behind and the seat.

Only those closest to the heat stove at the front of the car seemed capable of movement or conversation. From her position in the middle of the train car, Gerda watched the three men on the benches at the front. They had also boarded in Stuart that morning, rushing ahead of the two women more like unruly boys than grown men. It was an impression they still generated as they alternated between boisterous shouts and shushing one another, their attention on a game of some sort, dice or cards; she couldn't see what they had between them. Despite their boyishness, they had the look of working men. They shared the ruddy complexions born of working in the extremes of the cold and heat typical to the plains. The homespun everyday nature of their clothes brought to mind the clothes she first made and then often mended for Fritz.

He seemed continuously to outgrow his clothes so that they were always and ever a touch too small. He was a big man, her husband, six-foot-three and as broad at the hips as he was at the shoulders. Like the men at the front of the train, he had a roughness of movement when indoors, as if he were uncomfortable with anything but sky above him. These men were farmers maybe, or railroad workers, men used to hard physical labor. They looked like most of the men from home, familiar as a neighbor she'd seen but not met. Perhaps she'd passed them on the street or at the mercantile in town.

The rumble of wheels on the track and the rattle of the railroad car covered the sound of the men's conversation, and to Gerda they were simply a place to rest her eyes. Though they were good at hiding it, she saw they passed a bottle back and forth. She lowered her eyes when they looked up to see who was watching.

The man wearing the black homburg got on somewhere near Pilger. He took off the hat as he walked down the row, an action that seemed both natural and refined, but once he took his seat near the heat stove at the front of the car, he put it back on, too cold for such politeness. A dark-eyed, broad-shouldered man, he reminded Gerda of one of her uncles, though she couldn't say for certain which one. Her father's brothers, Joseph and Ambrose, had that same look of having made money in America, the look that showed in the way they held their heads, upright and aware of their own spine.

It was just outside Wisner that something started to change. She had been looking out the window and had seen the depot come into view as the train made the long sweep toward the south. First the red-shingled building was small, then it grew larger and then she couldn't see it any longer and only white land and sky were left to be seen outside the window. How small humans are in this big world, and how far away from everything they seemed to be out here on the plains. Gerda shivered at the thought and when she looked back at the men in the front she noticed the three younger men had moved closer to one another. Their shoulders were hunched and their heads tipped close together. The man in the black coat sat settled back into his own seat with his hat pulled forward, but something about the scene made her think he had just stopped moving.

Not knowing quite why, she reached out and tucked the blanket more firmly around the children. Leo drowsily crawled out from his place between his brothers and into her lap before falling back to sleep. Out of the corner of her eye she saw one of the young men stand up and begin gesturing at the man in the black coat, and then the other two stood up and started shouting at him too. Something told her not to look directly at the scene as it unfolded. She couldn't understand most of their words, slurred and angry sounding as they were, and the ones she did she didn't want to hear. Curse words she'd heard only once or twice in her entire life filled the air. The faces of the young men were contorted and flushed. The older man sat with his palms up and outward, trying to placate them it seemed.

In the seats around the group, people began to wake and sit up, though no one moved to join in. What happened next happened so quickly there was no time to speak out or reach up to the brake cord and stop the train. There really was no time, Gerda was certain of this, it all happened so quickly. It would take longer to say it than to live it. One moment the young men were shouting and the next they were hitting and dragging the other man down the aisle toward the door. His black wool coat, already pulled off one shoulder, caught on the edge of Gerda's seat as they dragged him past. One of the men jerked not the coat free, but the man's arm, and she heard a grinding snap. He cried out, a scream like a throat-cut sow. Another of the men grabbed his head and smashed it against the seat back. Blood splattered, droplets of it hitting the blanket under which her children slept. Gerda's hand reached out—she told herself later it was to stop them or to help him, but what she did was draw the blanket back, pulling her children closer to her. She protected what she could.

They threw him from the moving train as easily as they would a bundle of rags and that's exactly what he looked like as he rolled down the incline beside the tracks and disappeared into the whiteness beyond. Gerda turned so quickly toward the window she nearly dropped baby Leo. "No!" she cried, and reached to grab Leo with one hand while with the other she reached for the stranger outside the window.

Everyone in the car was awake then, some looking around in shock, others looking scared and confused. The woman across the aisle, her sharp nose red with fright, looked at Gerda as if to rush toward her. The three men came back inside, the metal door clanging behind them. They walked unsteadily now that their mission was accomplished.

"And that's what we'll do to any of you damned Germans if you think you can get away with criticizing this great country," one of them shouted.

Poof, like a bubble bursting there were smiles then and laughter. All around the car people began clapping, began shaking hands with the young men who were suddenly taller and stronger than anyone else in the car. One of them said, "I don't need to wait for the uniform before I start protecting this country from Germans."

"We'll take care of those dirty Kaiser-lovers!" someone called, and another voice answered, "Krauts don't belong here!" The bottle the three men had been secretly sharing was passed around from one willing hand to another. Gerda felt a shrill of cold climb up from her hands and feet. As the blood left her extremities, she felt paralyzed by fear. Across from her, the lone woman shrank back against her seat, pulling her coat up around her neck and sinking into it until only her eyes showed. She kept her gaze on the floor. There were tears.

Awakened now to this excitement, her boys let their blankets fall to the floor. Ray and Frank, their faces so round, so German, peered at her and at the mayhem around them. "Why are they laughing, Mama?" Frank asked, and she shushed him. She pulled the children toward her, into her lap, and whispered into Frank's blond and wispy hair, "Sh-sh-sh. Just be still." Ray pulled away from her, the better to see the activity around them.

They're too young to know what's happening, she thought, too young. She didn't want to explain any of it. She didn't want to let the world do what the world would most surely do to those dear hearts.

They were miles from home now, and the war, the one she had so confidently said was too far away to have any effect on them, had suddenly found Gerda Drueke Vogel and her three small boys.

CHAPTER TWO

Dr. Ed Gannoway heard the screaming just before his foot hit the bottom step of the hospital's north stairwell. He stood suspended for a moment gathering the information the sound would offer.

It was a woman, the screams coming from the male ward—not a patient.

The shrieks rose at the end of each exhalation indicating a question or disbelief, not physical pain.

In the guttural moan that came with each intake of breath he recognized the desolation that mourners often manifested. Of the two patients in the ward, one was a childless widower brought in by a neighbor who had found him sick with pneumonia. The other, a young man whose left leg Gannoway had been forced to amputate two days ago in an effort to stop the upward march of gangrene from an ill-cared-for wound on his foot.

The screamer would be the young man's wife.

Gannoway continued up the steps, casting off his greatcoat and preparing for what came next. Death has its rituals and mourners have their needs. It never failed to unsettle him when those needs involved such public displays. Grief, he believed, was a private matter, and there is nothing private about a scream of misery. No good ever came of abandoning oneself to such display, no dead ever rose up from the deathbed in response, and there was always the morrow to be reckoned with when the mourner had to recognize both the loss of the loved one and a part of oneself. It mystified him, though it did not keep him from offering compassion, and so when the young woman flung herself into his arms he knew to hold her, and when she began to hit him, her fists battering his chest, he knew to let her.

"The young man died after all." Gannoway scribbled the words on a fresh sheet of tissue-thin stationery while he waited for his wife, Miranda, to ready for Mass. He would mail the letter to his brother, Lark, first thing the next morning, as he had each Monday for nearly three decades. On Friday, a letter that Lark, also a doctor, had mailed the same Monday would arrive at Gannoway's door.

Though they hadn't seen one another in person for more than ten years, they knew more about one another's daily lives than anyone else they knew. Their letters to each other were long and rambling, more like journals than letters. Gannoway filed the letters by date with an index at the front of each box noting specific topics. They both started a new one each week, adding to it as time would allow, relaying to one another information about the cases they worked on, news about the patients, the weather, insights on anything from foot rot to what was happening in Washington. They learned as much from each other about the current state of medicine and politics as they did from the journals available to them. Lark worked now down in Fort Riley, Kansas, though prior to the war, he had worked and studied in Omaha and Chicago, with short stints down south, once as far as the Panama Canal. The variety of postmarks on his brother's letters sometimes stirred an unwelcome wanderlust in Gannoway.

"I admit I thought I had sacrificed the leg but saved the man. However, he took a turn for the worse late yesterday afternoon. His fever spiked and not even the chipped ice brought up by the bucketsful from the river could bring it down. If only they had called for me a day earlier." Gannoway put down his pen and rubbed the ridge of his eyebrow. The young man had been chopping wood and the hatchet had caught a knot, bounced off, and hit his ankle with all the force he had first held in his arms and shoulders. Had he been fortunate enough to sever his own foot completely, perhaps the family would have brought him to the hospital right away. As it was, they waited for what the young man's father had called "God's healing hand."

The wound had festered and the flesh blackened almost to the man's knee by the time Gannoway arrived. The small cabin where the family lived was set back in the bluffs northwest of Stuart, and the call for help had come in the midst of a heavy snowstorm. Gannoway had to walk a good distance beyond the navigable road, carefully placing his own snowshoe track atop the track of the man who had come for him to reach the place. He knew as soon as the cabin door opened and the fetid smell of rotted flesh rushed to greet him that what medicine could do would be limited by what faith had wrought. He moved quickly and gave instructions brusquely on how to move him with the least amount of added pain. He would not do surgery on a dining room table.

Gannoway thought about the way the man's blue eyes, cold as marbles, glared at him when his uncles carried him down the long path to the wagon. He had said "No" clearly when Gannoway said "amputate," but he hadn't the strength to fight beyond that, and his wife and mother were frantic for anything that could save him. Gannoway could only guess at the nature of the arguments that had taken place before medical help was finally sought. The father, a burly, clean-shaven man, had stood to the side when Gannoway came in, though the others kept glancing at him before moving to respond to Gannoway's requests. He could decipher neither respect nor fear in their demeanor, and the man didn't follow his son into town.

They would all curse the father now, Gannoway thought, though at some point and to some degree the gaze of their sorrow would settle on the doctor and the nurses who had been with him in the end. That was to be expected. The pain of any trauma needed a focus, a person or place to hold the anger and sorrow of life gone inevitably awry and Gannoway was no stranger to that fact. As a man whose life's work strode hand in hand with mortality, he knew he could be vilified before breakfast by one grief-stricken family and deified by another whose loved one he had saved by nightfall.

For his part he believed his rightful place was somewhere in between the two extremes. He made his medical decisions based on education and experience, blind to the doubters or disinclined, or even to those who complied with his orders and died anyway. He had said as much and more to Lark many times in letters previous to this one, so there was no need to ramble on about it now.

He lifted the letter to his lips and blew softly to dry the ink.

The road in front of St. Boniface Catholic Church was strangely empty for a Sunday morning. Gannoway walked with his wife's arm looped through his own and helped her around a snowdrift at the edge of the street. The howling wind that had come through late the previous afternoon had covered the town with long dune-shaped drifts that ended abruptly in curling waves. With a little imagination you could see a desert or an ocean right here in the middle of Nebraska. He always enjoyed the silence that came with fresh snowfall, and he didn't mind the cold. Left to his own resources he would have walked the short distance to church with his coat open and his head bare—the cold would clear his head.

Today, however, he wore his coat tightly buttoned up to his chin and a wool hat snugly pulled down around his ears. That would be Miranda's doing. Before they left the house for church she had bundled him up the way she would a child, handling the buttons roughly and chiding him for his obstinate refusal to admit defeat to the vicious season. Satisfied with her efforts, she pulled on her own heavy coat, wool gloves, and her latest pride and joy, a beaver-skin hat ordered from Sears and Roebuck last fall. He had not told her about the young man, nor would he unless she asked. They had learned to live together without such conversations.

"Never had such a fine warm hat in all my life!" she said as she did nearly every time she put it on, and then she offered him one of her rare smiles. She had a chipped tooth, the result of a sledding accident when young, and her lips were crooked—pleasingly full on the bottom, but on the top one side thinned out and disappeared in the corner. She appeared to be permanently preoccupied and sucking on her lip, the better to concentrate. However, when she smiled her lip straightened and filled out so that her entire face took on a pleasing symmetry.

"A lazy wind," Miranda said when they stepped out onto the road. "Too lazy to go around you so it goes right through you."

The bell began to peal just as they reached the steep front steps of the church. Johnny Kaup, the self-appointed caretaker of all that needed doing at the church that didn't involve the soul, had cleared a narrow path up the center of the steps, well away from the handrails at the side that most parishioners would need to climb the icy steps. Ed and Miranda paused and considered their choices for making their way to the front door: through the snow with the handrail for balance or free-form up the center.

"Johnny should have been an artist," Miranda said. "His talents seem wasted on maintenance duties."

"An artist?" Ed replied.

Miranda waved her hand to indicate the way Johnny had shoveled the snow, not tossing it randomly but fanning it precisely so that the cleared path appeared to flow upward between twin cascading piles of snow. The lines formed by the dark handrails he had so carefully avoided and the cascading piles of snow lining the path converged at the massive oak doors. The line marking the center of the two doors marked the precise center of the path, where, Ed now realized, Johnny had left a thin white line of snow on each step. Even the gravel Johnny had sprinkled on the icy steps looked more placed than scattered. Looking up the twenty steps to the door, Ed felt oddly pulled upward toward the church doors, and the feeling bothered him. He tugged a bit at the scarf around his neck and took a deep breath as if in preparation for something.

"Putting the path next to the handrails would have made more sense." He placed his foot carefully on the bottom step and offered his arm to Miranda.

Before taking it, Miranda looked around at the empty street. Normally there would be people hurrying to get seated before the ringing ceased and the organ began, but today the Gannoways were the only parishioners to be seen.

"There'll be no room at all for us, or we'll have our choice of seats," she commented dryly. "If it's the latter, the new priest is going to be a bit upset about our unholy community." A new priest had been installed the previous Sunday, and this was to be his first solo sermon.

When they stepped inside the church, the organist was just getting started, gallantly pumping her feet and hands trying to fill the big church with its airy notes. Miranda and Ed, with their choice of seats, walked up the center aisle to their customary pew to the left of center, in front of the statue of St. Boniface. Gannoway sat down, turned his face toward the front of the church and began waiting for Mass to be over.

As the new priest started in, Gannoway thought about Father Hettwer, the priest who had led St. Boniface's parish for the past decade. The old priest had been a baritone whose singing voice registered somewhere deep in the animal part of Gannoway's brain. When Hettwer sang "Kyrie eleison" during the Introductory Rites of the Mass, Gannoway felt the penitent in himself respond. The sorrows that arose, however, were not in response to his sins, but to his losses. There was a moment each Sunday as the priest intoned the prayer for mercy when Gannoway's greatest loss rose up in him and grief fired in his chest and throat. Though each time he tried to fight it, the combination of incense and the priest's voice would overcome his defenses and he would close his eyes and slowly, solemnly recall his little girl. She had been no bigger than his two cupped hands, and her stillness had formed a vast universe of starless nights. He supposed it a form of prayer, this moment of recall, though to what or to whom he didn't know. All he could say for certain about the Divine was that the Lord had shown no mercy the only time he had ever asked for it. With that thought he would open his eyes and continue to wait for the end of Mass.

The new priest was a much younger man than Hettwer and seemed by virtue of his age to promise a fresh and vigorous energy. That assumption was dispelled when Gannoway met him at his installation.

Father Jungels was a big man with a strangely boyish face. He kept his thick curly hair tamed with a heavy-handed use of hair oil. His small mouth was made to look smaller by the thickness of his cheeks and neck, and he had a disconcerting tendency to sniff between sentences. On this first Sunday, he had not yet found vestments to fit him and he looked almost comic with his arms and legs exposed by the too-small garments Father Hettwer had left behind.

Gannoway was not the kind of man to be biased by appearances. Still, as Father Jungels lumbered up the center aisle behind the altar boys and approached the altar, Gannoway did wish he had someone with whom he could exchange glances. The seams of the vestment pulled so that when Jungels genuflected, Gannoway held his breath in anticipation of a ripping sound. Such was his entertainment for the day.

It was a long hour, that first Mass with Jungels. His voice droned a dangerous monotone that seemed designed to lull people to sleep, rather than to worship or pray. To exacerbate the situation, his Latin pronunciation was deplorable, and he was, apparently, tone deaf. He spoke and sang the Latin as if he'd never heard it pronounced. Gannoway found himself wincing more than once at particularly egregious mistakes. If anything about the Mass had given him joy, it was the sound of the Latin phrases chanted so reverently by the priests, but Father Jungels was depriving him of even that pleasure.

At the beginning of the homily, Jungels stepped from the altar to the pulpit and glared out at the nearly empty church. His thick fingers gripped the pulpit so tightly that Gannoway thought he might pull it free from its mooring. He didn't speak for several minutes, though it wasn't a true silence. His breathing was audible. Miranda glanced at Ed out of the corner of her eye, but aside from that gave no indication she saw anything amiss. Ed looked over his shoulder and did a quick count. Twenty, no the Kroger family was on the other side, twenty-six parishioners aside from the Gannoways. Not a good count, but given the storm that had closed the roads coming into town, it wasn't a bad count either.

He looked back up at the priest's sweating face. No, he had to admit it; it was a bad count, and a poor showing of how pious the members of the Stuart community really were. He decided to take it upon himself to explain to

Jungels after Mass the probable reasons for the absent parishioners. Though he'd been a member of St. Boniface's parish for nearly two decades, Ed was not a religious man. He attended church because it was expected of him and his standing in the community depended too much on the opinions of the people who would be his patients. To be a doctor in 1918 was no guarantee of success. The medical profession had little uniformity in terms of education of its practitioners and even less power in protecting its good name. Charlatans could call themselves doctors and there was little to stop them. Quacks traveled the country offering cures in the form of miracle elixirs for everything from hiccups to goiters to virility. One smooth-talker came through not long ago advertising a cure for "lost manhood" problems. It took all of Gannoway's powers of persuasion to keep one or more of his patients from agreeing to undergo a transplant operation that involved having goat glands inserted into their testicles. Goat glands!

In such a world, a legitimate professional, which Gannoway considered himself to be, prospered according to his abilities not only at the sickbed, but at everything from casual conversation on the street or after church to his behavior at dinner parties. It rested, in the end, on how well he expressed his beliefs—political or otherwise—or kept them to himself.

Jungels had drawn himself up so that the too-short vestments grew shorter, and he glared down at the parishioners long enough to cause the pews to begin to squeak and to draw a few coughs from the back. Finally, he spoke. "Thank you for coming." Sniff. "I hope it wasn't too much trouble to pull yourselves out of your warm beds and come to worship the Lord in his own house." Sniff. "The evil sower, of whom Paul spoke in his letter to the Colossians, is the Devil. He sows the dark cockle, which, as you probably do not know, is a violent poison." Sniff. "It seems the Devil has been here, sowing his poison in this bucolic community." Sniff. "The poison of laziness and apathy."

He didn't get any kinder as he dressed down those who had come because of what he considered the sins of those who had not. Gannoway found himself sitting farther and farther back in the pew as the priest talked and sniffed. At one point Gannoway uncrossed his legs, set both feet firmly on the ground, and placed his hands on his knees as if to rise. Miranda gripped his elbow, though she didn't look at him. He wasn't planning to get up, he'd just been trying to get comfortable, but her action reminded him to be more careful about how he appeared. He settled back again against the back of the wooden pew and waited.

Gannoway would have liked to see the look on each of the parishioners' faces as they received Communion from the priest that day. Kneeling at the Communion rail, each congregant raised his or her face dutifully as always toward the priest, but when they rose to their feet and turned back toward the pews, their faces were masks. Though some chewed the Host, others kept their mouths still, and none of them gave themselves away. The oddest moment came when the last of them had returned to their seats. Gannoway had never taken Communion, though Miranda did, having grown up in the Catholic Church. When everyone had settled back into their pews, Father Jungels stood holding the chalice, looking at Gannoway. It seemed as if he thought he could force him to repent and become a full Catholic there and then. Gannoway merely watched him until he turned and walked back to the altar to turn the Concluding Rites into a curt dismissal.

The Gannoways were the last to reach the narthex, and by the time they got there the priest was alone. The big wooden doors had not closed properly behind the last to depart, and the narthex was so cold the priest's breath hung in white clouds around his mouth.

"What is your name?" Jungels said without preamble.

Miranda looked askance toward Ed and stuttered, "I—I'm Miranda..."

"This is my wife, Miranda. I'm Dr. Gannoway," Gannoway finished for her. "We met last week at your installation, though I don't blame you for not remembering. You met nearly a hundred people then, didn't you?" He tried to make his voice sound jovial, though he didn't feel it.

Jungels raised his eyes up from Miranda's frightened face to look directly at Gannoway. Perhaps it was the discomfort of the situation, but up close Gannoway couldn't help but notice that Jungels's eyes were set closely together and seemed unnecessarily small. A lesser man might call them pig-like.

"So, Ed," Jungels said. "You didn't come up to receive Communion. Though I suppose I'm to be grateful you came at all."

Gannoway paused to button his coat before answering. "Don't take it to heart, Father," Gannoway said. "I recall many a time when Father Hettwer preached to a church even emptier than this one. They come when they can, you'll see."

He placed his hand again on the small of Miranda's back to urge her out the door, but Jungels wasn't finished with him.

"And you? You don't receive Communion because you've committed exactly which mortal sin?"

Miranda gasped and looked up at her husband. Gannoway said nothing for a minute, simply gazed at the priest trying to gauge his stance. With all the reasons the church dictated to not receive Communion, why Jungels chose that particular affront gave him pause. Somewhere not far from here a grave was being dug for a young man with marble blue eyes.

"Welcome to Stuart, Father Jungels," he said quietly. "I'm sure you'll discover that this community isn't quite so heathen as it looks today. They've all got their good reasons for not coming, I'm certain." He stepped toward the door, his body pressuring Miranda to move in that direction as well. When they stepped out onto the high steps, a gust of wind caught the door and whipped it open, sending a blast of cold air and snow into the church.

The cold walk home against the wind gave Ed a chance to think about the situation more calmly, but through dinner with Miranda that day he could think of nothing to say that didn't seem mean-spirited, so he said nothing at all. Miranda sat at the other end of the table with a novel, the incident seemingly forgotten as far as she was concerned. Their conversation consisted of china cups clinking against china plates, the slide of paper on paper as Miranda turned each page, and an occasional cleared throat.

After lunch, Ed went into the parlor and dropped a small chunk of coal into the stove to take the chill off the room. He rolled the top up on his desk and set out the letter, his pen, and his inkpot, but he didn't uncap it. He rubbed his finger along the stains on the surface where, in his enthusiasm to get to the next page, he had turned a sheet face down before the ink had dried. If he looked carefully enough he could make out a word or two of some long ago letter, but mostly the stains looked simply like stains. He traced his finger across them now but could find no way to start in. If he told anyone what he felt it would be Lark, but what did he feel?

He went to the big picture window and stood looking through the filigree of frost onto a ground blizzard that cloaked the backyard and garden. There was no excuse to venture out and he felt caged. In the spring, summer, and fall he could always sneak out later in the day to work in his garden.

His true passion was the physical world. The garden, more than a hobby but less than a vocation, intrigued him, but it was the human body that truly fascinated him: about how it worked, what made it work, and when it didn't work, what kept it from doing so. He considered it a beautiful machine and he was in awe of the simple physicalness of his patients. He was grateful, when he gave it thought, to have a profession that allowed him to study the very thing with which he was most enamored.

For all that, he considered the body to be merely a vehicle for the mind and he didn't spend much time or energy worrying about what happened to either—mind or body—after one died. To his thinking, all humanity was physical in nature at its deepest level. Though the mysterious life-principle eluded the grasp of the wisest scientists, Gannoway considered this a temporary condition, and he saw no reason to consider the spark of life as indubitable testimony of Divine Power. He was interested in the *how* of the world; he let the priests worry over the *why* of it. Though years ago he and Lark had spent many hours discussing the meaning of life, especially after their mother died too young, once he'd grown to adulthood he saw no good reason to debate the issue, or even spend much time considering it. Until now.

Exactly which mortal sin have you committed, Jungels had asked, that prevents you from accepting grace and seeking redemption.

Two days later Gannoway knocked on the rectory door. The conversation between the two men that day took place on the small, unsheltered stoop of the priest's home, Jungels having declined to offer him entry. In a situation that bore no resemblance to the usual casual conversation between townspeople, Gannoway said things he hadn't intended to say, things he hadn't said aloud to anyone since he was a boy and had Lark as his only audience, things about his faith, or lack of it. In response, the priest's words grew louder and louder until the air around the two men grew brittle. When it was over, Gannoway walked briskly the few blocks to the hospital, tapping his gloves in the palm of his hand. Soft, silver-white clouds papered much of the sky, but the cerulean patches grew larger until the sun emerged full force and an unseasonable burst of warmth caused the ice on the trees and eaves to loosen and fall with a twinkling of something almost like music. Gannoway didn't hear it. He still found the young priest pompous and unreasonable, yet he was intrigued by the conversation. Father Jungels had threatened him with the fires of hell for his carelessness of tongue and soul, the mortal sin he referred to that first day became plural, a series of sins unatoned, but this time as Gannoway walked away he was not angry. What Jungels lacked in intellect he made up for in passion of belief. He recalled the words of a philosopher he and Lark had long admired and often quoted: "We have arranged for ourselves a world in which we can live—by positing bodies, lines, planes, causes and effects, motion and rest, form and content; without these articles of faith nobody could now endure life. But that does not prove them. Life is no argument. The conditions of life might include error."

Perhaps he himself had arranged for Jungels to come into his life. The thought of pursuing the conversation sparked a cutaneous sensation down the length of his arms and legs, a feeling that might have been excitement or might have been fear.

CHAPTER THREE

"There was no reason for you to come," her father said to her by way of greeting. "You think you're going to bring back the dead by showing up here?"

Gerda's knees nearly buckled with gratitude when her father spoke. She thought he knew about the man on the train. She would not have to describe for him the horror of the trip.

"He's really dead then?" She had hoped he was only injured, that the men had only thrown him from the train, not killed him.

Her father, stooping to grab the trunk from the depot's platform where the porter had left it, stopped in mid-motion and looked at her. "Whose funeral did you think you were coming for? Mine?" He shook his head derisively and headed for the buggy with her trunk.

Her misunderstanding and his sharp words seemed to close the door on hers, on what she had to say, even though it had been the thought of saying them to him that had kept the red terror within her from spilling out in the long hours after it happened.

"Sh-sh," she had said to the boys. "Your grandpa will be waiting for us at the depot and everything will be okay. Sh. Sh. Papa will take us home." She repeated the phrase into Leo's dark hair until everyone returned to their seats and the boys stopped squirming. The two older boys had stood between her knees and the back of the seat in front of her like sheltered guardians. They watched her face as much as they studied the others around them until the excitement shrank back to that circle around the heat stove where the three men now openly passed the bottle back and forth until it was empty and their eyelids grew heavy enough to silence them.

How strangely quiet the train car became then, even the roar of the engine and the click of the wheels on the track seemed to recede until the only sounds were those created within the car—a man in the back coughed, a bag was clicked open and shut again, something metal hit the wood floor, feet shifted, gravel grating between leather and wood. The woman across the aisle sniffed abruptly. Gerda looked at her, but her expression revealed neither ally nor foe.

She would tell Papa what had happened and he would know what it meant. He would make sense of it for her, and so she began recalling each detail, even those that didn't seem to fit or matter: the way the man wore his hat, for example, or that he got on alone at a stop that wasn't even a depot, one where there was no stationmaster to set the flag to stop the train. She would tell her father those things and he would explain it, make it make sense.

She had left home that morning a grown woman, but when she stepped off the train in the dark at West Point, she felt as young as the boys whose hands she held. The streets and buildings of a town she knew by heart spread away from the depot platform and even in the dark she could find each building and name its purpose, who owned this, who lived there. The brightness of the cold winter air was softened by the ever-present smell of hops from the brewery. The gristmill down by the river would be sending billows of steam into the sky during the grinding season. How could she have forgotten this is how it smelled, this is how it felt? Home. She breathed it in and felt steadied by it. Without her noticing, Fritz and the farm in Stuart receded to the other side of the great chasm that had formed during the time on the train. The chasm would be almost too wide to cross back before she realized it was there.

Her father had stood at the edge of the circle of light cast by the depot's ticket window. His back to the oncoming train, the collar of his greatcoat turned up against the cold and a heavy wool hat pulled low, yet she knew it was him by the slope of his shoulders. The sight of him stung her eyes. When she first saw him, she nearly left the children standing alone and rushed to greet him.

She could feel the crackle of tears gone solid when she heard his harsh words, *no need to come.* Watching his solid back as he walked toward the buggy, she felt the ice settle deeper and harden the words she wanted to say to him until she could think of nothing to do but follow him.

The two oldest boys, tired from the trip and nearly asleep on their feet, seemed not to hear his gruff words. The baby Leo was wide-eyed but mercifully quiet and too young to understand. Gerda felt incapable of finding the words to describe what had happened. No one else had gotten off the train at West Point with them, so she had arrived to this dark cold as a lone witness. She bundled the boys beneath heavy robes in the back of the buggy before she climbed up beside her father and found her voice. She wanted to say, "Something happened on the train," but instead she answered his challenge that there was no need to come. "I came because Katherine's wire said Mama needed me. Elsa was her only sister. . . ."

He interrupted, "I know who Elsa was." He slapped reins to the horses' backs and hunched his shoulders to his ears. Of course, Gerda thought, this is how he has always been, why had she thought he would be different?

She grabbed hold of the seat side and held on as the buggy lurched across the tracks. "I know you know who Elsa was, Papa. I didn't mean that." She looked over her shoulder at the sleepy boys. "I wanted Mama to meet my babies. I wanted them to know you. I haven't seen you in so long." Her words, coming out in puffs of white breath, were hard for her to say and didn't match at all what was on her mind. She didn't know if the man from the train was alive or dead along the train tracks somewhere. She didn't know what would happen to the men who had beat him, to the witnesses. What ligature had formed in the chaos of that moment? She thought of the woman across the aisle. Though it was a crime, she knew it was—if it wasn't, what could possibly be considered criminal?—no one on that train reacted as if it had been wrong. And what of sin? The Fifth Commandment censures all forms of abuse. *We are only stewards of this life and must render an account for its use and abuse.* What could she say to her God or her father about that man, about her silence?

The silence—even the porter had kept his expression flat and unreadable when he came through to tell Gerda her stop was coming. He came from behind her and startled her by tapping on her shoulder. When she looked up at him, he held out a small card that read "West Point," but he said nothing. Did he not know? Was it only the people in her car who had witnessed it? By the time they had reached her destination, the others in the car had settled down to their own thoughts, the three men still asleep on the floor near the heater, oblivious to the rocking of the train. She had been ashamed—*ashamed*—to meet the gaze of anyone, and so she left the train with her eyes on her Ray's blond hair, her hand on Frank's shoulder.

"I need to speak with you about that man," she had whispered to the porter when he retrieved her trunk. "The man—something happened. . . ." When he didn't turn to look at her, she placed her hand on his arm to get his attention. He looked at her hand first and appeared startled to see her standing so close. He stepped back involuntarily, then pointed abruptly at his ears and shook his head. Only then did Gerda realize his ears were little more than flaps of mangled, bright red scar tissue, the result of frostbite or fire, she couldn't tell. He pulled a pad of paper and a stubby pencil from his breast pocket and offered them to her. Gerda stared at the small square of white in his hand for a moment as if he'd handed her a small animal. She shook her head. She could not imagine writing words about thoughts she could not think.

And now her father seemed no more capable of hearing her words than had that porter, but she had to say them. "A man wearing a homburg hat got on somewhere near Pilger," she began, though even as she said it she knew she was bringing to fore the wrong details. In her mouth the words had such weight, but they sounded thin and light when she said them into the air surrounding her father. He was a strong man and he expected others to be strong too. When she was little, too little really, he would take her with him when he did chores. He taught her how to harness a team of horses, to reach between their patient legs to attach the martingale to bellyband, how to grind grain using the full weight of her body to turn the wheeled handle, how to feed the cattle by spearing the piled hay lightly so that layers lifted free and she could lift and pivot safely with no wasted movement and drop it through the trap door of the hayloft. One day she lost her footing and fell with the pitchfork in hand to the hard-packed floor below. Looking down at her through what was now a square in the ceiling above her, his face showed more anger than fear. What had she done wrong, he wanted to know. Had she tried to lift too much at once? Had she not listened when he told her to stand well away from the open trap door? The tine of the falling pitchfork had pierced her right leg and pinned her to the floor, but she felt fear, not pain. "I'm sorry, Papa," she said. "I'm sorry." She pulled the pitchfork free without telling him and hid the wound until it became infected. She remembers waking from a fever, a doctor bent over her, murmuring, "What were you thinking, child?" His ministrations felt gently accusatory, as if he was cut of the same cloth as her father.

She kept talking as they rocked toward home even though the effort to form sound into words felt like hard physical labor. She told him about the man, about the blood, and the sound of bone breaking. She studied her father's profile when she finished. The facts of the story hung invisible, vibrating the night air around them.

He had a long, straight nose, thick dark hair that swept up off his forehead, and a downturned mouth, all of which she had inherited from him. She knew his face as well as she knew her own. Seven years it had been since she'd seen him last, surely time had lessened his anger at her. She had named a son for him, was there no softness in him? What she knew was that he kept his eyes forward, his hands on the reins, and he wore his silence like a rebuke. Had he heard her?

She wanted to reach out and touch his arm, his shoulder, to feel the warmth of him. What she wanted was to be enfolded once again against his chest and assured that the world was not the terrifying place she suddenly felt it to be. She looked down at her hands, encased in mittens her husband had made for her out of cowhide and rabbit fur, and willed them to move toward him, but his silence held them down. They continued on, riding into the dark away from town. The light of their swinging lantern illuminated the trail a short distance ahead of the arched gray heads of the Percherons and cast moving shadows alongside the road. Once out of sight of West Point, theirs was the only light to be seen. Tufts of grass poking up from the snow rattled in the night breeze. Clouds obscured the stars. There seemed nothing in the world but them in this moving circle of light.

He broke the silence at last, but once he'd spoken, she wished he'd kept it to himself. "Katherine shouldn't a sent that wire. You shouldn't a been on that train at all. It's not safe. You were wrong to come. And you've better things to do than waste that Vogel money on train tickets for no good purpose." He spit to the side and added bitterly, "The little he has of it."

"My *husband* and I are doing okay, Papa." She wanted to spit the words the way he had the tobacco. "And I'm glad Katherine sent the wire. I wanted to come."

He sniffed loudly. "You think the war's got nothing to do with you? Didn't that *arme Teufel* have enough sense to know that this was going to happen? Does he even know there's a war going on?"

"Papa, he's not a poor devil! How can you say that?" she asked. "How could anyone have known that would happen? Of course we know about the war. Fritz had to register for the draft last June." How did that brave fact become little more than an arrow to shoot at her father? How quickly he was able to change everything.

"But he didn't go to soldiering did he? What's the matter? The army wouldn't have him?"

"He turned thirty-two in November, Papa." Her voice got higher and she cleared her throat to bring it back down again. "He's a farmer with a family. It had nothing to do with him. It's the army's rules. You'd rather he'd gone to war? You'd rather he'd left me and the children, *your* grandchildren to fend for ourselves? Having him gone or dead would suit you, wouldn't it?" She suddenly didn't care that she was shouting and she no longer felt like crying. It was not as a daughter or a wife or even as a mother she felt then. It was something else altogether and she could have no more named it than stopped it. "Would you have me be a widow, Papa? Would you feel at last that you and you alone were right about my marriage? Would you? Tell me, would you?"

Papa Drueke snorted derisively when she said the words *widow* and *marriage* but didn't answer her directly. Gerda shook her head in frustration. How did they return to this argument so quickly? "Yes, my *marriage,* Papa? It's a *marriage,* Papa. In the eyes of the law *and* the church I am *married.*" These were the same words he'd not heard seven years ago when she said them before she moved west with Fritz. They had married in the courthouse, not the church, because the Druekes had made sure of that, but a visiting priest who had no interest in local or familial politics blessed the union. Still, she could not force her father to take as proof those facts he refused to see.

She didn't want to talk about her wedding, even though the unresolved feelings surrounding it were part of why she had come. She wanted now to tell him how afraid she was about the war, about what was happening in this country, what had happened on the train, about how afraid she was that she could lose Fritz to all that. She tried again to speak, but he talked, louder, drowning out her voice. Wrapped up in his own war, he reminded her of all the sins she had ever committed, and the anger of a disappointed father proved no match for her desire for peace between them.

A sudden night wind caught Gerda's scarf and pulled it back off her head, and some of her hair came loose from its pins. She no doubt looked as she felt, like a wild thing, and she threw her head back and cried out to the night sky, not a word, just the sound of pain. Her father, for once in his life, looked at her. Dark as iron their eyes met.

"What do you want, Papa?" Her voice dropped to a whisper. "To be told you were right? I can't do that, Papa." She wanted to say something about love and about Fritz and how she felt about him, but she knew he would see it as something so completely and unforgivably frivolous that it would become so in his presence. "Look at my children." She held her hand in the direction of her sleeping boys. "And that man on the train, this war . . ." She looked back at the boys, afraid she had woken them, and she felt her chest go hollow, as if the fear and anger had scoured out some part of her. She slumped against the back rail. Her father said nothing, but his eyes were closed. His jaw had gone loose, and maybe trembled.

ࣻ

Europe's war, as they'd been calling it for the better part of three years, had become America's war too in the spring of the previous year. It had seemed so far away for so long and of no direct concern to everyday Americans, then suddenly it leaped around the globe. America was in it, her money supporting it, her men fighting it. It had become, truly, a World War. Gerda first learned of America's involvement on a day in late spring. She and Fritz had been trading in town and were starting home, the family up in the wagon. A rare treat it had been, all of them together in town, and the children were giddy and loud. Gerda shushed them, but the boys kept shoving one another, testing her patience. Katie crawled across Frank and sat between him and Ray to settle them down. Ah, my Katie, Gerda was thinking, when they heard the shouts. She turned and looked up toward the school expecting school kids, but it was from the *Advocate*'s office, where the newspaper was printed and telegraphs were sent and received, that the ruckus emanated. Everyone on the street looked frozen in that moment, all turned in the same direction. Even the blacksmith's dog rose from the shadow of the smithy and ambled to the center of the street.

"War! War!" Young men Gerda didn't recognize were running down the street. "Wilson's declared war!" As one of them ran past the family, he snatched off his hat and used it to slap the rump of the Vogels' big bay horse. "Gonna kill me some Germans," he shouted and ran on by. Soldiers, Gerda had thought. He meant soldiers, but the light had gone crystalline around them and nothing seemed to mean what it had meant moments before.

ࣻ

The rest of the ride from the depot to the Drueke home passed in a silence broken only by the jangle of the harness and the squeak of the buggy. When they turned off the main road, Gerda turned and spoke softly to the boys in the back. "Wake up, little boys, we're . . . here." She had almost said "home." During the week of the funeral Gerda wrapped herself in a cocoon of activity, always doing what was needed even though her parents seemed not to notice. The requirements of ritual gave them all a kind of unsatisfactory respite. It surprised her how quickly the kitchen and everything in it had returned to feeling unthinkingly familiar. The pickle jar in the corner with the oaken lid, the massive crock used for dough making, the seasoned cast-iron skillets of varied sizes and shapes that hung like heavy and useful art on the brick walls of her mother's kitchen—these were the things she had chosen to forget when she set up her own small kitchen. To remember them was to become aware of her own poverty, and really, where was the sense in that?

After breakfast the first morning Gerda took on the job her uncle, Elsa's husband, had assigned to their house. Her mother, ghostlike in her grief, hadn't had the strength to do it herself or even pass the task to someone else. Katherine said it had to be done, should have been done yesterday, but she too seemed unable to begin. Instead she dried the dishes over and over again before stacking them back in the cupboard. "I can help Katherine with the dress," Gerda said, and Mama Drueke left the room without answering.

Gerda sent the boys into the parlor and bade them to be quiet. She stoked the fire to high heat. She placed the flatirons in an efficient row on the stovetop before helping Katherine bring the heavy ironing board in from the back porch. They balanced it on the backs of two chairs. She set to wiping down the heavy sailcloth that covered the board while Katherine went upstairs to get Aunt Elsa's dress from the hook on the back of the door in their mother's room.

"She's sleeping," Katherine said quietly when she came back down. "The doctor gave her some sleeping powder and that's been a help."

Gerda nodded and dipped her finger in the water pail. She flicked droplets onto one of the irons. The water spots slid down before evaporating, so she set it back on the stove to continue to heat. The tiny pleats on Elsa's dress would take the hottest irons. Gerda stood with her back to the room and watched the stove, as if her attention could hurry the heating.

Elsa's burial dress, like all her clothes, was finely tailored and well cared for. The heaviness of the black fabric of the skirt reminded Gerda of the coat the man on the train had been wearing. How could she remember the very weave of that fabric, she chided herself. She had not been close enough to see that well.

Only for a moment: when she closed her eyes she could see that coat caught on the back of the seat just inches from her face. She shook her head, trying to clear the image.

"Does it bother you?" Katherine asked from across the room.

Gerda turned and looked at her with surprise.

"Ironing Aunt Elsa's dress, I mean." She trailed a long empty sleeve in her hand and let it drop. "Do you think about her wearing it?"

If Katherine were her daughter, Gerda would have gone to her without hesitation, would have wrapped her arms around her as an answer, but this Katherine was almost a stranger to her, her shoulders so broad and straight leaving small evidence of the slight girl Gerda had left behind.

"I'm not sure," Gerda answered as truthfully as she could. She took the dress from Katherine and unfastened the hooks that ran from the high neck to below the waist and pulled the garment inside out. She splayed the bodice on the tapered end of the board so they could iron the heavy pleats first.

"Do you want to iron or hold?"

Katherine looked at the dress and then at the irons. She pouted her lower lip and looked as though she would decline both tasks.

"I'll hold," she said at last. "I've never been very good at the detailing."

They set in then, working in silence for a long while, the kitchen growing steamy as they first sprinkled the cloth with water then pressed and smoothed the hot irons across the fabric, switching irons as each one cooled.

"Mama won't talk about Elsa," Katherine said after a while.

Gerda wiped her forehead with the back of her hand. Even in winter this was hot work. Gerda's first memories of her mother included Elsa at her side. The Fishers had traveled from Germany together as young girls, married men from their hometown in Germany and raised their families within a quarter of a mile of each other in the New World. Elsa had been tall and thin, and Mama wore enough weight for both of them, though that wasn't the only way they differed. Elsa started talking when she got up in the morning and kept it up until she went to bed at night. Her husband once claimed she talked in her sleep too, though there'd been an awkward silence around his comment. The private image of the two of them in bed together pressed against the limits of acceptable knowledge.

"No," Gerda replied. "Mama's never been one to say much, no matter how much needs to be said." She recalled the silence in the house the day of her wedding and had to decide again to let that hurt go.

Katherine gave a short laugh. "I'd say she's been true to herself then. Since Elsa got sick she's folded up on herself like she's got no tongue. Hardly talks to anyone."

"What about Papa?" Gerda asked. The hot iron sizzled and the sour smell of wet wool crinkled Gerda's nose.

"Oh, you know Papa. He talks all the time, but I can't tell if he's saying any more now than he ever did."

Gerda laughed and stopped her work to look up at Katherine. She hadn't expected that kind of assessment from her little sister, from the little girl Papa had so doted on when Gerda lived here. My, my, she thought, my, my.

Gerda's only time alone with her mother was on the ride to the funeral. "You've come home to us then?" her mother asked. Her voice, like her physical presence, was weak and thin. She seemed to have aged decades since Gerda had last seen her. She took her mother's hand and held it between her own hands, trying to warm her.

"Just for a week." She started to say she didn't think Fritz could stand for her to be away any longer, but she knew her mother would see it as weakness, not love.

"Just a week," the older woman echoed and looked out at the lands they passed on the way to the church. They were turning the corner just north of town and they could see the cemetery at the top of the hill. Elsa's grave had been chopped out of the frozen earth and the black hole against the white snow was shockingly visible even from that distance.

"So many years . . ." Her voice trailed off and Gerda didn't know if she was talking about how long they had been apart or how long it had been since they'd been to this cemetery together. Gerda was five when they buried her oldest sister.

"Aunt Elsa was a good woman," Gerda said. Her mother turned and looked at her steadily for a moment. The strength her mother was known for was in that gaze and Gerda thought, now, now is the time for her to say all the things she's not said in the letters they've written over the years. She felt her breathing quicken and she forced herself to look back at her.

"You're a lot like her, you know," her mother said, then abruptly closed her eyes as if the effort of looking at her daughter was too much for her.

Gerda waited. When they arrived at the cemetery, her mother pulled herself forward in the seat with tremendous effort, accepting Gerda's proffered hand only at the last effort, and alighted onto the frozen ground in silence. Gerda watched her walk away and for the first time since she'd read the telegram felt the hard twist of a deeper sorrow. The one that comes of knowing exactly what has been lost.

Was it enough, that moment? Never mind, that's all there was between them.

After the funeral dinner, her uncle found Gerda alone in the kitchen. He stood awkwardly in the doorway for a moment until Gerda looked up from the ham she was slicing. She set down the knife and wiped her hands on her apron before turning to face him. It was the first time they'd spoken to one another alone since Gerda's return.

"I'm so sorry about Elsa." She said this because it was expected, but as she looked up into his dear face, she realized she wanted him to hear her sorrow, to know he was not alone. She wanted to ask him something, something about the nights, about the silence in the house. Did Aunt Elsa still talk in her sleep during those last nights they shared a bed? What did she say? How do you let go of what you had?

"Are you okay, Uncle?" she said into the stretch of silence between them. His hair had gone gray and thin in the years she'd been away, and he'd grown so stooped she was not sure she'd have recognized him in an unfamiliar setting. He looked around the kitchen instead of answering, his eyes lingering not on objects but on the spaces between them. He cleared his throat and stepped into the room with such a careful lifting of each foot that it looked as though he were moving from one shifting surface to another.

"Have this." His words came out in a hoarse growl. He thrust a large, dark bundle into her arms. Gerda recognized the bundle as her aunt's coat, a sealskin fur, and she took it without thinking, as if catching something about to fall. She was struck first by the weight of it, then the incredible lushness of the color, and the softness, oh the softness. Cradled against her chest, the fur tickled her chin and she noticed how the fine hairs moved in response to her breath. Then, only then, did she truly recall her Aunt Elsa.

"I can't take this," she said quietly. "It's . . ." She started to say it's too beautiful, and she realized she could no longer imagine herself wearing anything beautiful and so rich. She swallowed. "It's Aunt Elsa's."

Her uncle didn't quite meet her eye. "Take it." He turned around with that same careful lifting of each foot. The way he reached toward the doorjamb when he walked out made it seem as though the kitchen itself was tilting. Gerda could feel it too, and she pressed her hip against the solid counter to stop it. He had said nothing about need, neither Gerda's nor his own.

In the mornings, it was Gerda and Katherine who rose before the others and they worked side by side to ready breakfast for the family. Katherine was slender and not as tall as Gerda and she moved around the kitchen easily as if she was used to doing the work there. As they worked, Gerda often felt Katherine's eyes on her, but they found little to say to one another.

First thing each morning, Katherine made coffee in the same speckled blue enamel pot that Gerda remembered from her childhood. Even the rusty chips in the enamel along the bottom edge were familiar to her. One morning, Gerda picked it up first and started to fill it, but Katherine reached to take it away from her.

"I'll take care of that." Their hands held the metal handle together for a moment before Gerda released the pot to her sister's grip.

"I know how to make coffee." Gerda wondered what stories about her and Fritz that Katherine had grown up listening to. What did the Black Sheep she had become by marrying Fritz look like to her sister's eyes? Katherine had been the one to greet them when they first arrived. She must have been watching for them. She had come out of the house carrying a lantern and wrapped in a buckskin robe, and Gerda thought she couldn't have looked more like a queen if she'd tried. She pulled first Gerda and then each of the boys into an embrace that enveloped them in welcoming warmth. She had smelled of lavender and fresh bread.

Katherine gazed at her appraisingly before looking over her shoulder toward the stairs. "I don't doubt it," she said quietly. "But if Papa found out how much coffee I used every morning, he'd be doing St. Vitus's dance right here in the kitchen." She leaned in toward Gerda. "Don't you tell on me, but I make mine first, then water it down for him."

Gerda caught her laugh in the palm of her hand. "Make mine like yours. I almost gagged on that warm brown water we've been drinking!" They both giggled, like ice breaking.

It was from Katherine that Gerda learned that her and Fritz's names were never used in that house. "When Papa can't avoid it, he mutters something about 'your mother's daughter and her *arme Teufel.*'

"It's bad enough that you married a poor man," Katherine explained, "but you were to be the bride of Christ, you know. Fritz didn't just steal his daughter, he stole Papa's key to heaven." They were washing dishes when Katherine told her this. Their mother had gone to bed, sick with one of her headaches—she had so many the week Gerda was there. Gerda's children were settled in with pillows and blankets in the parlor—using them to build, not to sleep—and Papa Drueke had gone outside immediately after another awkward and quiet meal. "It would be as easy for him to pass through the eye of a needle as it would be for him to forgive you."

Gerda walked to the window and pulled back the yellow gingham curtains. Mama Drueke always kept them pulled closed as if the out of doors was something best ignored until forced to go out into it. She saw her father standing in the yard beside a tall-sided corn wagon, his two oldest half-brothers up on the high seat. They were the first offspring of grandfather Anton Drueke's first bride, Papa the last of his second. The difference in years and maternal lineage rendered them as distant as mere neighbors, though hard times of any sort provoked a kind of circling. Gerda hadn't seen them since her wedding day; they had been at the church when she and Fritz passed it on the way to the courthouse.

Papa was talking, the Uncles watching his face, occasionally arcing tobacco juice to the side, seemingly in response to what he said. He had his hand on a horse's rump, patting it now and again distractedly. Both horses, matched dappled Percheron geldings, stood at rest, one hind foot raised and heads lowered in the harness.

"Fritz is not a devil," Gerda said as she watched the men, the phrase *arme Teufel* ringing in her ears, "and we're no poorer than anyone else around there." She wiped the cup in her hand slowly until it was dry and then she wiped it again. She caught herself holding the cup in the palm of her hand, one of the vine-patterned Bavarian cups her mother used every day, measuring the weight of the delicate china against the memory of the mug she knew Fritz would be using back home.

"The truth is—I thought Mama would forgive me, at least Mama. I named my daughter after her." She turned to look at her sister. "After you too, I guess. We still call her Katie, like we did you, when you were a baby. And when our Frank was born, it was Fritz who said we should name him after Papa." She set the cup on the shelf and picked up another from the drying rack.

Katherine shrugged. She had a funny way of lifting first one shoulder and then the other so that although she remained upright, her body appeared to sway, like reed grass moving in water. Gerda admired her sister's gracefulness even as she was dismayed by her glib response. "They're just names. Did you really think words would make a difference?"

Outside, the two men stepped down from the wagon to stand beside Papa. Gerda was struck by the care with which they negotiated the descent, their age showing in the slow stiffness of their movements. She untied her apron and smoothed her hair.

"Grandma Norma would be seventy-eight today if she was alive," Katherine said, the subject of Gerda's *arme Teufel* exhausted for now. "At least if I've done my math the way it should be done and Mama had the dates right."

Gerda checked her image in the glass on the wall to be sure she had no flour marks on her face—she hated discovering such things after she'd finished a conversation with people whose opinions she cared about. "Grandma Norma? How on earth would you remember a thing like that? She was dead and buried long before you came along."

"Oh, when I was little, Mama always told me I had her nose and Papa always told me to take care she didn't come back for it. For some reason I always thought her birthday was the most likely day she'd do that. I could never sleep the night before, I was so frightened! When I told Papa that, he just laughed. You know how he is."

No, I don't, Gerda thought. The Papa she knew would never have made a joke like that. Or any joke at all. "I see the Uncles are here." She pulled a shawl off the hook by the back door and wrapped it around her shoulders. "I'm going to go see if they've time to stop for a while." Aside from the conversation she had with Papa when she got off the train, the longest conversation she'd had about what had happened was with Katherine. "That must have been frightening," Katherine had said, but the bread wanted kneading, and she bent to that as though it mattered, so the conversation ended.

If anyone in this community knew about what had happened on the train, it would be the Uncles. They'd lived in the West Point area longer than anyone alive, aside from a few Pawnee, though with the divided history of the two races the natives didn't figure in the story the town told about itself, and so it was left to the Uncles to be the town's forefathers. They sat on the town council and any other board that formed, including the local chapter of the Knights of Columbus. They were the muscle in the order known as "the strong right arm of the church."

Katherine walked to the window and peered out. "They certainly won't come in without an invite, and Papa surely won't think to offer it."

The Uncles, Joseph and Ambrose, were both widowers, their wives succumbing in childbirth after the eighth child for Joseph and the tenth for Ambrose. Neither had remarried, though Ambrose had kept the same housekeeper for the past twenty-five years and people often mistook her for his wife. Or Joseph's, they were never sure. With their houses no more than a stone's throw apart, both men depended on the short, stout woman of indiscernible heritage (everyone called her Nana Taylor) to care for their children and their homes. For the most part she had succeeded: two boys lost to scarlet fever, a girl in a threshing accident, and one of the babies failed to grow, though that last one took place before her time and was never held against her. One of the sons had gone into the priesthood, two girls into the convent, and aside from the two still at home, the rest were farmers.

They were solid men, these two Uncles, standing wide-hipped and feet planted firmly in the soil when they stood still, and when they moved, others got out of their way. In Gerda's youth they had seemed taciturn and mysterious men, rarely speaking in her presence, no more familiar to her than the men she had grown up seeing at church and in town in passing. Even her cousins, their children, had never been a part of her life, not in the way of the cousins on her mother's side where the children had grown up together like puppies in a litter.

When Gerda stepped out of the house, the three men were deep in what passed for animated conversation in this part of the world, but as she approached they stopped talking and turned toward her, moving out of the circle they had formed to stand in a straight line facing her. They could be oak trees, Gerda thought, and for a moment she considered changing course and heading toward the henhouse. The distance between the house and the yard hadn't seemed so long when she started toward them, but by the time she reached them she'd had time to recall their history and her place in it. It would have been their doing that sent the priest who'd promised to marry her and Fritz back to Omaha the day before the wedding. They sided with her father, and it seemed they had the power to move mountains, or at least bend the church to their will. She wanted them on her side of whatever battle might be ahead.

"You've come home, then," Ambrose said as he replaced his hat. It was uttered as a statement, though it was a query she had been answering in nearly every conversation she'd had with family and neighbors all week.

"Yes," Gerda answered, "just for the week." The Uncles nodded and looked down at their boots. "Would you like to come in for a bit? We've got a pot of coffee on, and Katherine has a cake cooling on the side table."

"There was trouble on the train," Joseph said in answer. "On your trip home." Again, questions phrased as statements; no wonder she had such trouble conversing with them when she was younger. She felt as though her words were building blocks that she set out only to have them blindly bull through them with statements of their own.

"Yes." She pulled her shawl more securely around her, wishing she'd slipped her arms into Aunt Elsa's coat rather than throwing this thin fabric so carelessly around her shoulders. "Do you know what happened to that man? The one they threw off the train?"

Ambrose stretched his neck up and rubbed his chin. "He was German, you say."

"That's what *they* said," she answered, "the men who threw him off the train."

"There were Germans on the train," Joseph added. "Besides the man."

Gerda wondered whether he meant her and the children, and what he meant by pointing it out.

"There are Germans all over Nebraska," Papa spoke up. He was the youngest of the brothers by more than fifteen years, and in their presence Gerda could see that family order still mattered. Papa seemed younger standing beside them, still the little brother despite the decades. A long silence followed his remark.

Joseph and Ambrose didn't even look at each other when they decided to get back up onto their wagon and head home. After they left, Papa walked to the barn and Gerda stood for a moment in the yard, looking around. What just happened, she wondered. The wind picked up again and ice crystals bit her face.

That night she woke up sweating. When she threw the covers off, the winter chill hit her like a judgment. The memory of the young man slapping the Vogels' horse, shouting, "Gonna kill me some Germans!" got mixed up with the image of the porter's mutilated ears, and she lay awake trying to sort out what was real from what was the nightmare. The thought of boarding the train alone with the boys chilled her to the bone, and she grabbed blankets around her again and slipped from the darkened bedroom into the kitchen. *We are only stewards of this life and must render an account for its use and abuse.* The words of some long ago sermon repeated themselves in her head. Leaning her forehead against the frosty window, she tried hard to see herself and the boys getting on the train. What she could see, she could do, but the image froze each time she lifted her foot up onto the bottom step of the train platform and she could not will it to move farther.

When the morning finally came, an exhausted Gerda made the coffee and poured a cup for her and then for Katherine. She was adding water to the pot when Papa Drueke came in from the outside. The cold air rose from him as if he were the source of it. Since the night she had arrived he had said little to her. The children she had hoped he would learn to love seemed to excite little more than irritation in him. "Settle down and mind your manners," was the longest sentence he'd uttered to any of them, and that to Ray when his elbow caught a glass of milk at the supper table. Gerda supposed she should be grateful he hadn't backhanded the boy, as he had been known to do to his own children for similar offense.

Papa Drueke stood staring at his daughters, chewing on the edge of his untrimmed moustache as if frozen in place until Katherine said, "Papa, the door." He looked over his shoulder at it, then closed it and turned again to stare at them. Gerda and Katherine looked at each other then back at him.

Finally, he spoke. "You'll stay." He dipped his head in agreement with himself and began to unbutton his coat. Again Gerda and Katherine looked at each other.

"What are you saying, Papa?" Katherine asked.

"Her." He nodded toward Gerda. "And her young ones. They don't get back on that train. West Point's a good German town. They'll be safe here."

Gerda held the water pitcher above the coffee pot, no longer pouring, just holding. When she understood what he meant, she felt filled with a strange kind of exhilaration, nothing akin to joy, just the feeling of being suspended between two places, as if she'd slipped once again through the hayloft door as she had so long ago. In a trick of memory surrounding that first fall, she could not recall the actual slip through the door or the landing on the hard-packed floor below. It was only the moment in between that stayed with her, the moment when she floated, light and free as the dust motes in the air around her. That lightness returned to her now.

From the parlor came the high-pitched screech of one of the boys, followed by another's shushing sound and then giggles sliding into silence. A log in the kitchen stove burned through and split, dropping in a burst of whispery sparks. She pictured her daughter, Katie, in the kitchen back home, how careful she was when she opened the firebox door, always standing far back and leaning only as close as necessary to replenish the cobs or bank the fire. Fritz needed a woman in the house, even if that woman was only eight years old. He wouldn't eat if someone weren't there to see to it that he did. He wouldn't take the time even to fold meat between bread and stand at the table and chew if Katie had not stayed behind to care for him. He needed her.

"You will come home again, won't you?" he had whispered. How certain she had been then of her answer. How frighteningly welcome the sensation of floating felt now.

Gerda turned toward him, setting the water pitcher on the table as softly as a bird about to fly. The shadow of the Uncles' visit lingered like a solid wall at his back. She felt outnumbered.

"I need to be taking my boys home." Even as she said it, other thoughts crowded the back of her mind. Papa didn't argue with her, and his silence was more frightening than any words he could have used. As if Gerda had only herself to convince.

She spent the day preparing to leave, but it felt as though a curtain had been drawn across the morrow and she couldn't see herself opening her own front door. She remembered her mistake of watching the Stuart depot slide from sight and the fear that had clung to her that day came back to her. Had she set this in motion even then?

Sometime later, well after the lanterns had been lit, Katherine found her in the parlor where her travel trunk stood open and partially packed. She picked up one of the boys' freshly laundered shirts and began folding it. "Do you want to stay?" she asked.

Gerda looked at her with surprise and not a little fear. "I can't stay here?" Her own voice betrayed her by turning her statement into a question. She cleared her throat. "My life is there now."

Katherine looked at her out of the corner of her eyes. "If you want to go," she paused. "I'll take you to the depot." She dropped the shirt she was folding into the trunk. "You know Papa, he won't take you." Here at last was evidence that Papa was still the same man he had been when Gerda left with Fritz. Gerda sat down on the bed and brushed her hair back from her face with both hands. It had been Fritz who stood up to Papa and the Uncles before; he had been the mountain of strength. What if they try to stop her again?

"I'm afraid," she whispered.

"You have reason to be," Katherine said, and closed the door. "Get your things ready, but don't let Papa see your bags. Stay in this room as much as you can. I'll take care of Papa."

For the second night in a row, Gerda didn't sleep. Once the boys were in bed, the house seemed unnaturally silent, and she wandered about the darkened rooms and listened at the closed doors. Near sunrise, the snores from Papa's room were as loud as they had been all night. Gerda dressed in the cold and quietly stoked the fire in the stove before waking the boys. She was pulling a clean shirt over Leo's head when Katherine came in from the outside.

"Have you been out there all night?" Gerda asked in surprise.

"I just went out," Katherine said, but that didn't seem to be an answer to the question. "Are you ready?"

Gerda nodded toward the stairs to the upper bedrooms. "Papa's sleeping so late, but surely he'll be up. What will we do?"

Katherine smiled and held up a bottle. "Papa's whiskey works as well as Mama's sleeping powder. I brought him a double shot when I took up Mama's night glass. You know how he hates to waste anything, so I imagine the glass was empty before long."

Gerda stared at Katherine as if at a stranger. "But he had a glass before he went to bed."

"I told you I would help, and this is what help looks like," she said. "Do you want to go home? Or not?"

"Will he be okay?"

Ray came into the room then, yawning and rubbing his eyes. "I'm hungry, Mama." Katherine reached out and ruffled his hair. "I'll get you something. Your Mama has to get your things packed before the hired man comes in to get your trunk."

We are only stewards of this life and must render an account for its use and abuse. There it was again, that reminder of the long ago sermon. Gerda turned to go up the steps to check on Papa, but a knock at the door stopped her. Her first thought was that it was the Uncles here to stop her now that Papa couldn't, and she felt the urge to run toward the door and lock it to keep them out so that she and the children could run out the back way. She would run all the way home if she had to.

Katherine opened the door, and the old man who had worked for her father for more than thirty years stood waiting on the other side of it. "I've come for your trunk, Mrs. Vogel. The horses are ready."

Gerda ushered the children before her across the snowy platform between the depot and the train tracks. Their footsteps screeched in the hard-packed snow, a sound as cold as the air around them. The two older boys hopped from one foot to another, digging the heels of their boots in with each step, the shriek of snow giving voice to the feeling Gerda held as a lump at the base of her throat. Leo twisted backward in her arms, pulling away from her until her arms ached, and she feared she would drop him.

A sudden gust of wind-driven snow whipped her skirt back against her legs and took the breath from her lungs. She pulled the baby closer to her neck to protect him from the cold and for a moment he let her. Compliant in his need for warmth, he nuzzled the soft fur of Gerda's coat. A belch of white steam billowed up from the smokestack, and another stream screamed out from beneath the engine. It looked for a moment that the train was leaving, stranding them on the platform. Ray and Frank spun in the wind toward their mother. Their scarf-wrapped faces turned toward her, eyes wide open. She couldn't tell if they were happy or frightened. The ch-ch-ch of the engine sounded like the huffing of some great beast. Gerda pushed Ray's shoulder again to urge him toward the waiting train, though she too wanted to turn back toward something behind her that promised safety. Directly on her heels, the hired man followed them with their trunk slung across his back and bags under his arms. He looked more like a pack mule than a man.

She hustled the boys onto the coach car while Katherine saw to the stowage of their things in baggage before coming to see that they were settled. The two older boys were kneeling on separate seats with their faces pressed to the windows when she caught up with them. Gerda tried to move them together onto one seat, but with the baby twisting to see what his brothers were doing, it took both arms to hold him and they found it easy to ignore her. Katherine stepped up behind her and smiled at the boys; she settled them as if they were bewitched, and they both dropped down onto their bottoms.

"Got your tickets?" she asked hoarsely. Her cheeks were flushed and her eyes sparkled, but Gerda could see the hours leading up to this one had taken a toll.

"Yes." She patted the handbag that held them. She looked around at the other passengers as if to memorize them or sniff out their potential for trouble.

"You got something for those young ones to eat? It's a long trip and they'll need it."

She nodded and pointed to the basket at her feet that she had packed the night before, before Papa had come inside: hard-boiled eggs, sliced ham, and dark rye bread wrapped in flour bags.

Katherine turned to the boys, who were looking up at her uncertainly from beneath their caps. "You mind your mother, you hear?" The boys looked at Gerda. She pointed up the aisle where she wanted them to go, and they slid without a word off the benches and followed her direction.

"Katherine," she started, but the train whistle pierced the air at the same moment, drowning her voice. The baby threw himself back and bumped his head on the upright seat back and let out a high-pitched howl.

She held the screaming baby to her neck and looked at Katherine. "Papa," she began again, then the conductor called in that practiced singsong, "All aboa-rd who's going aboa-rd! All aw-ff who's getting aw-ff."

Katherine hugged her, quick and hard. The baby pulled away from her neck and screamed again. The train jerked forward and Katherine stepped out through the open door without saying another word.

Gerda stared at the empty space where she had been and swallowed hard. Frank leaned against her. "Where do we sit, Mama?" She turned to walk down the aisle between the seats, the baby still crying, the basket bumping her legs, and outside the window Katherine walked toward the buggy without looking back.

Gerda found a place for them as close to the heat stove as she could, but still the car was cold. She herded the boys into the seat and placed the baby, now recovered from his bump, between them and bundled the three under a thick wool blanket. She looked around at the other passengers, hoping for, and afraid of, recognition.

As the train pulled away from the depot, she took a smaller blanket out of the basket that held the food and covered her own lap. She settled back to watch the landscape slide by the window and murmured the prayer her mother had taught her when she was a little girl. "Oh most gracious Virgin Mary . . . ," she murmured. The rhythm of the train said the trip was over, the trip was over, the trip was over. She was taking her sons back to Stuart, to her daughter and her husband.

I am going home, she thinks. Home.

It is then that she sees her father, hatless in the wind, standing at the crossing on the west end of town. His horse puffs great clouds of white beside him. A chill of fear slides up her arms and prickles the hair at the back of her neck. He can stop the train, she thinks, and as she watches, he steps toward the tracks, his hands raised. The train rumbles past him, and her last glimpse of him is of a man bent over against the wind, bent over as if in grief.

CHAPTER FOUR

"When I say something, I see one thing and you see another, and yet the same moon shines on us both at night. In the morning the sun, the same sun wakes us." Ed Gannoway stood beside Father Jungels and spoke calmly, because he felt calm. "You feel winter cold and in the spring I know you hear the turtledoves, the meadowlarks, as I do. You smell the wild ginger, the sage, and indigo when they bloom." He waved his hat out to encompass the world around them. "We live in the same world, but I am wary of ascribing to some great unknown the very laws of nature. To my mind there are only necessities; there is no one who commands or obeys, or trespasses even. The shadow of . . . of a god isn't necessary for life to exist." He shifted his weight from one foot to the other and held a hand out as if offering Jungels a gift. "As one of my favorite philosophers said, science arose from poetry, and I think the same is true of religion. Times are changing, Father, and someday the three can meet again on a higher level as friends. Perhaps you and I, personally, will never be *friends,* but we can get along."

Father Jungels ignored Gannoway's last statement. "Religion—is not—poetry. *I* see God's glory shining all around. Not just the moon and the sun." He placed his emphasis on the word *I* in each sentence. "When *I* wake up and hear the birds, *I* know they're joining in my worship of God's creation—and the flowers that will bloom in the spring, they too worship God in their way." Jungels was not calm and his words were not spoken calmly. "It is only you, Dr. Gannoway, who seems unable to recognize that which is so clear to me, and to all believers, that the world is a manifestation of God's love. It exists because of God and for no other reason and in no other way."

Mass had been over for fifteen minutes, but still the two men talked on, paying no attention to time or even the cold gusts of wind that whipped sand and snow up the street now and again. Miranda had walked her friend Mary Becker and her husband to their automobile, declining their offer of a "lift" home, preferring to keep up the façade that the odd motion of autos made her nauseated, rather than running the danger of appearing envious of the gleaming machine. (That envy did have a home in her heart was no one's business but her own.) She had stopped and talked with Johnny Kaup about the Red Cross drills he ran for the Boy Scouts. Johnny was a pleasant enough sort, but so obsequious toward her that she ran out of things to say to him too quickly for him to help her pass the time while her husband and the priest held what Ed characterized as their "weekly theological discussions."

Today they were still going strong when she got back to the base of the wide church steps. She waited for a time at the bottom of the stairs gazing idly around at the day. Across the street someone had spilled what appeared to be ground corn, or maybe millet, golden against the snow, and a flock of birds of varying sizes and colors were fighting over the crumbs.

She always meant to study up about birds, about which ones migrated and which ones lived here year round, for example, so that she could identify the earliest stages of spring, but she never quite got around to it. Birds, though pretty enough to watch, were just winged things, a part of the great outdoors that she could take or leave. If pressed, she would have to admit that her interest in studying birds lasted only as long as a conversation with her husband about the possibility of studying them. Ed was a voracious learner, so hungry for knowledge that he would never learn enough in one lifetime with his one mind. He seemed always to be pressuring her to learn something new, as if her mind could be a storehouse for knowledge that he didn't have time to pick up or hold on his own. When she said she was interested in a subject, whether it was birds or manufacturing or wind direction, his face would light up and he would begin peppering her with questions and suggestions. At first it was exciting, but over the years it had grown tiresome more often than not. Could he not have a simple, pleasant conversation?

She looked up the steps where he and the priest stood and she saw the warning signs of color creeping up from beneath his blue wool neck scarf and that false, tight smile he got when something upset him. Sometimes she felt she knew him better than he knew himself, at other times she felt she didn't know him at all. The priest's face, as usual for these discussions, had been red since Ed approached him. It was time to put a stop to this one. She began walking slowly, purposefully toward them. For such a smart man, Ed seemed distressingly unaware of what constituted appropriate conduct in social settings.

Gannoway was saying, "You tend to the people in your care—"

"To my flock," Jungels interrupted.

"Yes, your flock," he conceded. "You care for them by praying and leading them in prayer—"

"I show them the *way*."

Gannoway stepped over that phrase. "I too care for these people, my patients, your flock. I care *for* them and I take care *of* them to the best of my ability, Father. And I believe that is enough for this world, and the next."

"No! No! No!" Jungels said loudly, not quite shouting. "That's where you're wrong." Miranda pulled on Ed's arm. She looked around to see if anyone was still within hearing distance.

"You are doing yourself and your patients a tragic disservice. You are a man they look to for physical care, yes, but they also look up to you. You aren't simply a doctor; you are a model of *how* to *be* in this world. Your rejection of the Truth endangers your patients *and* my flock. I must ask you to stop spreading lies and blasphemy!"

"Lies and blasphemy?!" Suddenly this conversation that had been as interesting as a chess game with a mediocre opponent took on a dark and sinister tone. Gannoway's calmness slipped away from him as easily as a man's reputation in the face of vicious rumors.

Father Jungels's face remained red, but he lowered his voice. "I am sorry to be so direct, Dr. Gannoway, but I fear I must, I must do what I can to save my dear and vulnerable flock."

"My good man," Gannoway began. "You need to understand something about this community and your place in it. I have been here for nearly two decades building a practice and caring for these people. You . . . you have just arrived. You don't even know the names of 75 percent of your parishioners—"

"I know their souls, and that's what matters."

"I know their names and I care for their bodies. I care for *them*. You care only for their so-called souls." Gannoway was beyond caring about social politics. He couldn't remember what had possessed him to try to have a relationship with this . . . this imbecile.

"So-called souls?!" Jungels roared. "So-called *souls?!* Do you not see the error of your ways? Do you not understand that the gates of hell are opened by the likes of men like you? You are a, a . . . *heathen*, Dr. Ed Gannoway."

Miranda plucked at her husband's arm, but she may as well have been a fly landing on his coat sleeve. He had worked for twenty years to build a place of respect in this community. It was his dollars that built most of the bell tower under which they presently stood, but he was no fool. He knew how easily loyalties can change. Did he not see it all around him as this war wore on and the Germans, even in this community, had grown smaller and smaller in their influence, staying away from town more and more? He knew the dangerously thin ground he stood on. "Father, please, I want you to know that I . . ."

The approach of a young couple stopped him from going on. Miranda took the opportunity to pull Gannoway away before he did further damage.

When younger, Gannoway and his brother, Lark, had spent hours discussing such issues as the nature of medicine, the importance of scientific training, the need for community—the meaning of life, really—and he missed those talks.

Breathing deliberately to calm himself as he and Miranda walked home, he thought about how long it had been since he and Lark had last talked. There were the phone calls at Christmas once the phone lines came to Stuart, but their voices sounded so tinny and distant to each other that they never moved beyond pleasantries shouted into the receiver. Perhaps he had lost the ability to have meaningful conversations, to debate a topic without getting emotional. (*Emotional! I'm a better man than that.*) He had no practice at the skill.

The Gannoways paused at the corner of Fourth and Parnell Streets to allow the Beckers to pass in their automobile. Mary Becker clumsily rolled down the window and called out over the rattle of the engine, "You should be glad you said no to our offer, Miranda. You would have been obliged to help push us out of the drift over on Fifth Street."

Miranda stepped closer to the car, unconsciously pulling her collar closer around her ears. "Heavens! Are you all okay?"

Mary laughed, but her reply was lost as John Becker continued down the street, the car lurching across the tracks left by wagons and sleds.

Ed took his wife's arm and they continued toward home.

"I'm not sure why anyone would want one of those contraptions," Miranda commented. "It certainly isn't something a man in your position could depend upon. Anyone who had to travel when *needed* and not just when the weather allowed, I mean."

Ed glanced up the street to where in the distance the Beckers were backing up and taking a second run at the small drift at the end of their lane. Miranda had a way of offering unexpected praise that never failed to ease the tension he too often held in his neck. He twisted his head a little, stretching his neck beyond his collar, testing it for the newly offered release.

"That contraption is going to change the world," he replied. "Think of how the roads will have to be changed. In winter there'll need to be plows out, opening the way after every storm. That reminds me of an article I read just last week . . ." and he was off, putting aside his anger at Jungels and his fear or discomfort at where their conversations led. The subject of roads was one that may or may not have intrigued him for years. It didn't matter—it caught his attention now.

While Miranda set out the cold cuts and potatoes the cook had left for their noon dinner, Ed pulled out maps of Nebraska to show her where the towns were and the existing roads between them, explaining how the roads themselves would have to change in time. She tried, she really tried to be interested.

They ate in the kitchen on Sundays when they were alone in the house. No need to heat the dining room those days. Once a month they hosted the Sunday evening whist games. In the summer there were concerts in the band shell in the park, and in deep winter groups met down on the river for ice skating, but February was an in-between month—a midwinter thaw ruined the ice for skating, but didn't last. The day yawned before them empty of plans they could agree on.

"It will be warmer to eat our dinner here in the kitchen," Miranda said, "but if you'd rather leave the maps out, I suppose we could go into the dining room with our plates."

Ed looked up to see her standing with a plate in each hand, surprised that it was mealtime.

"Oh," he said, looking between the maps and the plates. "I guess I could put these away for a while. Or maybe I could move them to the dining room?"

She tipped her head in a way that could mean yes or no and stood her ground with the plates.

Perhaps it was the wind that came just then, the way it sent a smattering of snow crystals against each window and down the chimney, causing the fire in the kitchen stove to flare and crackle and the house to shudder, even the walls seemed to pull in around them; something made their aloneness that day so profound, so remarkable that when Ed looked up from the maps' spidery lines, he saw Miranda's lips widening into balance and he could think of nothing more than touching her. She had that effect on him, even now after all these years, after all their shared and separate sorrows.

He held his hands out and took the plates from her.

"I do believe I forgot to mention something this morning before we left for Mass."

She knew what he was going to say, and she could feel the slight flush moving up her cheeks. The man made her feel like a schoolgirl at times.

"Really, Dr. Gannoway, you forgot something? That does surprise me as I've noticed you so rarely forget anything." This being one of their favorite jokes between them—his focus on ideas rendering him too often at a loss for the practical considerations in life. More than once she had teased him that he'd not be getting an automobile until they invented one that would remember its way home when he was lost in a daydream.

"Come with me," he said, walking with the plates and all up the steps to their room, "and I'll tell you what I meant to say this morning when first you opened those eyes."

She laughed and followed him slowly, her hand trailing the banister. For his part, he stepped sideways so that she stayed in his sight, holding the plates as if to entice her, though the food would grow cold before they touched it.

Behind closed doors, Miranda was not one of those women who were shy about their bodies. She stood still in the center of the room as Ed unbuttoned each button from her chin to below her waist. She pulled the pins from her hair and shook her head to let it fall in loose curls that tickled his hands. With a fluid shrug she let the dress drop from her shoulders to the floor, and when she stepped out of it, she stepped toward him as something she'd been born to do. She cupped the back of his hand to guide him to each ribbon, each bit of lace that needed undoing, and when she was completely free, she reached toward his clothes with confident smoothness. In the cold light filtering through the filigreed windows, her skin prickled and pinkened, but there was no hurry. Each action was a kind of ritual that she would not rush.

It was only afterward, when Ed buried his face in the thick of her hair, their bodies and their breath settling back to normal, that she could not hold back the inevitable sorrow. Her eyes burned, and she turned away from her husband, trying to hide what he could not keep from knowing. How closely tied is this act to our final fate as humans. We are mortal, fragile.

Memories rose like spirits in the room. How easily what is made can be taken away.

CHAPTER FIVE

"Here it is," Fritz said, rattling the paper between his big hands. "Headline says: 'Local Boys Take Patriotic Matters into Their Own Hands.' Now listen to this, 'When a German gentleman—and we use that term,'" Fritz stuttered over the word, "'iron . . . ironically here—spoke out against this good country, he got his comeuppance. "We picked him up by his britches and tossed him off the train," one of the young men reported. It seems the kraut believed the freedom of America included freedom to tear it down. However, he should have been more careful in exercising his "freedom." Those young men he spouted off to were on their way to Fort Riley, Kansas, en route to Europe with the U.S. Expeditionary Forces. Perhaps the man's roll through the snow was just the civics lesson he needed.'"

Fritz spread the paper out in front of him and smoothed it across the surface of the table. He tapped the small article with the palm of his hand and nodded abruptly once like a man who had satisfied himself in relation to the facts. "You made me think the whole train car got involved and turned it into a bloody riot."

Gerda turned from the stove where she was stirring a pot of boiling water filled with white garments. The steam flushed her face and curled wisps of hair at her temples. The wooden stick in her hand steamed in the cool air near the window.

"I was there, Fritz! I know what I saw!" Her shock at the article and his response showed in her face. "That man was bleeding when they dragged him down the aisle. His white shirt and collar were soaked with blood. And when he fell, they kicked him! I heard the sound of a bone breaking." She looked wild and disconcerted by Fritz's refusal to believe. "They were shouting! All around us people were shouting. They said, 'Kill the kraut!'

about a man they knew nothing about!" She tugged at the neck of her dress in frustration and stared at Fritz, her mouth open. "You saw the blood on our blanket!"

"How do you know they knew nothing about him?" Fritz asked, though he turned away before she could answer him. "You just think that's what happened, and you got all worked up because you were scared when you saw a little blood. You always get worked up when you see blood." He took his coat off the hook by the door.

Gerda closed her eyes and saw again the young men at the front of the railroad car, how it seemed that one moment they were talking and laughing, and the next moment one was holding the man's arms while the other two pummeled him with their bare fists. He had tried to defend himself, she recalled, and grabbed for the poker by the stove, but the other three were stronger and faster, and they got it from him. They hit him with it again and again. Gerda could still hear the sickening sound of it thudding against his back. His eyes, when they dragged him down the aisle past Gerda and the boys, were rolled up inside his head, and he did not resist them anymore. The snow bank where he rolled when they tossed him from the train was streaked with blood, red on white so vivid she knew she would never forget the sight of its trail.

"No, Fritz." She swallowed hard before going on. "No. That paper is wrong. I know what I saw. They didn't just grab him by the britches. There's something wrong there, I know it."

Fritz buttoned his coat and pulled his mittens on before answering. "Don't be borrowing trouble, Gerda. You and the boys weren't hurt." He opened the door, and snow crystals blew across the floor. Over his shoulder he said, "That has nothing to do with us."

Gerda didn't trust her voice. Anger felt like a white noise in her head, and she couldn't separate it into words. Instead, she slammed the spoon down on the stove, opened the fire door, and jammed wood into the fire. She hadn't told Fritz about what had happened in West Point when she told her father about what happened on the train, and at this moment she wanted to shout that information at him. She wanted to say her father loved her enough to protect her. "At least my father believed me," she said to the empty kitchen. "He believed me." She thought about how close she came to willingly staying in West Point, and the memory chilled her even though the kitchen was steamy with heat.

"It doesn't concern us," Fritz announced when he came in from the barn at suppertime. It was the first thing he said when he came in after chores, and though it had been hours since they'd last spoken, they both knew what he meant. He grabbed the newspaper off the table, roughly twisted it in his hands, and stuffed it into the wood stove where it caught fire immediately and burned brightly for a few minutes before settling into flat ashes. He sat down at the table and turned his attention to the plate of food Gerda had set before him. Gerda attacked the trail of dried mud and sand he had left on the floor, sweeping hard as if she could erase something. Katie sat huddled halfway up the stairs, her nightgown pulled tightly around her knees. Ray's pale moon face peered over her shoulder.

"Get to bed," Gerda said gruffly. For a long while the only sounds in the kitchen were the straw broom scratching across linoleum and silverware clinking against the bone china.

"I saw what I saw, Fritz," Gerda said at last.

Fritz slapped his fork down on the wood table. "Did you not look at the words, woman?" he shouted, though he didn't mean to. "Don't make more of it than what happened!" He abruptly stood up from the table and glared at her. The room seemed brighter for a moment as it had when the paper first burst into flames, and the two stared at one another. Gerda felt suddenly aware of their difference in size, but Fritz looked away first. He pulled his wool coat on over his overalls and clapped his winter cap on his head. His outerwear made him seem bigger and farther away from Gerda, though he hadn't yet moved toward the door. "Don't be getting worked up over things that have nothing to do with us." His overboots jangled as he clumped from the table to the back door and left without another word.

He stepped out of the light, letting the door fall shut behind him and looked up into the sky where a slivered crescent moon of seemingly perilous beauty lay beneath a milky spill of stars. A coyote yipped in the distance and another answered from nearer the barn. Fritz pulled his coat closer and walked farther into the dark, the gravel and snow crunching beneath his boots echoing in the vastness of the night. It was time for bed, not barn work, and he didn't know what he was doing outside at this hour. A quick breeze picked up snow crystals and sent them swirling. He felt dizzied by the feeling the whole world was spinning out of control.

He thought back to the day he first learned of the war, back when he worried about crops and weather and getting his work done. He still could imagine the sound of his neighbor's voice coming to him from a field just out of sight. How occasionally in a quirk of wind and placement in the hollows he would hear the soft calls of "haw" and "gee," though the closest farmer would be near to a mile away. Fritz had felt both companionable to the man, whom he knew to be Dan Liable, and in competition with him. Neither could control the weather that would cause these seeds to grow or not, but each had the ability to try to get ahead of the other. Plant this field in wheat, that one in potatoes, another, nearer water, in corn. Enough to feed a family and sell the rest, prosperity stretching like planted rows toward a distant horizon.

That was how far the future stretched for Fritz that remembered day in April of 1917: to the horizon, to the end of his own land where it joined with a neighbor's, whose name he knew and whose habits he could anticipate. It was a knowable future, peopled with men like him and work he understood. How could he imagine the changes ahead? Tonight he could still remember the feeling of familiar men around him, the sense they were all moving toward the same goals—to plant, to provide, to thrive. Something had happened since that day, and he wasn't sure what it was. Men were still working, families still growing, but something, something had been sent spinning, and he couldn't quite see what it was.

He thought about the other things he'd read in that paper, the things he hadn't read aloud to Gerda. The Germans had started gassing the Allied troops along the western front. He could picture the line of the river there on the maps he had studied, though he could only imagine the reality of the trenches that paralleled it now. When he dug an irrigation trench last summer, he tried to picture it wider and deeper, big enough to hold an army, but his imagination failed him. The words and pictures in the paper were enough. Now his imagination wouldn't let him free from the images of the bodies that lined those same trenches. Ninety-five percent of the men in one company gone in minutes without a shot being fired. How does that happen? The thought took his breath away even here, half the globe away.

And there was other ominous news closer to home. There was the notice buried between news of a cattle sale and an ad for W.N. Coats. (*We want your trade and will use you right!*) "Adolph Gottlieb of rural Stuart went to Valentine last week to take charge of the ranch owned by his son, Otto, who has been drafted."

Last time Fritz saw Adolph he'd told him Otto had a big spread out in the Sandhills. "Doing *gut*," he said, his accent still as thick and guttural as it had been when he first arrived in Nebraska some twenty years before, and his conversation was sprinkled with German phrases. He leaned against the horse rail as he talked to take the weight off his game leg. "That Otto's got his first little one on the way any day now. The missus is going to be a grandmama at last. *Ja*, lots a happy at our home."

Fritz had read the notice and put his hand over it as if he could make it go away or say something else. What was he to make of such news? The paper had said farmers and family men were exempt from the draft—what was Otto Gottlieb if not a farmer and a family man? Fritz knew the answer to that, though he couldn't let himself think it, not even now, or maybe especially now, alone in the dark with his family behind him. The Gottliebs had come over the same year the Vogels had, perhaps on the same boat, though Fritz had been too young to recall.

Morning brought a snowstorm. A wind-blown whiteness cloaked the countryside and there was again, for a short time, only Gerda and the children and the work at hand. Even the cold wind battering the house tendered a kind of solace, a separation from things they could not change.

Frost formed thickly on the windows and entranced the children with its spidery geometric designs. Katie and Frank scratched out math problems in the thin whiteness, laughing delightedly to find a fresh slate each morning. Fritz came in from chores feeling like a snowman covered in crystals he shook off on the rug by the door. His woolen coat steamed as it dried, and the sour smell of wet wool mingled with the smell of wood smoke and cornbread baking. Though there was still silence between them during the day, or maybe because of it, Fritz slept with his arms wrapped round Gerda, his body curled into her as if he was afraid she'd slip away again. They lived cocooned in their small house, the cold and the world held at bay by the fire and their closeness, though Fritz could not forget the other articles he had not read aloud to Gerda.

President Wilson says this war is for a noble cause, the paper reported. "We fight not only for ourselves but for all future generations. Americans cannot shirk their duties and every one of us must be prepared to give the ultimate sacrifice." A second draft, the article went on to say, would begin soon: 95,000 American men will be called up for training.

Fritz was thirty-one years old when America joined that war, just over one third of the years allotted to him, but he couldn't know that then. He had, as we all do, only one window through which he viewed an ever-changing Now. Two months after the war started, Fritz registered for the draft, one of the nearly 10 million men between the ages of twenty-one and thirty-one who did, according to the news reports. His draft number, registered with the Local Board of Holt County, Nebraska, was 837.

The way it works, he had explained to Gerda when he came back from O'Neill, where the registration was held, is that they give you a number. "The one here," he said, pointing at the number in front of his name on the forms he had brought home, "is your serial number. Everybody has got a serial number and that's how they'll know who you are if you get called up."

"But what if they make a mistake and they give two men the same number?" Gerda asked. Fritz brushed the question away.

"That's not going to happen," he said. "The way it works is every state has so many numbers, certain numbers that only that state has. Then the state divides those numbers up by each county, so it works out that once you know a guy's number, you know what state and county he lives in. Doesn't matter where he goes in the world, that number will tell the government where he's from." He patted the form flat on the table. Gerda had cleared the supper dishes and wiped the table clean so that Fritz had room to show the paper and tell the story of his trip to O'Neill. Frank and Ray were leaning over their father's shoulder looking at the form, and Katie sat on her knees on a chair opposite Fritz. Gerda stood at his shoulder. His stories were welcome to a family hungry for news, and this news, this news of the draft, was especially interesting. It had been talked up at school and at church. There'd even been a band playing in town the last time they all went, just to remind men to register, and the front page of the paper held two or three articles every week about why and who and how it was all to be accomplished. William Owens, the owner of the general mercantile in Stuart, had been selected to be what he called a "four-minute man" charged with educating the public about all things patriotic. Four-minute men, both appointed and self-appointed, had sprung up all over the country. Along with the speeches provided by the War Department, Owens had prepared a vast number of four-minute speeches that he gave to any available audience, and all his customers were considered available. The Vogels had more than once witnessed his enthusiastic orations. Excitement hung heavy in the air whenever they went to town and when Fritz went alone they waited eagerly for his return.

"The line there at the courthouse snaked all the way out the front door by the time we Stuart boys got there. Good thing it wasn't raining, cuz some of them boys had been there since dawn, it turns out." Fritz took a sip of coffee.

"Don't know what their big hurry was; the board guys said they would stay there until everybody in the whole county who was eligible was registered."

"Tell me again what 'eligible' means, Papa," Katie asked.

"It means if the government needs you to go be a soldier, then you need to pack your razor and go." Fritz tried to keep it light, to pretend that it was just another trip to town and when he put the form away things would get back to normal. He would go out and do his chores, plant his crops, and walk his land. The war would stay over there and he would stay over here. He felt confident of this not only because the papers said the country needed its farmers to farm, but because he was on the edge of being too old for service. If he was not called up before November when he turned thirty-two, then he would be free of the possibility of conscription, he believed. He was not against serving his country, but he was afraid of what would happen to his farm and his family if he were drafted.

"How do they decide who they need to be a soldier?" Frank asked.

"Well, they'll hold what they call a lottery." Fritz began folding the form carefully, matching side to side, creasing the paper with his thumb.

"And then what?" Gerda asked.

"Well, when they pick your serial number, they put it in order with all the other numbers they pick. Then they give you another number; it's your order number. That means boys go in the order they're picked." He took his wallet out and tucked the paper in beside the two dollars he had to his name. He stood up and the two boys clung to his neck, dangling and giggling. Fritz shuddered like a bear and they dropped to the floor.

"How do you know you've been picked? Does someone come get you?" Gerda unconsciously glanced out the window when she asked these questions.

Fritz considered his answer carefully before he spoke. "No, they will publish the names in the local paper. They'll tell you where you have to go and when." Gerda glanced at the newspaper that Fritz had brought home as if it had developed the ability to bite her right then. He understood the sentiment.

Unlike those back in the old country who were caught up in the swiftness of the war's onset in 1914, American men like Fritz had time to think about what the war meant to the country and her citizens for a long while before President Wilson committed resources to fighting it. Fritz hadn't believed Wilson would drag America into that business over there. He'd argued with Aloys about it more than once, and he'd voted for Wilson a second time because he'd kept America out of the war during his first term.

Aloys had told him he was a fool. "That war over there," he'd said, "is a hungry beast that ain't gonna be stopped so easy." Though it had been a full year since Wilson's declaration, Fritz still felt the shock of it.

Before the war, he hadn't been easily interested in what they were doing in foreign countries. He believed in the dream that was the story America told about itself—look to his own life for proof of that. He had started out with nothing but a back and arms as strong as his desire for a better life, and look at him now—thirty-two years old with a section of land, three sons, and a daughter to his name. It was exactly the life his father had envisioned for him and his brothers when he brought them to this country. Fritz believed in America, not as a country with streets paved in gold like something from a children's book, but as a land where men could stand up as individuals and dreams could be lived. His ideas grew out of a farmer's experience of self-sufficiency and a progressive's belief that the world must improve itself with each generation. He thought America could let the old world take care of itself. War, especially one fought on foreign soil, was a form of lunacy. Freedom meant nothing if not the right to work one's own land and live as a man ought.

After the weather broke near the middle of March, Fritz started in on his early spring chores. Cleaning out the barn, he loaded manure into a spreader wagon and fertilized his fields. Gerda sent the older children out after school to collect corncobs from the pigpens to use for fuel, and he moved the sows from pen to pen so that they could work in safety. Each step of each chore was familiar to him and it offered him a kind of comfort, allowing him to settle into a pattern he understood. Only when he let his mind drift did he come back to his fears. He was certain Otto Gottlieb was a little older than he was, but that didn't make sense. The age of eligibility was thirty-one. As Fritz understood it, Otto shouldn't have been drafted for his age alone. What about being a farmer and a family man? Isn't that what the paper said—that farmers and family men would not be called to serve? He wanted to ask someone about the rules of the draft, but the questions sounded suspicious even in his own mind. For all he knew, it was a question about the draft that got that German fellow, the one he and Gerda never talked about anymore, thrown off the train.

One of the changes he had not anticipated when the war began was the number of things he stopped imagining he would say to Gerda. He missed her now as much as he had when she had gone to West Point. Though she may be in the kitchen baking bread, or out in the brooder house caring for her chickens, she seemed to be miles away. No, it wasn't distance. It was as if some part of her, or maybe of him, had ceased to exist. When she came home from her visit with her family with that story about the German on the train, he could not find the words to talk to her. Worse, he couldn't understand the words she used to talk to him. They had become foreigners to one another. Sometimes he thought it was the fur coat she was wearing when she got off the train. It was as if her family, her father, had wrapped her in something he could not break through. He was glad when the weather warmed so the coat could be packed away.

He realized he was beginning to compose sentences in his head for which he had no audience. The flurry of information around them created the illusion that everything a man needed to know was available to him. It seemed at first that the careful man picking through the words could surely find the truth of anything, but Fritz realized instead that the noise of all that information created a new kind of silence. He felt keenly the pressure of things not spoken. In back rooms and on side roads, rumors and news were passed back and forth between men who perhaps trusted one another, and perhaps, like Fritz, found themselves adrift in a sea of confusing information and unknown consequences. Conversations once friendly were now terse and cryptic. Fritz felt eyes on him even miles from town, and in town it was worse.

"The problem is with non-declared alien males," William Owens was explaining to the men gathered around his counter once when Fritz walked in. Endorsed by three prominent businessmen—Fritz never did learn exactly which three—Owens had taken seriously his job of educating the public. He was prepared to whip up enthusiasm for the war and to encourage patriotism in the population of the small community of Stuart. His speeches had the fervor of someone who believed he was in the service of an altruistic cause, but his passion when he spoke embarrassed Fritz as much as anything else. Fritz felt cornered when Owens launched into a long four-minute oration.

"These are men without citizenship papers, immigrants, who are automatically exempt from the draft. They don't even have to register!" Owens was saying this time. A few of the men murmured quietly to one another. "These miserable specimens of humanity remain smugly at home to reap the benefits of the life work of our young citizens."

Again the murmuring passed around the small crowd, though it sounded a bit like a growl to Fritz. He wanted to turn back around, but Owens looked up just then and caught his eye. "I'm talking about immigrants, Mr. Vogel, noncitizens who live here in this great land taking what we've got and letting our boys die to protect them."

Fritz felt a flush rise on his face. "Yeah," he said. Pride kept him from adding, "I am a citizen." He glanced around at the men standing there. Aloys Baum's was the only familiar face. He wondered where these strangers came from. How was it that he had lived in this community for years and not met these men? They looked hard to him. And they didn't look like Germans.

Fritz stood by the door and waited for Owens to finish. It seemed a long four minutes. His "central idea" this time, the phrase that always signaled he was about to wrap up, was that each man held responsibility not only to register for the draft if he was eligible, but to make sure his eligible neighbors were registered as well. Fritz turned and left without talking to Aloys and without picking up the supplies he had come to town for.

On the way home, he sat hunched over on the wagon seat, letting the rain drizzle from his hat in a steady curtain in front of his face. He thought about what he wouldn't tell Gerda when he got home.

Owens was a wealthy man of sorts, and Fritz knew he considered himself not only more American than the immigrants in the community, but more even than America herself. He often told people that his family had arrived on America's shores before the revolution that defined her had been fought. Even before this latest war, he had made clear his belief that it was not tradition but principles that bonded Americans one to another. Those principles must be transmitted to each of the ethnic groups that moved into a community. He liked to say this for the benefit of the "ethnic groups"— also known as Germans—who came into his store. It wasn't birth or choice that made one an American, it was like-mindedness against a common enemy, and education was the key to a true American. The war seemed to have fired Owens's passions, and the need to transmit information and education became even more urgent. As near as Fritz could tell, Owens believed civilization itself hung in the balance and he saw himself and his place of business as a fulcrum around which it would be saved. In any case, he clearly took it as his duty in every encounter to educate toward a commonality of thought. Though he had always been a storyteller, keeping his customers as much through the tales he would spin as through his service, the war changed the tone of every interaction with him. There was no room in such a dangerous world, Owens opined, for a plurality of views.

Fritz found Owens's store nearly empty the next time he stopped in, and for a while it felt like old times. They traded stories the way they used to, taking turns talking and waiting, but when it was Owens's turn and he started in with a story about rabbits going through his garden faster than he could plant it, he said "trenches" when he meant to say "furrows," and both he and Fritz stopped laughing at once. Whatever had seemed funny about the story of the rabbits in the garden stopped being about rabbits and became something else altogether. Both men's smiles froze on their faces and the war and all the changes it had wrought rushed into the room like an icy blast. Each saw mirrored in the eyes of the other not his own reflection, but the reflection of his nightmares. Each saw the image of trenches and death and a war that seemed endless and hungry. Their laughs, cut short, hung in the air with the dust motes and smell of feed and seed and leather and something else just beyond the reach of identification.

Fritz felt the tightening of muscles at the back of his neck and up into his jaw that he felt so often now when he talked to neighbors or townsmen. So here we are again, he thought. He could have been on his way home by now; his family had already gathered in the wagon to wait for him. He had already signed the bill of sale and had his hand on the stack of seed sacks, ready to sling one over each shoulder and return to the work that always needed doing back home. It was high spring and the demands of the season seemed to press up under his boots whenever he stopped moving, but he knew the trading of goods and money was only part of any transaction in town. Talk was the currency of real trade.

Owens stared at him across the counter, the word *trenches* still hanging in the air. Fritz turned his chin hard to the left in an effort to get the kink out of his neck. Through the door he could see his horses dozing in their harness. He looked down at his hand atop the seed bag, noted the black crescents of soil beneath each fingernail, and thought about the manure still needing to be spread in the field in the northwest corner of his section. He was not a man, nor was this an era, given to irony. The job simply needed to be done, though he knew it would have to wait until this transaction was complete.

"I hear they're running short of hip boots," Fritz said at last. "Up near Verdun the water level's so high the trenches turn to rivers when it rains."

Owens nodded curtly, familiar with the territory Fritz referred to because he had pored over the same maps, studied the same news stories.

"Foot rot is taking as many men out of combat as artillery guns some
days," Owens said, and Fritz knew that he saw his chance to educate an immigrant, for that's what he saw when he looked at Fritz nowadays—a German immigrant, not a man or even a customer he'd known for years. Owens
reached under the shelf and pulled out a pair of six-buckle overboots and set
them on the counter. "Can you imagine this being the difference between
victory and defeat?" he asked in a voice that had gone suddenly louder as if
to address a larger crowd. The light in Owens's eyes flattened as he spoke,
but brightened somehow too, so that it was hard to see in him the familiar
store owner.

He shook the boots a little as if to rattle them to attention.

"Seems hard to imagine that such a noble endeavor as this war for peace
should hinge on such humble items, but it's as true now as it ever was. 'For
want of a nail the shoe was lost, for want of a shoe the horse was lost, for
want of a horse the battle was lost,' and so goes the kingdom." Owens was
a small man with a big voice, and when he warmed to a topic, he seemed to
swell and take more space than seemed likely for a man who could wear the
boys-sized clothing he sold off the back shelf.

"You understand, Fritz, that every one of us has a responsibility to this
great country." He leaned toward Fritz, both hands on the counter. "In a
way, we're all like these boots."

Fritz's gaze shifted down toward the boots and back up to Owens's face.
He decided to smile agreeably. Owens stood eye to eye with him when he
stood behind the counter and that always made Fritz laugh a bit. Owens
had built up the floor all along the back of the counter, putting him at eye
level or above with all his customers. Fritz towered over Owens anywhere
but here in Owens's store. That was okay, Fritz thought. He had no problem
with a man working his property to his own advantage. It was the image
of Owens stepping out from behind that counter and dropping down suddenly to below shoulder level that kept Fritz from feeling the anger that
could have come as Owens continued his "four minutes."

"If you think about how the little things matter," Owens went on, "you
can understand the need to make changes in how we do things in our everyday lives." Owens turned and picked up a catalog off the shelf behind
him. "When I place orders now for any equipment, any supplies, I take care
who I'm buying from. Of course, our nation no longer has commercial ties

with Germany, but I need to be careful about buying from any Kaiser-loving business. How do I do that, you may wonder. I pay attention to the small print—the German language in the description is the giveaway. If they use any Hun-loving words, I don't order it." He nodded emphatically and slapped the catalog closed. "Which brings me to my central idea: the subject of schools. Did you know our university right down there in Lincoln is still teaching that vile language to unsuspecting students?"

Fritz felt his tolerance fading and he crossed his thick arms in front of his chest.

"We simply cannot be a united people, a United States, if we're talking different languages. We'd become like the Bible story about the Tower of Babel—not understanding each other and the whole country failing. The schools need to understand that. My central idea is that we need to educate our children to be Americans."

Owens's face had taken on a sheen, not quite a sweat, just the moisture of his own enthusiasm. The two men stood facing one another—storeowner and farmer—and if a clap of thunder hadn't startled them both, there's no telling what would have happened. At the sound, they both started and turned toward the door. Fritz could see Gerda and the children in the wagon, gazing west. The two men reached the door at the same time. Owens fell back to let Fritz exit first. They stepped out onto the street and looked up at the sky. Rising towers of thunderheads loomed dark and foreboding. A gust of cool wind carried sand up the street toward them and spattered against the storefronts.

Within minutes Fritz and Owens had the wagon loaded. The horses strained against the harness, as edgy as the children in the back about the storm that was heading toward them. Fritz set his foot up onto the step, but paused before climbing up. He didn't like leaving anything, even conversations, unfinished. He too believed little things mattered. He fumbled in the pocket of his overalls as if searching for the right words to say and pulled out a red gingham handkerchief. He blew his nose and carefully refolded the cloth and turned toward Owens, who stood patting the haunches of the nervous, smaller gelding. He looked at Fritz warily. They stood on level ground now, and he had to tip his head back to look up into the big German's face. His lips were pursed, the salesman's smile gone.

"Your son," Fritz said and stopped to clear his throat. He was not a man to show feelings. He lived, as so many men do, on an island of self, not always aware of his own isolation, and when he became aware of it, the distance between himself and others seemed too far ever to cross. There were trenches within him too, he realized. They had been laughing about rabbits and furrows, and now Fritz was looking at Owens across a gulf so wide that he wasn't sure his voice would carry.

"Your son," he repeated, his voice booming unexpectedly, "he's leaving for Fort Riley soon?" He had seen the boy's name in the paper some weeks back, along with several other familiar names in that list he always read with trepidation. He felt strangely aware of the muscles in his face, as if they were capable of mutiny, turning his lips upward in a smile when he wanted to be somber. He wanted Owens to know he too feared for the boys going over there. He wanted to say he was an American, and he was embarrassed by the urge to say it.

Owens palmed his fine-boned hand across his face as if he too were trying to control mutinous muscles. "Yes," he said. "Soon they'll be taking in another batch of boys." He paused. "He's good with machines, you know. Always has been. Knows what makes them run and likes to figure out what keeps them from running. That'll keep him back from the front but still doing important work." He nodded, confident in his vision of how things work.

Fritz nodded too. "They need their mechanics, that's for sure." The memory of something he'd read surfaced and he offered it now. "It'll be the mechanics who win this thing, if it can be done."

"Yep," Owens said. "Mechanics will win the war." He must have read the same article, though Fritz couldn't say for sure because so many of his words sounded practiced and composed nowadays. "But we need farmers to feed them too. To every man, a job to do." Owens didn't shake his hand before he went back inside. Fritz wondered if it mattered. Though the day had started out warm, a cool wind followed the Vogels home, and the horses fought the reins in a hurry to get back to the barn before the storm hit. The unpredictability of weather was the one constant Fritz could count on, it seemed.

CHAPTER SIX

The new priest had fingers like sausages. His ample chin fanned around his neck and folded over the edge of his collar. With skin smooth and unblemished as a young boy's under dark hair, thin and retreating, he looked like a middle-aged child, Gerda thought. When he said Mass, he mumbled the Latin, no articulation of the individual words, just a kind of singsong chant. The mystery of faith grew more so in his services.

He was not really a new priest. He had been at his previous parish in Boyd County for nearly a year before he came to St. Boniface, and he'd been here for months now, but Gerda still thought of him as new, unproven. Father Hettwer, his predecessor—now there was a man of God. Without her asking, he had waited with Fritz during the births of her last three children, ready to baptize or offer Last Rites, because he knew of Gerda's fears. He said the Mass with such joy, as if the words he spoke were new each time he said them. After Mass he would stand in the vestibule and shake hands with everyone, even the children. Katie, Gerda suspected, was a little bit in love with him. When the bishop called him home to the Omaha Diocese, the Vogel women, mother and daughter, were among the saddest to see him go.

And now Father Jungels muttered his way through another Mass. Outside, March had given way to April, and the songbirds trilled the joy of it. Gerda regarded the sunlight streaming brokenly through the stained glass window to her right and tried to feel the presence of the Holy Spirit. The scent of incense lingered in the air and Father's voice droned on. The congregation knelt and stood at the appropriate moments, but there seemed to be no life at all in the small church anymore. It didn't seem right to have lost Father Hettwer just when they needed him most. The war, that frightening war, was taking the boys from the farms and sending them across the ocean, some of them never to come home.

Gerda placed her hand over her eyes and said no, she would not think about the war, not now. Church is for praying, not worrying, her mother would have told her. And so she began to pray. She stopped following the words of the service and descended into her own prayers. She didn't even notice when Father Jungels began his homily. When she looked up, she saw him staring down onto the congregation as if waiting for an answer to a question she had not heard him ask. For a long moment he stared, his soft, round face seeming to grow thinner and stronger in the silence he created. Fritz had begun to doze; planting season was upon him, and there were too few hours in a day. The boys fidgeted in the pew beside her. Only Katie kept a calm demeanor. Her steady gaze met Father Jungels's silence expectantly. Suddenly he slapped his hand down hard on the lectern it echoed throughout the small church, and Fritz and all the farmers around him sat up hurriedly. Some of them looked around sheepishly at their neighbors.

"Then God smites his hands together," Father Jungels shouted, "and strikes out a soul as a spark, into the organized glory of things, from the depths of the dark." His words echoed, and he waited again for silence to reign. "From the beginning of time humans have understood this truth and have expressed it in one form or another.

"According to Greek myth," he went on in a quieter tone, his goal of gaining the attention of all seemingly achieved, "Prometheus formed a human image from the dust of the ground, and then, by fire stolen from *hea-ven,* it was animated with a living soul. You must know that even the myths of *pre-Christians* agree: *Hea-ven* gave life." He tapped his palm on the lectern with both syllables each time he said "heaven."

"Scientists try to convince us that life came of spontaneous generation." He emphasized the sibilance of the words. "And now the idea of natural evolution is popular. Some believe that the impenetrable mystery of life is evolved from the endowments of nature, and they build their imperfect theory on observations of the concrete. Scientific investigations are *restricted* to the concrete," he rephrased for emphasis, "but is proof *only* what can be seen with the human eye?" He shook his head in disbelief before going on in a louder tone. "But every function indicates purpose, every organism evinces intelligent design, and *all,*" he pressed his fist into his hand as he uttered that word, "*all* proclaim Divine Power." He paused and appeared to look at certain individuals in the congregation. Gerda tried to see without seeming to look which members squirmed under his gaze.

"Something cannot come out of nothing. With man's ability to reason, we know *chance* is an impossibility. We, therefore, must accept the display of wisdom in nature as indicative of the designs of God." He struck the lectern with the palm of his right hand, as if the word *God* needed the emphasis of thunder. "Thus 'has He written His claims for our profoundest admiration and homage all over every object that He has made.'

"If you ask: Is there any advantage in considering the phenomena of nature as the result of Divine Volition? We answer that this belief corresponds with the *universally* acknowledged ideas of accountability; for, with a wise and efficient Cause, we infer there is an *intelligent* creation, and the desire to communicate, guide, and bless is responded to by man—by *good* men—who love, obey, and en-joy."

Again he paused and looked directly at someone near the front of church. Gerda stretched to see around Mrs. Havranek's hat, but the pillar between the pews blocked her view.

"Nothing is gained by attributing to nature vicegerent forces." Father shook his head as if he was answering a question. Who was he talking to? Gerda looked around her to see what the others thought, but all their faces appeared placid, as if they had become stones in a river and the priest's words were water rushing over them. She looked at Fritz, and though he seemed to be listening, he did not look at her, did not share in her consternation. This was not a sermon, Gerda thought, it was an argument, but with whom?

"Is it not preferable to say that nature *responds* to intelligent, loving Omnipotence? Our finiteness is illustrated by our initiation into organized being. Emerging from a ray-less atom, too small to be seen by the human eye, we gradually develop into conscious beings, the exercise of which provides irrefutable evidence of our immortality. We are pervaded with invisible influences which, like the needle of the compass trembling on its pivot, point us to immortality as our ultimate goal, where in the sunny clime of Love, even in a spiritual realm of joy and happiness, we may eternally reign with Him who is All in all." Father paused for breath here. "Can you not see that?"

His right eyebrow lifted in deep bewilderment, and he held out his thick-fingered hand in supplication for a moment. A baby in the back began to cry, and the sound seemed to bring the good Father out of the reverie his words had sent him into. He glared out at the congregation, looking for a moment as if he had forgotten they were there. He straightened his shoulders and said, "Let us pray to God, our almighty father."

In gathering up the children's coats, Gerda missed seeing who occupied the pew that had seemed the focus of Father Jungels's attention. She whispered to Fritz as they made their way toward the door. "Who was he talking to?"

"Who?"

"Father? Who was he talking to?"

Fritz shook his head. "Well, to all of us, I suppose. Who does a priest usually talk to?"

Gerda wanted to shake him. Did men notice nothing of what went on around them? And then the pretty Mary MacGewan, Dr. MacGewan's wife, was beside her. "Mrs. Vogel," she said brightly, "you're looking particularly lovely this morning. I don't know how you do it, all these children and yet you stay so fresh." Immediately Gerda was aware of the strand of hair that had pulled free from her twist, of the smudge of mud on the hem of her skirt and Ray's uncut hair.

"Good morning, Mary," she said quietly. In front of them, Ray and Frank were pinching each other's backsides, each trying to make the other squeal. Leo, the baby being carried by Fritz, stretched his stiff body out past his father's shoulder and wailed for Mama.

"I can hardly hear you, my dear Gerda, you're so quiet!" Mary laughed and hooked her hand inside Gerda's elbow and squeezed, as if they were the best of friends. Before Gerda had a chance to reply, Mary moved forward in the line to be closer to Fritz. Her green taffeta dress, such a rich dress for this parish, rustled against the children as she pushed past them. She reminded Gerda of a peacock, so proud of herself, always preening. When she saw her take Fritz's arm and smile up at him, and he back at her, Gerda felt her face grow warm. A line of sweat trickled from her armpit down her side. Of course men notice some of what is going on around them, she thought.

They were among the last to reach the vestibule. Only Dr. Gannoway was still before them. With Mary holding Fritz's arm and laughing, Gerda almost missed the exchange between the priest and the doctor. Father Jungels's face was red, and he looked cornered. Dr. Gannoway was smiling, but there didn't appear to be much humor in his smile.

"I'm a man of science, Father. I make no apologies," Dr. Gannoway was saying as he turned from the priest toward the Vogel family. "Good morning, Fritz!" he said pleasantly. "And to you, Mrs. Vogel, as well." He studied her face a moment before looking down at the boys. If she let herself think about what Dr. Gannoway knew about her—he had delivered three of her children after all—she could not look him in the eye, so she chose instead to look at the peculiar pattern of the flush that crept up his neck as he took her hand.

On the way home Fritz whistled a lilting tune, one he played often on the mouth harp in the evenings, and the sound calmed something that seemed always to be fluttering in Gerda. The boys in the back leaned over the side trying to reach the grass heads as they passed. Katie read a book she'd brought along, and the baby Leo in Gerda's lap passed a stick from one hand to the other. She would need to stop thinking of him as the baby soon. He could walk, though he preferred to be carried. He spoke only a few words, but he said them clearly, speaking as distinctly as a military man. Gerda listened to the jangle of harnesses, watched the wide shifting haunches of the two horses as they slowly pulled them home.

Despite the peacefulness of the moment, she felt a lump grow in her throat as she considered these children of hers. She looked around at the world she had brought them into. The sun was shining. The trees were leafing out so that there was a haze of green on the newly planted shelterbelts they traveled along. It was not a bad world, she told herself.

They turned the corner then off the county road onto the lane that led to their farm. A sign on a fence post caught her eye. The neighbor needed a new hired hand, the sign said, because his man had been drafted. It was the small letters at the bottom that caused Gerda to jump. "No krauts need apply." She looked up at Fritz to see if he'd seen it, but he was whistling and dangling a grass stem for Leo to grab. The children in the back hadn't seen it either. Had she thought it wouldn't come this far, this rolling wave of hatred? What had happened on the train had been out east. The changes Aloys saw too, those had been east of here. Stuart would not have such things, she thought. We know each other here. She looked up the road that separated their land from this neighbor's land and perceived it as a kind of fireguard. Surely the spark would not leap. Please, God.

"Margaret and Aloys stopped by yesterday," Gerda said. The smell of the bacon she was frying mingled with the smell of wet wool that steamed from Fritz's coat hanging on a hook by the door. The hot grease sizzled and popped as she placed the press across the strips in the pan. She opened the fire door to check the level of flame, and then turned to the counter where she began to mix yeast and water. "Margaret tells me there's a new clerk in town at Kroger's." Fritz stood at the table over a large cutting board where worn leather harnesses draped onto the floor. Straps of newly cut leather were pinned to the board with vises, and Fritz leaned his weight into a leather awl making holes for the buckles. "Huh," he said by way of answer.

"She says she's not too pleasant either," Gerda went on. "Made her and Aloys wait a good ten minutes before she'd even wait on them."

"Huh," Fritz said again, though it could have been just a grunt of exertion as he twisted the awl through the stubborn leather.

Gerda paused for a moment by the window and looked out toward the apple orchard. It was raining hard and steady, a "soaker" her father would call it, and the heavy gray clouds didn't appear to be moving. The house seemed to be growing smaller the longer spring took to arrive. "There're rabbits getting at those trees again." She shook her head, thinking about how best to protect the fruit come summer. "Saw four or five of them yesterday." Fritz abruptly pushed the pile of leather straps to the side, and one strap caught the box with the buckles, sending it to the floor with a crash. Baby Leo in the high chair screeched in surprise, Fritz cursed under his breath, and Gerda turned to pick up the scattered buckles. Katie, bless her heart, came down the stairs dressed and ready for school and took the baby from the chair.

"This would be easier in the barn," Fritz muttered before he stooped to pick up the box for the buckles.

Gerda said nothing, though she recalled having said that very thing to him last night when he set the cutting board up on the table and brought the harnesses in. The leather was easier to handle when it was warm, but the work surface in the kitchen wasn't designed for such tasks. "Breakfast is about ready anyway," she said when they finished picking up the scattered pieces.

On her father's farm the work shed was as big as the house. It had a heat stove at each end. Every tool had its place and when the tool was not in use it was in that place. Gerda chided herself for remembering that now, but once the memory entered her mind she couldn't let it go. The shed was orderly and clean, and Gerda had been allowed in it only when her father accompanied her. A misplaced tool meant a beating and the Drueke children treated the work shed with the same respect they did a church. It smelled of leather and oil, smoke and wood, and the light from the lanterns strung up on a pulley system on the center beam made it bright as day inside when her father worked there. Her father could hit the brass spittoon by the door from anywhere in the shed without seeming to aim. The floor was composed of thick oak slabs raised nearly a foot above the ground. A pipe that could be attached to the back of the stove sent heated air into that space between earth and wood, and to walk into the shed on a cold winter day was as pleasing as walking into a warm kitchen. One wall was hinged and swung open when needed to bring in equipment for repairs so that the Drueke men could work in comfort.

Fritz dragged the pile of leather straps to the woodpile and dropped them roughly. Gerda placed the box of buckles beside it and stepped out of the way so that Fritz could take the cutting board, a center slab from an oak tree, and lean it against the wall. She wiped the table and began setting dishes out before she realized the bacon was burning. She scooped it up with a slotted spoon and decided it wasn't too bad, though the smell of it was of ashes, not food. They had too little to waste.

The morning, like all mornings, slipped into afternoon, and work continued. Fritz took his outside, and Gerda busied herself with hers. Busied herself? No, it was the requirements of the work itself that kept her moving. Even though the rain gave her reprieve from outside work, there was always something to be done, some need requiring her attention. She hauled in water from the well house to heat for washing. Checked the bread in the oven and twisted dough into rolls to go in next. Time passed without her noticing it.

Looking up from the task at hand, she gazed out the kitchen window to see the rain had finally let up and a sliver of blue sky showed along the horizon. In the pale sunlight the grasses seemed to be greening as she watched. Through the trees she glimpsed the mail wagon heading north up the lane from the county road. Her heart quickened as it always did when she saw the familiar blue wagon. Even if it held no letters from home, there would be newspapers and maybe a catalog. She and Katie liked to page through the Sears and Roebuck's in the evening. They had nearly worn out the Burpee Seed catalog that had come a few months back. Reading about plants and flowers made the winter more bearable.

She glanced over her shoulder at the children. Katie sat at the table bent over her slate practicing letters. Ray leaned against her side, watching carefully the slow loops she made, white on black. In their hunger for learning they were like twins, though they were two years apart in age. Frank and the baby Leo were still napping. She had taken her frustration out on them when she put them down, shouting when she had meant to be silent. They were babies, both of them, their smooth beautiful faces so free of blemish, and yet she had lost her temper at them. She had slammed the bedroom door to silence them, knocking a picture off the hall wall. What kind of mother would behave this way, she wondered? They had been frightened into silence, and, really, what kind of mother was she that the fact of their fright satisfied her as a means to an end? She wanted them to remain asleep awhile longer because it gave her room to work without interruption. Sometimes it seemed there wasn't enough air in this house for all of them. She stepped to the foot of the stairs and listened for sounds of movement in their room, but all was quiet. Now was her chance to get away, if only for a few minutes.

She wiped her hands on her apron, leaving streaks of white, and pulled it slowly over her head. She stepped toward the door and quietly pulled her big coat off the hook and slipped her feet into a pair of buckle boots Fritz had left on the floor. She moved slowly and deliberately, the way she would in a corral of spirited horses, careful not to spook them. She wanted to be almost gone before her children noticed her leaving.

How like animals they were at times, she thought, so full of unbridled needs and fierce with their emotions, too easily provoked and so anxious to keep her in their sights.

Sometimes she just wanted to fly, to get out of the heat of the kitchen, of the closeness of the house and breathe, just breathe. That's all it was, a chance to get some fresh air. She turned the doorknob slowly, the grinding of springs startlingly loud. Only Katie looked up. Gerda placed a finger to her lips and smiled before closing the door.

Her children safe behind her, she raised her face toward the sky and inhaled deeply. The smell of soil set free of the frost flowed toward her like a river. The coat she had wrapped around her like a shawl felt too warm for such a day as this, so she draped it over the fence, tying the sleeves around the top rail. The sunshine and breeze felt as soft as an apology.

Early spring was her favorite time of the year. A flock of finches littered the calf pen, scavenging for seeds or worms. The jangle of buckles on her boots scattered them as she approached, and they disappeared into the trees lining the drive.

They came back every year, robins, jays, finches—all the birds, all part of the cycle of seasons, nothing to get excited about, but still the sight of them made her happy, gave her hope. Sentimental nonsense is all it is, she chided herself. Still, she felt uplifted by the sight of the small birds and the whistle of the meadowlarks.

She walked slowly, watching her feet when she got out onto the lane, taking care not to slip into the muck, and she was almost to the mailboxes before she realized the mail wagon was still there.

She looked up and smiled at the man leaning against the backboard of his wagon.

"Good afternoon, Mrs. Vogel," Charlie Burke said with a slow smile. "You're a fine sign of spring."

She blushed and looked away.

"You look like some great bird coming toward me down the lane, Mrs. Vogel." He held a stack of mail out to her.

Gerda told herself not to notice the way Charles Burke's smile spread slowly across his face. She told herself the dimple on his chin was no concern of hers. She kept her head tilted down as she looked at the stack of mail he handed her.

"It's the way the wind caught your dress, I mean," he went on. "It looked like wings." He spread his hands and arms out at his side in imitation of her. "Or maybe it's an angel you remind me of?"

Gerda felt her cheeks warming, and she pressed her lips together to keep from smiling. "Bird," she said abruptly. "That's what my name means, you know—in German 'Vogel' means 'bird.'"

"She talks!" He looked pleased with himself. "A talking bird, are you, Mrs. Vogel? I wasn't really sure if you had a voice at all, you know. Or maybe you don't talk to simple public servants like me? Maybe I should be offended by your silence?" He raised an eyebrow at her.

"Oh no, it's not like that at all," Gerda put her hand up in protest. "I mean, I . . ." Her face grew warmer. "I didn't mean to offend you! I didn't know you wanted me to talk to you. I didn't know . . . ," her voice trailed off to silence though her mouth didn't quite close.

"Didn't know I wanted you to talk to me? Come now, Mrs. Vogel, what red-blooded man wouldn't want a beautiful woman to talk to him any chance he had for such an occasion?"

Did she actually say "Yawp"? She hoped not. She was so stunned by his words she wasn't sure what she said. She simply stared at him a moment and then she spun on her heels and took a step back toward the house, but then immediately turned back toward him and simply stared at him, her hand on her neck.

The sudden bawl of one of the calves up near the barn took their attention away from the space between them for a moment and when they looked at each other again, Charles was still smiling. "Will you talk to me now and then, Mrs. Bird? Just talk, it'll give me something to look forward to on this long route."

Gerda looked back up toward the house.

"When I see you, of course I'll talk to you, Mr. Burke. I . . . I didn't mean to be rude." She felt a fluttering in her chest as if a winged thing had suddenly awoken inside her.

He nodded agreeably. "Well, you've been rushing out to meet me for weeks now. I decided it was time to break the ice. You can talk to me anytime. I'm sure we'll see each other again soon."

"Oh, but it's my sister," she stuttered in explanation. He looked around as if looking for her sister and raised a quizzical eyebrow. For the first time she realized that it was her actions that had started this exchange, that he had misunderstood her intentions and thought she was coming to meet him. "My sister. I've been writing to my sister, and she has been writing to me. We write letters. I visited her this winter, I mean, I went to my aunt's funeral and she was there and now we write to one another." She couldn't seem to stop her mouth, as if someone she didn't know had taken control of her voice. "I want her to come for a visit, you see. It's not you. I didn't mean to meet you. I simply can't wait for her reply."

"Not me?" Charles looked hurt, or perhaps he was only pretending; Gerda didn't know. Men made so little sense to her.

"No, it's the letters," Gerda said and held out an envelope as proof. "The letters from my sister, I'm sorry."

Charles put his hand on his chest. "Another broken heart. What's a poor young man to do?"

Gerda looked at him from the corner of her eye. "Mr. Burke, I do believe you are pulling my leg."

He smiled again, devilishly. "May I call you Mrs. Bird from now on?"

Gerda shook her head in the same way she did when her children misbehaved. "What does your name mean, Mr. Burke?"

"Burke? I don't really know. It's just a name. An American name."

Gerda's smile froze on her face. How quickly the tenor of a moment can change. Of course, Gerda thought, American names were enough in themselves. Only immigrants had names with two meanings. To be an American, your name was just your name and that was enough for America.

She nodded. "Of course, American." She vowed never to tell anyone again that "Vogel" meant "bird," that it meant anything at all. "I really must be going, Mr. Burke. Thank you for bringing my mail. Our mail. Good day." She turned and walked away, her face still burning.

"Mrs. Bird?" Charles called out. She turned back to face him. "Goodbye!" He tipped his hat and bowed ceremoniously to her before climbing into his wagon.

Gerda walked quickly back toward the house, wondering what on earth she was thinking when she told Charles Burke her name meant "bird" in German. Was there not enough trouble in this world without her going out of her way to bring it on?

"I know the way to town, Fritz," Gerda said. She sat on the floor in front of the wooden egg crates, carefully wiping each egg with a damp cloth before nestling it into the papier-mâché tray.

Fritz walked from the door to Gerda and back again. He looked out the window to where Dan Liable's hired hand waited in a wagon.

"I can tell Liable's man I can't do it today," Fritz said. The bright sunlight outside made him squint. "His work is no more important than mine." He sniffed loudly, then took his kerchief from his back pocket and blew his nose.

Gerda finished cleaning the last egg and draped the flour cloth across the top of the crate, then slowly stood. She placed her hands on the small of her back and leaned back, stretching the stubborn muscles there. "I know the way to town, Fritz," she repeated. She felt such fatigue, but she tried to hide it from Fritz. If he knew how exhausted she really was, he'd surely decide against helping the Liable family and stay home to drive her into town.

Forcing a bright smile and an industriousness she didn't really feel, she gathered up the rags from the floor and walked to Fritz. Up on her tiptoes, she kissed his cheek and opened the door to usher him out. He stepped, still squinting, across the threshold.

"Oh, wait, I forgot," she said, though she'd planned to say it all the time. "If you could carry these eggs out to the wagon for me I'd appreciate it."

Given a definable task, Fritz moved quickly. Once out the door with the crate, he felt the pull of his neighbor's need and could accept Gerda's decision to go into town alone. He set the egg crates where the shock of the wagon ride would least jostle them, then turned toward Gerda. "Right as rain," she said with a smile and patted his arm. They walked to the other wagon where Liable's man waited.

"Mrs. Liable said to be sure an' tell you how grateful she was for you taking the time out of your chores to help her," the hired hand said. "Mr. Liable's been real sick."

Fritz climbed up beside the man before he spoke to Gerda again.

"When you get back, if I'm not here, you just leave the team hitched up," he called to her. "It won't hurt them to stand for a while."

Gerda smiled and waved and wished they would just go already. Dan Liable's hired hand had arrived nearly an hour ago, just as Fritz had brought their team up to the front of the house to load eggs and milk for the trip into town. Though Fritz had scowled at her when she said it, Gerda had invited the man in for coffee. She couldn't have a neighbor, even if it was just a hired hand, go away from the door without having felt welcomed. The man had come in and sat down gladly. Between loud slurps of coffee he told the Vogels that Dan Liable had some lung illness, "a fluenza, the doctor's callin' it, and I've been doing the work of two men for goin' on two weeks now."

"The doc's been out to the place three or four times now." He slurped his coffee. "Sounds like he's getting better, but it hit his lungs, ya see, and the doc says he needs ta rest a few days more. And Mrs. Liable, ya know, thinks that Dr. MacGewan could walk on water if he'd a mind to, so it don't matter what ol' Dan thinks he needs or don't need." He let out a laugh that sounded more like a bark than anything else, then sipped loudly again. "Mrs. Liable won't let ol' Dan out of the house—MacGewan's orders, ya know."

Fritz leaned back in his chair and looked out the window as if to check the position of the sun. MacGewan was the one Gerda called "the other doctor in town." He made his house calls in a Ford and a tailored suit. "I wonder if he takes that suit coat off to deliver babies, or if he just stands back and watches so as to keep clean," she had once said. "Or maybe *his* patients don't get dirty." It was as close to being spiteful about the wealthy people in town as she got. The hired man went on.

"You know Mrs. Liable. There's no changing her mind once she's got it set, and it don't matter that the work takes two men to get done, one of those men is *not* going to be ol' Dan." He barked a laugh again. "Less'en he climbs out a window."

The man finished the last of his cup of coffee and looked toward the pot on the stove. Fritz looked at Gerda and almost imperceptibly shook his head. She raised an eyebrow in equal degree, and Fritz stood up.

He'd agreed he had a few extra hours today and told Gerda he'd take her into town tomorrow to do her trading.

"Yes," Gerda said. "You go and help them, but I'm going to take those eggs in today. Everything's ready to go, and I'll take them."

The hired hand stood up and said, "Thank you, ma'am, you're almighty kind." He handed her the coffee cup with both hands and moved toward the door like a man who knew things had swung his way. "I'll wait out by the wagon for you, Mr. Vogel. I'm much obliged for your help."

The plan was in motion before Fritz had a real chance to argue, and now he was headed down the lane with the hired hand and his Gerda was standing at the door giving work and behavior orders to the children. By the time they were out of sight, Gerda was tying a scarf around her hair and considering the choice of a coat or a sweater. It was warm and it was May, but it was also Nebraska, and the weather was always changing. She scanned the horizon; a smattering of thin clouds paled the southern sky, but for the most part it was all blue as far as she could see. She opted for the sweater and hurried toward the wagon before she had a chance to consider that yes, she did, as she had told Fritz so confidently, know the way to town, but in truth she had never before gone there alone.

When she got to the end of the lane and turned the team south toward the main road, a breeze swept up from the south and the riffled the horses' manes. They caught the scent of the river, or maybe it was of adventure, and they broke into a trot. Gerda had to grip the seat to keep her balance and use more of her strength than seemed reasonable to pull the team back down to a walk. The breeze, the sun in her face, the jangle of harness, it all formed a kind of music and made her want to laugh out loud. Her fatigue and worries forgotten in that moment, she set the horses at an easy walk. She was going to town.

She stopped the horses near the back door of the Kroger's Grocery, near the spot Fritz had been stopping every month for years. She set the brake on the wagon just as she had seen Fritz do a thousand times, though what he did with one hand smoothly, she needed both hands and most of her body weight to accomplish. She climbed down and patted the dust from her skirt and retied her scarf. Several strands of hair had come free during her ride, and she tucked them back into place before going into the grocers'. She resisted the urge to sing out, "I did it! I came to town all by myself!" when she walked in the door, but she couldn't keep the smile from her face.

The new woman Margaret had told her about stood behind the counter. In her excitement Gerda didn't look closely at her but instead waited her turn by walking up and down the aisles. The new clerk moved about the space behind the counter efficiently and confidently, and she chatted easily with the farm family ahead of Gerda as she finished wrapping up their goods. The family—Gerda was never good with names—had lived in Stuart for several years but didn't attend St. Boniface. Gerda nodded politely as they turned to walk past her. She thought how Fritz would no doubt find a way to start a conversation and she envied him his ease with people. Though she had plenty to say to people she knew, she could never think of anything to say in moments like these.

It didn't matter, Gerda realized with some relief. The family, a tall man and woman with two tall girls in a line heading for the door, didn't stop to even return her greeting. Gerda noticed one of the girls, probably the youngest, who looked to be about thirteen, glanced over her shoulder at Gerda. An odd glance, Gerda thought, as if she hadn't simply looked at Gerda, but had pulled her skirt away from her in passing to keep them from touching. Gerda automatically reached up to smooth her hair and wondered if her face was covered with dust. The door closed behind the family and Gerda turned back to the woman behind the counter.

"Good morning," Gerda said. "I'm Mrs. Vogel. Gerda Vogel." She smiled and waited for the woman to reply. It was in that moment of silence that recognition came. She had seen the woman before. She had been on the train to West Point. Gerda felt the air leave her lungs but she forgot to breathe back in and the two women stared at each other for what felt like a lifetime to Gerda. She gasped for breath and whispered, "We've not met."

As soon as she said it she wanted to take it back. It was a lie and she didn't know why she had said it. They both had been witnesses. Suddenly it seemed as if time collapsed and they were together on that train again. Gerda was pulling the blanket closer. Gerda was looking away from what the men were doing. She remembered the fright on this woman's face, the tears she didn't wipe away. She had wondered even then what bond had formed in the chaos of that moment, and now a part of her wanted to reach out and touch the woman's hand, while another part wanted to run. Guilt at her own silence rushed over her.

The woman crossed her arms and stared at Gerda. Gerda's mouth formed words she didn't say. *Do you think about it all the time too?*

The news of her accomplishment, coming to town all by herself, seemed foolish against the stark red-on-white image of the man falling into the snow. She felt faint. She wanted to go back out and get into her wagon and go home; she wanted Fritz to be standing beside her. She pointed toward the door she had just come through. "My wagon is outside. I've brought eggs and milk." She didn't want to look at the woman as she waited for her to respond, so she studied the contents of the bins along the counter. She hoped the woman would call for the boy who worked in the back to come around and unload the crates and barrels, but as the moments ticked on and nothing happened, she looked up. The woman still stared at her. "For trading." Gerda spoke more slowly this time. "I've got eggs and milk in my wagon outside." When nothing happened, she swallowed hard and said, "I'm Mrs. Fritz Vogel, and I've brought milk and eggs for trading." She didn't know why she was repeating herself, but she didn't know what else to say. She pursed her lips and went on. "I would like some help unloading the wagon if I could."

Again Gerda and the woman stared at each other for what felt to Gerda like a long, long time. Strangely, she found herself wanting to laugh and cry at the same time. Perhaps it was because she still felt the thrill of a new independence and she was in a store she had shopped in for years, and knew the warp and waffle of the hard wood floors in each aisle, and it was as comfortable as any business in town could ever be for Gerda, but despite the connection between her and the woman, Gerda simply did not expect what happened next.

The woman shook her head and said, "So Frau Vogel wants help does she? That's rich."

Gerda was so shocked by the woman's words she laughed outright. It was a short yip of humorless laughter that she caught quickly and tried to take back by placing a hand over her mouth, but it was too late. The woman raised her chin and glared at her. "What's so funny?"

Afterward Gerda wondered what she would have said if Mr. Kroger had not come in the front door at that exact moment. Gerda spun toward him, not sure now from what direction an attack would come. The woman immediately turned around and began to rearrange things on the shelf behind her.

"Mrs. Vogel!" Mr. Kroger called jovially. "I thought that was you I saw coming into town, but I said to myself, that can't be Mrs. Vogel—there's no Fritz up beside her."

Gerda's hand was still over her mouth and she couldn't think for a moment what to say. She looked at the woman industriously working behind the counter, inexplicably moving items from one shelf to another. "I—no, he—Fritz didn't come," she finally managed to say. She pointed toward the back door. "Eggs. Milk. I have them." She knew she must be sounding like an idiot, again or still, but she couldn't get her mouth to form the words she meant to say.

Mr. Kroger didn't seem to notice her discomfort and simply walked behind the counter and pulled out the book where he kept the trading records. "Fine, fine, Mrs. Vogel, I'm happy to hear that." He pulled his glasses from the front pocket of his apron and perched them carefully on his nose. "Emily," he said to the woman beside him, "did you call Ambrose out? He'll need to bring the goods in." The woman, Emily, straightened her shoulders and walked toward the back room without glancing again at Gerda.

"Oh." Mr. Kroger looked up absent-mindedly. "I forgot to introduce you to Emily. She's my sister-in-law's cousin from St. Louis." He leaned toward Gerda and lowered his voice. "A widow, you see, come out here because we're all the family she's got. She came out for a test run in February but gave up and went back to St. Louis. She ran out of money before she got there, though, so she turned around and came back to us. I'm training her to help out around the store." He leaned over the counter toward her and lowered his voice even more. "Because my wife says she's not much help around the house." He winked at her, as if they now shared a secret.

Fritz hadn't kept track of the time. He looked up from his labor to wipe the sweat from his forehead with the big kerchief from his pocket and that was the first he noticed that time had passed and weather had changed. It had grown increasingly hot and humid as he and Liable's man worked, typical of a spring day, but a sharp breeze had kept them cool by drying the sweat on their backs and they had made quick work of the two-man projects the Liables needed doing. In truth, Fritz lost track of the time when he and the hired hand had rumbled down the drive. That was his way when he worked—he gave himself entirely to the task at hand with no concern for what came before or after. His concentration ended only when the job did.

He stretched a bit as he stuck the kerchief back into his pocket and looked around. A woodpecker had rattled the tin stovepipe a few times earlier in the morning, but it had settled in on a branch of an old cottonwood above them and kept them company most of the day. Fritz realized it had gone silent and had been so for quite some time. He looked up to where the bird had been working and realized that the chirp and chatter of all the birds had ceased. He noticed too that the breeze had disappeared and it felt breathlessly still in the farmyard. As he looked around, the Liables' dog, a big shepherd, suddenly jumped up and yipped a couple of times. Fritz looked at the dog and then turned to look toward the west, already knowing a weather change would be coming. He'd lived on the plains most of his life and was as accustomed as anyone to the weather and its sudden changes. Still, what he saw shocked him so much that he stepped backward, almost stepping on the hired hand who had come up behind him.

"That don't look so good." The man's voice seemed loud and sudden in his ear. Fritz studied the storm clouds boiling in from the west. Thunderheads rose what looked like miles into the air. They rolled up and out across the blue sky like a rush of dark smoke from a fast fire. Every part of the storm front was in motion, layers of clouds going in different directions, though the entire mass moved from west to east like an army. The base of the storm was black as night. Streaks of lightning crawled along the lower edge where a wall of clouds had formed.

It looked to be a few miles off yet, but it was moving fast. Fritz calculated the distance between where he thought the storm was right now and his farm. He figured he could beat it there if he could borrow one of Liable's horses. He could bring it back in the morning. He turned to tell the man his plan, and that's when he remembered Gerda wasn't at the farm. Gerda was in town, alone. He spun back to look at the clouds, trying to see if the storm would have hit town yet, as if his vision would let him.

"I need a horse," Fritz said, and he would be forever grateful to the man for how quickly he moved to help him. No questions asked, just action. Fritz didn't wait for the saddle, though he needed to guide the horse up along the fence to where he could climb up and swing his leg over the draft horse's wide back. At seventeen hands tall, the horse was like a mountain, and once on his back Fritz could see even more of the storm. He slapped rein to rump, and though the horse resisted, wanting only to return to the barn, Fritz pulled its head around and kicked him into obedience.

As he crossed the river, the horse's hooves pounded across the wooden bridge making its own kind of thunder. It was only then that Fritz realized the decision before him. When he reached the main road, he must either turn west toward town and Gerda, or east toward home. A nonsensical nursery rhyme that Gerda sometimes quoted to the children flitted through his mind: "Ladybug, ladybug, fly away home. Your house is on fire and your children are alone." He thought about Gerda with that team of horses, how small she sat on the wagon seat. Even with the reins wrapped around her hands she could lose them, lose control of the horses, or hold the reins too long and be pulled from the seat. He saw this so clearly in his mind it was as if he were witnessing it at that moment, and he kicked the horse's sides, urging him toward Gerda.

But just as he reached the turning point, he thought too of the children at home. Had he taught them what to do in bad weather? Could Katie lift the heavy door to the fruit cellar? Would she even know to go there for protection? He thought of the Easter tornado, the one that wiped out much of Omaha just a few years back. He remembered the pictures in the newspapers, the brick buildings blown apart as if cannonballs had hit them dead on. He remembered the pictures, he remembered the papers, but he couldn't, he *couldn't* remember whether he had shown them to his children, whether he had told them what to do in a storm. He wanted to shout, he felt such anger at the storm, at himself for not being there, for not remembering to teach the children how to save themselves, and finally at Gerda, God forgive him for this, at Gerda for going to town with this storm coming.

He kept his eyes turned to the west. He could see the lightning at the front of the bank of clouds looking like fiery spider legs creeping across the plains. He thought again of Gerda, of the horses, of the wagon out of control—he knew his horses, he knew they would be terrified and would want to come to the safety of the barn. He knew they would run as fast as they could unless strong arms held them back. He did shout then, not a curse, because he was not a cursing man, just a raw sound of frustration and fear.

He pulled the horse's head around in the direction he needed to go. He made a choice, he knew, between his wife and his children. The cold air that came with the storm front hit him then with the force of a cold wave. The horse's coarse hair whipping in the sudden wind brought tears to his eyes. He buried his head for a moment in the horse's mane, the wind-driven rain chasing him home.

Mr. Kroger had been as friendly as ever, and in his presence Gerda felt her heartbeat return to normal. He peered at Gerda over his reading glasses and asked about the family and the size of her garden this year, how her fruit orchard had fared during the past winter. He had lost a few big apple trees to the ice storm last fall, he told her.

"The branches just snapped off and dropped around the base of the trees like they were kids getting ready for their weekly baths and leaving their clothes at their feet," he said. "I darn near cried when I saw that. They were my sweetest apples, you see."

Gerda arranged her face in sympathy and tried to think of something to say in response, but Kroger was the kind of man who didn't need a response. He did enough talking for two or three people. Though some days Gerda grew tired of his ramblings—she had already heard the saga of the fruit trees twice—today the familiarity of his voice and stories calmed her.

Emily had apparently sent the boy out from the back room, but she didn't return to the counter while Gerda was in the store. She couldn't shake the feeling that the woman was lingering just out of sight, a cat waiting to pounce, and Gerda felt her shoulders stiffening to the point of pain as she finished pulling what she needed from the shelves.

It had been more than three months since Gerda had seen the German thrown from the train, but his face and the dark looks of the other passengers in the car still haunted her. How quickly things can change, how easily people can turn on one another.

When Mr. Kroger helped Gerda up into the wagon, his voice droning on in a comforting hum, Gerda glanced up to see Emily in the shadow of the doorway watching them. She felt a stab both of fear and of shock. Until this moment, she had seen this war as a man's war. War was something in which women were merely bystanders, or perhaps helped where they could, like the British women she'd read about taking over the factory jobs when the men went to war. But they were not combatants, they simply were not.

The sight of Emily, one hand on her throat and her gaze dark and malevolent, filled Gerda with foreboding. The hatred for Germans sweeping across the country had arrived in Stuart, Gerda realized, in the form of a woman.

Mr. Kroger stepped away from the wagon and looked up to the west. "There's a storm coming, Mrs. Vogel. You best be heading right home."

That's all Gerda wanted, to be home, in her own kitchen, with her family around her. She kept her eyes on the shifting rumps of the horses as she left town. She didn't look up to see what was chasing her. She knew she couldn't change what was happening around her, but she couldn't bear to see it, and so it was that the storm took her by surprise.

The horses strained against the reins from the moment Gerda released the wagon brake and set out for home. Boss, the younger of the two horses, pulled sideways in the harness, tossing his head and jumping as if trying to jerk free of his bindings. Gerda was glad Fritz had harnessed Ol' Blue along with him. She wasn't sure she could have held him in without the old gelding's calming influence. As it was she had to brace her feet against the footboard and push back with her whole body, pulling hard on the reins just to keep them in check on the streets leading out of town.

It had grown unmercifully hot in a short time, as it does so often just before a big storm, and she wished she'd taken off her sweater before releasing the brake. She felt wet with sweat before she'd gone a mile. It dripped between her breasts and under her arms. The dust that the rose up from under the horses' hooves hung in a cloud that threatened to choke her.

She was within sight of the lane leading north toward home when a burst of cold wind caught her, and then the rain followed. The drops hit like small stones against her face, and she thought at first it was hail, but it was raindrops coming down so hard it hurt. That lasted only a few seconds before the skies opened and poured out rain so heavy and fast that she had to lean forward and down to catch a breath. The horses were terrified, and she had no strength to stop them. She lost hold of the wet leather reins and the wind-driven water came so hard she couldn't see the direction they ran. She held on to the wooden back of the seat and screamed, but her voice was as nothing to the roar of the storm. When the horses got to the turn toward home—how could they know?—they were running full out, and the wagon tipped perilously into the turn. Gerda was tossed to the edge of the seat, fingernails clawing at the wood to save herself.

Fritz said later it was Ol' Blue that slowed them down. The old gelding, he said, had suddenly planted his forefeet in the mud and the wagon hitch, pulled forward by momentum and the second horse, caught him on the hind leg causing a wound that would never heal, but it was just enough to keep the wagon upright. Fritz was standing at the barn door when it happened. He could see little more than the dark shapes of the wagon and the horses. Offering a prayer seemed his only hope, and so he did—the fierce prayer of a man unaccustomed to the task. He swung the big barn door open and the horses rushed in, Gerda clinging rag-like to the seat.

CHAPTER SEVEN

When the Knights of Columbus called a meeting in the middle of the day, it was generally conceded to mean that the group had taken on a job for which they wanted women's participation. This time, the meeting was not only to commence at 2:00 p.m., the traditional starting time for meetings of the local women's clubs, including the Altar Society, the Ladies' Aid Society, and the Red Cross Women's Club, but had a stated end time, which made it clear the meeting would be over early enough for the homemakers to get home in time to prepare the evening meal.

The meeting's focus was to be the War Library Fund and was one of the seemingly endless fundraising projects that had sprung up within days of war being declared last spring. Despite the overload of such meetings, this one involved a matter for which Gannoway held a special affection. Well-read citizens were imperative to a healthy democracy, he believed, and he'd long been interested in making books widely available. This particular project involved bringing books to the soldiers, both in the camps at home and overseas.

William Owens was to start the meeting off, the notice had read, with a discussion of the Traveling Library that had "graced Stuart residents with access to knowledge since 1914." Gannoway, who had heard Owens's four-minute talk about the importance of ridding that library of all German-language books, could already guess the tenor of his discussion.

A speaker from Omaha would follow Owens, a Miss Charlotte Templeton, and it was her talk that interested Gannoway most today. She was the executive secretary of the Nebraska Public Library. A colleague of Gannoway from his college days in Lincoln had written to encourage him to do what he could to help her with the project she spearheaded.

Gannoway had read his letter aloud to Miranda when he received it. "She's in charge of organizing the Nebraska libraries, even the traveling ones, in the war effort to get books to our soldiers," the colleague had written. "Not an easy job, as you might imagine, even in ordinary times, but these are not ordinary times, and the poor girl is having quite a time with some of those communities."

"I'll wager that's true enough," Gannoway said. He knew without the need to have it spelled out that one of the problems would be working with the people who would jump on board only to advance a separate agenda. How easily efforts can be sidetracked by those who would hook their car to any engine even if it meant the whole train would be slowed to a stop. "There are men like Will Owens all over this country who can't see past the so-called dangers of the German-language books to see the real dangers of sending men to camps without recourse to healthy pastimes." He talked as much to himself as to Miranda. "'What is good for me is also good' is one of the great errors of intellect according to Nietzsche, and Owens seems pretty convinced that getting rid of everything German is good for him."

Miranda stood at the table folding towels as he talked, and she peered at him through squinted eyes. "I trust you've enough sense to keep some of those opinions to yourself," she said. "Remember, honor has not to be won; it must only not be lost."

Gannoway went on as if he'd not heard her. "And they certainly can't see the opportunity presented by an effort of this nature. The library is offering an education to men who in peacetime would have no access to it, wouldn't even know to go looking for it. If this effort is successful they'll have information at their fingertips," he paused, "literally, at their fingertips."

Miranda picked up a pile of folded towels and walked to the chiffonier in the upstairs hallway. Gannoway followed her. "This drive has been going on for months—months! Did you know that? Since right after America entered the war. Stuart is way behind in getting started."

"Who has time to plan how to improve the world when they're so busy pointing out the flaws?" Miranda said.

"Exactly!" Gannoway replied.

Miranda turned to him. "I was referring to you."

He tipped his head. "All right, make fun if you will, but you have to admit this War Library is a noble cause." He looked down at the letter in his hand again.

"Ed," she said, placing her hand on his arm. But she didn't go on.

As they walked toward the meeting hall, he thought about what his colleague had told him about the fund drive for the War Library led by the Lincoln Commercial Club down in the capital city. "If you can't give a book, give the price of a book" had been their slogan and Gannoway liked the sound of that. He thought he'd suggest it for use in Stuart's campaign. Easily meeting that city's quota, Lincoln had raised several thousand dollars in just one afternoon without even canvassing the residential areas. Gannoway didn't imagine a community like Stuart could come up with a lot of cash, but it could certainly do its share. The quota for each city was determined by the population and Gannoway made calculations in his head of the potential donation for Stuart if it had 100 percent participation in a similar campaign, 75 percent, and then 50 percent in terms of the population based on the census data from 1910. Thinking in numbers helped him clear his mind. The community had grown in the last eight years, but he had no accurate figures as to how much, and he was not one to hazard guesses. Lincoln residents had ready access to books in general and a wealthier populace, but still he thought there was no reason why Stuart couldn't do its part and he was determined to do what he could to make it happen.

It was Owens's face on his mind when they stepped through the door, not so much as an enemy to overcome but as a rut in the road to be aware of, so it surprised him when Dr. James MacGewan rose from his chair and hurried toward him before Gannoway even had a chance to look for Owens in the room.

"I'd like to talk with you before we get started," MacGewan said as he gripped Gannoway's elbow and steered him back out the door he'd just come through. Miranda dipped her chin at him when he pulled his arm away testily. Gannoway smiled to hide his irritation. Miranda had insisted they cultivate a friendship with MacGewan and his wife when they first came to town, "to size up the competition," she said. Gannoway didn't like to think of MacGewan as his competition; there was more than enough business in Stuart and the surrounding community for both of them. In truth, when MacGewan had first arrived in Stuart ten years back, Gannoway had welcomed him as a colleague. He was a graduate of the University of Nebraska, as was Gannoway, and Gannoway assumed that since they had had the same teachers they would have similar philosophies about patient care.

MacGewan, however, had apparently spent more time socializing than studying down in Lincoln and showed little aptitude for the actual practice of medicine. He had learned early that the appearance of knowing something would take him as far or farther than actually knowing it. He was a man who used many words, but in the end said very little. He was charming, though, and handsome, and not above stepping in between Gannoway and his patients to try to lure them away from the older doctor. Despite Gannoway's welcome, and Miranda's efforts, they had not, in short, become friends.

"Have you been made cognizant of the purpose of this gathering?" Mac-Gewan asked.

Gannoway nodded. "The War Library Fund, as I understand it."

"It's the War Library Fund," MacGewan went on as if Gannoway hadn't answered affirmatively, describing in detail the history and goals of the fund. He didn't so much converse about it as lecture on the topic.

Gannoway watched MacGewan's handlebar moustache wiggle up and down as he spoke. He had to concentrate on not reaching up to grasp the handles and tug them. Finally, he simply had to look away to avoid the temptation. He pulled out a kerchief and wiped the sweat that had formed on his brow and neck. The heat was oppressive again today, as it had been for weeks now. The country felt baked under a heavy sun. It wasn't yet high summer, but the prairie had long lost the fresh green of spring and turned brown again. In town, wind-driven dust had coated everything; even the trees looked gray at first glance, as if the chlorophyll had leached from the leaves.

As MacGewan talked, Gannoway tucked his kerchief back into his pocket and looked around at the colorless world and thought about the patient he'd just left resting after gallbladder surgery. He thought about the pattern of stitches he had used and the way the young man had squeezed his hand when he came out from under the ether as though he'd awoken to the sensation of falling and had grabbed for something to hold onto. He thought about the beef and potato stew his wife had instructed the cook to make for supper tonight, about the catalogs Miranda had spread across the table that morning. He might have gone on to think about the weave pattern in his suit coat if MacGewan hadn't finally gotten to his point and reached out to grasp Gannoway's elbow again.

"I simply must ask you to support me on this," MacGewan was saying. "It is one thing to keep the men entertained. I'm more than willing to assist in financing the purchase of such dime novels as those penned by Zane Grey or Owen Wister. I'm certainly not averse to spending time with a rousing tale on the subject of the Old West." Gannoway considered how many words MacGewan could say before taking a breath. "However, it has come to my attention that certain communities have sent informative literature of the textbook variety." He spluttered his last words, "*Medical* textbooks!"

MacGewan's meaning finally came clear. Gannoway rubbed his hand across his face to hide a smile. MacGewan was an advocate of keeping patients in the dark as much as possible about all areas of treatment. He'd even followed Cathell's advice in that silly book *The Physician Himself* and had taken to complicating his prescriptions with the Latin terms for common items—*phenicum* for "carbolic acid," *natrum* for "sodium." MacGewan's habit had always seemed an insignificant practice to Gannoway, and a harmless one, and so he ignored it unless one of the patients specifically asked for clarification.

Gannoway removed his hat and fanned himself a few times before replying.

"James," he said patiently, "let's not worry too much about overeducating the public. I think there's little danger of that." He held his hat up to his ear when MacGewan started to speak, as if using it to help him hear a voice in the distance. "I believe I hear Mr. Owens calling the meeting to order, and if you'll excuse me, I believe I'll go find a seat before Miss Templeton steps up to the podium."

He left MacGewan pacing the small square of shade outside the hall.

Miss Templeton was a slight woman whose spectacles had a tendency to slip down her nose as she spoke. Nonetheless, her eyes held confidence and she moved with businesslike grace to the front of the room when Owens finally ceded the floor and introduced her. She gave a prepared speech, glancing only occasionally at the papers in her hand, and remained admirably unflappable when the residents of Stuart said what they came to say.

The president of the Ladies' Aid Society spoke up first, hardly waiting for Miss Templeton to call for questions. "I'm not accustomed to speaking in front of the gentlemen, so forgive my nervousness, and of course I speak only for myself," she glanced pointedly around the room at the other women in the society, "and pardon my slang as well, but," she pinched her lips together before going on, "nothing doing. Our society has been sidetracked in the service of the Red Cross, and until someone can devise a way to increase the number of hours in the day—not just resetting our clocks, mind you—we simply cannot do any more. I wish you luck with your endeavor, Miss Templeton."

Dr. MacGewan's wife stood up so quickly her chair nearly tipped over. "The humanitarian efforts of the Red Cross are needed and noble causes.

We have cooked meals, wrapped bandages, made packages of toiletries, and raised money for our soldiers. I publicly apologize if our service to 'Uncle Sam' has interfered with anyone's sleep."

That's what passed for civility during the rest of the meeting. When the men joined in, chaos ensued. There was shouting and chairs pushed aside to accommodate roving speakers.

"Nothing is worse than active ignorance," Gannoway said quietly to Miranda, and if Philip Larue had not overheard him, the phrase might have remained a private joke between them.

"You are quite fond of the German philosophers, aren't you, Dr. Gannoway?" Larue said loudly. A pocket of silence developed around them. Gannoway looked quizzically at Larue, but said nothing.

"That was Goethe you were quoting, wasn't it?" This time both of Gannoway's eyebrows went up. "Yes, I've read some philosophy too," Larue went on. "We are not all rubes in this town." He nodded his head in a way that seemed not only to indicate the people around them, but also to include them. "The difference between you and the rest of us is that we recognize danger when we see it. The Germans are dangerous, Dr. Gannoway, make no mistake about it."

Gannoway opened his mouth, but strangely, no words came to him. A rush of thoughts went through his head, thoughts about justice and prudence, and it occurred to him that if the threat of death were imminent, his slowness, this characteristic tendency to think before speaking, would lead to his own extinction. How interesting, he thought, what that would mean for humankind. No retort divided itself into specific words to offer in response to Larue's comments. Miranda grasped his arm and pulled him around to face her. "Good day, Mr. Larue," she said over her shoulder. "Please give my regards to your wife. I'm sorry she couldn't be here."

By the time they got to the door, Miss Templeton, of all people, had restored order in the room. "Please take your seats," she said, and had he been in the mood, Gannoway would have noted how sheepish and childlike the adults were in obeying the order. When the room had quieted down Templeton looked around the room with a schoolmistress's practiced glare. "When I took this job, I was warned there would be difficulty in securing concerted action from the many communities in Nebraska. But I believe in the cause, and I believe in you, my fellow Nebraskans." She folded her hands in front of her, and though she looked sincere, Gannoway couldn't help but admire the succinct duplicity of her next statement. "I refuse to believe what my colleague from South Dakota claimed about our state, that certain communities cannot be counted upon to remain loyal."

The unseasonable heat had grown even more oppressive and the sun lingered high in the sky when Ed walked Miranda home. They did not discuss the generous donation Ed had made to the War Library Fund, nor the small number of others in the community who had joined him.

When they got home Ed couldn't bear to go inside. He stood at the bottom of the porch steps and removed his suit coat and loosened his collar. "I need to check on how Mr. Thomas is doing without his gallbladder," he told Miranda. She studied his face a moment before going inside alone.

He kept to the shade of the buildings as best he could on his walk back into town. Deep in his own thoughts, he saw little of the day around him. It was the sight of Gerda Vogel sitting on the wagon near the mercantile that brought him back. A straight-backed, square-shouldered woman, Gerda had a kind of quiet dignity that was unlike any of the other women in the community. She was herself only, recognizable even from a distance. He had not seen her since early spring, a memory that still made him flush. Gerda had been standing beside a wagon looking up at her husband. She had been crying silently. Gannoway could see the tears glistening on her cheeks and his hand reached instinctively toward her to console her even though he was yards away and not part of this moment at all. He had watched as Fritz reached down, his big hand cupping her cheek. With his other hand, he caught one of her tears on the tip of his finger. What he did next shocked Gannoway, as if he was witnessing their lovemaking. Fritz took the tear from Gerda's eye and placed it in the corner of his own. Gerda placed her hand on Fritz's arm and leaned her face against it. Her children clustered about her like sepals around a flower.

Gannoway walked toward her now as to a destination, a smile forming on his lips. Only a few steps more and he would cross the street and she would turn toward him, he thought, her face luminous with that mysterious inner light that made her otherwise plain features beautiful. In his mind's eye he saw again the look of her face when Fritz had taken her tears and made them his own.

He stopped to wait for a horse and buggy to pass, waving absent-mindedly at the driver who called out a hello. Gannoway only looked beyond him to Gerda, impatient for the delay. Suddenly he realized Gerda was slumped on the seat and he felt a jolt of fear run through him. He started to dash toward her around the back of the buggy. It was then that he saw Fritz standing by the wagon, tossing bags into the back, and the picture cleared. Gerda was not slumping, merely leaning awkwardly over the back of the seat helping her children.

Gannoway stopped again, this time in the middle of the street, another horse and buggy going around him, the driver asking him if he was okay.

"Heat getting to you, Doc?"

Gannoway looked up but didn't recognize the man. He smiled weakly. "No, no, I'm fine. Sorry to be in your way." He stepped back to the side of the street opposite the Vogel wagon. Standing in the shadow of the bank, he realized with a start that after seeing Gerda he had fastened his collar and put his suit coat back on. His reflection in the plate glass window held the expectant look of a suitor. He felt himself falling and reached out to grab the brick wall beside him. He looked around to see if anyone else had seen. The image of Fritz's hand on Gerda's face seemed to be everywhere and he felt heavy with something he didn't understand. Not desire, exactly; need, perhaps.

That night, he dreamed of snakes. Snakes covered the floor, the dresser, and the bed. Writhing coils draped on every surface. He was under them. Buried in snakes, he couldn't move his arms or legs. The weight of them crushing him, his chest felt filled with fire. He struggled with all his might to push one arm free and clawed his way out from beneath the undulating mass. The smooth, silent sliding of skin on skin terrified him and when he opened his mouth to scream, snakes began pouring forth from him. They were choking him. He couldn't breathe or make a sound. One coiling rope looped around his neck and he clutched at it with both hands and strained against it to pull away. Standing, he awoke to hear Miranda ask, "Ed, are you okay? What's the matter?"

He rubbed his eyes and face trying to rid his mind of the dream images. "Nothing," he said. "Go back to sleep." Miranda sat up and straightened the blankets he had tangled in his nightmarish struggle and looked at him one more time before turning back toward the wall to sleep.

He pulled one of Miranda's crocheted blankets off the quilt stand at the end of the bed and wrapped it around his shoulders before going downstairs. In the kitchen he opened the fire door on the stove and poked the embers before adding kindling. He sat hunched in front of it, watching the lick of flames.

He'd had the dream before. When he was a child, it came often. He remembered once pulling his brother, Lark, out of bed, nearly spraining his arms in an effort to get him away from the danger. Lark was younger and at first the intensity of the dreams frightened him too, but when he realized they were merely nightmares, he teased Ed mercilessly. One night he brought a bull snake to bed with them and let it out of the flour sack just after Ed dozed off. Ed killed the snake and then almost killed his brother before he came completely awake. It was the only time Lark played that trick. Now the dream came only once a year, and when he awoke from it, he knew what the day would hold. Because he swore each time it would never happen again, he never prepared himself for it, and it might as well have been the first time each and every time.

The sun was coming up before the fire in Gannoway's chest cooled and he could let go of the feeling of snakes sliding on his skin. He was still sitting in front of the stove when Miranda came down and started breakfast, moving around the kitchen without speaking.

She set his breakfast in front of him. He could feel her eyes on him. It was unusual for him to be home still, unready for work so late in the day. He typically drove himself to the limits of his endurance, whether it was through work or studying the latest medical journals.

He ate the food methodically. Eggs and fry bread were the only things Miranda cooked, and those not very well. The cook didn't come in until midday. Ed could never be certain if he would be back from his rounds at noon, so dinner was usually a bowl of sweetened milk bread, which he ate standing at the stove because the kitchen table would be laden with the cook's tools and the dining table would be covered with Miranda's things—catalogs, yarn, or fabrics. Supper was the main meal in their home, and it was served in the dining room with full china every night. Miranda adored the delicate bone china gifts that Ed gave her and she used them as often as possible. Sometimes Ed would watch her hands as she held the fragile pieces and he would remember when she touched him with such care, but mostly they ate their meals in silence, not looking at one another at all.

Finally it was time to go. He had delayed as long as he could. He stood in front of the mirror adjusting the knot on his tie, loosening it because the dream still felt so fresh, and he knew he could not change what he was about to do. It was not the dream that delayed him. He couldn't pretend that it was.

He smoothed his hair back carefully and straightened his collar once, again. He looked at his reflection dispassionately. He saw a man, forty-five years old, trim and muscular. Though he was going soft around the middle, his height, six feet, hid the excess weight well. His wavy hair had gone gray at the temples and sideburns. Gray eyes, dark-rimmed with flecks of black, gazed back at him, and he stared into them as he promised himself: this would be the last time he did this thing. Just today, just one more time, and then he would be free. Once he'd made that promise, he forgot all the promises that came before it, all those years of making it, and he wanted only to get outside and be alone.

He stepped out into a morning where the bowl of sky hung so low and blue it made his throat ache to look at it. White tufts of clouds trailed sweeping wisps across the firmament. Like tails in search of horses, he thought. If his daughter had lived, he would have called her to come see. There is a herd of horses without tails just on the other side of the horizon, he would have told her, and the two of them would have galloped across the plains to witness the moment of reconciliation between sweep and bone, earth and sky.

If his daughter had lived.

When he closed the door a host of sparrows scattered in a whirlwind of feather and sound from the yard in front of him. They disguised themselves as acorns in the oak trees as he watched. The wooden plank creaked in the stillness as he stepped off the porch. He followed the stone steps set in the ground from the corner of the house to the edge of the yard where lilac and spirea bushes formed a half circle around a stone bench. In late spring the space would be blossom-filled and bee heavy, wild with color and scent, and in winter it was quiet except for the rattle of branches when the breeze blew. In all seasons it was a place of solitude. He walked to the bench he had built eighteen years ago and looked around, then he draped his coat on the bench and placed his hand on it to help himself down into kneeling position beside it. His lower back spasmed in protest, a pinch in his sciatic nerve sending sharp stabs of pain up his hip and down into his leg. He gritted his teeth, trying to control the pain by refusing to accept it, and waited it out. Then he closed his eyes and began.

He listened for the sound of his heart beating. He followed the whoosh of his own breath filling his lungs and diaphragm, then whooshing back out again in a steady rhythm until *Now* fell away and he found what he needed.

He brought his hands up and cupped them together and, one more time, he willed her into being. The weight of her body rested against the soft pink pads on his palms and fingers. The silken down of her scalp, the warm scent of musk and blood that was hers and hers alone, her bowed lips, the fringe of lashes on milky white cheeks, her impossibly small fingers, pinpricks of nails, a birthmark the size and shape of a teardrop on her shoulder—all of it came back to him as if it were happening again. The snake-like cord he had pulled from her neck still pulsing.

She would have been eighteen years old now, and he would have been the father of a young woman, not a little girl. For a moment, and only a moment, he breathed in the pain of a loss so sharp and heavy it could easily have been new. He made it new.

He had delivered dozens of babies before her and twice as many after. Some had lived and some had not. The power of life and death was not his. He was a man only of medicine. He believed that, but he could see her in his mind, feel the weight of her in his hands, blood-covered and still. Everything he had ever learned had not prepared him for the searing emptiness of her small body. In the grove on this blue day, he bent low over his image of her and blew air into the palms of his hands. *Forgive me,* he breathed. *Forgive me.*

It was as useless now as it had been then, but when he had no more air in his lungs to give, he held them both in the space between breathing out and breathing in as if he could change the past. When he could no longer hold it off, he gasped for air, breathing in, he let her go again. He looked up from his hands and flung the memory of her away as forcefully as he had pushed away the women who came to bury her.

His head jerked back. His long-fingered hands covered his gaping mouth. A searing white heat filled his chest and had he been standing he would have fallen. The burning spread, it filled his cells with warmth, sparks of self rico-cheting off one another so violently he felt aglow. Frozen in time and pain, he stayed like that as long as he could, for a minute, an hour, a lifetime, her lifetime, his baby girl's one and only lifetime. When he opened his eyes, he saw again the sky, lone witness to his remembering.

Today was his daughter's birthday and death day and now she is gone, he told himself. She is gone. She is gone. She is gone.

CHAPTER EIGHT

"Look, Mama! That bird is walking on water!" Ray called. His full-moon face turned toward Gerda to be sure she saw this miracle-performing bird before he ran toward it waving his arms and shouting, a flurry of little-boy energy in hand-me-down, too-big pants. The thin puddle that held the bird splintered as he ran through it, and water, bright splashes of it, wet his boots and hers. She held her tongue between her teeth, considering her response.

"Little boys with wet boots have to stay inside by the stove until they're all dry," she warned, but Ray wasn't listening to her. A new calf had trotted to the fence line to watch the commotion and the two of them, moon-faced boy and white-faced calf, studied each other with a seriousness that made her want to laugh, that took her breath away. Her babies made the world new again, every day.

"He thinks you've got milk to offer," she said. "Put your fingers out." Ray lifted his hand as if in a trance, doing as told but with an unmitigated uncertainty. The calf, for its part, mirrored the boy's attitude. It planted its forelegs in a wide stance and stretched its neck cautiously forward. Its fat, pink lips sought Ray's chubby fingers, pulled them in slowly, sucking lightly at first, then with intensity as if every object had the potential of becoming nourishment.

Ray stood awestruck, watching the calf work his fingers like dry teats. When he looked up at his mother, she wasn't sure if he was about to cry or smile. She leaned against the fence rail, waiting for him to decide.

A soft breeze picked up a smattering of sand from the cattle yard and rattled it against the fence, startling the calf and Ray alike. They jumped apart, spell broken.

"It was going to eat me, Mama!" Ray held his hand up for inspection.

"I wouldn't let that happen." She laughed at the earnestness in his face.

Ray was Fritz's boy, through and through. His hair, though thinner and finer, held the same wave across the crown as Fritz's. It curled around the edge of his ear given any chance to grow long enough. It was long enough now, and she added a haircut to the list of things she needed to get done before church on Sunday. Gerda always looked forward to Mass, though Fritz didn't seem to care either way. She liked bringing the children into the church, seeing them there among the holy things. They always seemed to look more angelic in the light coming through the stained glass windows. Her father's phrase *arme Teufel* still stung, and she was determined that her children would never look like or be the poor devils he predicted she would have.

The morning spread out around her like a promise. The weather had been unusually warm all month. The air blowing up from the south carried with it the sound of the No. 6 train heading east and the smell of the river. The combination always reminded her of home—would she never stop thinking of it as *home*?

Through the branches of the apple trees she could see her garden, and she felt that familiar itch to get out there and get started digging and planting.

"Mama! Mama!" Ray called. "A robin redbreast!"

"Yeah," she answered. It made her feel suddenly tired to hear his voice. The need to attend to him, to all of the children's needs, seemed so overwhelming. Inside the house Katie and the two boys were supposed to be cleaning up the breakfast dishes, but how could she know they were doing as told? Katie, the oldest, was still only eight, and the boys listened to her or not according to some whim Gerda could never predict.

"See? See?" Ray shouted.

"Yes, yes! I see it." She snapped at him. What is it that sent her skittering from one extreme to another? First melting with love when she looked at her son and then wanting to scream at him to just leave her alone. Give me some peace, child! she wanted to shout.

The breeze from the river came again, and she felt an almost uncontrollable urge to run toward it, to follow it east until she found her way home again, to her mother's house where she could forget all about this *arme Teufel* and these children. *Oh Mama,* she thought. *I get so homesick sometimes. Don't you miss me too?* Tears bit the back of her eyelids, and she wanted to shake herself. This was nonsense and she could not abide nonsense in anyone, least of all herself.

She shook the empty egg basket in a fit of anger. She didn't see Ray so close beside her until it was too late. The cold metal caught him just above his left eyebrow. He screamed. She screamed, and they both began to cry. She knelt beside him, not even noticing the horse pies in the lane where they stopped.

"Let me see, little one," she said. "Let Mama see. There's blood, oh no! No! There's blood, Ray! Let me see. Let me see!"

Ray's pudgy hands covered his face and he curled into a comma on the ground in front of her. Crimson seeped around his fingers and dripped onto her skirt. His cries were pitiful and loud. She pulled him into her lap and pried his hands away from his face expecting the worst, but found instead a simple red welt on his forehead. The blood that smeared across his face bubbled from his nose. There was no cut, only a red welt already darkening into a bruise on top of the bone that protected the temple.

"Oh Ray, you have a bloody nose. Mama didn't cut you. It's just your nose." She felt weak with relief. Why hadn't someone warned her how frightening a child's bloody nose could be? After four children the sight of blood on one of their faces still sent icy stabs through her heart. Bloody noses were common occurrences, but she always feared they wouldn't stop. With the first sign of blood she imagined a flood, a gushing away of life while she stood by helplessly. This was her nightmare, her worst fear, to lose a child, to not save what God had given her to protect. She clutched him to her chest, the blood smearing both of them now.

"I'm so sorry, little one. Mama's sorry," she murmured into his fine, fine hair.

Ray's sobs turned to whimpers and then sniffled to silence. Crisis passed, she could breathe again. "Come on, Ray. Help Mama gather eggs." She helped him stand and straightened his coat.

"Why did you hit me?" His bottom lip trembled and his gray eyes dripped tears.

She bent down to look directly at him. *Moon-faced child, why do you torment me so?* She smoothed his hair and tried to smile at him.

"I didn't mean to," she said. "I was just careless. See what happens when someone is careless?" She pulled a big red handkerchief out of her apron pocket and wiped his face. "We must always be careful. Remember that, my little boy. We must always be careful. Remember when Mama told you about that little boy from Atkinson?" There had been a story in the paper some weeks back about an accidental shooting where a young boy had killed his cousin. She spit on the corner of the kerchief and scrubbed at the blood already drying on the boy's chin. "That little boy wasn't careful and look what happened."

Ray struggled to get out of her reach. Like all children, he hated to have his face cleaned, especially with spit. "Mama don't!" he wailed, the welt on his forehead already forgotten.

"Well, all right then, but let this be a lesson to you. You must be careful at all times." Even to her own ears she sounded exactly like a mother.

Ray pulled free and raced ahead to the chicken coop. Gerda stood and looked around her. The calf continued its inspection of her and the boy. The great barn door stood open like a gaping mouth. The whitewashed outbuildings shimmered in the morning light. A cardinal whistled from the shelterbelt back of the house, a two-story white with black shutters and trim. In full summer the yard around the house would look like a jungle—or at least what she imagined a jungle would look like: morning glory vines creeping the walls and fence lines, hostas, lilies, hollyhocks, irises, roses, daisies clamoring for space. She closed her eyes and pictured it as it would be in the summer ahead, as it would be when the trees and shrubs that she had planted that first year would grow to full height.

She took a deep breath and felt the straining cloth of her dress across her chest. Suddenly she knew. Her tiredness, how close her tears seemed always to be, and when she moved her shoulders back to accommodate the intake of air, her breasts felt tender and full.

But of course. Another baby. How could she have not known? Time flew so quickly, weeks running one into another, she hadn't noticed the missing months. She waited for some feeling to come with this realization that the growing season was within her, but all she felt was tired. She opened her eyes and looked around again at this place they had built, she and Fritz. This is a good life, she thought, but even as she thought it she felt the sense of something wrong and hurtful lurking just out of sight, of a darkness waiting to pounce.

The memory of Ray's face with blood on it caused her to gag. She brought her hand to her mouth and murmured a prayer, fighting back the sickness and fear. "Oh most gracious Virgin Mary . . ." It was the prayer Elizabeth had tried to teach her, and with the words came the memory of her sister, came the fear she could not shake. Her head was bowed, and she didn't hear Fritz step up behind her. He placed his hand on her shoulder, and she jumped.

"Oh Fritz! You startled me!"

"You look as though you have the weight of the world on your shoulders, Gerd—is that blood you've got all over you?" His blue eyes widened, and he reached toward her. "What happened? Are you okay?"

"Yeah, yeah, I'm okay," she said, waving him off. The fact of the baby was still hers and she wasn't ready to share it. "Ray got a bloody nose and . . . ," she hesitated, not wanting him to think her weak, but she so wanted to lean on him, just for a moment. She felt suddenly so tired, these waves of fatigue surprising her. She tried to keep her tone light. "You know how I am. I started thinking about that Helme boy from over in Atkinson, that one who died of a bloody nose last spring." She caught herself before Fritz could start to laugh. "I mean he died of the gunshot wound." She looked away, still shaken.

Fritz patted her shoulder roughly as he turned to go. "Gerda, Gerda, Gerda. We've enough sorrows in the world without borrowing from strangers."

She watched his broad back disappear into the darkness of the barn, wanting to call him back, wanting him to just go away. Don't borrow trouble was his answer to everything, it seemed.

"Twenty-seven." Ray interrupted her reverie as he gingerly placed the last egg in her basket.

"Twenty-seven!" she exclaimed. "How did you learn to count that high? You're too young to count that high."

"Nu-uh," Ray said solemnly. "I'm old enough to count to a hundred if I wanted to."

And he was, she realized, old enough to count and read and force her to admit that time was flying by and her babies were growing up. She felt a pinch somewhere in the vicinity of her heart, something that was neither joy nor sorrow. Little boys become men, she thought, and she tried not to think of what came next in a world at war: men became soldiers.

I love you. I love you. She could say it a thousand times and it wouldn't make any difference. These are not magic words with healing properties. She knows this. And still she says them. She holds her hand to the rise of her belly. *I love you. I love you. I love you.*

And then she tries not to cry. *What baby would want to have a mother like me?* she thinks. *I cry. I shout. I attend to the washing with more tenderness than I show my children. My living children.*

Her living children. She holds her hand to her abdomen. She whispers, "I love you."

It is the fear she finds hardest to bear. The tiredness will pass. The aches and strains of carrying a child, these she can handle. She never suffered like some women with the stomach ailments. Sometimes the pressure against the other organs causes burning in her chest, but she never has to rush to the slop pail. She's lucky.

Lucky. She's lucky. But so very afraid every waking moment.

"I love you," she whispers to the quickening, to the flutters just below her right rib.

When Elizabeth died, her mother screamed. Like a madwoman, an animal. Under the bed Gerda held her hands over her ears and tried to keep out the sound, that howl of misery that came not from her mother at all but from some demon that had entered her body. She threw herself onto Elizabeth's body. The weight of her sagging the bed until the metal pressed against Gerda's face, trapping her beneath her mother, her Elizabeth, and the baby. She screamed words Gerda could not understand, grunting garbled phrases that made no sense. Gerda thought she was possessed.

After a time, a few moments, or an eternity, someone dragged her away from Elizabeth. Gerda could hear her father pleading with her, softly first, then shouting. Twice they picked her up to carry her away and twice she broke free and returned to cling to her dead daughter's body. Gerda saw her from her hiding place beneath the bed. Blood covered her mother's hands and arms, soaked the front of her dress. Blood, so much blood. The dress clung wetly to her legs.

When they closed the door, Gerda was alone with Elizabeth. She knew she was dead. She knew what dead meant. She had seen farm animals die. She was five years old and she knew about death.

When she slid out from under the bed, she bumped Elizabeth's hand. She reached out to stop its swinging. How quickly the warmth leaves the body. She dropped it as if burned. She stood by the bed and looked down at Elizabeth. She was naked. There was light coming through the south window and it shone on her face. Her eyes were open. Her legs, smeared with gelatinous red, were pulled straight. Her belly, and her breasts too, bloody. She thought at first Elizabeth was wearing a red dress, or had a red blanket spread across her. Gerda couldn't understand why there was so much blood.

It spread across the baby too. That's why she didn't see it at first. Its black hair matted and slick, it lay in the crook of Elizabeth's arms. Hardly a baby at all, a worm, curled into a ball beside Elizabeth.

The air in the room vibrated with silence like a string plucked. The hum of what had happened here not yet ready to be past. Even then she thought some aspect of this moment would be a part of all her future Nows. She would never again be free of this image, her sister's face whitened in death, the baby curled beside her.

The smell of blood and afterbirth filled the room with a cloying sweetness so thick she could almost taste it. Without warning she vomited. The corn and beef of the last meal still undigested came up in one wave. The wet splat of it on the floor clapped loud as an explosion in the quiet room. She wiped her mouth with the back of her hand, and she saw the blood was on her. She began to scream. One long keening howl until her breath was gone and then another. Someone burst into the room, threw the door back with such force the window rattled. Someone scooped her into her arms and ran with her from that room.

The blood on her face came from a tiny coil of a laceration. She must have caught the head of a loose nail when she crawled out from under the bed, her aunt reasoned, and Gerda believed her. When it healed, the curled cut became a scar shaped like a backward *S*.

S is for *sister,* she told herself. Reversed, it means goodbye.

They never said "I love you" in the house back home. She had never heard that combination of words, *"Ich liebe dich!"* that her mother had cried. Even in English it was a foreign language.

"Ich liebe dich!" Mama had screamed, but it was too late. Elizabeth was gone, and she never heard it this side of the grave. Gerda would not make that mistake. "I love you," she whispered, pressing her hand against her stomach, letting the vibrations of the words travel down her arm to enter her womb. "I love you," she said to the rise in her abdomen.

CHAPTER NINE

She married Fritz because she loved him. She married Fritz because she believed he would be a good father and a good husband. She married Fritz. She is the mother of four children; she carries another within her. And yet she cannot stop smiling as she walks back to the house, the mail tucked under her arm.

Charles Burke is a just a boy, a young man so very full of himself. He means nothing of what he says and simply likes to make women laugh. She didn't pretend anything more was meant by these . . . flirtations. She was not a goose.

Still.

When she talks to him, she remembers she is a woman; is that so wrong?

She had hurried to the mailbox with a letter for Katherine, but she nearly forgot to give it to him when he started teasing her. Really, the whole thing was nonsense. Her face burned as she walked back toward the house. Her skirt had two round circles of mud in front where she had kneeled in the garden earlier stringing a line for the beans she had planted. She hadn't noticed them when she talked to Charles, but now she could see them even without looking down. They could have been lamp-lit they stood out so. She reached up to smooth her hair and felt that a pin had come loose and a thick curling strand hung down her back. Good heavens, she thought, Mr. Burke must be having a good laugh right about now.

She chuckled and did her best to shake it off. She looked through the mail in her hands and found a letter from her sister. The back of the envelope showed a cluster of overblown pink roses surrounding a heart. "To my dear sister" was printed on the heart. Katherine always had some new stationery or postcard to write on. Gerda used the same paper for lists as she did letters, a pad of lined notepaper that she bought at Kroger's two or three at a time.

Her sister's sprawling handwriting covered the front and back of the pink paper and Gerda read the letter as she walked back toward the house.

"Oh my," Gerda said aloud, and broke into a run.

"Katie's getting married!" Gerda met Fritz at the door, her face alight with emotion.

"Our Katie?" he asked incredulously.

Gerda smacked him on the chest with the letter in her hand.

"Of course not, she's only eight years old." She stepped back to let him in and looked at the letter in her hand. "I mean Katherine, my baby sister."

"Well that's a relief," Fritz said and turned to the basin to wash his face and hands. "I didn't think I'd been out in the field that long that my little girl would grow up and get married on us." He reached out and ruffled Katie's hair as she went past with a bucket of water and began to pour it into the reservoir on the stove.

"I'm not getting married, Papa," she said over her shoulder. "I'm going to be a Sister."

"You're already a sister," Ray piped up. "You're my sister."

"Not a *sister* sister, a sister *nun,*" Katie said with a frown.

Gerda stomped her foot, though even as she did it, she wished she hadn't. "Oh, now you're all talking nonsense. This is about my sister Katherine, who is twenty years old and who has written a letter to me saying Johnnie Hoffman has asked her to marry him." She held the letter out for them to see but not long enough for them to read. "You remember the Hoffman family, don't you Fritz? They lived over south of the church? Had that big brick house you could see for miles when you came north out of town?"

"That little pipsqueak?" Fritz said. "Why he's nothing but hot air and big teeth. Why would she marry a blowhard like that?"

Gerda scowled and looked at the children. "That's no way to talk about someone you don't even know."

"I do too know him," Fritz said as he ladled gravy onto his bread. "You just said I know him. He lives just south of the church in that big brick house you can see for miles." He winked at Ray and Frank. "His name is John Hoffman, and he's asked your little sister, that would be Katherine, who is twenty years old if she's a day, to marry him. What do you mean I don't know him?"

"Whether you know him or not is not the point," Gerda said. She could feel her face growing hot and she wanted to stomp her foot again and to shout at him for behaving like a . . . a dunderhead. "You shouldn't talk about people that way!" She could feel her voice growing shrill and she hated it when that happened.

Fritz looked up at her, his expression flat and complacent. He chewed slowly, swallowed, and said, "What way?"

Gerda stared at him as she would a madman. She turned abruptly and grabbed the slop bucket from the corner and marched outside to the pigpen and dumped the contents into the trough.

Why? Why? Why? she railed silently, *could we not have even the simplest conversation about the simplest things?* She flung the bucket against the fence, sending the pigs on the other side into a snorting frenzy.

"Oh, do shut up," Gerda muttered. She placed her hands on her hips and looked around at the farm, at what they had built here. After a moment's contemplation she went into the brooder house where the baby chicks Fritz had brought home earlier in the week huddled under a heat lamp. She checked the level of the kerosene in the lamp then pulled a stool close to the fenced enclosure. She sat down carefully so as not to frighten the small things and watched the downy yellow chicks peck and stumble about. She watched them until her heart returned to its normal pace, then she sat up and looked out toward the house. Fritz had not yet come out after his noon meal, so she decided to watch the chicks a little longer.

"Papa doesn't much care for John, though he tries to hide it," Katherine wrote in her note. "I think it's because John is not afraid of him the way the rest of the young men around here are. Were they always that way? Not John. I remember seeing him talk to the men after church even when he was still in short britches. I tell you what, when John talks to Papa about business, Papa has to sit up and listen whether he likes it or not. Did you know the Hoffman family practically founded this town? They certainly own enough of it now, or so it seems."

Katherine went on with the news about the greatness of her soon-to-be husband, his family, his pets, and his every thought. Gerda wouldn't have been all that surprised to read that the Hoffman family outhouses didn't need ventilation.

How unlike her own experience, Gerda thought, when it was her turn to fall in love and start a family. Fritz too had been unafraid of Papa Drueke, but that hadn't inspired respect.

࣭

"What do you want, Gerda?" Father Bestal had seemed to read the question from the catechism in front of him and Gerda searched her own copy for the proper response. They were seated in his study in the back of the rectory. The two kerosene lamps on the wall and another on the desk between them were not enough to dispel the shadows of those dark autumn nights. Gerda often had to squint to read during their sessions. Bookshelves laden with dark leather-bound books lined the walls floor to ceiling and two small windows of dark stained glass allowed in little light even in the middle of the day. An easy chair near one of the two wall lamps offered the only comfortable reading light in the room, but for her sessions with Father, the two of them always sat across the desk from each other, a single lamp between them.

Gerda perched on the edge of her straight-backed chair, leaning into the circle of light cast by the lamp, though she never quite felt that she had reached it. The words in each line of her catechism seemed to cast shadows on the words below them and Gerda read uncertainly, never quite sure she was catching each word, much less its meaning.

Finding nothing on the page that matched his words, Gerda blinked up at the priest. The old man chuckled. "Don't be so frightened, *mein liebes Kind*," he said. "I've seen less startled looks on the faces of rabbits I've chased from my garden."

He closed the book in front of him, leaned back in his chair, and folded his hands across the wide expanse of his belly.

With the priest's face in deeper shadow, Gerda felt the bands around her chest loosen, and she slid back a little in her own chair. The shadows across her face gave her a sense of safety. Her thoughts, which Father Bestal had a disconcerting ability to read, felt private, were hers to keep.

"I'm sorry, Father," she said. "I thought it was part of the lesson that I'd missed. I didn't—I don't understand your question."

At nineteen, Gerda Drueke's smooth skin glowed as if lit from within by some holy light. Her dark hair swept back off her forehead in soft waves. Though she kept it pinned up neatly, it always seemed to threaten her efforts.

The lustrous coils caught the light in such a way that her hair seemed to move on its own despite the pins that held it. Unlike other young women her age, she had the habit of looking directly into the eyes of whomever she spoke to. This habit always caught Father Bestal off guard, and even though her father had delivered her to these lessons once a week for more than three months now, the old priest was still a little taken aback when she looked up at him.

She would make a formidable Mother Superior, he thought, if the Lord called her to such a life. It was the question of that calling that had prompted his inquiry. Gerda attended to the lessons, obedient and polite, but by the second one he knew she was only going through the motions. She did not have a true vocation to the cloth. Though the church needed women like her to carry its mission forward into the next century, Father Bestal believed only those who were truly called should be allowed a life of the veil.

"What is it you want, Gerda?" He repeated his question softly, and though he couldn't see her face clearly, he could see the tension in her shoulders loosen as she settled deeper into her chair.

"I don't know, Father." Other young women might have stuttered disingenuously, but Gerda spoke calmly and with assurance. "My father believes I will take the veil, that I will be his greatest gift to the church, but I don't know that I will be a gift of any sort. I fear the weight I feel in my chest whenever I think about the life he has chosen for me will weigh down any good I would ever do in the world." She leaned forward, bringing her face into the slight circle cast by the lamp on the desk. "Is that a sin, Father?" she asked. "Is it a sin to not want the way of life your father believes is best for you?"

Father Bestal gazed at her earnest face. Her brown eyes so dark he felt pulled into them.

"No," he whispered, then cleared his throat abruptly. "No," he said again. "We each serve the Lord in our own way. We must answer the individual call He gives us." He stood up and held his hand out to Gerda. "Let us pray together for a moment, Gerda. I hear your father's wagon outside the door."

Gerda obediently rose to her feet and took the priest's hand. She felt like smiling, though she wasn't sure why. She kept her head tipped low and away from the light so that the priest couldn't see her expression.

When Father Bestal told Gerda's father he didn't need to bring Gerda back for instruction, Frank Drueke looked as though he would strike the old priest where he stood. Instead, he nodded curtly and slapped a whip to the horses' rumps before Gerda had completely gained her seat. She grabbed a seat back for balance and sat down as far from her father as the buggy would allow. She rode home beside him cowering in silence, certain that as soon as they were out of sight of witnesses, he would take the whip he used on the horses and wield it against her.

He didn't whip her. He didn't speak to her again for days, and when he did, it was only out of necessity. Her mother, who at first had seemed to understand that it was inevitable for Gerda to build her own life, slowly shifted to seeing only what Frank wanted to be true. She too stopped talking to Gerda and the house became as silent as a tomb. They worked in silence. They ate in silence. They attended church together in silence. When Gerda tried to speak to either one, they silenced her, her mother with a raised hand and her father by slamming out of the house, the very air around him roiling with violence. Her uncles stopped by, but didn't come in the house. Gerda felt them watching her, though they never spoke directly to her.

When Gerda could take it no longer, she went back to the old priest. This time, alone in the confessional with the priest, Gerda was clearer about what she wanted.

"Bless me Father for I have sinned." Gerda's mouth formed the familiar words, but hardly a breath of sound passed her lips. Her knee joint shifting against the hard wood of the kneeler popped loudly in the small space of the confessional. She cleared her throat and tried again.

"Bless me Father for I have sinned," she whispered. "I have committed the sin of disobedience."

"Was your disobedience to God or to your father or mother?" Father Bestal asked quietly. Through the screen that separated them Gerda could see his white head bowed over the ever-present rosary he held in his hand. He always told his catechism classes he carried a rosary with him everywhere. "That way, if I find myself with spare time, I can say a rosary. None of God's time is wasted if you carry a rosary with you at all times." Gerda had been fifteen the first time she heard him say that and she had wondered if he said the rosary while he did his business at the end of the path out back of the church. She had not said this aloud to anyone, but the image still made her want to laugh. Not this time though.

"My papa," she whispered.

"You're going to have to speak up a little, Gerda. I'm an old man."

"My father," she said a little louder. The screen separating them gave only a symbolic anonymity. "I have sinned against my father. I have been disobedient. I did something he told me not to do. I have angered him." Once she got started, it wasn't so hard to speak.

"Father Bestal," she went on. "I don't know what to do. I have disobeyed my papa, and I will do it again. I know this, but I can't help it."

"Can't? Or won't?"

She sighed. "Okay. I won't."

"Is this about your vocation, child?"

"I don't have a vocation, Father! I want to be a wife and a mother. I am almost twenty years old, and it is time."

Father Bestal nodded his head slowly. "Fritz is a strong Catholic man." He surprised Gerda. She didn't know anyone outside the family knew that Fritz had spoken for her.

"Yes," she said bitterly, "but he's poor. Papa doesn't care if he's Catholic. He thinks only of money. Of getting ahead in the world."

"You do your father a disservice talking like that, my dear girl."

"But it's true," she insisted. "He let my sister marry a Protestant because he had money."

"Your sister? I didn't know you had a married sister," he said.

"She died," Gerda said quietly. "A long time ago, before you came here."

Through the screen she could see Father lift his hand, the one that held the rosary, to his ear. It almost appeared he was listening to the beads.

"Your sins are forgiven," he said abruptly. "Say ten Our Fathers and ten Hail Marys and you will be right with God."

He slid the partition across the screen before she had a chance to reply. When she stepped out of the confessional, she saw that the line of those waiting to confess had grown from only a few to more than ten. They all looked up at her as she moved to the back of the church to say her penance. Her face turned hot as she realized what they might think about the length of her confession. As if feeling dismissed by Father Bestal wasn't bad enough.

The next day during Mass she realized the old priest had not dismissed her concerns, but had taken them into his heart and had something to say about them. Yes, the priest had made her right with God, but her own father never forgave her for what he said.

"Honor thy father and thy mother, the Lord tells us," his homily began. "But what if your father behaves dishonorably toward you?" The old priest stood at the lectern looking out at the congregation. Even in her surprise, Gerda could see a new unsteadiness in his hands, and he paused for a long moment. He fingered the top of his head for a moment, and he seemed to draw strength from the birthmark there. Gerda remembered he had called it his angel's kiss. He held the rosary when he prayed, but his hand reached for that spot on his head when he felt the need for guidance.

"I would like to talk today of the three paths to heaven that are open to each child." He nodded and his voice grew stronger as if he'd found the tone he'd meant to strike. "The shortest, most direct way is the religious life. The second path trends away to the right, but its slightly circuitous route also leads to the same bright, eternal goal. That path is the state of the unmarried in the world. The third road leads away to the left, into a hilly region. There are many pleasures and joys to be met with on that way, but also much toil and many sorrows. That is the married state. All these three states, I state most emphatically, are ordained by God; it is not a matter of indifference to the almighty God which state in life we chose for ourselves, but when we are called, we must take on willingly the vocation God has given us. Marriage, like the religious life, is a true vocation."

Gerda felt as if everyone in the church could tell he was talking directly to her and she felt her ears start to burn. When she realized where he was going with this line of thought, she began to pray that no one else would recognize his target.

"If you, Christian maiden, have attained a suitable age, feel yourself called to the married state, and receive offers of marriage, the important questions arise: whom should I marry and to whom ought I become engaged, and to what ought I principally look? I will endeavor to offer practical answers to these questions. Always look in the first place to religion. Look only to virtue, uprightness, devotedness to our holy church."

Gerda stole a glance at her papa. He stared forward. She couldn't tell if he was listening or not.

"St. Jerome relates the following anecdote in regard to St. Marcella, who was left a widow while still quite young. A man of good family, Cerealis by name, wished to marry her, promising to make her sole heiress of his fortune if she would accept his hand. Her mother urged her to close with the brilliant offer, but she replied, 'If I had not determined never to marry again, I should look out for a *husband,* rather than a *fortune.*'"

Father Bestal nodded, pleased with the story he had found to relate his point. "You, Catholic maiden, and your family, ought to be of the same opinion. When the time comes to choose a husband, do not think too much about riches and temporal interests. Pay all the more attention to another point, which is perhaps the most important of all: marry only a Catholic. On no account conclude a mixed marriage."

Gerda's father sniffed loudly and crossed his arms in front of his chest.

"No offense to Protestants is intended when Catholics are warned against marrying them," Father Bestal went on. "Protestants ought to hold similar opinions, looking at the matter from their own point of view, and indeed, they frequently do. A mixed marriage is always a sad mistake. Anyone who forms such a union must make up his mind to experience a good deal of trouble. God does not smile on such a union."

Gerda closed her eyes and tried to imagine herself growing smaller and smaller until she was small enough to slip beneath the pew, to disappear entirely.

"No one who is earnestly concerned about his own salvation and that of his children ought to contract a mixed marriage." Father began to wind up his message. "Yes, honor your father and your mother; it is the fourth of the great commandments of God. But fathers and mothers, you too must be faithful to those selfsame commandments. Place no false gods before you, in your duty to your children and in your life entire."

Father Bestal straightened his spine and smiled out onto the congregation. "Praise be to God," he said and turned back to the altar.

Though her father marched past Fritz after Mass without so much as a nod, Gerda whispered to him before she ran to catch up with her family, "Yes, yes! I *will* marry you."

ʔ

She pulled the letter from Katherine out of her pocket and looked at it again. Katherine is getting married. She studied her sister's handwriting, how the letters looped so evenly across the page in just the manner they had been taught back in school. A shadow fell across her lap and Gerda looked up to see Fritz standing in the doorway. She couldn't see his face, so she waited for him to speak.

"I didn't mean to make you so mad, Gerda. I was just having some fun."

Gerda brushed the hair that had fallen loose from her bun and pinned it back in place before she spoke.

"I don't think I've told you my news," she said.

"You mean there's more to that letter you've got there than just Katherine getting married?"

Gerda looked down at the paper in her hand. "No, it's not in the letter, Fritz." She spoke so softly he had to step closer to hear her. "It's me. There's another baby on the way." She looked up at him. The light of the heat lanterns reached his face and she could see he didn't quite know what she meant. She put the letter back into her apron pocket and stood up. "There's another baby on the way here. You and me, we've made another baby."

God love him, Gerda thought, as the slow light of realization on his face turned to joy. Fritz smiled and grabbed her in a bear hug and spun her around, her feet flying like a little girl's. When he set her down he kissed her clumsily.

"Well now, Mrs. Vogel, I reckon we'd both better get back to work so we can feed this new baby. We're going to have quite a flock, aren't we?" He took her hands and led her out into the sunshine. "Quite a herd, quite a gaggle, a school, a bunch, a bouquet, a lot, a bushel of babies, me and you, Mrs. Vogel, me and you." He spun her around again, more slowly this time, as if they were dancing in 3/4 time, then he let go of her hands and returned to work, whistling as he walked away.

"Wedding date set for late October, dear sister! It will be after harvest, I'm sure. That matters to the farmers, I suppose. Johnnie hardly gets dirty doing his work. Love to you, dear one!"

Gerda thought about her sister's words and decided Fritz didn't need to see them. He was so touchy about being snubbed or looked down on by the people back home. Sometimes, she thought, he brought some of that on himself. He had always seemed to enjoy playing the hayseed farmer around her father and brothers. It had always infuriated her when he would act the bumbling fool and her brothers would puff themselves up to make him look even dumber—both sides believing they had the last laugh. She had never told Fritz the story of her escape from her father's house. Because she hadn't told him right away when she came home, the fact of it became a secret, one she could not think how to share with him now. First, he wouldn't believe her about the man on the train, and second, she knew there was no way she could tell him what had happened with her father that wouldn't make everything worse between them.

Men were so frustrating at times, she thought. It's no wonder the world was at war; men could be so determined to see things their own way and only their own way. Women seemed so much more capable of finding common ground and keeping peace. That entire thought had scarcely formed before she remembered the woman at Kroger's.

Emily Davies. Gerda had learned her name from Margaret. She was a widow, as Kroger had said. She'd married Mrs. Kroger's cousin out in St. Louis several years back, though the Krogers had never met her before the cousin died and Emily Davies found herself homeless and penniless.

The cousin had been a sailor who signed on with the American Expeditionary Forces nearly before the ink had dried on President Wilson's "acceptance of the state of war" speech. When Gerda had heard that, she wondered if he had done it to get away from his wife, but she'd bit her tongue to keep from saying it aloud. Turns out he was one of those killed before they even got to the war front. A German sub had sunk the ship he was on, the oil carrier *Vacuum*, just off the coast of Ireland. He was one of six sailors who died. Most of the men on the ship had gotten to the lifeboats and drifted into Cork one foggy morning. The locals there helped drag them to shore, half-drowned and hungry. The Americans didn't look then like the saviors they were supposed to be.

Somehow or another, and Gerda wasn't sure if the confusion was in the story as it got passed around town or in Emily herself, but it seemed Emily held the Irish as responsible for her husband's death as she did the Germans. The fact that he'd gone down with the ship within minutes after the Germans blasted a hole in the hull and had never come within two miles of Ireland didn't matter to her. They said that when the train that brought Emily out to Stuart passed through O'Neill, she'd opened her window, leaned out, and spit toward the sign the city elders had just erected, "Welcome to O'Neill, Nebraska."

It was, according to the gossip reports, Dr. MacGewan who saw her do this, and though he'd seen her ticket read "Stuart" as her destination, he introduced himself and asked her where she was bound.

She'd answered his question with one of her own. "MacGewan. That's Scottish, isn't it?"

"Long time back it was," MacGewan had answered. "Been American now for generations."

She'd looked at him through squinted eyes and asked, "This town of Stuart, is it filled with a bunch of krauts, or is it just my late husband's family that bears that shame?"

That was Emily Davies's introduction into the society of Stuart, though the story of it had been around in circles by the time Gerda heard it. Of course it had been Aloys Baum who had brought the news of it out to the Vogels. Fritz had acted as though he'd never heard of the woman.

Gerda cried out when she heard the story, "That's the woman I told you about! The day I went to town, remember?"

Aloys kept talking as if Gerda hadn't spoken. "She's a dried up old apple of a woman, I'll tell you that much. Old Kroger is going to be losing some business if he doesn't watch how she treats his customers."

"I thought she was downright scary, if you ask me," Gerda said, but of course the men weren't asking her. Though Fritz didn't dismiss Aloys, he wasn't interested in what Gerda had to say about the woman at Kroger's.

"She's no concern of ours, Gerda," he'd said after the Baums left. "Don't go getting yourself all worked up again. It's not good for the baby."

Being told to not get herself "all worked up" almost always had the effect of getting Gerda "all worked up." She tossed the towel she was holding onto the counter and left the kitchen in a huff, letting the door slam behind her.

She heard the mail wagon coming, and she didn't stop to brush herself off. She could feel her skirt billowing out as she rushed toward the wagon and she couldn't keep from smiling at the image. "Mrs. Bird," he said, and they both laughed. She traded a letter of her own for the stack he held out to her. He bowed deeply. She curtsied. Then she smiled all the way back up the lane. Such a silly interaction, but something she looked forward to each time.

Fritz startled Gerda as she walked the path back toward the house. He stepped out from behind the chicken house so suddenly that she almost screamed.

"You're in deep," he said. "Something good in the mail?" He held tools in both hands, so Gerda didn't hand him the letters, though she felt as though the impulse to tuck Katherine's letter into her pocket without him seeing it showed on her face. She felt flustered. She wondered if Fritz had seen her talking to Charles Burke and her agitation brought warmth up her neck.

"You all right?" he asked. She brought her hand to her neck and opened her mouth to speak, but the two little boys raced around the corner just then. Frank shrieked that Ray had stolen his toy and they were all suddenly immersed in the routine of family turmoil.

For weeks after that moment Gerda didn't have time to think about the mail or what Fritz might have seen. It was summer at last, and there was more work to do than hands to do it. Soon her belly pushed her out of her regular clothing, and when she thought of herself again, there was little left of the woman who had blushed at Charles Burke's silly flirtations. Pregnancy always took all her attention; even her other children receded from her thoughts. It was as if she moved to an island of sorts where she could see her family, but only at a distance. As the days passed, she grew more and more alone with the growing form inside her.

CHAPTER TEN

The Vogel farm on the northeastern edge of the Sandhills of Nebraska was as flat as the palm of a man's hand. Trace the contours of your own palm to know how deceptive that flatness can be. Level fields, like smooth skin, drop abruptly into gullies and draws caused by seasonal water flow. Land pillowed and sloped so gently, the horizon seemed distant on all sides, the line of it marking the empty edge of an overturned blue bowl. A short walk in any direction, however, can swallow a human figure from sight.

The highest point of this particular farm, say at the base of the thumb, marked the watershed between the Elkhorn River and the Big Sandy Creek. The Elkhorn, flowing east to meet the Platte River, the Big Sandy winding north toward the Niobrara, they all join the Missouri eventually. The rise between them was Fritz's favorite spot on his farm, perhaps in the entire world. Working this field he always felt lighter and younger, closer to that wide blueness above that was, he believed, God's true home.

On this particular Sunday morning he had used the excuse of needing to check the ripeness of the wheat before Mass in order to arrive here just as the sun tip-kissed the world. The moment never failed to fill and tighten his chest. He faced east, patiently waiting for it to come again. Light, lighter, gold! Wheat heads shimmered and glowed. The entire field moved like the back of a well-stroked cat.

Fritz smiled for the sheer joy of it. For this one sacred moment his blessings were without reserve or qualification. Gerda, six months' pregnant, was round and clumsily graceful as a mare about to foal. His wheat fields were heavy with grain, his potato vines thick and thriving. His cattle lowed in the near distance. Life was a suspension of pure promise and Fritz felt almost giddy with the beauty of it all.

The whinny of a horse nearby startled him out of his reverie. His own team was back at the barn and the sound of a horse so close, though not an unfriendly sound, seemed so out of place and unexpected that it caused a cascade of images in his mind that robbed him of his elation.

Gypsies, he thought, and he worried about what would be gone when he returned from church. A few hens missing and the cows milked dry would be bad enough, but lately the Gypsies had gotten bolder. Raven-haired children had been seen roaming the alleys in Stuart and victory gardens denuded of harvest. The neighbors just to the south lost a pig a couple of weeks past, and little could they afford it what with Daniel still sick from the illness that put him down last spring. Fritz didn't mind the Gypsies as much as others did; the family group that came through last spring had proven to be fine pot menders, and the price they'd charged was reasonable enough.

For Fritz, the problem wasn't so much what they did or how much they lifted from any given farmstead—it was their strangeness. They seemed to appear in or disappear from communities without actually traveling the roads between them. He would go to bed one quiet night and the next morning wake to the smell of a campfire, and there they were again just across the road. Or evenings, after a long day of working in the fields, he would step out to look up at the stars after supper, and he would hear their jangling music and laughter come up from a camp near the river. They would be settled in before he even knew they were there.

Not today, he thought, not this season. They could not stay. With another baby coming and no sign of the war letting loose its stranglehold on a farmer's profits, Fritz simply didn't have enough to share. Telling them to move along wouldn't be easy—no telling what they'd do—but a man had to do what he had to do to protect his own. He headed for the ravine where they had last camped and from which he'd heard the whinny.

Where he expected to see three or four of the weathered green wagons, he saw instead the gleaming black of a new buggy. He stopped to study the scene before him. The upper branches of the cottonwood saplings crackled in the morning light, but darkness still bowled down in the draw where a dapple-gray mare stood uneasily in her harness.

Fritz recognized the mare, a delicate-looking Arabian, as one that belonged to Owens, the local storekeeper. Not quite sure what he'd stumbled upon, he waited and listened. He thought he heard the muffled sound of a man's voice and then the clink of glass on metal.

"Hello the buggy?" he called out after a moment. The horse turned and looked at him and Fritz noted the arch of her neck. He'd always dreamed of owning a fine horse like that and if he were the envious type, it would be for something like her. She'd cropped most of the grass within easy reach and Fritz surmised she'd been standing there quite some time.

He heard a rustling sound and again a man's muffled voice. The buggy squeaked as a man rose from the ground on the other side, pulling heavily on the wheel for support. It took a moment for Fritz to recognize the figure as Owens. His usual neatly slicked hair was in disarray, a hank of it standing up at the back and another lopped across his eyes. His black suit coat was twisted off one shoulder and his starched white shirt hung untucked. Thinking him hurt, Fritz started toward him, but before he'd taken a step Owens barked out a command. "Stop!" He pointed his finger at Fritz and narrowed his eyes. "Stay away."

Fritz froze in mid-step. "Are you all right, Owens? Have you had an accident?"

Owens continued to point his finger at Fritz, sighting down the length of his arm as if aiming a pistol.

"Owens?" Fritz said, not sure what to make of the other man's behavior. After a moment, Owens dropped his hand to his side, bent over, and vomited abruptly. Fritz started toward him again, but Owens put his hand up to stop him.

"Leave. Me. Alone. You filthy German bastard."

Fritz settled his weight evenly onto both feet, the better to meet whatever was coming.

Owens stared at him through narrowed eyes. He wiped his mouth with his sleeve, elbow to wrist, an action so out of character for the fastidious man that it startled Fritz out of his anger. Neither man said anything for a stretch and the only sound was insects in the grass and meadowlarks trilling from tree to tree. Owens fumbled in his pockets and pulled out a small bottle; shaking hands tipped it to his lips.

Even from this distance Fritz recognized the amber liquid. His father had been a drunk and he knew there was no point in talking or arguing about anything with Owens now. Whiskey logic had no ears. He considered walking away then, acting as though he'd seen and heard nothing, but something didn't feel right to him. Fritz didn't pretend to know everything about Owens's life, but the man had no reputation as a drinker and in a town like Stuart that would be a secret impossible to keep.

The sun topped the rise behind Fritz and the morning glared fully onto Owens's face. A day's worth of stubble stood out darkly against his pale skin. His eyes so bloodshot they seemed about to bleed. Dried spittle streaked his chin.

Long ago Fritz's father had destroyed any sympathy he might have felt for a drinking man. He felt little more now than curiosity as he watched Owens. What Fritz had learned from his father was that a man in the clutches of the drink was not a man at all, but an animal trapped in a man's form. The confinement made him wild. He still sometimes had nightmares about his father turning into a wolf, his teeth growing longer, his hair shaggier with each swallow of the foul-smelling liquid. He could see that creature in Owens now as he spun suddenly and flung the empty bottle into the trees, his movements feral and unpredictable.

The bottle thudded impotently in the grass beyond, and Owens bent over again, his hands on his knees. His face contorted, and Fritz thought he was going to vomit again, but instead Owens cried out, a sound of desolation that seemed to come up from the darkness at the center of the earth, not from the small broken man standing in the shimmering light of morning. The gray mare startled and lurched forward, but the front wheel was lodged firmly against a rock and the phaeton creaked and shuddered but didn't move.

"My son," Owens cried. The two words strung together in a long, keening moan. "My son! They've killed my son! Those lousy German bastards have killed my son." He slumped onto the ground and pressed his face into the sandy soil.

Fritz closed his eyes and saw the face of Owens's son, a young man in a new and ill-fitting uniform when last he'd seen him. The faces of his own sons replaced Owens's, and he saw them growing older as the world marched endlessly toward war in search of peace. He felt the air pressed out of his lungs and a sudden weakness nearly buckled his knees. He moved toward Owens slowly and dropped down beside him. Tender and slow as only a man who has worked with animals all his life can be, he put his arms around Owens. He must have felt like a bear to that grieving man so small in Fritz's massive embrace, but Owens did not struggle to pull away.

Kneeling there on the yielding, familiar soil, Fritz held Owens close to his chest, awkward and careful and so afraid of what the future held. He looked up to the top of the hill he had just come down. The close horizon formed a deceptive, ever receding line. On the other side of it, Gerda and the children waited.

CHAPTER ELEVEN

Summer bloomed hot and dry. The heat thrummed through the days from June to August. Mornings, hot and muggy, dried out in the face of a persistent wind, and by afternoons the air was filled with dust that coated her skin. Gerda felt thick and dirty, and tired more often than not. Washing clothes seemed wasted time when the air hung so thick with the same dirt she washed out of the fabric. The garden soaked up every drop of water she and the children could haul to it. By the time they got back from the well with one bucketful, the evidence of the one they'd hauled before was already gone, the topsoil dried and beginning to blow.

Gerda taught the children how to cover the plant rows with straw to hold in the moisture, but even that wasn't enough on the hottest, windiest days. The wind picked up the straw and sent it flying. She had the children collect the clumps the fence caught and spread it again in the evenings when the wind died down.

She began to feel the wind had an individual spirit—it certainly had a voice, whistling and howling most days and half the nights—but this particular spirit seemed to have directed its hatred at her; its gusts felt sometimes like fingers tugging her places she didn't want to go, or sometimes like fists battering her and the world until she thought she'd go mad.

The "cool weather" plants she'd started early because they grew best in the spring before the summer heat came hadn't fared well in the spring that didn't last. She stood at the end of the row assessing them as she waited for Frank and Ray to return with another bucket of water. With her back to the wind, her skirt and blouse billowed out in front of her. She could see her shape in the shadow on the ground beside her. She tried to smooth her skirt and blouse closer to her body, but the wind was relentless, and her efforts seemed to emphasize the size of her belly. I could be pregnant with the whole world, she thought, at the rate I'm growing anyway.

Ray and Frank's voices preceded them up the path. They were arguing, of course, this time about whose side of the bucket was heaviest and thus who was the stronger of the two. Their contest, Gerda noted, had caused much of the contents of the bucket to end up along the path to the garden. Next year, she decided right then, she would plant flowers on both sides of the path. Zinnias—they could take the heat and the dryness, because the boys wouldn't always be little, wouldn't always be arguing and spilling water. She reminded herself of that as if it would help.

She had dippered the water out the bucket onto the tomato plants and sent the boys back for more when she heard Fritz's voice calling her name. She turned in the direction it came from, but he was on the other side of the orchard, so she couldn't see what he needed. She tossed the weeds she had pulled onto the weed pile at the edge of the garden. Between the fast-growing crabgrass and the bindweed, her garden seemed under siege from unwanted plants. If it's not the wind, it's the weeds, Gerda thought. She held her hands out away from her body and rubbed them briskly together, letting the wind be her ally for once and take the soil and dust that caked her fingers.

Fritz had hitched Boss to the wagon and was straightening the leather on the harness when Gerda found him. Ol' Blue stood at the fence whinnying nervously. The wound on the older gelding's leg had not healed properly, and Fritz no longer double-teamed unless it was unavoidable.

"You called for me?" Gerda asked.

"The last damned belt is broke on that grinder." Gerda looked toward the granary where parts lay in a row beside the grinder, an explanation for the cursing. "You said you wanted to go in and see that priest," he said. "I need to go in to Owens's store. If you're ready when I leave, you can go."

"How soon?" Gerda asked, slipping immediately into thoughts of what needed to be done.

"Now's good," Fritz said, then walked into the barn. Gerda rushed to the house where she gathered up the children hurriedly and put Katie in charge of seeing that faces were clean and clothes weren't too dirty.

"After you've done that," Gerda said as she rushed around the kitchen, "you get out there to that wagon and keep your father from leaving without us."

"How?" Katie eyes were wide with fright.

"I don't know." Gerda's attention was on the work at hand. "Set one of the boys in front of the wagon. That should slow him down some." She rushed out of the house with a basket in her hand.

Katie looked dubiously at the boys. Ray, standing behind the other children, pointed at Frank. "Him first," he mouthed to Katie.

She scowled at him. "Go! Go!"

Gerda had hoped to pack the basket more neatly and would have chosen a day when the produce was at its peak, but she had to take a ride to town when she could get one. She hadn't been back alone since the storm in the spring.

Just that morning she had told Fritz she wanted to stop in to see the new priest. She couldn't seem to stop calling him "the new priest"; he still felt new to her though he'd been in the parish for nearly six months now. She wanted to talk to him about baptizing the baby.

Traditionally, parents brought the new babies to church as soon after the birth as possible for a formal baptism in the baptistery, but Gerda didn't want to wait. With all her children, Father Hettwer had arrived shortly after the doctor and blessed her babies with holy water before the vernix had dried on their small bodies.

Elizabeth's baby had died with only a midwife's blessing, and Gerda prayed every night for that small soul trapped in the purgatory of the unbaptized. She did not want her own babies to suffer such a fate.

It had been Father Hettwer's idea to leave instructions with Dr. Gannoway to have him called as soon as he went to the Vogels to assist in delivering her babies. Gerda still loved him for how kind he had been, how easily he had set aside her fears.

She wanted to talk to the new priest—to Father Jungels, she forced herself to say his name—to ask him if he too would come and bless her baby when she or he first came into the world. The basket of produce, a jar of canned beef, another of sauerkraut, and two more of jelly seemed a meager offering in exchange for eternal salvation, but it was all she had to offer. She realized after loading the basket that the bread she'd planned to bake was still sitting on the counter as dough rising under a cotton towel. She left the basket in the path and ran back into the house and punched her fist into the middle of the rising mound. She kneaded it down to less than a third of what it had been and then set it on the table. At least there, when it rose so much that it overflowed the bowl, it would land on the table. It would not be the best bread she'd ever baked, but it would not be ruined. She checked the kitchen once quickly then rushed back outside.

Fritz was in the wagon when she reached the edge of the yard. He was shouting at Ray to get out of the way. Katie and Frank, holding Leo by the hand between them, stood beside the horse. Ray had planted himself under the horse's nose. He had his back to his father, his small arms crossed at his chest and a look of pure terror on his face when Gerda rounded the corner and saw them. If she hadn't been so surprised, she would have burst out laughing. Ray waited until she was within a few feet of the wagon before he stepped out of the way of the big horse.

It was a long quiet ride to town. Gerda reached back and ruffled Ray's hair every few minutes, but Fritz nearly threw sparks he was so irritable. In town, he stopped the wagon at the corner between Owens's store and the grocer's. It was two short blocks to the small house St. Boniface's parish used as a rectory. Fritz jumped out of the wagon and walked into the mercantile without glancing at his family. Watching him walk away, Gerda had to resist the urge to throw a pebble at his back. He could be such a stuffed shirt at times, she thought. Instead of resorting to violence, she turned around on the seat and smiled at the children.

"Thank you, my dears, although," she paused a moment and looked at each of their upturned faces, "we need to be more careful about which of my orders you follow to the letter from now on. Okay?"

"Told ya," Frank said and kicked Ray's foot. Ray just scowled at him.

Katie stood and helped Leo out of the wagon—sometimes she mothers him better than I do, Gerda thought. When Katie had her littlest brother on the ground, she looked up at Ray. "I thought you were brave, like St. George. He was a knight, you know."

"You were all brave," Gerda said. "My knights in shining armor."

And they were off then, out of the wagon and chattering as if nothing had happened. The two boys carried the basket between them toward the rectory. When they reached the porch, Gerda released the children. "When you see me come out, you get back to the wagon," she said. "So don't go any farther than the ball field there."

She knew the priest's parlor wasn't much bigger than a horse's stall, and she didn't want the children filling the small space with noise and nuisance. She waited until they were gone before she turned the key to ring the bell.

Through the screen door Gerda could see all the way through the house to the kitchen. The back door lined up with the front. Fritz would have said you could shoot a cannonball through the house and not break anything, or he would have before the war started. No one joked about cannon fire anymore. The parlor, off to the right, was dark. Heavy drapes covered the windows.

Gerda rang the bell and turned her back to the door. She considered it polite to not look in until someone had responded to her ring. She knew someone was home because she'd glimpsed movement in the kitchen and could hear even now the rattle and bang of pans. The noise didn't stop with the sound of the bell, so Gerda tried again and then knocked on the wooden door.

"Hello?" she called into the house. She saw what appeared to be the new priest—Father Jungels—peering from around the corner at her. The light from the door behind him threw his face into deep shadow, though, so she couldn't be sure it was him.

"Well?" he said. "Don't just stand there." And he disappeared back into the kitchen where the bang and rattle of pans began again.

Not knowing what else to do, Gerda let herself in, clumsily holding the door with her foot and dragging the basket in behind her. Inside, she found the new priest waving a knife around with one hand and stirring something on the stove with the other. It smelled like food, but she wasn't sure what kind. The kitchen looked as though a strong wind had emptied the cupboards onto the table, counters, and floor. The priest, with the sleeves of his black cassock rolled up and missing the white collar, looked like something out of a picture book, one of those with a crone stirring a smoldering cauldron muttering incantations. Gerda started to say she was sorry to interrupt him, for stopping by unannounced (Father Hettwer had never minded), but before she could speak, he turned toward her and said, "It's about time you got here. As you can no doubt imagine," he waved his knife around to encompass the chaos of the kitchen, "I don't have any experience in cooking. My training is in theology. Not cooking. Not domestic duties. I hope you're prepared to work." With that he dropped the knife and the spoon and grabbed a rag and began wiping his hands. "I'll leave you to it," he said and walked abruptly from the room.

Gerda stood in the middle of the room, dumbfounded. The contents of the pot on the stove suddenly boiled up and splattered into the fire below. The spitting and hissing made her jump and she automatically reached for a hot pad to move the pot off the fire. He had tossed the wooden spoon too close to the flame and its handle began to smoke and blacken. She pulled that away, blew on it until it cooled, and turned to look at the mess around her.

"Father Jungels?" she called out. She walked to the hallway and called again. In a moment the priest came out again, his sleeves rolled down and buttoned, his collar in place. He was smoothing his hair carefully when he came back in the room.

"I think there's been a mistake," Gerda said. "I'm not here to be a housekeeper." Father Jungels looked her up and down and she followed his gaze. A smudge from spilled gravy ran down the side of her skirt and mud from her garden clung to the hem. She scolded herself for not taking more care before coming into town, but she'd had no time. The image of her little son standing in front of that massive horse passed through her mind. She went on, "I've come to talk to you about baptism." She pointed at the basket near the front door. "And I've brought you some produce and the like from my garden." She looked at the man, but he remained silent, simply looking at her. "I'm sorry I didn't have time to welcome you properly when you first came to St. Boniface's." Somehow she felt an unconfessed sin weighed heavily on her at that moment. "We left home in a hurry, and I'm afraid my garden isn't doing well in this heat. Though I try," she hurried to assure him, "I try to keep it watered and the weeds down but . . ."

"You mentioned something about baptism, Mrs. Vogel. It is Mrs. Vogel, isn't it?"

"Oh yes," Gerda went on, happy to have a chance to get right to the point. "You see, I want to talk to you about baptizing our baby."

"Your baby? Why that child is two years old if he's a day. That's not a *baby.*" The priest brushed past her and walked into the parlor. He picked up a book off a table and opened it as if to start reading, though it was far too dark in the room for that. "Are you aware you are risking that *child's* immortal soul by waiting so long to wash him clean of his Original Sin?"

Again, Gerda felt completely dumbfounded by the priest. Then she realized he was talking about Leo. "Oh no," she said brightly. "That's not the baby I mean. I mean, that baby is already baptized. I mean this baby," she held her hand on her stomach. "I want to talk to you about the new baby."

Father Jungels's eyebrows dropped into a scowl. "You are with child? Is that what you're trying to say to me?"

"Yes," Gerda said. And then, before she could lose her courage or he could change directions once again, she told him what she wanted, what Father Hettwer had done for her previous babies, and what it had meant to her.

She even mentioned Elizabeth's name in her onslaught of words, though she knew even as she said it the name meant nothing to him.

When she left the rectory, she wasn't sure whether he had agreed to help her when the baby came, or simply agreed to accept the gift she had brought to him. In any case, her ever-present fatigue got the better of her and she wanted only to get out of that house and back to the wagon. She didn't even stop to wave the children over; she simply walked to the wagon and let them find their own way to her.

Heat shimmered the distance and thrummed the air around her. The grasses lining the road toward home looked watery at the edges of the horizon. Grasshoppers chirred and snapped against the baked storefront. Trickling sweat followed the curve of her collarbone and dampened the neckline of her dress and heaviness pressed her against the backboard.

She stared at Fritz through the glass of Owens's store where he stood at the edge of a group of men. She willed him to turn and look at her.

"Come," she whispered. "Come out now." He didn't move. She looked away with a deep sigh.

The 4:35 from the west blew its whistle at the edge of town, the rattle of cars and the roar of the engine filled the town with a sense of industry. Kids appeared as if from thin air and headed toward the track at a trot. Her own brood, limp in the wagon, rose like marionettes pulled up by strings.

"Mom?" Frank said.

"No," she answered. "Your father will be here in a minute and we need to get home to chores. No time to chase after kids chasing after trains."

Frank slumped back and pulled his hat over his face. She could see his jaw moving and she could guess the silent curses his mouth formed. She considered rebuking him but decided all her strength was needed just to wait here in the sun.

At last the screen door creaked open and Fritz came out with one bag slung over each shoulder.

"Look to yourself," he said as he slung the bags into the wagon, leaving the children to scramble for safety. He looked in a darker mood than when he'd arrived. She closed her eyes and tried to think of the prayer the new priest had given her to say when in her last confession with him she confessed to anger. The new priest had given her at least that, she reminded herself as the family headed home.

It took Fritz most the way home before he spoke, and he spit mightily into the weeds beside the road before he did.

"Owens has moved to O'Neill." Gerda waited for more. "That Davies woman is minding his place for him." He slapped the reins to hurry the gelding into a trot and Gerda almost didn't hear him above the creak and jangle of the moving wagon. "She says they don't give credit no more. She runs a cash business now."

Gerda watched the road in front of them, thinking about the Davies woman on the train. Perhaps if she had reached out to her then in those terrifying moments when they were just two women alone, things would be different. She wondered about her silence that day, how like an unsaid prayer it had been.

The baby kept her up nights, woke her early in the morning. The baby swims all day inside her, Dr. Gannoway says. Women, he said, are amazing machines. Your body will make everything the baby needs, not just now while it is still unborn, but afterward too. Your breasts will grow heavy with milk to feed this child, just as they have for all your babies.

Her face grew warm when he said that. She was a grown woman, a mother of four, and still certain words in a man's mouth, even a doctor's, could make her blush. The breasts themselves didn't make her uncomfortable. It was the word *breasts*, the bubble of air forming behind the lips on the opening consonants, bursting with a small puff of air then turning at the "st," a sound that reminded her of a snake's hiss. The word held a kind of naughtiness in it that never failed to call attention to itself when she heard it pronounced. She never said the word. Made no conversation that required it, and there was Dr. Gannoway using it as if it were just a word, unladen.

He knew so much about what she thought and felt without her having to say it. How could he not see this? Sometimes she felt he deliberately baited her, as if the sight of her red face was one of his great delights.

She felt the baby move. She had been feeling it kick for days now, though sometimes she couldn't distinguish the kicks from gas. It always started this way. Her pregnancies followed a pattern she could draw out and lay across the fabric of her life. First the fatigue, that was the easiest sign to ignore, then the backaches and restlessness, the spreading waist, and then this, the movement of life inside her.

She placed her hand on her abdomen and took a deep breath. This was real. There was a baby, a being within her. She jerked her hand away, as if she had been burned, and in panic looked at the palm of her hand: no *S*-shaped scar at the base of her thumb. That was not her scar. "Oh Elizabeth," she murmured. "Oh my Elizabeth."

Yes. Always the same pattern. The fear she would wear like a cowl, a weighted, invisible hood she would peer out from under at the world around her. Between her and everything she saw and heard and felt would be the vision of Elizabeth, the silence that settled when it was all over. She had learned her prayers. She had made up for her mistake when her sister needed her. She knew them all by heart.

"O most gracious Virgin Mary that never was it known that anyone who fled to thy protection, implored thy help or sought thy intercession, was left unaided. Inspired by this confidence I fly unto thee, o virgins of virgins my mother. Before thee I stand, sinful and sorrowful, despise not my petitions, but in thy mercy please answer them, Amen."

"Hail Mary, full of grace, the Lord is with thee. Blessed art thou among women and blessed is the fruit of thy womb, Jesus. Holy Mary, Mother of God, pray for us sinners now and at the hour of our death, Amen."

She said them dozens of times each day. Unconsciously murmuring them as she worked, consciously chanting them when she first awoke and then again when she closed her eyes each night. She had not known the prayers when Elizabeth needed them. That was her personal Original Sin. Such simple prayers, why had she not learned them when Elizabeth tried to teach her? What punishment awaited her for this sin? For all her sins.

CHAPTER TWELVE

Charles Burke stepped down easily from the bright blue mail wagon onto the sandy trail beside the mailboxes. He still stood nearly a head taller than Gerda. She noticed, though she told herself she wouldn't, that his eyes were as blue as the paint on the wagon he drove, like the sky of a cloudless dawn.

"You've come looking for a note from your sister, I suppose?" Those eyes held the devilish light of someone who knew something she didn't. He held the stack of mail with both hands against his chest.

"Of course I did, Mr. Burke." She smiled and tilted her head to the side (good heavens, where had she learned to be coquettish?). "I'm trying to convince her to stop in Stuart when she and her new husband come back from their wedding trip next month."

"They're going to see the sights in Yellowstone, are they? 'How I long to see the geysers and the wild creatures there!'"

"Oh, so do I! I—Mr. Burke! How did you know my sister was going to Yellowstone?" She placed her hands on her hips. "Have you been reading my mail?"

Charles laughed and tapped the mail against his chest. "Why, Mrs. Bird—how could you think such a thing? I'm a man of honor." He held a single postcard out to her.

"Only the postcards." He winked and waited for her to read the postcard from Katherine.

"'How I long to see the geysers and the wild creatures there.' Mr. Burke, you not only read it, but you took her words as your own!"

"I only *borrowed* them." He tapped his finger on the card in her hand. "See. I put them right back. No harm done."

Gerda laughed. She felt lighter out here at the end of the lane, as if not only the baby shifted to make it easier for her to breathe, but the air itself held her suspended. There was so little of that feeling of ease in her life anymore.

"You are a scoundrel, Mr. Burke. You know that, don't you?"

He bowed that silly, courtly bow and solemnly replied. "Thank you, Mrs. Bird. You are so very kind."

"By the way, did you see my name in the *Advocate* last week?" He held out the rest of her mail—two more postcards and one letter and something else she couldn't quite see, an advertisement of some sort. It seemed an odd thing to be sending through the mail. When she reached to take the stack, he pulled it back, closer to his chest, and she almost, almost, stepped closer to reach it, but she checked her forward movement and simply waited.

"Ah, Mrs. Bird, you are exactly the kind of woman I hope to marry one day." He laughed and handed her the mail. "Well, did you see it? I feel famous; tell me you saw it."

"No," Gerda said, genuinely sorry. "I've not had time to read the paper this week. It's canning time, you see, and the tomatoes and beans and beets, well, the whole garden it seems is ready at once." She surprised herself by listing the vegetables and she bit her bottom lip before she went on about her other chores. "My friend Margaret is coming over to help tomorrow, but I've much to do before she comes."

"Ah, but you have time to walk down to get your mail just when I come down the road." Again he laughed, that joy-filled sound.

Gerda's face flamed and she put her hand to her cheek. Did he misunderstand her motives, or worse, had she misled him?

"I . . . I . . . ." She couldn't think of a thing to say. Around them the meadowlarks trilled and a redwing blackbird landed on the fence line just beyond Charles's shoulder. Its red patch shimmered like a warning and she felt the urge to turn and run. In fact, she did turn away from the wagon and began walking back toward home.

"Wait!" Charles said in surprise. "I didn't mean to chase you away, Mrs. Vogel! I look forward to handing you the mail. This is a long route and the day gets pretty empty—once I get everyone's postcards read, I mean."

She looked at the postcards in her hand and then turned back to look at him. He smiled disarmingly, teeth even and white against his sun-darkened skin. "I just need the fresh air, Mr. Burke," she said without returning his smile. "Sometimes the children's voices—though I love them dearly—sometimes their voices are so . . . loud. I just like to stretch my legs and listen to the birdsongs instead. I meant nothing by coming to get my mail."

Along the lane up ahead were the trees she and Fritz had planted the first year they moved here. Backbreaking work that, though the soil was sandy and soft. She had carried water to each tree every day until they put down roots to find their own water. The cherry and apple trees in the orchard up nearer the house had begun to show a crop this year, though it would be a few more years before their fruits were beyond her reach while she stood on the ground. The trees they had planted surrounded her home. The home she and Fritz had made.

She looked at him solemnly and his face settled until it mirrored hers.

"I've been drafted, Mrs. Vogel. That's why my name is in the paper. I leave at the end of the month for Fort Riley." He rattled on then, telling as much as he knew about where he was going, building up the danger and adventure, because he was young and so full of life he couldn't imagine that anything ahead of him could be any less than his wild dreams allowed him.

Gerda listened without response. Charles would be the first man she knew personally who went to war, though she had recognized many of the names of the men called up. She looked around at the familiar countryside, recognizing each tree and birdsong, but with the mailman's news, everything felt shifted, and shifting. She felt lost, as unsure of where she was as what she should say. It seemed for one strange moment that she and Charles stood not at the end of her own lane, but on the brink of something else altogether. It was as if the world, the world of soldiers and guns and gas and trenches had suddenly rushed forward, like water filling a submerged bowl. If she walked a few steps in any direction, she would see it: Italy, England, France, just over that near horizon.

Gerda heard the musical tinkling of glass clinking against glass, and she knew Margaret had arrived with canning jars. "You boys finish filling up that wood box now and bring in another pail of water." She waved her apron at them like they were cats to be shooed. "Then you head out to the barn— your dad will be needing you." She quickly finished drying the dishes and set them in the cupboard. "Katie, in the garden with Leo. You two can weed while it's not so hot." She pulled her big blue canner off the high shelf in the summer porch, feeling the stretch in her side.

"Gerda, *achtung!*" Margaret called. "You wait yourself a minute while I get unhitched from this wagon and let me get that! *Ich bin gleich da!*"

Margaret struggled with a knot of twine at her waist. She had improvised a harness so that she could pull the jar-filled wagon behind her and leave her hands free to carry the canner. A farm dog that had followed her over stuck his nose into her hands and she swatted at him. "*Geh!* I don't need your help. I'm having enough trouble, *dummkopf.*"

By the time Margaret got the knot undone, Gerda had unloaded the wagon and was setting the jars by the sink where she had pans of soap water ready. Margaret bustled into the kitchen, paused a moment to allow her eyes to adjust to the dim light, then started in working quickly alongside Gerda. Both of them knowing what needed to be done when.

"Be sure you drink a lot of water today," Margaret said. "How have you been feeling? Any strange pains? *Und das Kind?* Have you felt it move to-day?" Her questions came at Gerda in a steady pulse of concern.

"Goodness, Margaretha," Gerda chided her. "You're like an old mother hen." Though in truth, Gerda felt pleased to have someone caring for her that way. The longing to be mothered, to be loved with such tenderness, never really left her.

"I told you that name was a secret. I'll be accused of having Gypsy in my blood if you're not careful—as if being German weren't bad enough. You didn't answer my questions. Any spotting? That's a bad sign you know."

Though she had promised not to use that name, Gerda often thought of her friend by it, *Margaretha.* It had such exotic beauty, yes, but something more too. The breathy syllable at the end seemed full of promises, of life. It fit the spirited woman that she knew still breathed inside the plain and unassuming body that outsiders saw.

Some days, if it hadn't been for Margaret Baum, Gerda feared she would drown in her own thoughts. Maybe it was the loss of her only daughter that made Margaret such a good listener. She told Gerda once, not long after they met, that she'd been a hard mother to her own children, always worry-ing about how to feed and shelter them.

"They were little more than mouths to feed and hands to help when they got old enough." She told Gerda this one bright day when they were out picking sand cherries west of town. The men had pulled a wagon out into the river and were fishing for bullheads from the comfort of the wagon seat. The children thought that looked like more fun than walking the hills, so Gerda and Margaret had time to themselves, walking along the bank and filling buckets with the tart and sticker-y berries.

"When my daughter married and moved away, the house got so quiet I thought I'd gone deaf!" She laughed with the telling of that story, but her smile didn't hold. After a while she went on. "Her son changed that. All he did was holler that first year we had him. It got so I wished I was deaf!" She shook her head. "Poor little guy cried enough for the both of us. When my daughter passed . . ." She paused for some time. Her daughter had died giving birth and the son-in-law took off to get a drink and never came back. "Left us with a baby to raise when we were both old enough to be put out to pasture." Gerda looked out to see that grandson, twelve years old now, out in the wagon with the men and the Vogel children. She could hear his laugh ring out now and again; probably over some practical joke he'd played on Katie. He took such delight in trying to upset her serious expression.

Gerda told her then that she'd lost a sister in childbirth. A story that had taken her years to tell Fritz just rolled off the tip of her tongue in Margaret's presence.

"Was your sister the mama or the baby?" Margaret asked.

Gerda started to say, "The mama," but suddenly she remembered the stories she'd heard her mother and Aunt Elsa whisper back and forth when they thought Gerda wasn't listening. "I guess you could say both," she said thoughtfully. "I mean, Elizabeth, my older sister, she died and so did her baby when I was about five, but I think Mama lost other babies. There were graves back home that she put flowers on, but she wouldn't tell me whose they were." Gerda rubbed the scar on her temple as she talked. It was a habit of hers to touch the jagged backward *S* there whenever she was worried or deep in thought.

"Childbirth's hard. Tiny graves the world over prove that. It's a wonder any of us make it out alive," Margaret said, then she barked a laugh. "Well, we don't! I guess it just takes some of us longer than others to die." The idea seemed to cheer her up, and she began humming as she walked.

Canning day with Margaret reminded Gerda of working with her mother and her aunt. Her mother, usually stern and quiet, grew chatty in the presence of her sister. The two women told stories and laughed at the oddest things, private jokes between them that made the workday seem more like a party than a chore. Gerda could still see their faces streaked with sweat and tears of laughter. Canning days were exhausting, and sweltering no matter the weather outside. Even though they used the cook stove in the summer kitchen, it still felt stifling in the house. When they finished, well after supper, Gerda asked Margaret to stay a little longer. "Wait until it has cooled off," she said. "Your menfolk won't starve without you there for one meal."

They went outside then and sat on a bench at the edge of Gerda's garden until long after sunset. The children stretched out on blankets on the grassy area behind them. The heat finally lifted with the help of a soft breeze and the sliver of a new moon offered the only light. They watched for falling stars—August was thick with them—but the children had long since quieted down and Gerda thought only she and Margaret would see the shooting stars this time. The dark nights of August were her favorites of the summer, though they reminded her of her father, how he'd bring her out to the grassy knoll south of their house to watch with him when she was a little girl, and so such nights had a bittersweet quality to them. There was a time when he had loved her in a way that made her feel loved. Still, it was beautiful, the night sky, the falling stars. She kept her head tilted back to watch for the fleeting streaks of light. She stretched her arms above her head and felt the heaviness of her breasts.

"I do have some spotting, by the way, but not the kind you were asking about." She placed her hands on her breasts, and she and Margaret laughed.

"Your body's getting ready to feed that little one," Margaret said. Gerda recalled Dr. Gannoway saying much the same thing and she blushed at the memory.

"I know I have a ways to go, but I feel like the baby already has crowded out all my insides." Gerda placed her hand at the base of her throat. "I think my lungs are sitting about right here and my stomach not much lower." She breathed in wearily. Shortness of breath and fear of what was to come was a part of every moment now and they surged inside her at times, threatening to overflow, especially now with Margaret's kind heart beside her, making her want to open floodgates of words, hoping that letting them go would free her somehow. Out of her whirling thoughts she recognized the image of baby Marie folded into Elizabeth's arms and guilt burned like indigestion in her chest. What if she told Margaret that she bore the shame of not knowing the prayers that might have saved her sister's life? She recalled the feeling of horror that had come over her when the words Elizabeth had tried to teach her would not come when Elizabeth most needed her to say them. Gerda struggled to get air as the fear that she had brought God's punishment down upon them in that room rose up from deep inside her and squeezed her lungs. It could happen again, and because of that, pregnancy terrified her. Even as that fear formed the words in her mind, she knew she wouldn't say them. For if she said them, others might spill out as well, words she couldn't even think:

what if she had remembered the prayers, would any deity have listened? She looked up at the vastness above them and shivered. No, some secrets were so closely guarded there was no way to reveal them, even to herself.

"You know," Gerda went on after a moment, "how most of your life if you think about *how* you're doing something, whatever it is, if you think about the *how*, a part of you is always thinking you could do it better if things were just a little different, or if the time was right, or you were stronger or better?" She looked at Margaret to gauge her expression. Her friend nodded. "That's how it is with me anyway. I'm always thinking about the next thing I need to do, or the last thing I did. I'm never really—whole." She stopped to think about how to say what she meant. "But with having babies, there's this moment after each birth when I see the baby for the first time and I hear that first cry and I smell the blood and the—I don't even know what it is. That new baby smell and when I look into the baby's eyes for the first time and see . . . I see . . ." She knew words weren't enough for what she meant. She didn't know how to say how in those first moments of seeing this new life, this new *soul*, she felt for that one moment complete joy. She knew she would never be a better person than she was at that one moment in time. She wanted to say how all that she is goes into that moment . . . her touch, her breath, her eyes looking into that one tiny new *being*. She looked up at Margaret again, feeling a little embarrassed at what she was about to say. "For that moment I know I am as close to God as I can ever be."

Margaret's eyes glinted in the dim light.

"*Verstehen Sie?*" Gerda said. She seldom used German phrases, but sometimes with Margaret they simply came to her mind and felt a natural part of the way they spoke to each other.

"*Ja*, I understand."

Behind them a branch snapped in the darkness and both women jumped. Katie sat up from the pile of children and looked around, but she lay back down when Aloys stepped out of the shadows.

"I thought I'd stop on my way back from town," Aloys said. "Thought you might still be here."

"And here I am." Margaret stood up and stretched her back muscles. "A ride home will be *gut*."

"You mean 'good,' don't you?" Aloys said gruffly. "Better be learning English." He walked back in the direction he'd come. Gerda wondered if he'd heard any of their conversation, if the order to speak English was directed at her as well.

"He's always like this now when he's been to town," Margaret stage-whispered to Gerda. "It's that woman that used to be at Kroger's—seems she's taken up the war educator job where Owens left off after his son died. You know he's taken a new job in O'Neill and isn't at his store much, don't you?"

Gerda flushed at the mention of the woman. Even her name seemed to have some power over her. "Fritz says she's working at Owens's store now."

"Well she gets more four-minute talks in in a day than Owens did in a week! My goodness that woman can talk!" Margaret shook her head. "And she's got a voice that carries half a mile. She doesn't care who listens, either, but she makes sure everyone hears."

"What does she talk about?"

"I don't really know, but if you ask me, she's not educating, she's just stirring up hate." She looked at Gerda out of the corner of her eye. "She don't like Germans, ya know."

"What's she doing here then?" Gerda asked. "Who does she think she's talking to?" She sat up straighter and blew her nose, her inner pendulum swinging now toward anger. "More Germans in Stuart than anyone else."

"That's the funny thing," Margaret said, though her expression showed no humor. "Like Aloys says, seems like there are less Germans in the county all the time, 'cept nobody's moving away."

Gerda looked at her, puzzled. Margaret went on. "They say there're some laws being changed. Stick your neck out for a German and you can go to jail for treason."

"What?" Gerda whispered. She looked over toward the children. "What are you saying?"

"I don't know how much of that is true," Margaret lowered her voice too, "but like I said, that woman's voice carries half a mile." She went on to tell Gerda what she knew about some of the woman's favorite topics. She seemed determined to personally stomp out the use of hyphenates— German-Americans, Italian-Americans, Russian-Americans and the like. "'You're either an American or you're not,' she's said more than once. 'And if you're not, you should be shot.'" The two women shuddered and leaned closer together. There was more, and by the time Margaret was finished, Gerda felt she'd never sleep again for all the fear she felt in her gut, or if she did fall asleep, it would be into nightmares.

Margaret leaned back into a loud yawn.

"I'd better catch up with Aloys or he'll leave me to walk yet." She patted Gerda's hand and started after her husband. Gerda sat awhile in silence, looking up. Two meteors streaked the sky, one at the dome of heaven, the other on the horizon. Gerda placed her hand in the dish of her back and rubbed the ache there. This is now, she told herself, tomorrow is tomorrow.

Then she stood and called to the children. "Come," she said, "your own beds are waiting for you."

In the morning, Fritz stood at the table reading the front page of the Omaha paper that Aloys had dropped off the night before. "That Kaiser's army is just eating them up and spitting them out." He shifted a toothpick from one side of his mouth to the other. "Not going the way anyone expected it would, I guess. Thought Americans would just go over there and get things done, one-two-three." He continued to read, his reading glasses perched on the edge of his nose. "Nope, not going the way they expected at all." Suddenly he leaned closer to the page and ran his finger along the lines of an article. He took his reading glasses off abruptly and snapped them back into their case. Instead of setting the case on the shelf above the door, where he put all things he wanted to keep from the children, he slipped the glasses into his breast pocket. The paper he folded roughly then tucked it under his arm.

Gerda looked up from her ironing and watched him. She couldn't tell what was going on behind his wide face, his jutting jaw. Did he worry about his brothers disappearing into the maw of that hungry war? Did he imagine it dragging on, soaking up the years until his sons reached the age . . . or was it only her borrowing troubles?

"That hay won't be getting mowed without me," he said, and he grabbed his hat off the hook. Gerda heard something in his voice she couldn't quite place.

He stepped out on the back porch where Katie and the two bigger boys were snapping beans into a large crock bowl. "You pick those tomatoes for your ma when you're done here," he said. "You hear?" He didn't wait for an answer—once he got headed for work, he didn't like to stop—but instead of heading toward the barn, as Gerda expected, he started off down the lane. She watched him walk away, confused by his strange behavior.

The August heat lay like a weight on her skin. She didn't think the sunny garden could be any worse than standing over this ironing board. She used the cook stove on the porch to heat the irons, but the air still held the radiant warmth until it seemed the house itself had caught fever. She had put this task off as long as she could, hoping for a break in the heat wave, but none had come and the entire family was nearly without clean, pressed clothes. The tomatoes were ripe. The peas, the beans, the carrots, and beets all ready, waiting to be dug up or picked and cleaned and cut and canned, everything in the world it seemed, pushing up or out. Trying to live.

"There've been some changes I think you should know about," Fritz said when he came back in after chores. His voice sounded strangely flat and she couldn't read the expression on his face. She set aside her needlework to watch him, but he turned his back to her.

"I don't want you to worry." He took his hat off the hook by the door, put it on his head, then took it off again and put it back on the hook. He came to her and wrapped his arms around her, chair and all. He cupped her belly in his big hands. Gerda tried to settle into the curve of him, but she felt stiff with fear, though she didn't really know why.

"It's about the draft, the military draft," he murmured into her hair. Gerda felt a tingling sensation on the backs of her hands and tops of her feet. It moved up and in, turning into the icy feeling of fear.

"It was in the paper that some changes have been made in Washington," Fritz went on. "Seems this war isn't wrapping up the way they thought it would."

Gerda said nothing. She feared that if she spoke she'd spook him and he would stop telling her what he'd set out to tell her.

"Now, they say the country wants its farmers to keep on farming, so you just keep that in mind."

Gerda pulled away from him. "What are you saying, Fritz? What does the draft have to do with us?"

He walked over to the sink, dipped a cup into the water pail, and took a long, slow drink before going on. "Probably nothing. They say there'll be no changes in what they call the 'agricultural exemption.' The changes probably won't affect me."

"Well?" Gerda asked. "What are the changes? Who do they affect?"

"Lot of men." Fritz started moving around the kitchen. It occurred to Gerda that his halting way of telling her the news had little to do with her. He was simply trying to make sense of things before he said them out loud, but still it frustrated her. She wanted him to just talk, to say what needed to be said. "Lot of men. The government has changed the draft age to include men aged eighteen to forty-five."

"Forty-five?" Gerda nearly shouted. "Are you sure? Forty-five?"

"You think I'd make something like that up?" he snapped. He shifted his weight awkwardly from one foot to the other, looking like a man who wanted both to run away and to run into her arms. "I'm going to catch a ride into O'Neill with Dan Liable in the morning. I need to file for another exemption, just to be sure, now that they've changed the age." He looked at Gerda. "It'll be okay," he said. A heavy silence hung in the air between them. Fritz broke it with a smile. "We'll be taking Dan's new Ford. We'll be *motoring* our way to O'Neill."

"Motoring?" Gerda said. "In a motorcar? Are you sure that's safe?" Even as she asked it, she knew how ridiculous the question must be, but she felt hollowed out by Fritz's news, and she could think of nothing else to say.

Fritz answered with a puff of air blown through closed lips. "Safe? 'Course it's safe!" He took the change of subject as an opportunity. He called to the children. "Guess what your ol' Pa is doing tomorrow," he said. "I'm riding in a motorcar all the way to O'Neill." The children danced with excitement. "Me too! Me too!" they cried.

Though Gerda felt as if the air had left the house when Fritz told her of the change, it was as if in celebration that she and the children waved goodbye the next morning. She tried to smile at the men in the car as she waved along with the children, but before they had turned the corner at the end of the lane, she was back inside, grabbing work to do as if it were a lifeline.

Fritz would keep the form the man at the draft board gave him in his wallet. It was the only place he knew that it would be both safe from loss and Gerda's eyes. He folded it into thirds lengthwise and then in half by width so that it fit in the fold with the dollar bills he never had enough of. Sometimes, for minutes at a time, he forgot it was there.

He had walked into the county courthouse with the three other men from Stuart, still exhilarated from his first ride in an automobile, anticipating nothing but a long line and a confusing form to fill out. When he looked around at the tables set up, he was shocked to see William Owens sitting behind one of them. He hadn't seen him since the day he'd found him in his field just after Owens's son had died. For a moment, the two men locked gazes. Owens looked away first. Fritz removed his hat, looked at the inside of it as if he could find the words he could say printed on the sweaty band. That moment in the field had been unlike any other in his life. He didn't know a man could cry like that, could lose himself in such grief. He had half carried Owens to his buggy and lifted him into the seat as he would one of his own boys. The caught wheel had been easy enough to dislodge, and he got the buggy back up to the road. The jostling caused Owens to vomit again. Fritz stopped the buggy to hold onto him as he leaned into the painful sound of dry heaves. When Owens sat up, it was as if a demon had been exorcised and he was himself again, straightening his spine and looking forward over the horse's head.

"All right," he said. "You can go now."

Neither man seemed capable of looking at the other. Fritz handed him the reins and stepped down from the buggy and set out across his own field toward home. If Owens had been changed by that day, it didn't show. He sat behind the table looking as self-important as he had when he launched into a four-minute speech.

Someone bumped Fritz's shoulder and he realized he was blocking the movement of two lines. He stepped aside and looked around for his neighbors. When he looked toward the tables again, Owens was gone and another man had taken his place.

The lines moved quickly, the county having worked out the problems that had slowed it down in the early days of draft registration. There was lots of talk in those early days about what the draft rules were and who would be in charge of upholding them in each individual county. Some states let men apply at the nearest post office, but Holt County required a trip to the county courthouse. What looked sensible enough on paper coming out of Washington didn't always translate efficiently when the men lined up. The fact was there were many men who couldn't read at all, Fritz could see some of those now in the line in front of him, holding the form up as if to get a better light, not wanting to admit to illiteracy, or worse—a poor grasp of the English language. It made for slow work. Fritz recognized a couple of farmers from over by Atkinson and he nodded in greeting, but there was tension throughout the great hall and men spoke only softly to those they knew well. The men behind the tables, the officials, were on a platform of some sort, so as each man came up to the front of the line he had to look up as one would in a courtroom toward a judge. The men filing looked smaller when they got to the front, and it made Fritz think of Owens's store with his raised floor behind the counter. He looked around for Owens again and saw him standing behind a pillar talking quietly with someone. Both men were watching Fritz. Just before it was his turn, the other man walked to the table, spoke to the man collecting forms and walked away. If Fritz were another kind of man, one who distrusted others, he would have felt a prickle of fear when he saw that, but Fritz was a man who steadfastly believed in the goodness of others.

He handed the form to the man at the table. The man looked it over quickly, glanced over his shoulder, then stamped it and handed it back to Fritz.

"Exemption denied" stamped in red ink across the center of the page.

Fritz read the words, not quite understanding what they meant. He looked then at the man behind the table. "What does this mean?" he asked.

"It means you'll need to watch for the notifications in the paper for the date you report for physical examination." He answered slowly as if Fritz couldn't understand the language at all. "Sometimes they send a letter, but it's your job to know the date, so don't wait for them to come looking for you."

"But," Fritz blinked and squinted at the paper in his hand, "I'm a farmer. There's that exemption for farmers."

"Not all farmers." The man's face grew guarded. He hunched his shoulders and leaned over the table as if protecting something. "They had to make some changes because people were going out and buying garden plots just so they could qualify for that exemption. It's like the marriage exemption; a whole bunch of men ran off and married the first woman they saw, just so they wouldn't have to help out when the country needs them."

"But I been a farmer all my life. I been married for nine years. I got kids, ya know." Fritz could hear the desperation in his voice and it angered him.

The man reached his hand out to take Fritz's form again. He looked at it more closely this time. Fritz noticed that the room around them had gone strangely quiet. "Vogel. That's German, isn't it?" His voice was a bark in the newly silent room and his expression flattened into a kind of curtain. Fritz stood looking up at him, his mouth open ready to speak words that wouldn't come to him.

Someone grabbed Fritz's elbow and he jerked it away before recognizing Dan Liable.

"Come on, Fritz," Dan said. "Let's go."

The man looked down at Dan. "You two together?"

Dan Liable had never recovered from the influenza virus he'd caught that spring and in the dim light of the courthouse he looked pale and old, though he was only a year or two older than Fritz. They'd known each other as neighbors and as friends ever since Fritz and Gerda had moved to Stuart. They'd helped each other through at least eight harvests and countless smaller chores. The man behind the table stood up. Dan looked up at him, then at Fritz. His expression went flat, and he turned around and walked out of the courthouse. The last of the Stuart men to follow Dan tipped his head at Fritz, encouraging him, without open commitment, to follow them.

How had a room full of people become so quiet so quickly, Fritz wondered. It wasn't so much fear that walked him out the door as it was shock. He didn't know what else to do.

He didn't tell Gerda. With the baby so close to coming, she was tired all the time, and he couldn't give her this new burden to carry. Perhaps the war would end before his number came up, he thought. His silence, he knew, was the biggest lie he would ever tell Gerda. He took to getting the mail before she could get to the mailbox at the end of the lane. He stopped waiting for Aloys to bring the paper and would invent reasons to go into town on Thursday mornings, the day the paper was published. Please God, he found himself murmuring when he was alone, please God please. But what he was praying for seemed too big for either of the languages he knew by heart, so he never got beyond the murmuring sound of beseechment. Each breath he took seemed a kind of waiting.

Gerda set a plate of gravy bread in front of Fritz and watched over his shoulder as he cut into it with his fork. He quartered the square of bread neatly and then cut each smaller square into triangles before taking the first bite. He chewed slowly, looking down at his plate.

"Food all right?" Gerda asked.

Her question startled him into action. He looked quickly at her, then dug heartily into his dinner. "*Ja, ja*, it's good," he said. "You're a good cook, Gerda. I tell you that Margaret Baum can't make good gravy to save her soul, you ask me." He rattled on about the merits of gravy and the difference between beef and chicken gravy.

He'd been behaving strangely all week. When he came home from O'Neill that day, Dan Liable had dropped him off at the end of the county road. He'd walked the last half mile home, so Gerda hadn't heard him return, though she'd been listening for the rattling sound of the engine since midafternoon. She and the children were in the barn finishing up the milking. Ray's chubby fingers were at last long enough to grasp the teats and pull milk from young Bess, the smallest cow, and each of the three older children could now have their own cow to milk. Leo, still small enough to stay in the hay trough out of harm's way, tried to feed hay by the handful to the cows locked in their stalls. Passive and calm, the cows mostly ignored him. Katie and Frank, already adept at milking and balancing on a stool and steadying the pail if the cow moved, could be left on their own. Gerda sat beside Ray, her head against the cow's flank to steady her while her boy squeezed and pulled out trickles of milk that made him smile each time. Gerda's hands over his, she taught him as she had taught each of the other children, reminding him to be gentle, praising him as the milk slowly covered the bottom of the pail.

When Fritz's figure darkened the doorway behind them, it startled them all. Gerda grabbed the bucket Ray had painstakingly filled before it went over, but on the other side Frank landed on the floor when he lost his balance on the one-legged stool. Leo squealed with delight to see his father and clamored to be picked up. Even the cats jumped down from their perches where they waited their share of the milk and meowed loudly.

What struck Gerda in those first moments was the way Fritz didn't move toward any of them. He simply stood in the door and watched them as if they were on a stage and he was the audience. He didn't look at any one of them in particular, but seemingly all of them at once. He squinted at them, as if to assess them in some new light, she thought.

Fritz worked in frenzied spurts all week, though Gerda would find him again and again, as she had now at the dinner table, motionless, lost in thought. She reached out to touch his forehead with the back of her hand. He pulled away testily.

"I'm not sick," he said in answer to her unspoken question. "Kids, you ever notice how much your ma acts like an old mother hen?" He set his dishes in the washbasin and turned to her, squatted down, and put his arms out in imitation of a hen. "Cluck, cluck, cluck-cluck," which made the children laugh, so he kept it up, wrapping his big arms around her and two-stepping her around the kitchen.

"Enough! Enough!" Gerda said. "I'm too tired and too big for dancing." She pulled away from him and sat down, her hands cupping her belly. She could feel the baby moving, a foot or a hand making a small bump against the bigger roundness. Frank and Ray jumped up and began prancing around the table, their hands tucked in their armpits and flapping their elbows. They clucked and Katie took Leo's hands to clap in rhythm with them. Though the room filled with motion and noise, Gerda wasn't fooled. Fritz was smiling, but his eyes had a flatness to them that told her there was something behind them he wanted to keep hidden. To ask would lead only to denial that there was anything at all, so she waited, a kind of sadness and fear nestling into the back of her mind.

Days settled into weeks and work kept their hands busy and their bodies tired. Gerda watched Fritz, and though it seemed that he too was watching everything and everyone intently, as if to memorize, she never caught his eye. She was reminded of the shells the cicadas left behind on the trees—they looked complete and real, but they were only shells. Sometimes she reached out to touch him and he jumped, startled to see her so close.

The Baums were already alighting from their wagon before the Vogels noticed their arrival. Gerda was the last one out of the house to greet them, her movements so heavy and slow now. The children milled about one another before taking off in the direction of the orchard, but Aloys took Fritz's arm and walked him toward the barn with hardly a glance toward the house. Margaret fussed with the cover on the pie plate she held in her hand. She never arrived without some small gift of food. Gerda watched the men walk away before turning to Margaret.

"What are they up to?" she asked.

Margaret looked toward the children. "I don't know. What makes you think they're up to anything?"

"I mean the men," Gerda said, pointing to where Fritz and Aloys had disappeared from sight. "What's going on?"

Margaret shrugged. "I don't know. Aloys came home from town this morning gruff as an old bear. When I told him I wanted to come over here to see how you're doing, he jumped up and said let's go." She handed the plate to Gerda. "It's not much, but it's all Aloys would give me time to put together." She looked at Gerda closely, walking around her and studying her profile. "That little thing is getting into position, my friend."

"I know," Gerda replied. "I can breathe again, but I spend most of my time running to the outdoor room." Margaret made it easy for Gerda to laugh again. She had been with her through the births of her three boys, and Gerda felt no shame telling her things she would never admit to anyone else. With Margaret's help, Gerda could think only about the baby. She could let go of the mystery of Fritz's behavior and simply be a woman preparing to give birth.

Aloys walked all the way into the barn before turning toward Fritz and handing him what he held under his arm. It was the Omaha paper, the daily one that published first the list of men called up for the next draft. The Stuart paper wouldn't come out with it for two more days. The article was above the fold.

NOTICE OF CALL AND TO APPEAR FOR PHYSICAL EXAMINATION

Local Board, Holt County
Nebraska.

The following named persons are hereby notified that, pursuant to the Act of Congress approved May 18, 1917, they are called for military service of the United States by this Local Board.

The serial numbers and the order number of each of such persons are shown below. They will report at the office of this Local Board for physical examination on the 25th day of October, 1918, at 8 o'clock a.m.

Any claim for exemption or discharge must be made on forms which may be procured, or the form of which may be copied at the office of the Local Board, and must be filed at the office of this Local Board on or before the seventh day after the date of posting of this notice.

Your attention is called to the penalties for violation or evasion of the Selective Service Law approved May 18, 1917, and of the Rules and Regulations which may be consulted at this office.

Serial No.	Name	Address on Registrat'n Card	Order No.
258	Lewis Scott Taylor	Stuart	1
458	Harm McInert Franzen	Stuart	2
436	Harm Ostendorf	Atkinson	3
854	Ward B. Roberts	Dustin	4
1095	Ercie Wingert	O'Neill	5
1455	Gregorsos Bothols(?)	Karparili,Thevon, Greece	6
83	Claude H. Gunn	O'Neill	7
1117	Richard Charles Hoffstein	O'Neill	8
837	Fritz Vogel	Stuart	9
337	Harry Phillip Schroeder	Lynch	10
676	Fred Charles Yeutter	Atkinson	11

There were more names, but Fritz didn't need to read any further.

"Did you know?" Aloys asked after Fritz looked over the list and folded the paper again.

"I figured as much," Fritz said. He didn't trust his voice to say more.

No, he hadn't known, hadn't even let himself imagine it could happen. He had concerned himself with worries about Gerda, about how she would react to the news of the denied exemption, but he had not really considered it a possibility that he would be called up for the draft. Standing in the quiet, musty darkness of his own barn, he felt strangely light and buoyant, as if gravity had lost its hold on him and he was in danger of floating upward. He imagined himself grabbing at the rafters, trying to get back to solid ground. Aloys's voice seemed to come from a great distance. Fritz could make no more sense of the words he was saying than he could of the squeaking chirps of the barn swallows that flitted about between shafts of light.

He recalled the look in William Owens's eyes when he stepped up to file for his exemption. It was hatred he saw there, he now knew, but he hadn't understood how deep the hatred ran. He understood it was directed at more than just Fritz's place of birth. It came to him then that the day he had found Owens in his field drunk and broken, he had made a terrible mistake. Fritz should have turned and walked away. Owens could forgive him for being German, but not for witnessing that raw, personal, and brutal grief.

That night, Fritz curled himself into Gerda, wrapping his arms around her, cupping the child they had made, so grateful for the bulk of her and the baby she carried he wanted to weep. Only in the dark could he form the words to tell her. When he told all he knew the silence took shape and weight around them. It pressed against Fritz so that he felt the air squeezed from his lungs.

Into that solid, corporeal silence, Gerda said, "No, you will not go."

Fritz held her tight, his face pressed into her hair, memorizing the scent of her. She sounded so certain, and he wanted to believe her. He wanted to believe her faith could save them. Focused as they were on the evil of war, they never saw the nearer danger coming at them, the devil rising even then from the plains of Kansas.

CHAPTER THIRTEEN

The late September midday would hold the heat of summer, but on the morning of the first death, autumn was on the rise. A light fog lay in the hollows until after the sun topped the horizon. Daylight revealed skeins of snow geese following the ancient flyways south. Gray threads against the azure, they were almost invisible between the feathered wisps of high clouds and only when the earth held its breath could their haunting calls be heard. Cottonwoods shimmered yellow in the breeze. In the meadows along the river, flocks of red-winged blackbirds dipped and rose like smoke. Just the week before, they had perched separate and alone atop reeds, but something in nature, theirs or the earth's, had alerted them to shed their independent ways. Now, en masse, they skirred the contours of grass and tree line. A trio or so of meadowlarks tagged along at the road's edge, flitting between stalks of heavy-headed goldenrod and stands of bluestem. Their whistled "See you! See yeers!" to one another felt like good company to Gannoway as he traveled along the lane south of the river.

The communication of birds, Gannoway thought as he rode toward a new patient's place, was a strange and beautiful mystery. He felt reminded that he was glad to be alive and of late that was a feeling he sometimes forgot. "Nothing is worth more than this day," the philosopher Goethe had written, but that was a thought Gannoway knew he would need to keep to himself. The war was so far away and yet it was everywhere. Even here people had turned strange, neighbors not sure if they could trust neighbor. Posters lined the storefronts reminding everyone of their duties to the country. "After you register for the draft, make sure your friends do too." "True Americans buy war bonds. Have you bought yours?" Patriotism seemed the only safe topic on the streets. Even the schools weren't exempt. The Bureau of Education had issued a statement that "patriotism, heroism, and sacrifice" should be the themes of the study plans for elementary school children, the idea of education as the art of making man ethical no longer paramount in this fear-driven time.

The War Library Fund he'd hoped to see succeed had fallen apart before it ever got started. In the slang of the day, "nothing doing" had been the most common response. Unless they could be sure that no German-language books would be purchased, most of the townspeople would hand over no money. Owens publicly condemned German as "a language that disseminates the ideals of autocracy, brutality, and hatred" and claimed that once the money left Stuart, there was no way to ensure that those in charge didn't buy Hun-loving books. MacGewan simply hitched his own wagon to that mule and between the two of them they squelched what enthusiasm the rest of the town had been able to drum up.

There was too much anti-German sentiment, Gannoway thought. It was as if all hatred and anxiety common to human nature had found a place to settle and it didn't matter anymore what was true, it only mattered what everyone seemed to believe. The whole town was paralyzed by fear even as people continued to live normal lives on the surface. Victory gardens were safe, and war bonds, but if it couldn't be proven to be completely free of what the woman at Kroger's had called "the Kaiser taint," no one in town could get behind it.

Today, however, the birds reminded him of beauty and he felt lighter as he headed south out of town in the early morning. His day had started with a call from the Paulson place. Amanda Paulson had sounded frightened when she called, but Gannoway had grown accustomed to doing what he could for his patients without adopting their terrors. He was not worried about what lay ahead of him. It was too early in the season for much illness. Viruses, he noted, seemed to wait for the cold to set in good and hard before maturing into sickness. Even his business had been changed by the war in Europe. It had sent a tremor through the population here at home so that a new stoicism had taken hold and no one wanted to admit to weakness by claiming to be sick or hurt. Medical calls had dropped off. Just last week a man over in Atkinson had nearly died from a mower cut on his foot because he hadn't wanted to report to a doctor. He lost his leg from the knee down to gangrene because he wanted to be a Good American, one who didn't take supplies needed for the soldiers. The same sentiment could explain why

Amanda Paulson waited so long to call about her husband, but Gannoway didn't know the couple personally, so he couldn't say.

"He's never sick," Amanda had whispered into the phone when she called Gannoway from his sleep just before sunrise. He had stood in the hallway listening to the murmur of guilt and fear in her voice, his mind on the cold floor beneath his bare feet. He calculated how long it would take him to drive out to the Paulson place while he reassured her that things would be okay.

"I think I'm too late, doctor." Her voice was raspy with fear.

"I'll be there, soon as I can," he said. His voice was deep, the kind that carried reassurance across the telephone wire. "Soon."

When he turned off the main road toward the Paulson ranch, he noted no smoke rose from the chimney of the house at the top of the rise, and it was then he felt the first itch of foreboding. Autumn had been mild, but even if they weren't yet heating the house they'd need a fire for cooking, Gannoway reasoned. A flock of starlings rose from the calf pen and took up a silent post on the telephone line leading toward the house. He rode beneath them feeling watched and exposed. The restless lowing of cattle and the syncopated pop of horses kicking the stall walls told him the chores were undone. The place seemed strangely deserted. Not even chickens out in the yard, the brooder house off to the back closed up tight, and Gannoway knew that whatever illness had struck here had come at night after the chickens had gone in to roost and their hutch closed up. It must have come hard and fast, he reasoned, and he contemplated the possibilities of what he'd find inside. There had been those letters from his brother about an illness down in Kansas at Fort Riley, but he had no reason to suspect it had spread this far, so the memory of those letters didn't come to him then, not then.

He set the brake on his buggy and stepped down slowly. As he walked across the yard, he half hoped someone would come out to greet him. The windows, curtain covered, were like blank eyes. No one answered his knock, though he tried twice, so he let himself in.

"Hello?" he called into the darkened house. "Dr. Gannoway here. Mrs. Paulson?" The house smelled of camphor and body wastes, the peculiar, sweetly pungent odor that lingers in the homes of the sick. He felt his way toward the table in the center of the room. In the dim light from the window he saw a darkened shape on the kitchen floor and from it came the rattle of phlegm-filled lungs. He stepped closer and pulled the curtain back to let in a shaft of light. At first he thought there was some mistake. The figure on the floor was that of a colored man, not the Norwegian he expected to see. A rustle of movement behind him startled him, and he turned to see Amanda Paulson leaning against the doorjamb, a cloth pressed to her face. She tried to speak, but the effort turned into a violent cough. She could give no help and she waved her hand helplessly before leaving the doctor to his work.

On his own, Gannoway found a lamp on the side table. He took a long tapered stick to the stove and poked the coals until a spark caught and flared. With the flame wavering on the stick's end, he lit the lamp, and what he saw in the flickering light shocked his breath away. It was Lloyd Paulson on the floor, he could see that now, but he'd never seen anything like what was happening to him. Mahogany spots had formed along his cheekbones and spread outward so that his entire face had darkened. Gannoway surmised at first that violent coughing had broken blood vessels under the skin, but closer inspection told him something else was going on. It was cyanosis that blotched the skin around the base of the man's ears. His lips too had darkened to an oxygen-starved blue. His mouth hung open and his breath came in great shuddering gasps.

Gannoway knelt beside him and opened his satchel. Suddenly the man began to flail about, grasping as if the air he needed in his lungs could be caught and held in his big, calloused hands. The gurgling sound in his chest brought Amanda in from the other room, but she was doubled over with her own weakness. She too had the strange illness—Gannoway could diagnose that by the dark bluish circles beneath her eyes. Lloyd grabbed the doctor's arm and tried to pull himself up. Gannoway held his hands with practiced firmness and spoke softly to him. Where he could not save, he offered solace. Lloyd fell back. His head struck the hard wood floor. Amanda winced at the sound, but too weak to come forward, she simply lingered by the door, watching her husband take his last labored breaths. Gannoway then turned his attention to Amanda. He placed a poultice on her chest and wrapped her in blankets until she stopped shivering. He made a tent of blankets around her bed and set a pot of boiling water with menthol and eucalyptus on the floor to help her breathe. He rubbed her arms up to her shoulders until her skin pinkened, but within hours she was dead too.

Lloyd Paulson was thirty-five; Amanda was twenty-eight and eight months' pregnant with their first child. Gannoway knew the couple only by sight. He'd never treated them before, though he knew of Amanda's pregnancy—the bloom of it showed in her face even before her belly swelled.

Lloyd was a big man, strong as the bulls he raised. Hale and hardy, when he laughed you could hear him a block away. They were not people who would die easily, Gannoway thought, and he was mystified by what he'd seen.

May the good Lord, if there is one, forgive him for this: his first reaction when he folded Lloyd Paulson's arms across his chest and smoothed the dead man's eyes closed, was of excitement. He felt on the cusp of some great and powerful lesson. He felt the same tingle of anticipation and dread that he had felt when he performed his first autopsy, or peered through a microscope for the first time. It felt as if he'd stepped through a portal to a place where mysteries could be solved, explanations would be given.

Upon returning home, he wrote immediately to his brother. Lark Gannoway was stationed at the medical officers' training camp in Fort Riley, Kansas. In the spring, Lark had sent him news of a doctor he knew from western Kansas. Loring Miner, who practiced in Haskell County, Kansas, was a man cut of the same cloth as Ed and Lark. He was an educated man who prided himself on his own scientific knowledge. Like most doctors, Miner had seen many cases of influenza, but in late January and early February of 1918, a number of his patients presented symptoms of unusual intensity. An influenza of sorts that was violent and rapid in its progress through the body. "Some of my strongest patients have been knocked down like they'd been shot," he had told Lark. The disease nearly overwhelmed Miner with patients. He took to sleeping in his buggy, letting his team take him home. (Such luxury, Lark commented dryly, was one reason rural doctors clung to the use of buggies well past the time when automobiles were readily and cheaply available.)

In late spring, though, the disease had disappeared. Gannoway had forgotten all about it until now. He told his brother about the strange case of the Paulsons and mentioned Miner's reports from early in the year. Yes, Lark wrote back, that sounded something like the strange illness they were starting to see down there, though he didn't seem overly concerned at first, mentioning it only as a kind of postscript when describing the conditions at camp:

"They used only partially cured lumber when they put the building up, you see. The cracks in the walls are big enough to insert a fist through if you've a mind to, so you can imagine how many mosquitoes get through at night. To fix it before the cold hits, the enlisted men have been put to work lining the insides with newspaper and tarpaper and scrap lumber they've scavenged from Camp Funston down the road. That keeps the most severe winds out, but not the mosquitoes, and not the pneumonia. I don't know if the state of our cantonment is responsible for the severity of this new illness or not, but something is sending it through the camp like a prairie fire. You'd probably enjoy yourself down here now, interested as you are in learning about diseases. This one, I have to say, seems preternaturally virulent. And you're right, it does bring to mind Miner's stories. Influenza usually kills through a slow-moving bacterial pneumonia, but this one seems to attack the lungs directly. It's almost as if the lungs are being burned up inside the patient. Pneumonia, that 'captain of the men of death' as they used to say back at school, is on the march here."

Gannoway had read the letter a half dozen times, each rereading diluting that familiar twinge of regret and shame he'd always felt about being left behind. Lark, his younger brother by less than a year, had joined the army months before most Americans knew the country was headed for war. Both brothers saw the medical corps as the perfect marriage of civic duty and wanderlust, and though Lark had ended up stationed only as far away as Kansas, there was always the potential for more.

Gannoway knew he was doing what he needed to do here in this small town on the lip of the Sandhills, yet when his brother enlisted, he felt as if the world had suddenly exploded with possibility—could he really consider war *possibility*? He couldn't help himself. He did. He felt something was going on somewhere and he was not doing his part. Not only had he not taken the uniform, but that letter reminded him he was missing out on excitement of the most profound kind, that of a new scientific discovery.

As a scientist, and he considered himself a scientist as well as a medical doctor, he believed a thing could be *known* if knowledge of it followed logically from the sound premises found through observation. The two most important questions in science are "What can I know?" and "How can I know it?" One must be in the presence of something to observe it, and sometimes he looked at the countryside around him where little stood between him and the horizon and he felt the poverty of experience. And yet, the world seemed to be growing smaller, or maybe closer. It was the war that did that. Things were changing; Gannoway could feel it. What he knew and how he knew it were about to expand beyond his wildest imaginings. Yes, war was Possibility.

And now there was this.

CHAPTER FOURTEEN

The congregation descended the wide steps of St. Boniface and scattered quickly under a sodden sky. Already, news of the strange illness had spread and the threat of bad weather and sickness kept neighbor from neighbor even here at church. In normal times this was the only social life many of the farm families enjoyed. But these were not normal times.

Only John Kaup lingered after the crowd was gone. It had been his custom for years. John made it his business to walk the length of the church checking the pews at the end of each Mass, making certain that the kneelers were in place and no items—scarves, bonnets, or even rosaries—had been left behind. If he found them quickly enough, most lost things could be returned to the owners immediately. John took a personal pride in keeping the box at the back of the church empty of orphaned belongings.

It wasn't simple generosity on his part. It was his habit to stay behind at any gathering, giving others a chance to leave first, lessening the chance that anyone would walk behind him. He'd seen the younger ones imitating his walk, turning the right foot out and sweeping it forward with a lurch. Marked by polio in his youth, he learned early that a clubfoot was nothing he could change, no more than he could change the attitudes of others around him. The best he could do was to arrange his daily habits in such a way that kept the ridicule of others at bay. (Thank God Christina had seen beyond the foot to see *him*. Not a day went by that he didn't remember to feel gratitude for that.)

"Thank you, Johnny," Father Jungels called to him before disappearing into the back of the vestment room. John waved and kept walking, the scent of incense his only companion. Christina would have taken the children on home, and by now she would be starting dinner. Their children would be playing a game of some kind. He could picture the scene in his home clearly and it made him smile to imagine it. He wished Father Jungels would have stopped to talk a moment, just so he could say, "Well, I need to get back home, my family is waiting for me." He liked this image of himself as a family man. There'd been a time when he didn't think this would be his lot in life. He was closing in on thirty when he met Christina, though she was ten years younger, and he had begun to believe—to fear—that family life, a family of his own, had passed him by.

Finished with the job he'd assigned himself, John pulled his cap on and stepped out onto the empty steps, thinking only of the dinner Christina had waiting for him. One buggy still sat on the street, the bay gelding in the harness stretching his neck to reach the foxtails coming up at the edge of the road. John recognized it as Doc Gannoway's rig. He assumed the doctor would be waiting for Father Jungels. The doctor and the priest often stood in the vestibule or on the steps discussing one thing or another after Mass, so he paid little attention to the buggy and turned toward home.

"Mr. Kaup," the doctor called before he'd gone far. Later, John would remember that, that the doctor called him "Mr. Kaup," not John or Johnny. "Mr. Kaup." He turned toward him in surprise.

"May I have a word with you?" The doctor stepped down lightly and came toward John, which surprised him even more. He was used to being the one who approached others. The doctor's greatcoat flapped open in the wind and John couldn't help but think of a great bird preparing to fly. He took a step back, caught himself, and then limped forward to meet the doctor.

"Mr. Kaup," the doctor said again and held his hand out. "I understand you might be available to help me." John took his hat off and held it in both hands a moment before realizing the doctor was wanting to shake his hand.

"Anything, Dr. Gannoway. I'd be happy to help you with anything I can." He pumped Gannoway's hand enthusiastically and his voice rose at the end of this statement, though he didn't mean to sound unsure of his own conviction. He meant it. He would be honored to help a man like Gannoway. Not simply because of his skills as a doctor, though that would be enough, John thought, but because of the way he acted toward John and his family. When the doctor came to their house, first to deliver their babies and then to help Christina through some female problems, he always treated John and Christina with the same respect John had seen him offer to everyone else in the community. Though the doctor never made him feel small, John never forgot the differences between their stations in life. He held himself straighter in the doctor's presence, worried he'd do or say something wrong, and talking to him always made him nervous.

Gannoway seemed not to notice the man's discomfort.

"I need a driver," Dr. Gannoway said. "I'm having trouble keeping up with this new challenge." He cleared his throat. "I mean this illness. It is taking its toll."

John knew about the illness. Everybody in town knew about it. Businesses were starting to keep shorter hours because the help were too sick to come in. The Mass he'd just left had been sparsely attended. Seemed like everybody was coming down with something. It hadn't worried him, though. He and Christina liked to keep to themselves and his kids were too young to go to school yet. They were a healthy lot. This here influenza seemed like something interesting to talk about, but not to worry about.

John felt ten feet tall when he arrived home. Christina had dinner waiting, and the children were playing just as he had imagined, but he felt different. He was now a man who'd been offered a job, a steady job making good pay—no more standing in line for seasonal work or begging for odd jobs around town. He called his family into the kitchen and insisted that Christina sit down before he told them what had happened.

"He called me 'Mr. Kaup,'" John said to the faces smiling up at him. "He said he needs a man he can count on, and he asked me." John felt his shirt had grown tighter, what with pride swelling him up so. The children laughed and clapped and danced around him. They may or may not have understood what it meant to a man like John to have the respect of respectable men, but they certainly understood the look of joy on their father's face and they felt it too. That Christina was silent did not register in John's mind, nor did the children pay attention to it. The three of them made enough noise through dinner and beyond.

It took her all day to start talking again. She loved her husband, of that there was no doubt, but she loved her children too. It was after they'd gone to bed before she said what she needed to say.

"You need that job driving that doctor from sick house to sick house," she said quietly in the dark beside him.

"Yes, I do!" John interrupted. "I want more for you and the kids. I want to provide more. I know you don't want lots of nice things, but the kids will be going to school soon and they shouldn't be looking like ragamuffins when they do." He rattled on about his dreams for them, he said things he hadn't said to her before, about all the things he wanted to give her. He said this was just the beginning. "Once a man like Gannoway is on your side, well, there's no telling how far you can go."

He was still smiling when she interrupted him.

"But we don't need that illness here," she said quietly. "For their sake, John, when you start that job, I want you stay away from the children." After tomorrow, she told him, he was not to go in to kiss them good night. Once he started the job, he could not hold his little Marie on his lap, nor wrestle with Jack, the way a man does with a son.

He didn't answer her; what was there to say to her request? He needed the job. She understood that and so did he, but there was something more, something he didn't know if he could put into words. The doctor needed him. The clubfoot had kept John from joining the service alongside his brother and neighbors had kept him from doing anything to be a man for his country. He ran the Red Cross drills, but the boys who followed his orders on the fields west of the church knew he was crippled, would never lead men in battle. He'd seen the VanNoys boy following behind him, imitating his walk. He'd pretended not to notice or care, but it bothered him. It did.

When the doctor approached him, he'd sounded desperate. "I need your help, Mr. Kaup," Dr. Gannoway had said. Mr. Kaup. How could he say no to him? It's not as though he would be doing anything truly dangerous, he wanted to say to Christine. He knew horses and he knew how to get a wagon or a buggy across most any kind of terrain.

"I can do that, Doctor," John had said. "I can get you anywhere you need to go, any time of day or night." It was a skill he knew he had, and it was a skill he could offer. He wanted to serve. He had been willing to make any sacrifice the moment America entered the war, but he was not fit for the military, for anything it seemed. His draft registration form had been stamped "cripple" and the word seared in him. All around him sacrifices were being made for this war, even his own brother was a soldier, but he'd been left behind, and now he'd been asked to help his fellow countrymen. He didn't know what sacrifices he would have to make, but he was willing to make them. He had decided on his walk home from church that he would consider himself a soldier from that moment on.

This is what it feels like to be a soldier, he thought as he lay in the dark beside his wife. This would be only the first sacrifice, and maybe the hardest. In the morning he kissed Christina and children goodbye and moved his bedding to the woodshed in back of the house. When the doctor called, he saluted his family and walked away.

His devotion to his job and to Dr. Gannoway did not flag and his admiration for Gannoway grew with each passing day. Gannoway worked like some kind of unstoppable machine, available twenty-four hours a day for the sick and dying.

John took to sleeping in the back of the wagon, not bothering to even go back to his shed and the austere cot he'd made for himself. He wanted to be ready when called. The doctor seemed never to sleep. He closed his eyes on the rides, but the roads they traveled were so rough and gutted by late summer rains that there was no real rest to be had. And yet the doctor kept going. He didn't have to say much to John, for John could see the gray face and dark circles under the doctor's eyes. He had to help the doctor up into the buggy more than once.

Yes, the good doctor needed a driver, John thought, but more than just a driver—and this realization settled inside him in ways that changed him for the rest of his life—"The doctor needs me."

CHAPTER FIFTEEN

"Please stop on your way back from Wyoming. Just for one day!" Gerda wrote to her sister. "Just long enough to clean up and rest after the long trip before you get back home and to work. Please, I miss you my dearest sister!"

She wrote every day, sometimes twice a day. Katherine had told her they would be traveling to Wyoming by train, passing through Stuart sometime near the beginning of October, and at first it had been a simple wish, a desire to see her only sister. But in the months since, Gerda had felt a growing fear that she would never see any of her family again. Her trip home had kaleidoscoped into a series of horrific nightmares that woke her, sweat-soaked and shivering. She pleaded until Katherine finally replied that she would try, she would ask her husband that small grace.

"He is such a businessman," she wrote to Gerda. "Everything relates to business or it's of no interest to him at all. Even our 'honeymoon' destination was chosen so that he could pursue a business deal in Wyoming. And that's as it should be. Yet I believe he will indulge me. He is so generous, I'm sure you will love him too. As he will you."

"As always, your loving sister," she had signed off above the postscript. "Father overheard me tell mother what I hoped to ask my new husband and he began shouting in German all around the house, but I simply pretended I didn't understand what he was saying. He's such a stubborn old bear. And he shouldn't be speaking German anyway."

Gerda could hear her father's angry voice and she couldn't imagine pretending not to understand him. She thought about her last image of him, standing by the tracks with the icy dawn behind him. She still believed he had the power to stop trains, to keep her from her family, from Fritz, and the memory of him standing there, his hat off in the cold wind, caused her to feel his power all over again. How close she came to giving in to his will, allowing herself to be protected by it even as it consumed her. Only now was she beginning to see that this was a daughter's lot. She had vowed to cleave to her husband, unwavering and loyal, which she did so willingly, but to cleave also means to split and that was the meaning she had resisted for so long.

Katherine had told her he tore up the letters Gerda had written, tossed them into the fire, and watched over them to make certain they became ashes before turning away. Nine, ten letters Gerda had written before Katherine told her to stop. "Papa will not bend and you are hurting mother," she had written at last. "Each time a letter comes she cries for hours." The distance between them was less than 150 miles, but it just as easily could have been a thousand. "If you go," her father had said when she and Fritz had boarded the train years ago, "you stay gone." The injustice of it drove her mad at times. He used to call her his "Little Bird," his *kleiner Vogel*, because she moved like a bird among her older, lumbering brothers. Did he not see how she had become what he had named her? She had thought she could change him, but it was she who had changed. In a nation at war, a world such as this, why? Why?

But now Katherine was coming west. What her father did or thought no longer hung like a noose around her neck, and there was a measure of joy returning to her thoughts of home. Gerda wrote to Katherine that she imagined herself lying down on the tracks before the eastbound train, forcing it to stop even if Katherine did not choose to. "I would line my children up beside the railroad tracks and shout at you—'See! See your niece, your namesake! And your three strong nephews! Aren't they beautiful?'" She considered adding a postscript of her own, "You could see what Papa is missing because of his bullheadedness."

Fritz read the letter from Katherine and pointed out that she had not promised that they would stop. She said simply that she would try to "present it" to her husband when he was "feeling most generous." He read her words aloud, exaggerating certain ones to show his distaste for the new husband he'd not yet met and for Katherine's lofty language. Still, Gerda prepared as if the answer would be yes. She rolled up the rugs and took them out to the clothesline and beat them furiously. She washed curtains and stretched them onto forms that lined the walls for days as they dried. She washed windows and walls as if a queen were scheduled for a visit. She baked pies and cakes and secured them in the coolness of the well house for safekeeping.

She couldn't sit still. Even during the meals she would pop up to wipe a spot clean on the wall or stove. Fritz threatened to tie her to a chair if she didn't settle down. In answer, she walked to the mailbox to look for more letters.

He told her to rest some, to save some energy for the visit itself. Had she forgotten the baby would be here soon?

The baby, as if she could forget the baby, she thought, though she didn't stop to answer him. The baby twisted and kicked until her rib cage ached from the inside out. The weight of her belly pulled on her back making her feel like a swaybacked old mare.

"I'm just going to be ready if she comes," Gerda snapped at him. "When she comes." He couldn't know how important this visit was to her and it was too late to explain it to him. She had hid the truth from him and now she was alone with it. She felt adrift in this indescribable war between two men she loved. If only she could see Katherine again, she would feel she had found peace in at least one war.

Katherine was coming! The very words made her feel as if her lungs were expanding and she could breathe freely again.

The train tracks ran along the river just a little over a half mile south of the Vogel farm. Some days the sound of the train was loud enough that she could hear the rattle and screech of the metal wheels rolling along the tracks even in the house with the windows closed. Other days she only noticed it if she was outdoors when the engineer pulled the whistle cord. Whether she was conscious of them or not, the trains kept a steady rhythm in her days, an external heartbeat. The Northwestern Railroad ran six passenger trains every day across those tracks nowadays, three eastbound and three heading west, and again as many straight freight and coal trains. There were more of them now than when she and Fritz first moved here, though she didn't remember the exact numbers or when they changed. The empty westbound hoppers heading back to the mines in Wyoming and Montana rattled loudest, but all the trains gave off a sense of hurry-hurry industry. They instilled in her a strange combination of comfort and fear. The trains were her lifeline home, a constant connection she could see and hear. Katherine would come on those tracks. But the increasing number of trains, especially since the war began, made her feel that the world was hurtling too quickly toward the future, an unknown and dangerous future, it felt to her. She didn't want Time to stop, just some days she wanted it to slow down.

She had awoken that morning to a sharp twist of pain in her lower back, and she lay with her eyes closed waiting for the next cramp. *Is it now?* she asked her body. When a second cramp didn't come, she rolled gingerly to her side and sat up on the edge of the bed. She felt the buzzing tingle in her pelvis that always came late in the pregnancy, but no further pain and no rush of water. *Not yet*, her body said, *not yet*.

The baby could come any time now, and though Gerda could not escape the heavy sense of fear whenever she thought about the birth, she was ready. Her body felt stretched out and weighted and she just wanted it over with. She looked down at her ankles. She had to stretch her legs out in front of her to see them. She noted that even this early in the morning, after a full night's rest, they were swollen and tight. Her hands reminded her of Father Jungels's sausage-stuffed fingers. She was, in many ways, unrecognizable to herself. She looked toward the east window where a glimmer of pink showed just above the dark horizon. Stars still dotted the sky. What will this day bring? she had wondered.

Katherine will be here soon, she thought, and she forgot the aches and the swelling and felt a flush of pleasure. Perhaps the baby will come while Katherine is here. She could help deliver her own niece—that would be a fine introduction to married life, Gerda thought with a smile. If she said that to Margaret, the two would laugh together, but alone with her thoughts like this in the early morning she couldn't help but remember Elizabeth. No, she told herself sternly, I will not think of that today. Instinctively she prayed, "Oh most gracious Virgin Mary . . . ," as she dressed in the dark room. Fritz's steady, heavy breathing assured her she had not disturbed him. She closed the door quietly behind her.

By Gerda's reckoning, Katherine and her new husband should be coming back from Wyoming that day or the next. Katherine had written before the couple left for their honeymoon with their general itinerary. She had promised to telegraph specifics when the time came. "We will be in the wagon-lit, of course, with a private sleep berth, so we will arrive well-rested and well-fed. Don't worry about us. We plan to be intrepid explorers on this trip, eating and drinking what and where the winds of fate provide. I will have seen the geysers of Yellowstone before I see you again—there is no telling how changed I will be by all this wild and wonderful living. Oh Gerda, I am so happy."

Gerda recalled her sister's letters and thought how she couldn't wait to see her Katherine, to hear her tell the stories of travel. Gerda had never been west of Stuart and only as far east as the Missouri River. The memory of the one boat ride of her life still gave her pleasure. Her father had taken her, she no longer remembered the reason, she only remembered standing on the deck of the steamboat, the wind blowing so hard she could lean into it and not fall down. The rolling motion of the boat stayed with her for hours after they got back on land. There'd been no further trips, life so full of work. Her younger sister, though, she would have adventures, a thought that made Gerda smile.

She heard Fritz stirring in the bedroom, and though she tried to be quiet, she knew her movements would bring him out even though he could use a few minutes more of sleep. She started her day as always, by stoking the fire in the cook stove. It was cool enough in the room that she welcomed the heat, holding her hands out, palms down over the small flame before beginning the morning's work. She had looked again to the east and wondered what the day would bring.

She heard the train's whistle crow longer than it should, and then came a sound like the high-pitched death squeal of a stuck hog. Her first thought was to wonder who would be butchering at this time of year, it was still far too warm for such work, but before that question fully formed in her mind, thundering booms shook the windows. The groan and scream of bending and twisting metal seared the air.

She stopped kneading the bread on the counter and rushed toward the door. Outside, the air still vibrated from the sounds, but now came the bawl of terrified cattle and men shouting, and Gerda knew what had happened. Without thinking, she started to run toward the south, but turned back before she'd taken more than a few steps. The two older children were at school, Ray and Leo sat on the floor playing with blocks.

"Come," she said to Ray as she pulled Leo out from under the table. "Hurry." She ran through the south orchard with Leo in her arms and Ray at her heels. Her breath came in shallow gasps and her heart pounded "Katherine! Katherine! Katherine!" in her ears. She stumbled once and went down on one knee. Leo, clinging to her neck, was strangely silent.

She felt as if she were running through molasses, slow and labored. By the time she topped the divide on the other side of the trees, other neighbors had arrived. She could see them on the road by the wreckage. The engine still puffed down the tracks a ways, seven or eight cars still attached behind it, some leaning precariously. The last of the upright cars held the cattle. The first of the twisted and wrecked cars—maybe all of them, Gerda couldn't tell—had been coal cars. Their black cargo spread nearly a quarter mile along the track and fanned out as far as the road. Men were standing, arms akimbo, in groups up and down the road. A few were seated and others were stretched out on the grass. No one seemed concerned about those who were prone. They must not be hurt, she thought, or they're already dead.

Gerda put Leo down on the ground beside her to catch her breath. She had a stitch in her side that made breathing painful. She cupped her hands on her belly and bent over to wait for her heart to stop pounding. The boys jumped up and down with excitement, dancing around her as if she were a maypole. Leo, too young to know what was going on, followed Ray's example and cried out begging to go down closer to the train. "Please, Mama, please!" they both cried.

"Hush," she said. "Hush! We need to stay back out of the way." With her attention on the scene before her she didn't see Fritz come over the rise, and when he shouted her name she turned guiltily to face him.

"What are you doing out here?" he shouted as he trotted toward her. "I came in from the barn and you were gone and I thought something had happened." The boys rushed toward him shouting, "Train wreck, Papa! Train wreck!" Gerda was grateful for their distraction. She knew Fritz was right to be worried. She was so close to her time and she needed to be more careful. She waited for him to reach her, his face so red with worry she couldn't meet his eyes. She pointed at the train below her. "I thought it was Katherine's train," she said weakly. "I didn't think. I just ran."

Fritz walked between the boys as though moving through tall weeds. She thought he would scold her, tell her she was silly, but he said nothing. Instead, God love him for this, he wrapped his arms around her and looked at the wreck below them. She tried to match her breathing to his as they stood silently on that hill.

"Looks like the 1:16; they don't have passenger cars," Fritz said after a moment. Only then could she let herself truly feel the relief. It came in a flood of warmth that made her knees weak and she would have folded to the ground if Fritz hadn't held her up. "Coal cars," he added. "That's all it is, coal." He turned toward the house with one arm around Gerda and picked up Leo in the other. Ray ran ahead, bouncing and excited, as if life's possibilities were endless and lay in any direction.

When the two older children came home from school, they rushed to the divide to watch the cleanup. Though Gerda wanted Katie's help, she knew the train wreck and aftermath was too exciting to miss.

"Don't go any farther than the top of the rise," Gerda warned. She looked directly at Frank when she said this. His adventurous spirit lit candles in his eyes and she knew he would be the one to push past the point of safety given even the slightest chance. And though she knew Katie would be the one doing the watching, she told Frank he needed to keep an eye on Leo. The baby might slow him down.

Fritz had gone down for nearly an hour, but with chores of his own to do, he didn't stay long. Gerda worked in the kitchen and listened to the pops and rumbles of the cleanup work. Part of her wanted to go with her children to see how the railroad crew went about cleaning up such a mess, but another part of her, a much stronger part, wanted her to just go to bed if she wasn't going to do the work that needed doing in her own kitchen.

The run that morning with Leo in her arms had pulled muscles in her arms and shoulders. Even her legs, strong from so much walking and work, felt rubbery. *Too much to do, too much to do*, the thought rumbled in her head, so she kept going without rest. She kept her mind on the tasks at hand—the rolling movement of the wash water as she turned the agitator, the whoosh of water dropping from the clothes as she pressed them through the double pins of the ringer, the strong smell of lye that burned her eyes when she leaned over the washtub. With such concentration she could work through most any pain.

The whinny of a horse brought her up out of her reverie. She pulled a towel from the hook on the wall and walked around to the front to see the bright blue mail wagon stopping in front of the house.

Ed Garret, the plump middle-aged man who had taken Charles Burke's job, stepped down slowly from the wagon and stopped to rub his back and stretch his legs before turning toward the house. By the time he'd loosened up enough to walk, Fritz had come up from the barn to stand beside Gerda.

"Afternoon, Vogels!" Garret called as he limped toward them. "Quite a mess down south!"

Fritz nodded agreeably and the two men began comparing notes about what they knew. Gerda simply listened. Two men swapping tales like that didn't leave room for a woman's voice.

"The train was still inside the switch," Garret said. "So the train traffic won't be blocked, but it sure made for a long mail haul, I'll tell ya! I've been on roads I never been on before today—roads that ain't even roads yet, just trying to get the mail through." He nodded vigorously as he talked as if he agreed with everything he said. "That's my job, though. That's my job." He stuck his chin out when he said that and it reminded Gerda of Charles Burke, how proud he was to be in charge of delivering the U.S. mail. Ed Garret seemed to feel the same pride in his work.

"They got a lot of men out there," Fritz said. "Shouldn't take too long to clean it all up."

Garret spit derisively to the side. "Most a those men ain't working. What you see down there is a bunch a Weary Willies who were along for a free ride on the freight cars. That wreck shook 'em up like they been offered work, but they ain't a workin'." Garret rubbed his nose with the back of his hand and looked around as if he were looking for something specific. Gerda figured he wanted some water, but she didn't want to leave until she heard what he had to say about the wreck. He sniffed and went on. "Then there's a bunch of railroad bulls just sitting around watching to make sure nobody makes off with any of that spilled coal until the railroad gets what they're willing to pick up."

"Their leavin's might keep a few local people warm this winter, don't ya think?" Fritz asked, and they both laughed.

"How fast you suppose that engineer was going when that hot box burned through that axle?" Fritz asked.

"From what I heard he was just hitting the taller spots of the rails when the smashup came."

Fritz nodded. "I thought he sounded like he had it going full speed ahead just before it happened."

Gerda finally stepped forward.

"Got any mail for us today, Mr. Garret?"

Garret grabbed at his pocket and turned red in the face. "I almost forgot why I came all the way to the house! You got a telegram, Mr. Vogel. It's from a Mr. Johnnie Hoffman. Something about a change of plans."

He handed the paper to Fritz and then turned to Gerda. "Mind if I step over to the well there and get some water?" He took a cup out of the wagon and held it out for her to see. "I brought my own cup—what with all this sickness in town I'm being careful about everything. You heard about the sickness, haven't ya? Bad stuff that, bad stuff."

Unconcerned about what she thought was old news, Gerda waved him in the direction of the well and stepped closer to Fritz, trying to read the telegram over his shoulder. He was maddeningly slow about unfolding the thin sheet. He held it out at arm's length, the only way he could read it without going in to get his reading glasses. She couldn't read it at that angle, but the look on his face told her it was bad news and she felt a sharp intake of breath. Fritz looked at her and asked, "Are you okay?"

"What does it say?" she whispered urgently, but before he could answer, Ed Garret was back beside them.

"Thank you for the water, Vogels," he said as he climbed slowly back into his wagon. "Nice and cold, just the way I like it. You stay well, folks. Stay clear a town if'n you can. No use risking your health for a little trading." Fritz stepped back and tipped his hat at the man, but Gerda kept her eyes on Fritz. "What does it say?" she asked again.

Fritz tipped his head to the side in sympathy. "Katherine's sick, it says. They won't be getting off the train when they come through." Gerda felt as though something was dropping in her chest. "No," she said. "No." Though she didn't know what she was saying no to.

She took the telegram from Fritz and walked slowly back into the house.

By the time Fritz came in after chores, the kitchen looked as though a whirling dervish had come through the house. Pans and jars and food littered every surface and the room was steamy from cooking.

"What on earth are you doing?" Fritz asked in a voice he must have struggled to keep quiet. "Have you gone mad, woman?"

Gerda continued to rush about the room. "They'll be on the No. 6 tomorrow morning. We can leave right after milking. The children will just have to be late for school one day."

"No," Fritz said. "We won't be meeting that train." Gerda stopped then and the two stared hard at each other across a wide gulf.

"I will meet that train, Fritz Vogel. With or without you."

Fritz's jaw worked back and forth and his fingers clutched into fists. "Gerda Drueke!" he shouted now, not even trying to keep his voice down. "You . . . I . . . No!"

Gerda said nothing. The thunder of Fritz's voice echoed in the room, but she did not speak and she did not turn away. She had the strange sensation that she was standing outside her own body, looking down at the scene. This is what Katherine feels like when she's defying Papa, Gerda thought. For what seemed an eternity neither of them moved. When Fritz finally broke the brittle silence, Gerda knew she had won this battle. "You're so close to the baby time," he said. He spread his hands out as if in supplication. "You're working too hard."

Gerda began slowly stirring the pot of soup on the stove.

"Katherine is sick," Gerda said quietly. "She needs me."

Fritz shook his head and looked out the window toward the south. He shifted his weight from one foot to the other and then back again. He looked at Gerda, out the window again, down at his feet. "I'll get Katie in here to help you with this. Would you just sit down?" He looked up at her with a mixture of love and irritation. Gerda's shoulders softened. She hadn't realized how stiffly she had been holding them.

"Yes," she said. "Send Katie in when she's finished and I'll sit down. For a minute." They didn't smile at each other, but the air in the room no longer sizzled.

"All that coal is going to go to folks who don't have a train to catch," Fritz said as the Vogel wagon rumbled passed the scene of the train wreck the next morning. Gerda didn't rise to his bait. She sat rigidly on the seat beside him, leaning ever so slightly forward as if to propel the entire family a little more quickly toward town. Her conversation since waking that morning had been limited to admonitions of "Hurry! Hurry!"

Fritz wanted to be angry with her. He knew this was a fool's mission, rushing to meet a train that would stop for less than five minutes, as if any good could come from seeing her sister for such a short time. He grew so impatient with her when it came to her family, especially her father. Yes, of course he was her father and as such deserved respect. Fritz believed in the commandment "Honor thy father and thy mother," but there came a point in a man's life, and a woman's too, he supposed, where he let go of his first family and lived with and for the family he had made. What was that Bible verse? He didn't pretend to know the Bible very well, but he'd been going to church long and often enough to have picked up a few verses. The one that came to mind now was the one from his own wedding—something about a man shall leave his mother and cleave to his wife. It was the word *cleave* that stuck in his mind. It didn't seem to mean what he thought it should mean. He thought to ask Gerda about that, but he looked at her out of the corner of his eye and saw the jut of her jaw and remembered he wanted to be angry. He slapped the reins to the horse's rump and settled back in his own thoughts.

Behind them, the children were oddly silent. That meant they knew he and Gerda were fighting. He didn't understand that, their fear when he and Gerda did what all married folks do—disagree once in a while. He thought about his own childhood, about his own father. Fritz spat out the side of the wagon as a bitter memory turned to a bitter taste at the back of his throat.

His father had been a violent man as well as a drinker, and Fritz hadn't learned to get out of his way at the right time until he was old enough to get out of his father's house altogether. His own children didn't know how lucky they were that he didn't drink. He was a reasonable man, easygoing, he believed, and he really couldn't understand the tight, frightened faces of the children on mornings like this. He wanted to shout at them and tell them to behave, but they were behaving, and he knew there was no way to explain what he wanted of them. Something, he wanted something of them, of somebody, but he didn't know what it was. He felt stifled by a hunger that gave him no peace even when he sat down to a meal.

The wagon wheel caught in a rut for a moment then jerked free, the abrupt movement tossing Gerda against his side, and he reached out to steady her. "You all right?" he asked.

"Yes, I'm all right," she snapped.

Fritz looked back at the children and caught Ray watching him. He wanted to shout at the boy to keep his nose out of his parents' business, though he knew the urge was childish. Ray looked away first and Fritz saw him glance at Katie. The children—like all children he supposed—had a coded language, one consisting of sideways glances and shrugs.

He felt accused by the two children somehow, as if they believed he was in the wrong. Not just about this argument about going to meet a train no one would be getting off or on, but about every exchange he'd ever had with Gerda. He sometimes felt that the children saw themselves as Gerda's protectors. As if she needed protecting from him. The thought filled him with a sudden sadness so powerful he wanted to shout, "I am taking care of your mother!" And then he came to the thought he'd tried to avoid, of the draft notice date and how soon his children might be Gerda's only protection.

He was just a little over two weeks away from having to check in for the draft physical. He'd heard some men left for training the next day; some men got extra time to finalize details, to take care of their families. Fritz didn't know how it would work for him. He thought again of the look of hatred in William Owens's face. It chilled him. Aloys Baum had told him, without Fritz having to ask, that he would take over his acres and get them harvested if he had to leave before then.

"And next spring . . . ," Aloys had started to say, though neither man wanted to think that far ahead. Surely the war would be over before that, they both thought, but Fritz wasn't sure about anything anymore. Each time he finished a job, he knew it could be the last time. He'd begun to clean his outbuildings and organize his tools and machinery so that another man could use them. Every action came laden with need to prepare for someone else to do it the next time. He looked back over his shoulder again to look at his sons, the little boys. He hunched his shoulders as if to hide some dangerously soft spot on his chest and pulled his hat down lower.

They were just on the edge of town when they heard the train whistle west of Stuart. Gerda turned to him, a look of terror on her face. "Please, Fritz," she whispered. "Please."

Whatever anger he'd felt toward her that morning slid from him, leaving only a lump in his throat that made it hard to swallow. "We'll get there," he replied. "I promise." He tried to smile at her, but his face felt wooden. "I'll lay down on the tracks if I have to."

The engine was just coming into sight when the Vogels arrived at the depot. The platform was usually crowded with people waiting to get on or to meet someone. The morning train was always the busiest, people leaving for day trips to O'Neill or Atkinson, where there were more merchants. Today, however, the platform seemed strangely deserted, only a few stragglers standing well apart from one another. That flu business had cut into everything, it seemed. Fritz tipped his hat toward a few familiar faces, but Gerda focused on the train. She had insisted on carrying the basket for Katherine, so Fritz merely stood beside her, his hand on the small of her back. Katie held Leo by the hand, while Ray and Frank dashed to the west edge of the platform to watch for the train.

The morning was still and cool. The steam from the engine formed a high, white column against the blue. Gerda had not been on a train since her return trip from her father's house. She clutched the basket tighter and watched as the engine glided past and the passenger cars came alongside the platform. Amid the steamy noise and busy movement as people rushed forward Gerda didn't hear Fritz tell her the wagon-lits, where the sleeping bunks were, were farther down. She rushed toward the conductor, calling out for directions to her sister's sleeping berth. The Red Hat turned his head toward her and said, "You don't get on this train without a ticket."

Then, and here was his mistake, he turned away. Fritz heard him and he stepped forward to plead Gerda's case, but Gerda didn't wait for permission. She turned and looked down the track where she recognized the sleeping car. She walked quickly toward it, her head down, as if by not looking at anyone she would remain invisible. Fritz blocked the conductor's view of her actions.

She set the basket inside the car and grabbed the handrail to pull herself up when a black man in an usher's uniform appeared above her. Gerda looked at him, startled and silent.

"If you'll step back, ma'am, I'll get a stool down for you," he said. Gerda stepped back, keeping her eyes on the man in case the conductor saw her and tried to wave her away. As soon as the usher stepped out of the way, she scrambled onto to the train and picked up her basket. "I'm looking for the Hoffmans' berth," she said to the usher.

The usher looked at her sadly. "That's not good, ma'am. You shouldn't be getting close to that one." He looked at her belly then away as if embarrassed by it. "In your condition, I mean. The Hoffmans is sick. You should just stay away. I'll deliver what you got for 'em if you please."

Gerda's hand shot out and grabbed the man's tie. "I want to see my sister!" she said through gritted teeth. The lonely craving and frenzied activity that had brought her to this train car on this day turned to acid in the center of her chest. "I will bang on every door until I find her."

The usher's eyes widened, and he took off his cap. "Oh no, ma'am. There's no need to do that. The Hoffmans is number three." He stepped back and let her pass.

Katherine's husband, Johnnie, looked up at Gerda without interest when she burst into the room. She saw immediately that he too was coming down with the illness and was too sick to care about propriety. He wore only an undershirt and trousers, the suspenders hanging about his waist.

"You must get off the train and let me help you," Gerda said. The room reeked of sweat and fear and something metallic and familiar from long ago that Gerda couldn't name. She felt the urge to vomit, but she swallowed and said again, "You must let me help you."

"No." Johnnie's voice was stronger than Gerda expected it to be. "My family is waiting for us. We'll be home by nightfall. We've a good doctor there."

"Please, my sister." She pointed at the woman on the bed and felt a wail flaring in her chest. What she saw twisted in the sheets terrified her.

"*Meine Schwester*," Gerda whispered. In the dim light Time folded beneath her. The basket slipped from her hand and she slid to the floor. On her hands and knees she crawled across the universe of the small room. She was decades too late. The woman on the bed was not Katherine. Matted hair twisted across her neck and her face shone white against the pillow like a bleached skull.

"Elizabeth," Gerda whispered into her ear. "My Elizabeth. I am so sorry." She tried to remember the prayer Elizabeth had taught her, but the nightmare held her in its grasp and no sacred words would come to her. Again, she could not save her beloved sister. "*Meine liebe Schwester.*"

Katherine opened her eyes and took a sudden gasp of air. Gerda grabbed her hand and stroked her smooth palm. "Katherine. Oh Katherine. You must stay. You must let me help you." Love and the desire for redemption burned like acid in Gerda's chest. "Please. Please. Please." She laid her head on Katherine's shoulder and closed her eyes. She breathed the prayers of her life into the body of her sister. She tried to save her this time.

Johnnie stood up and reached for a shirt. He began to dress as if to show his authority. "My wife and I are going on to West Point."

Gerda looked up at him. She heard the warning whistle and knew she had to move quickly. "Please, let me help you." She kissed Katherine's feverish forehead. "I'm going to put dry clothes on you, and then I want you to try to drink something. Can you hear me, Katherine?" She began to cough and Gerda held her up so that she could catch her breath. She could hear Katherine's breath struggling through mucus-filled lungs.

When the conductor found her, Gerda was straightening clean sheets around her sister. The man held a cloth to his face when he stepped through the door.

"Leave this train. Now." His voice, though loud, seemed uncertain. Gerda looked up at him, frightened not by his presence or his power over her, but by his apparent fear. When she stood he stepped back to prevent even her skirt from touching him. She brushed her hair from her beloved sister's face. "God be with you, *meine liebe Schwester.*" Without thinking, she gathered up Katherine's sweat-soaked clothes and held them to her chest as she left the train.

How could she know? Isolated as they were on that small farm east of that obscure town, how could any of them know they stood on the brink of a horrible history? Would Gerda have abandoned Katherine to her illness if she had known the strength of this demon flu? Did her actions that day on the train save her sister's life? What turns the tide of an illness so virulent, so malevolent? The Devil, rising from the plains of Kansas in the form of a killer virus unlike any the world had ever seen, had found a way to use the love of a family, of sisters, to spread destruction. Around the world millions would die of it in less than three months. While the world focused on a war in which Man killed Man with horrific abandon, Death slipped behind the battle lines and entered their homes, took their families.

CHAPTER SIXTEEN

Ed Gannoway and his brother, Lark, believed health and disease were physical conditions upon which pleasure and pain, success and failure, depended. Every *individual* gain increased the public gain, each individual loss a public loss. Lark had once told Ed that he felt the very prosperity of a nation was based on the health of its citizens. Health was essential to the accomplishment of every purpose, Lark had claimed, while sickness thwarted the best intentions and the loftiest aims. To become a doctor was not merely to become a part of some grand institution. It was a profession in which the labors were constant, its toils unremitting, and its cares unceasing. As their favorite professor, Dr. Pierce, had once said to them, "The physician is expected to meet the grim monster, break the jaws of death, and pluck the spoils out of his teeth."

They were soldiers in an army whose enemy was death itself. Secretly Gannoway thought of their work not as cures, but as conquests, and he knew his brother felt the same. The two of them had graduated side by side from medical school, and Gannoway could still remember the elation they had shared the day of their commencement when Dr. Pierce stood at the front of the auditorium like an admiral speaking from the deck of a ship to sailors about to go into battle: "Unto us are committed important health trusts, which we hold, not merely in our own behalf, but for the benefit of others. If we discharge the obligations of our trusteeship, we shall enjoy present strength, usefulness, and length of days; but if we fail in our performance, then inefficiency, incapacity, and sickness will follow, the sequel of which is pain and death. Let us then prove worthy of this generous commission."

Is it any wonder then that it was his brother's response to this illness as much as the illness itself that disquieted Gannoway into sleeplessness?

A month after Lark had written the letter in which he first mentioned the odd virus, he sent another letter.

"I can stand to see a few men die, you know that. (*They did not mention their mother's name, but she was always with them.*) But to see twenty and thirty men go, row after row of them gone in hours, it's just too much." Ed had never imagined Lark capable of fear. Sanguinity the very basis of his nature, Lark had never winced in the face of anything. This latest letter could have been written by a stranger, the loops and swirls of his familiar handwriting gone chaotic in his haste. He named his fear and Gannoway knew his younger brother was stretched to the limits of his endurance.

He wanted to go to him, to help him. Or die with him. But Ed was needed here. In Holt County the sickness continued unabated by the methods taken to contain it. The memories of his patients' deaths, more ghastly than any nightmare, would be with him until his own death. With each case he built the wall higher and thicker around his heart and he would not let himself consider them as anything but cases. Not people any longer, *cases*. He kept notes in a leather-bound notebook he carried in his left breast pocket, but he did not reread them. After the first week of what became the pandemic, Gannoway put feeling aside. Only his brother's letters found a way through the wall he had built around him, and then only for as long as the paper was in his hand. He could not afford to stop and consider the depth of this horror; his only hope was to keep moving, to outmaneuver the jaws of death even if he could not break them.

The wind had kicked up after the sun went down and the branches of the lilac bushes and cedar trees along the alley side of his house clicked and rustled like they were getting ready to move on. Gannoway stopped for a moment in the middle of his backyard and looked up at the spilled swath of the Milky Way. Later in the season he'd be able to see the Northern Lights from this spot. Though he'd seen the phenomena hundreds of times, it always felt magical to watch the buckle and sway of lights just above the horizon. Tonight, however, he had business to attend to, so he didn't stop long. He walked down First Street past the barbershop and the grocer's toward the back room of the bank where he knew the village elders were holding their monthly meeting. He hadn't asked to be put on the agenda, but he knew they'd let him speak. They would not like what he had to say, but they were reasonable men, he believed. They could be convinced of the dangers they faced. Gannoway practiced the words he would use as he walked. "Prudence requires that we meet our foes on our own grounds and rid ourselves of the dangers which threaten us." Phrasing it as a battle would aid him not only because of his own attitude toward the practice of medicine as a kind of war, but also because men in these times had war much on their minds. If he could make them feel a necessary part of some greater plan, they would follow. "We must turn all our attention and energy into practical common sense, the kind of sense I know each of you possess in great quantity and of which this community is in dire need."

He had lost two more patients in the last week. He wasn't sure what the death count was countywide, but he knew he was not alone. It was happening all around the country. He wanted the board to close the schools. If they would do that, he was certain the churches would fall in line and cancel services, though some would growl resistance.

"We cannot abandon God when we most need him!" Gannoway could imagine them claiming. Probably William Headrow would be the most vocal. A small man who habitually wore a big coat, Headrow seemed to store irritating mannerisms in his pockets. He would be the one who brought God into the discussion and Gannoway knew he'd have a struggle keeping the rest of the board on task. Since America had entered the war in Europe the previous spring, the war as a subject had consumed the attention of nearly every citizen in this community. In most communities, Gannoway surmised. It had replaced weather as a conversation starter. It had, in a figurative sense, become a weather system of its own, a dark cloud high on the horizon, zigzags of lightning hitting families with draft notices, thunder rumbling of more danger to come.

This new threat of a killing virus so close to home would be hard for them to understand. Either they would panic or they would try to ignore it. Gannoway's job, as he saw it, was to lead them to some middle ground. "We must take the threat seriously." He practiced the words in his head as he hung his coat on a hook by the door. "We need to take effective action against it, to be strong in the face of it." He turned and faced the men seated around the oak table. They looked to him that dark night so vulnerable, so innocent, gathered there in the small windowless room at the back of the bank, and he felt the heavy yoke of responsibility on his shoulders.

He simply wanted to protect the people in his care. He didn't want to wait for the State of Nebraska to lumber into action about this threat; he wanted to do what he could *now*. He knew this virus was passing from person to person, and though he couldn't stop it, he wanted to at least slow it down by keeping people apart. He wanted people to stay home, to hunker down as if behind bunkers. The battle against this virus felt as real to him as the battles being fought in Europe. And as deadly.

"Do you think it's the Germans behind this?" Neil Porter asked when Gannoway finished speaking to the men. Because he sat directly in front of the gas lantern on the wall, Gannoway could only see him in silhouette, but he knew that his eyes would be narrowed, that his opinion was already formed no matter how carefully Gannoway answered. Having lived in this community so many years, he felt he knew the individual quirks of each of its citizens; within his breast he concealed the disclosures of so much suffering.

"I have no evidence of that," Gannoway said carefully. "I have no reason to believe it to be . . ."

"I heard a story about a woman in Boston." Porter started speaking quickly and loudly over the end of Gannoway's sentence. "She says she saw a cloud, like one of those clouds they say drifts over the trenches when them Germans release the gases." Porter had the attention of the men at the table and he knew it. He liked it too. He ran the barbershop on First Street and Gannoway often thought he took up barbering because he liked to have a captive audience. Porter leaned forward in his chair as he spoke, his hands waving the air in front of him, unconsciously miming the motions of cutting hair. "She said it was dark and greasy lookin' and it came in over the harbor there and floated up over the docks." He placed his hands palms down on the table before him and looked around the table at the men seated there. "Next day half the people in Boston were sick. Sick and dying."

The room exploded with voices. The rest of the men put previous business aside and leaned into the new topic.

"My brother-in-law sent me a copy of the paper from out of Philadelphia. Says there on *page one* that the Germans snuck ashore all along the East Coast with vials full of germs and they opened them up in theaters at those Liberty Bond rallies."

"I say it's the German products we're using." Their voices rose and fell like the caw of crows. "The Germans've been getting ready for this war for years. They planted this here. They planted dev-ah-sta-tion among us." Another voice joined in. "Bayer aspirins are deadly. We're poisoning ourselves every time we take one of them there pills." Nods moved like a wave around the table.

"I believe you are all wrong," the man seated beside Gannoway opined plaintively. His voice, higher pitched than the rest, cut into the baritone cacophony and insisted on being heard. Gannoway winced and knew what was coming. "This is a plague brought upon us for our own wicked ways." William Headrow wiped his nose on the back of his hand and then pulled a worn copy of the Bible out of his voluminous coat pocket. "The book of Revelation spells it out clearly: first the world will be struck by war, then famine, and then with the breaking of the fourth seal of the scroll there will be the appearance of a horse, 'deathly pale, and its rider will be called Plaague.'" He drew the word out into a gravelly two syllables and seemed to terrify himself with his assertion. He fell back into his seat and closed his eyes.

Gannoway stared at him a moment. "Gentleman, I beg you. Remain calm, if not for the reason that others count on you to be leaders, then for the reason that I am tired." He placed his palm on his chest. "And I still have hours of work ahead of me before I can go home." He smiled at them woodenly. The skin on his cheeks felt fractured into lines. "Your job this evening is not to find the cause of this latest threat to the safety of our community, but to act in such a way as to protect this community. I repeat, for starters you must close the schools immediately."

At that Philip Larue snorted. "Not necessary." He was one of the few who had remained silent up to this point and Gannoway looked at him, waiting for an explanation.

"We can't mollycoddle these kids. If we let them out, they'll be roaming the streets like Gypsies. There's no way of knowing what trouble they'll find. We can't let these Germans dictate how we'll raise our children."

Gannoway told himself to breathe in twice before answering. He studied the quiver of Larue's jowls and thought about the nature of skin tissue as it ages. A lack of moisture leads to decreased elasticity and then gravity has its way with it. Larue had been a big man throughout most of his life, overeating a hobby it seemed, but poor health in the form of ulcers had put a stop to that. In the last few years he had shrunk to almost half his former size. The skin had yet to adjust to the smaller man it now encased.

"You're inclined to be too easy on young 'uns because you've never had any of your own," Larue continued. "They'd a been soft if you had."

Gannoway resisted the urge to reach across the table and tweak the flesh hanging from the older man's chin.

"Be that as it may," Gannoway said quietly, "the Health Department of the State of Nebraska has encouraged all schools to close down until this illness is controlled."

Neil Howard, seated beside Larue, tentatively raised his hand like a student in school. Howard was a mouse of a man, thin and prematurely gray, who was, not surprisingly, married to a cat of a woman. Nonetheless, the two of them produced children at regular intervals for nearly a decade and provided Gannoway with a large portion of his patient list. Howard waited to be invited to speak even though the meeting had until this point been run as an informal discussion. Gannoway neither liked nor disliked the man and he knew it was lack of sleep that caused him to be irritable and short-tempered. "Speak, Howard," he snapped. Did each man here have to be so damned obtuse?

"Is it really as serious as you're trying to make us believe, Dr. Gannoway? I mean with all due respect, shouldn't we be worrying about educating our young more now—in the face of this war—and not let fear mongers keep us from our task?"

Gannoway placed his fingertips against his eyes. They felt sandblasted by the wind. He knew he must look as bad as he felt, eyes reddened and bags beneath them. He realized he should have shaved before leaving home this evening. He slowly smoothed his hair back off his forehead before continuing.

"Let me review just the local facts. Five of your neighbors have died as a direct result of this virus since I first identified it less than two weeks ago. More than 50 percent of the homes in this county are affected by it. There is not an empty bed in the county hospital. We have two patients in a room where in better times we store brooms and mops. I cannot keep up with the needs of the ones who are sick. Our only hope is to control the spread. The State of Nebraska has issued an alert warning against the congregation of more than five unrelated people in a public space. Unless things change for the better, next week at this time a meeting such as this one will be illegal." He looked around the table at the men seated there. He had their attention and in their eyes he saw their fear. "Gentlemen, you don't have to understand it. You simply have to act. You must close the schools. You must protect the children entrusted to your care."

He wasn't aware of having stood up while talking or even of his voice rising as he spoke, but when he stopped the room echoed his words. The board members looked up at him in shocked silence. Gannoway picked up his hat and turned to leave. He was at the door when he heard Neil Howard say, "All those in favor of following the directive of the State of Nebraska and Dr. Ed Gannoway and closing the schools in the Stuart district until further notice, say aye."

They were quiet in their assent, but they gave it.

"The ayes have it," Howard said, and Gannoway closed the door behind him. He stepped out into the street and looked up at the stars. The first sliver of a new moon hung low in the west. His night was only beginning.

"Surely you don't mean we should cancel church services?" Father Jungels stood between Gannoway and the buggy where the driver, John Kaup, sat waiting. In the week since the village meeting, events had come to pass just as Gannoway had predicted. The state had outlawed all meetings, and still certain members of the community refused to understand. The priest stood in front of Gannoway with his arms crossed and his feet spread wide, his smooth, round face alight with umbrage.

An unarmed guard, Gannoway thought, as he passed his bag from his right hand to his left.

"No," Gannoway said. "We don't mean that."

Jungels tilted his head to the side, perplexed. He obviously hadn't thought it would be this easy. Which, of course, it wasn't. Gannoway continued. "You may continue to conduct the Mass as always. However, no one will be allowed to attend."

Jungels harrumphed and began to speak, but Gannoway held up his hand. "The directive is clear, Father Jungels. The *danger* is clear. The state Board of Health has ordered that all public gatherings both within and without of doors be dispensed with until further notice. Our differences aside, Father, I concur with the decision of the board, but even if I didn't, the facts would still be the facts. This disease is virulent. Immediate and drastic methods must be adopted to combat its spread. I have patients who need me right now, Father Jungels. Good day." Brushing past the priest, Gannoway settled his hat more firmly on his head as if proceeding into a stiff wind. He had no time or energy to fight this particular fight at this particular time.

Father Jungels did not give up so easily, however. He hurried to catch up with the doctor. "Your precious facts, doctor. You are always hiding behind them, scattering them in the path of those who would show you the true way. The soul is a fact despite your refusal to acknowledge it. I too am in the business of saving people. I care about their eternal life, and I will not allow you to force me to abandon my flock at this critical moment. I will not lock the doors of my church. I will not refuse solace to the hungry spirits of those in my care. You cannot, you simply cannot expect me to obey this outrageous directive."

Gannoway had reached the buggy by now, and John Kaup was gathering the reins, one hand on the lever to release the wheel brake as soon as the doctor was settled. He'd been hired to get the doctor from one place to another as quickly as possible and that is what he would do. When the doctor nodded to him, he slapped the reins to the horse's rump and they set off at a brisk walk. The priest hurried alongside, not finished with what he wanted to say. A heavyset man not used to physical exertion, he grew winded quickly. His long black cassock tangling between his legs impeded him even more.

"The Mass is a sacrament, Dr. Gannoway. You are a Catholic at least in name. You know in your heart this order is a sacrilege, a gross irreverence to God!" He was clutching his chest by now and Gannoway didn't have the heart to keep going.

"John," he called. "Pull up."

When the priest caught up with the buggy, he bent over, his hands on his knees, gasping for air.

"Father Jungels." Gannoway's voice felt tight in his throat, his desire to avoid this conflict throttling his anger. "Imagine, if you will, that we are a nation at war." John Kaup, whose brother had shipped out to France with the AEF just a few months back, looked over his shoulder at the doctor. "Imagine an enemy so strong, so devious, that it was capable of destroying each and every one of us in this town, in this entire country. Imagine it not as an army, but as a silent killer, invisible to the naked eye but nonetheless observable. Imagine it using our own way of life, our desire to congregate, to be together in our hours of need, as the method of its destruction. Imagine it clinging to the skirts of mothers, slipping from one to the next, depositing poisonous germs into the lungs of children." Gannoway was shouting, though he had told himself he wouldn't. "Imagine this, Father Jungels! And then remember that basic tenet that even I understand: the sacrament of Mass does not need the presence of parishioners to remain holy!" The priest's face had gone white, and for the first time Gannoway thought about how young the man was, the boy inside him suddenly evident in the soft contours of his face. Gannoway peered down at him from his seat in the buggy and saw that Jungels was afraid, terrified really. He felt his anger soften.

"At this time, there is nothing stopping you from visiting your flock, one on one, as I do," Gannoway went on in a softer voice. "They need you."

Jungels straightened his back, his big hands hanging uselessly to his sides. Gannoway tipped his hat and nodded to his driver to go. As the horse started off, he called out to the priest. "Wear a kerchief on your face when you enter a sick house. I beg you."

Jungels stood watching the buggy until the road dust behind it had settled again.

CHAPTER SEVENTEEN

Fritz moved through his days as though swimming through murky water. Most days were cloudy, the sun never seeming to rise before twilight set in, and then the darkness of moonless nights felt thick and dangerous outside the reach of their small lamps. He had divided his fields between Dan Liable and Aloys Baum. Between that and his military pay, his family might not starve. The bank was still considering what to do about his land payments. ("We like to help our soldiers, Mr. Vogel. Are you a citizen as well?") Aloys's grandson—just a few years older than his own sons, Fritz thought with a shiver—would move in with Gerda and the children. Between him and Gerda and the three oldest Vogel kids, they'd be able to keep the milk chores done on time. Gerda already took care of the chickens, and what she couldn't do there Katie was old enough to learn. It was time Ray put aside some of his young foolishness too. He was big for six, and he could be a big help to his mom. Though Frank was the older of the two boys, he took too much reining in to get a job done well without supervision. Ray seemed to have been born with an old soul, a man inside a boy's body.

Fritz took Ray with him into the fields. He showed him how to get the horse to lift its foot so that he could scrape clean the iron shoe. He pointed out the delicate frog in the hoof that needed to stay healthy and be cleaned carefully. Ray leaned over the horse's hoof and looked closely at what his father showed him. When he reached out to touch the leathery pillow in the horse's hoof , Fritz saw that the boy's hand was smaller than the horse's foot, and he felt for a moment as if he would begin to cry. He let the horse put its foot down and took the boy around to the other leg where the scar tissue on the horse's haunch was still raw and shiny. He told him to keep an eye on that spot and if it changed he was to get Aloys over to take a look at it right away.

"Don't let it fester, you hear?" he said to the boy, and his voice even to his own ears came out sounding gruff and angry. Ray's eyes, so alight with curiosity, darkened and his round face settled into a mask. Fritz wanted to grab the boy and shake him. "I'm going away!" he wanted to shout. "You have to take care of your mother and the family!" He turned away quickly so the boy could not see the rims of his eyes redden.

He took him to where the harnesses hung. He showed him the stool he had made that Ray could take with him throughout the barn to get at the things he needed that were out of reach. He reminded him that the stool needed to have all four legs on even ground or it would tip over. "You have to be careful when you're working," he said. "Your mom don't need to be worrying about you."

"Just about you?" Ray asked. Fritz spun toward him and the boy ducked, but Fritz wasn't swinging, he was reaching. He grabbed the boy so tight to his chest so quickly they both went down onto a pile of straw, and though Ray struggled to get away, Fritz wouldn't let go. He held his son there with his head tight against his chest until the boy stopped kicking and the two of them lay in the gloaming of that early October evening, crying together, each refusing to let the other see his tears.

The corn was in, the rye too. Harvest almost completed. Just the potatoes waited. A root crop, the vines were little more than brown tangles along the rows now and could handle the cold nights.

"I'll start digging potatoes in the morning," Fritz told Gerda. "I'll be done by the end of the week."

This was how they spoke to one another now. About what they did that day, what they would do the next, as if time stretched only so far in either direction and they no longer had a real past or a true future.

Gerda let her hair down at night, pulled the pins out so that her dark hair dropped, a thick rope down the center of her back. Before sleep, Fritz reached out and wrapped it around his wrist, a tether that would hold him to her through the night.

Sorrow and fear took on a physical presence and came to live on the Vogel farm that fall. Every room of the house knew its shape and it lurked in the recesses of the barn. It moved like a shadow from tree to tree in the orchard. After the schools closed, the children stayed home and worked alongside their parents, oddly silent, as if the massive, invisible weight of it held them all in some kind of stasis. The family seemed to have found itself stranded in a strange and unpeopled country.

When the Baums stopped over to visit, the Vogels felt as if their voices were trapped somewhere deep inside their bodies and they had nothing to say to their neighbors and friends. When Aloys relayed news from town, Fritz and Gerda nodded silently in unison. He could have been telling them about some native tribe from far away.

"Everything is shut down," Aloys said. "It's like a ghost town." Unconsciously each of the adults looked around as if the mention of ghosts had reminded them of something they didn't yet know or didn't want to remember.

"I saw Charles Burke carried off the train when I passed the depot," Aloys went on. "He got sick down in Fort Riley and they sent him home."

"To die?" Margaret asked. She put her hand quickly over her mouth as if to try to catch the question, to ward off the evil it implied. Gerda looked at her friend's face, noticed the heaviness of the bags under her eyes and deep downturn of her lips. Slowly what they had been saying began to make a new kind of sense to her. The danger that Aloys was telling about was not the war. She realized with a start that another monster had invaded their lives. She had thought only of Fritz's departure; this illness had just been gossip, a story Aloys liked to tell.

"What is it?" Gerda asked. "What is this sickness he's dying of?"

Aloys and Margaret both rose to her curiosity and told her about this virus—about the German plot to destroy America. It made no sense to her.

"But Germans can get it too, can't they?" She thought of her sister, Katherine, who was still recovering under the care of her husband's mother. "They're dying too, right?"

"It's all conspiracy malarkey, if you ask me," Aloys said. "I'm just telling you what I heard."

"It's bad, whatever it is," Margaret added. "You stay away from town until it blows over, Fritz. Don't be bringing this back to Gerda."

"They say they're going to be closing down the army camps soon if it don't let up," Aloys said. "That Burke boy might a been one of the last they let go home with it, from what the doctor was saying."

Fritz and Gerda walked with them back to the wagon and watched as the old couple climbed slowly back into their buggy. Margaret called out to her, "You send one of the older kids over to get me when it's baby time, right? I'll call the doctor and the priest before I come."

The Vogels waved goodbye. Gerda turned and looked toward the west where the sky blushed a deep pink. She took a deep breath of the cooling evening air and felt a sharp ache across her chest. She dismissed it as nothing and went inside to ready supper before going out to help with milking. Fritz, she noticed, seemed lost for a moment. He walked first toward the machine shed, then stopped, changed direction, and headed toward the milk barn. She wanted to go to him, to feel his arms around her, but she felt so tired, so filled with strange aches. Work to do, no time for anything else.

CHAPTER EIGHTEEN

Sometimes she felt as if the air in this room was a whirling eddy and she was caught in the middle of it. She didn't walk from stove to counter to table, but was spun by forces she couldn't see and couldn't stop. Swept toward the stove, she checks the level of cobs in the burner, settles the roast on the shelf above the low flames, and closes the oven door just before the force whirls her to the counter where her hands measure flour into a crock bowl. She mixes it with water, kneads it into dough, then pivots to the cupboard where, without thinking and without looking, she pulls out a stack of plates and sets them on the table. She does this because she's been turned to the stove. She does that because she's been spun to the counter. The dough now rising on the table behind her hammers its own heartbeat—or is it hers? No matter, time to cook, time to wash, to iron, to set dishes onto table, to ladle food onto plates, to spin toward the water pump to start all over again. Sometimes when the sun sinks out of sight she feels not so much tired as dizzy. This kitchen, these children, that man, a kaleidoscope of pale colors she can't separate one from the other.

She didn't think it would be this way. Her father told her not to marry this man, this *arme Teufel*. Said they'd come to no good if she followed the poor devil here. Her father gave his sons farms. One hundred and sixty acres to each of them to keep them near him, and keep them wealthy. His daughters he bought off, gave them cash, but he didn't realize that once the cash was in their hands in this new country, they could buy what they wanted, they could make their own choices. Gerda bought machinery; she bought cattle; she chose her *arme Teufel*. What her father meant she can't imagine anymore. What "no good" would they come to here on this farm with work and each other their only companions?

Fifteen years after her sister Elizabeth died, Gerda met Fritz Vogel. When he asked her to go walking after Mass one bright, crisp morning, she said yes without hesitation, though she knew her father would not approve. A body is not meant to be alone. Fritz's family sat on the opposite side of the aisle in St. Michael's from her father's family. The Vogels still spoke German to each other and fumbled over English phrases that came easily to her father, a second-generation American. But it wasn't words Gerda was wanting then. Words filled the air in her father's house, brags made and everything named, but nothing ever seemed to be said.

Fritz and Gerda had walked on the path that led to the cemetery, walking into the morning to get away from the crowd outside the church. When they got to the cemetery gate, Fritz took her hand in his without speaking. Her hand looked so small against his. For a moment, she felt like a little girl again, like the one she had been before she lay on the wood floor beneath her sister's deathbed. They didn't talk that first morning. But oh, her hand in his, just the memory of it makes her weak even now. She felt healed of an illness she didn't know she had, and she didn't look back when her father called her name.

And now she is here, spinning in this kitchen, her footsteps furring a path on the wood between stove and counter and table and pump. If she closed her eyes she could be her mother, or her dear Elizabeth. Of what was her father afraid? What did her rebellion bring her?

The first cramp took her after dinner when she bent to pick up the kettle of water for washing. She knew what it was, it was her fifth baby after all, but still it surprised her with its strangeness. She knew of no other pain like it. It started oddly on the surface, as if the skin of her belly was shifting to accommodate what was coming. Then the muscles tightened, starting at her back and moving around her torso like finger-spread hands, squeezing, squeezing.

Fritz and the children clustered about the door, pulling on coats and boots. Picking potatoes out of the sandy soil was a job simple enough even for the six-year-old Ray, but Gerda knew Leo would take more watching than Fritz liked to give this late in the season. It was his way of helping her. He knew her time was short and he always grew gruff and endearing at this stage. Today, however, she wanted—what? What did she want? She felt restless and caged. She wanted to not feel this pain. Since last evening, just after the Baums had left, she'd begun to feel the movement of each joint as if bone moved against bone. Her skin hurt to touch. Even her eyes moved grittily in the sockets. Today her chest ached with each breath and she knew the heat in her face came from inside, not from the stove she bent over.

"I will not be sick," she had told herself as she ladled stew into bowls and set them before her family. She believed it was just worry she had picked up from the Baums' stories. She didn't think about her visit with Katherine on the train, she just kept her mind on the work.

When Fritz and the children left for the fields after dinner, Gerda cleared the table, one hand pressed to her belly. The cramp kept her bent over for its duration, but when it released she stood and continued working. She warmed yeast in the bread bowl and set it aside while she finished separating the milk into cream and storing it in the well house to keep cool. The second cramp was a long time coming and she knew it would be a hard night. She lost her sense of time, wrapped up inside her own skin, and she worked without thoughts. The lowing of impatient cattle reminded her it was time to milk. She pulled her big wool coat on before she went outside, even though she felt so warm that perspiration caused her dress to cling to her back.

She walked to the barn seeing only a few steps in front of her. The cows, when she opened the door, jostled their way into their regular spots. She started with Bess, the youngest cow, not because she bawled the loudest, but because she was closest and Gerda didn't want to move any farther than she had to. She pulled the stool close to the big cow, leaned her head against its warm hide and grasped the teats. Her knuckles hurt with the effort and the cow stomped her foot with impatience, kicking the pail over. Gerda set it upright and tried again. Breathing hurt. She started to cry.

Fritz looked up from the row he was walking to see Aloys hurrying across the field toward him. The old man stumbled across the potato hills, his thin frame looking fragile out in the open like this. He was waving a newspaper and Fritz felt his heart drop. No good news could come of this, he thought. He told the kids to keep working and he walked toward Aloys. His head had been aching all afternoon and now as he walked he noticed an ache in his chest as he breathed. He counted out the days he had left before his physical and calculated the work still to be done. He would not be sick.

"Fritz!" Aloys called out as he got closer, as if he had to get his attention. Fritz swallowed his irritation and waved a hand. He was not a patient man by nature, and illness, acknowledged or not, made him even shorter-tempered. A frown creased his forehead by the time the two men met. The weather was turning colder and a breeze had picked up from the north since morning. It caught Fritz's cap and he spun to catch it before it got away. Aloys moved faster and caught it by stepping on it. He picked it up and slapped it against his leg twice to dislodge the sand his shoe had deposited on its brim.

"I told you it was going to happen!" Aloys said excitedly. "Yesterday I said it!" He shook the paper out in front of him, but didn't show Fritz which article he meant.

"You told me what, Aloys? I can't make sense of what you're saying." Fritz resisted the urge to just walk away. If it was just more gossip Aloys was sharing, he wanted no part of it. He had work to do.

"The camps!" Aloys cried. "They've shut down the camps! That flu has brought the army to a standstill!"

"What?" Fritz asked, disbelieving. "What does this mean?"

Aloys finally stopped shaking the paper in the air and held it still to point out the article on the front page of the Omaha paper. "Provost Marshal General of the U.S. Army Cancels Draft Call," the headline read. "142,000 men asked to stand down as camps declared under quarantine." Fritz couldn't read any more of the article without his reading glasses, but even with them his eyesight would have been blurred. He looked away from Aloys and wiped his eyes with the back of his hands and watched his children continue to work. Katie kept Leo beside her, holding out her basket for him to drop potatoes into. Ray worked ahead of them, driven it seemed to do more, do faster, do everything that needed to be done. The ache in Fritz's chest threatened to choke him and he began to cough, a dry and painful cough. "That's good news, Aloys," he said after he caught his breath. "But it won't get my potatoes out of the ground." Fritz went back to work and only after Aloys had walked back to his own land did Fritz think to say thank you. He imagined telling Gerda, though what words he would use wouldn't form in his mind. He just kept imagining her face when she heard.

The horses knew the path back to the barn and Fritz let them have their head. The wagon was so full there was no room for the children to ride, so he stayed to walk back with them. They were so silent, all of them, even their footsteps in the dried grass along the path seemed muted. The wind was the only noise, high and mournful. It rattled the trees and rustled the grass. When they got closer to the farmyard, Fritz looked up to see the horses standing patiently beside the barn. The pen beside the barn was empty, telling him the cows were in the barn waiting to be milked. It gave him a small pleasure to know that his animals followed familiar patterns and made his life easier. He almost didn't see Gerda before he moved toward the horses to lead them around to where he could unload the wagon. She was slumped against the doorjamb, half in, half out of shadow. Her nose was bleeding.

Fritz had never felt such horror. For a moment, he felt paralyzed and mute. His mouth hung agape and he reached his hand out toward her, but felt trapped in a nightmare where he couldn't move and no sound would come. "Ma?" Ray called out, and the sound of his son's voice released him. He rushed toward Gerda and dropped to his knees beside her.

"Fritz," she whispered. "I'm sorry. I tried to finish the milking, but I'm so tired. I can't carry the buckets." She wiped her nose with the back of hand but didn't seem to know it was blood that she wiped away. "I'm so tired, Fritz. So tired." She leaned her head against him. "Please don't leave me."

"I won't. I promise," Fritz said. He wanted to tell her something, but he couldn't remember what it was. He lifted her up from the ground and half carried her to the house. The three older children stood watching them walk away, Leo leaning against Katie's legs. A certain slant of light cast them in amber it seemed, as if they would always be there, waiting for the next thing.

CHAPTER NINETEEN

The morning began with the moon at the window and the shrill double ring of the telephone at the end of the hall. Ed Gannoway found himself awake at the head of the stairs not knowing what to do about the moon or the urgent ringing, and when his wife brushed by him to descend the stairs, he, for one stark and terrifying moment, didn't know who or what she was. Her white gown billowed and her hair, loose from its customary chignon, fanned out across her back, wisps of it rising like wings. Soundless and quick, she could have been a ghost. The silver light coming through the window turned the room around him—this familiar room, *his* room—into something insubstantial and otherworldly.

Where am I? He placed his palm on the wall. The plaster felt slick and cool to the touch. He slid his hand down to the wainscoting he himself had nailed into place years ago. His finger found the head of one square nail, then another a few inches over.

Here, he remembered, *now*, and he knew what the phone call would be. The *who* didn't really matter anymore. He ran his hand across his face, the rough stubble on his cheek tickling a scar on his thumb. He let his hand rest on his throat where he could feel the steady drumbeat of his heart in the carotid artery. He closed his eyes and pictured the dead first, then the dying, and finally the pale and fearful survivors. His hands held the acrid smell of poultice he'd packed on a young soldier's chest just hours ago. The man's fever so high the heat had risen from the bed as from a fire. His chest had rattled with each breath and when he tried to cough, he cried out in a pain that was beyond comfort and reason. Like the other victims, the man had retreated into himself, had become the illness that affected him, aware of nothing but his own pain and suffering. "Charles?" Gannoway had called to him. "Charles Burke? Can you hear me?" The young man's hollow eyes stared at the doctor unseeing. Only the heat of his body and the rattle in his chest showed him to be a living thing. The young woman entrusted with caring for him was nearly gone herself, her face as pale as that of the figure on the bed, and Gannoway knew it was only a matter of time before she too succumbed to the illness.

"Change this poultice in two hours," Gannoway had told her softly, his face close to hers to ensure that she heard him. "Try to make him drink some water. If he doesn't swallow, swab his mouth with wet cloth." He made the motions of how to do it as if he were talking to a foreigner who didn't know the language. "Do you understand?" he asked. The young woman looked at him pale with fear. Strands of her blond hair had come loose from the barrettes that held them and hung limply in her face. Her eyes glistened black like marbles in the dim light. After a long silence she nodded, but as he turned to go, her hand darted out and she grasped the doctor's arm, her fingernails like small thorns digging into his wrist.

"Is he going to die?" she whispered.

The doctor looked at the man on the bed. He didn't see the telltale blueness of cyanosis, but experience had taught him that final stage could come suddenly and the man could be gone within hours, or he could win this battle against death and wake on the morrow. Gannoway was no longer sure of anything.

"I don't know," he said quietly.

"He's only twenty-five," she hissed. "We're going to be married."

He gently pried her hand free and said he would come back again. "I have to go now." There are others sick, he wanted to tell her, but he knew she wouldn't hear him. Her world, made smaller by this man's illness, was now limited to this one room, this one man's labored breathing. The glass in the framed pictures along the wall reflected flickering firelight, and darkness, like the needs of others, pressed against the windows.

It could be them calling, Gannoway thought, or their neighbor, or their neighbor's neighbor. Town or country, rich or poor, patriot or foreigner, no one was immune.

The Devil, some were calling it, and that seemed as likely a name as any other, though influenza was the accepted title. However, it was influenza unlike any Gannoway had seen in his lifetime. Perhaps unlike any that had ever been seen. It was vicious and virulent, almost evil in nature. Influenza and pneumonia, as a rule, take the old and the weak. It's a fact of human biology, of all biology, that the young and healthy withstand harsher punishment. The strongest should be the survivors. The nature of evolution demands this. If it weren't true, a species would die before it could develop into complexity. And the human species was highly developed and complex—Gannoway found himself arguing these points with some nameless dark shape that lingered just outside his peripheral vision as he waited for his wife to get off the phone. This flu, this Devil, made no sense. It came too hard and hit too fast and most of all took the wrong people. The country—the whole world—was losing young and healthy men at a phenomenal and terrifying pace. First it was war, he thought, and now this.

Oh yes, he remembered where he was. He turned back to his room to dress, his night's sleep over. He lit the lamp on the dresser and splashed cold water into the basin on the stand. Some sloshed out and he reached without looking for a towel to wipe it up, but his hand found paper, not cloth. He forgot about the water and walked closer to the light to look at what was in his hand, though he knew without aid of the lamp exactly what he would find. He reread the letter his brother had sent along with Charles Burke just two days before. Lark had known quarantine was coming, and he sent one last missive to his brother. Gannoway had always admired Lark's scientific eye and clear prose. This most recent letter, however, read as if a stranger had written it.

"More than 5,000 sick here. We got them lined up on cots in the barracks, bodies stacked in the stable. It's hitting the nurses, especially the new ones, pretty hard. Sixteen dead last count. That's nurses, I mean. Lost count of the number of patients dead. Hundreds. Can't bury them because the undertaker is unable to acquire coffins quickly enough. I cannot describe the horror around me, Ed. I want to ask for your help, you're a good man and a good doctor. So much sickness here. We're beyond help. We're going under quarantine before nightfall and this letter may not reach you. Have you heard? The last group of recruits called up is being asked to stand down. They need them desperately in Europe, but the men are dying by the hundreds every day in every camp in the country. Remember when we used to wonder about the nature of heaven and hell? You said you didn't believe in anything that couldn't be proven. I think I've found your proof if you'll take my witness as such. It seems the prairies have become some lesser region of Hell, and the Devil is a virus we can't stop. Having met the Devil, I now await God."

Gannoway looked out the window where the Sandhills rolled westward under the dark sky. He had grown up out that way, in Cherry County where his father had homesteaded and built a ranch big enough to get at least two of his sons out of the country and into something where, as the old man liked to say, "the work wouldn't kill them and the pay, if they're good at it, wouldn't starve them."

He'd led a good life in the years since then, he thought. He'd brought babies into the world, set bones, lanced abscesses, cut out some cancers and let others win when he couldn't catch them in time. His study of physiological anatomy taught him that every organ, every *cell,* had a function to perform and by studying the functions he could know Life. The mysteries of living stemmed from a lack of man's vision and understanding. He believed if he could just see a little clearer he would understand everything.He kneaded his brow ridge and temple with the tips of his fingers and looked at the letter in his other hand. He realized again that the beliefs he had held all his life simply were not true. Before this illness, there was the war, and the war lingered even as the men fighting it died before reaching the battlefields. The force that had sucked America into that gruesome conflict across the Atlantic showed no sign of letting up, and now this illness was attacking the home front. No cause, no cause, Gannoway thought, could sanctify the wanton bloodletting of modern warfare and no explanation could steady the world now hit by this Devil Flu.

He put the letter down and turned to listen to his wife's voice at the end of the stairs. There was fatigue in her voice, irritation, and fear.

"I'll let him know," she said.

"Yes, he'll be there.

"Soon.

"Soon, that's all I can say."

The earpiece clicked softly back into place and then the stairs squeaked beneath her step.

"The Burkes?" he asked when she came into their bedroom.

"The Vogel family," she replied.

At the mention of the name he felt unbalanced, as if in crossing a stream he had placed his foot on an unsteady rock. The *who* didn't matter anymore, he reminded himself.

"Is it Gerda?" he asked, then cleared his throat before adding, "Mrs. Vogel?"

His wife pulled a pair of pants from the press and handed them to him.

"It's all of them, as near as I can tell," she said. "It was a neighbor who called. They're all sick. And Mrs. Vogel's in labor." She stood neither facing him nor turning away and wrapped her arms around her own shoulders as if warding off a chill. The curve of her spine held the sorrow of years. "You should hurry," she said softly.

A brisk wind carrying the bright smell of sleet rattled the tree branches, and the moon that had woken him was covered with clouds by the time John Kaup brought the buggy around. Ed climbed up into the seat and stared into the darkness outside the lamp's circle of light.

Death, he thought. I am moving toward death. He tried to shake the chill the image brought with it as he signaled John to proceed, but as the man slapped the reins across the horses' rumps and they jumped forward, Gannoway couldn't dispel the feeling that they were moving not eastward in the direction of the Vogels' farm, but in a direction uncharted altogether, into the morning of a world about to change.

The call had come from the Baum house, not the Vogels'. The switchboard operator couldn't quite make sense of what Mr. Baum was saying, his German accent was so thick and garbled. ("Why can't these people learn to speak proper English?" Lucy Miles thought.) She understood him to say his wife was in labor.

"That can't be, Mr. Baum," Lucy said slowly and loudly. "Your wife is sixty years old if she's a day." At twenty-five, Lucy believed she knew more about life than anybody she spoke with on any given day. She rolled her eyes as she listened to Mr. Baum start in again.

"*Nein*," Mr. Baum said patiently, thickly. "*Nein. Nein.*" Lucy wondered why he wanted her to ring up 99—Dr. Gannoway's house number was 47 and Dr. MacGewan's number was 27. She knew all the switchboard numbers by heart.

"It's Mrs. Vogel," Mr. Baum went on, though he pronounced the name "Fokel," the word so far back in his throat he almost swallowed it. "She's go to have baby. She needs a doctor. She's sick. Sick. The whole family sick. Flu."

The dreaded word finally seeped through what Lucy thought she was hearing. "Mrs. Vogel is going to have a baby or she has the flu?" she said slowly.

"*Ja*," Mr. Baum said with relief. "*Ja.*"

Lucy hit the switch to ring the doctor. "Let him work it out," she muttered. "I don't have time for these people."

Miranda Gannoway had taken the call. The sun not yet up, she wanted Ed to have the rest he needed, though the sound of the phone woke him. He was so tired, though, he had stood at the top of the steps staring down into the darkness where the phone rang as if it were some kind of monster coming for him. She could not protect him from anything.

"Soon," she had said to Mr. Baum. "He'll be there soon."

She placed the earpiece back in the cradle softly and turned toward the stairs. Darkness pressed against the window on the landing, her reflection shadowy beside the lantern. "Sleep," she whispered, but the floor creaked above her and she knew he was off again. His drive, which she so admired, would be the death of him, she always told him. But not yet, she prayed that morning, not yet.

His face appeared at the top of the steps, ghostly white.

"The Burkes?" he had asked.

"The Vogel family," she replied.

In the darkness she hadn't seen his expression, but she saw his hand clutch the rail, noticed how quickly he turned and readied himself to go. She stood at the window a long time after his buggy rolled out of sight, her posture one of resignation and despair.

An owl rose up from the south ditch at the corner of the Vogel quarter section with a mouse dangling from its claws. It flew low across the road and startled the team and John Kaup too. It stayed low as it crossed the potato patch on the backside of the shelterbelt. John watched its ponderous flight and noticed the undisturbed potato hills. Nearly half the patch was unharvested. The season was getting on and Fritz Vogel was late with his labors, John noted. He tapped reins to the horses' rumps to hurry them toward the house at the end of the lane. He noticed for the first time that Doc Gannoway, beside him on the seat, was sitting upright, his bag clutched in his lap, eyes wide open.

"You all right, Doc?" he asked.

Gannoway looked at him. In the pale light cast by their lantern his face appeared tight and dark. For the first time since he'd taken the job, John saw what looked like fear in the doctor's eyes. "You sick?" he asked quietly.

Gannoway shook his head. "No." Then he seemed to force himself to relax his shoulders. "She's pregnant, you know." He nodded toward the Vogel house. He didn't have to say more. They both knew the pregnant ones didn't survive this particular virus. John looked again at the house and imagined the two dead they would soon see, mother and baby, and he made the sign of the cross. He pulled the team up close to the house and sat waiting for the doctor to make his move. A breeze sent the rancid smell of skunk their way, but it was too light and too far away to be of concern here now. Watery predawn light silhouetted the trees and their shapes reminded him of soldiers. His brother was somewhere between here and France, he didn't know where, and he picked out one of the smaller trees, skinny as a boy, and hoped his brother was okay.

"The courage my mother had she took with her to her grave," Gannoway said quietly. He sat still as stone beside John. A rooster crowed off in the distance, its call muted beneath the whisper and sway of the windblown trees around them. A couple of other birds whistled—John could never keep straight which call came from which bird—and as the air grew lighter around them, the noise from wild things seemed to grow. John looked over at the doctor and waited for him to go on speaking, or get out and get moving. The restless energy that the good doctor wore like a familiar coat had disappeared. He seemed to have given up somehow.

"Did you need something, Doctor?" John asked gently.

Gannoway looked at him. "No. Nothing. I mean, just . . ." He clutched his bag in his left hand and moved to get out, placing one foot on the step. He stopped and turned awkwardly back to his driver. "Thank you, John. I . . ." He looked toward the house. "I don't think I've made myself clear to you. How grateful I am for getting me here." He cleared his throat, "For getting me everywhere I need to go."

John shifted the reins in his hands. Such talk made him nervous. This is what men do: they do the work that needs doing. They don't talk about it. They do it. John lifted his hat up and set it down again. He looked at the doctor out of the corner of his eye. He could see the doctor still looking at him, his right foot on the step, his left still on the floor of the buggy. He was clearly waiting for some response.

"Can I carry your bag in for you, Doc?" His voice came out louder than he'd meant it to. "You just wait here a minute while I tie up the team and I'll carry your supplies in for you." John wrapped the reins around the bar and pulled the brake lever in quick practiced motions.

"No," Gannoway said. He put his hand up to stop him. "I don't need help. I just wanted you to know." He stepped down lightly and turned toward the house. "You rest up while you can," he said over his shoulder. "Today will be a hard day."

The house ahead of him was two-story white clapboard with black trim and shutters. The shutters were the decorative kind, nothing that could be closed against inclement weather, and they always struck him as incongruous with the rest of the farm, where everything had a purpose. Even the bulk of the flowers Gerda planted each spring were marigolds, placed strategically at the edge of the vegetable garden to help keep the insects at bay, or spreaders that needed little in terms of water or care. Though there was beauty in the farm's utilitarian nature, nothing was wasted or frivolous. Gannoway wondered who had selected the shutters. Fritz or Gerda?

The kitchen window glowed with lamplight and the back bedroom window showed a flicker of light, but the rest of the house seemed dark. The only light upstairs came from the moon shining through one window and out the other. Inside, Gannoway knew, would be one man, one woman, four children. The phone call from the neighbor had said the Vogels were sick. "They're all sick," Mr. Baum had said. "And Mrs. Vogel, she be with child, you know." His German accent grew thicker in his haste and fear caused him to shout. Gannoway had heard the conversation even from the distance. "My wife say she have her time soon."

As Gannoway remembered Baum's words, Gerda's face came to mind. He could see her eyes, brown and kind, and beautiful, and the flutter of fear in his stomach threatened to send his breakfast back up. He stood with his hand raised to knock on the door, but suddenly he froze and felt a tightening around his neck. For a moment it felt as though snakes were about to choke him. He knew it was movement that would save him: rush forward, don't stop, pluck the spoils from death's jaws, but the weight of so many sorrows held him in place. "We are soldiers in an army whose enemy is death," he heard his brother say. He knocked on the door, and didn't wait for an answer.

There were boots and coats piled on the floor beside the door. A kerosene lamp on the wall spread a thin light throughout the kitchen and Gannoway made out the thin figure of a woman kneeling beside the wood box near the back of the stove.

"Gerda?" he asked, surprised to see her out of bed, but the woman who turned toward him was not Gerda. He recognized Margaret Baum. The old woman didn't rise to greet him, but instead pointed toward the wood box.

"I can't get him to come out," Margaret said. "He's burning up, but when I try to reach him, he just screams and holds tight to the far edge of the box." Gannoway walked closer and peered into the shadowy box. He could just make out the form of a small boy. "Which one is it?" he asked.

"Ray," she said. "The middle one. He's afraid to go to his bed, because he says that's where people get the sickness and he's afraid he'll die. I tried to tell him that weren't true, but he won't listen to me."

The old woman stood up stiffly. "They're all sick, Dr. Gannoway, not just him."

"Gerda?"

She nodded. "Water ain't broke yet, but she's ready to push."

"Go to her, I'll be in when I've settled the children." He knew Gerda well enough to know that the children would need to be cared for first before she'd consent to his ministrations. He took the blanket Margaret had been kneeling on and leaned in to cover the boy. He felt the boy's forehead and spoke softly to him the way he would a wild animal. The boy whimpered and brushed the doctor's hand away weakly, but the doctor leaned in and scooped him up before he had a chance to grab the side of the box. His small body shivered like a struck tuning fork. He twisted weakly, trying to get away, but he was too sick. The effort started a coughing fit and by the time he caught his breath the doctor had him in bed beside his brother. Both boys tossed fitfully but didn't try to get up. Gannoway picked up Katie from the floor beside them and settled her into her own bed across the hall. The youngest boy, still in a high-sided crib, tossed and moaned as if having a bad dream.

Gannoway gave each of the older ones pills to swallow, mashed the aspirin into honey for the youngest, and got them each to drink a little water. The oldest boy was the hardest to help. Delirious with fever, he kept spitting the tablets back out. "*Schmeckt wie feuer!*" he would cry.

Gannoway's understanding of the German language was limited. "No, not fire," he replied. "This will put out the fire." Finally he sat down beside the boy on the bed and tipped his head back across his lap. "These will make you better," he whispered. "No more fire." The boy was too weak to fight for long and Gannoway too practiced at handling resistant patients. The boy's eyes burned both with hatred and fever, but he swallowed the pills at last.

The silence from Gerda's room disconcerted him. Years of delivering babies had taught him that he could not anticipate how any woman would react to labor pains. Some of the most refined women he knew turned into cursing banshees, and women typically loud and brash in everyday life settled into a birthing process as if they'd been rendered mute.

Gerda had never been completely silent in the birthing room, but never loud, either. What he'd always loved about attending her was the way her inhibitions slipped away and her sense of humor came out to play. She called him "Doc" when she was in labor, the only time and the only person from whom the nickname felt welcome to him. She became loose and talkative, telling him funny stories about her children and Fritz. "Shh!" she would say to him before she started each story, "don't tell anyone this story." She seemed intoxicated by the process of bringing the baby into the world. When the cramps were at the worst, she would go silent, biting down on a pillow to keep from screaming, though she wasn't afraid to grunt when she felt the drive to push.

"Ah, Doc," she would say to him when she caught her breath. "How can you stand to look at a woman with love in your eyes after you've seen something like this?"

"It's because I've seen something like this," he would answer.

As soon as the birth was over and she was stitched back together, her reserve would return—even something as simple as the mention of the word *breast* could make her blush like a maiden.

He had heard Fritz coughing off and on since he'd arrived, but nothing from Gerda, and he wasn't sure what he'd find when he went in. If her skin had begun to turn blue, indicating cyanosis, he knew she had no chance of surviving, and he would need to make the decision to take the baby quickly if it were to survive, if it was still alive even now.

He was glad Fritz was too sick to ask him any questions when he helped him from the room where Gerda lay. He had been sitting on the floor beside the bed, his head resting beside Gerda's shoulder. The big German was on fire, and it didn't take a stethoscope for Gannoway to hear the fluid built up in his lungs. Gannoway half lifted him up from the floor. Fritz moaned loudly, "My head! It's goin' to bust open."

"I'll give you something for that, but first we need to get you out of here."

"No," Fritz said, and he turned to go back to Gerda. "She needs me."

Gannoway signaled for Margaret to help him by taking Fritz's other arm, and between the two of them they got Fritz turned back toward the parlor where he stretched out on the davenport. His feet hung over the edge, and there was little room for turning. It wasn't ideal, Gannoway thought, but it was the best they could do under the circumstances.

Pulling the blanket up around Fritz's chin, Gannoway finally replied to Fritz's comment, "Yes, Fritz, Gerda needs you. She needs you to live through this thing. You've got a family to raise." He patted the big man gently on the chest and then turned to the room just off the kitchen where Gerda lay.

She was bleeding when he walked in. It was one of the worst symptoms, and Gannoway was sure then that Gerda would never hold in her arms the baby she now held in her womb.

The baby—Gannoway felt a surge of that particular private grief he thought he had controlled—the baby could not survive this. Gerda's face was waxen, white, and shiny. The blood trickling from her nose pooled in her ear. Bleeding from the mucous membranes—epistaxis, a word he hadn't thought of since his school days until this flu hit—was one of the striking features of the strange disease. He couldn't tell if she was bleeding from the ears as well. Some patients did, some vomited blood, some hemorrhaged to death in a matter of minutes. It was a terrifying sight even to him, and the family members who witnessed it were traumatized for life—those who lived to remember it. He was glad Fritz was too sick stay with her.

Gannoway held the lamp closer to Gerda's face. He wiped the blood off her face and ear, leaning close to see if more came. Suddenly Gerda's eyes sprung open and her body bucked and twisted on the bed. Bloody water gushed from between her legs and soaked the bed. Gerda's face twisted into a grimace and she groaned with tremendous effort.

"Margaret!" Gannoway yelled. "I need you in here now!" There was no time to decide between Gerda and the baby. The baby's hour had arrived and there was nothing Gannoway could do now but let the imperative of nature take its course.

Father Jungels arrived with incense and holy water and as soon as he stepped into the room Dr. Gannoway knew the priest had never attended a birth, had perhaps never seen a woman naked. The priest held his rosary in front of him as if he were warding off the powers of Satan. He kept his eyes on the ceiling and Gannoway knew it was not the better to see God, but the better to avoid the corporeal being he served. The smell of blood and body wastes in the room was overpowering and the addition of incense stung Gannoway's eyes. He had been present for many Last Rites—the sacrament of Extreme Unction was no stranger to sick rooms even in normal times—but in the past month he'd heard it so many times he'd lost count. The Latin phrases so familiar now he could chant them in his sleep.

As a rule, Gannoway neither welcomed nor begrudged Jungels's presence in a sick room, a lack of distinction that had rankled Jungels and fueled their discussions, but this time when Jungels walked in Gannoway felt something fire inside him, something akin to jealousy. Even as he recognized it he knew he was wrong for feeling it. He tried not to look at Jungels, as if that would lessen his impact in the room, but out of the corner of his eye he could see the priest waving the cross about blindly, his gaze on the ceiling, not the body he blessed. As he anointed Gerda's eyes, ears, mouth, and feet with the Oil of the Sick, he did so with his head turned away. Gannoway felt the urge to shove him out of the way, to protect Gerda from something he didn't understand.

The effects of Extreme Unction, Jungels had patronizingly explained during one of their talks, are to comfort the pains of sickness, to strengthen the sinner against temptation, to cleanse the soul of the remains of sins, and restore health when God sees fit. "Such a tangled web," Gannoway had replied, "for such a powerful being."

How long ago those discussions now seemed.

This day, though, he had no time to consider the complexities of sacraments or science. He had a job to do and he would do it with or without Jungels's aid. The birth itself happened so quickly, at that moment Gerda needed no one's help. The baby, a little girl, slipped easily from Gerda into his waiting hands. She came into this world so quickly that he thought at first something had gone horribly wrong and the thing he held could not be what he hoped it would be. On one push the head had emerged and with the next the dark-haired baby lay cupped in the palms of his hands. She held her tiny fists close to her face, as if she had just finished wiping the vernix from her eyes on her way through the birth canal. Wide-eyed and wiggling, she looked as though she did not want to miss even a second of this wild and precious life she'd been given.

Gannoway breathed in the bright, indescribable smell of her newborn body and was filled with a strange sense of wonder as he held the small bundle of flesh and bone in his two hands. The roundness of her bottom settled snuggly into the hollow of his palm, the umbilical cord pulsed against his wrist. They were alone, this man and this baby. The room around them fell away and he felt himself in the presence of something or someone he could not see or understand.

The dead do not button their own shrouds. The words formed in his mind, but they were not his words.

He breathed in again. The smell of incense and ritual surrounded him. The feeling of someone standing over him grew stronger. Now was the moment of his own daughter's birth—the perfect body of that little girl became the perfect body of this one. Slippery and wet, this baby, his baby, nestled in his hands, and he could feel her alive, eternally alive, even as Gerda's baby stretched into her life in his hands. She lived and lived and lived.

The dead do not button their own shrouds.

Through selfish ritual he had held his little girl to this world. Each year on the anniversary of her birth he had brought her back to the time of her death. Never giving her a beginning, he kept her always at the end. In this Now, he swaddled Gerda's baby in soft muslin. In this Now, in this unknown presence, he buttoned the shroud on his own daughter. He let her go. He loved her and he let her go. Even as he held this wiggling, breathing bundle to his chest, he let her go.

"Dr. Gannoway?" Margaret whispered beside him. She was holding out the blanket she had readied for the baby. Gannoway looked at her, he felt aglow with the promise of new life, a life so much grander than any he had ever imagined, but when he saw the feverish brightness in Margaret's eyes he felt a renewed fear.

"No, Margaret," he said quietly but firmly. "Nothing you've touched can touch the baby." Margaret's shoulders slumped slightly. She didn't argue; she knew she was sick and she knew what that meant. With her head down, she pointed to the dresser behind Gannoway. "There are more blankets there."

Gannoway wrapped the baby gently and turned toward Jungels. He held the little one close to his heart while the priest murmured the prayers of baptism and made the sign of the cross on the baby's forehead. When the priest was finished, Gannoway closed his eyes and searched for answers in the storehouse of his lifetime of learning. He knew the only way to save the baby was to get her away from Gerda. He didn't think Gerda could be saved. He did the only thing he could.

"Take the baby," he said to the priest, his voice heavy with what might have been Faith. "You and John take the baby to town to Mrs. Gaines. She's a widow and she can help." Jungels took a step backward. "It's the baby's only chance," Gannoway said. "We must get her out of this house, away from this illness."

Jungels bowed his head for a moment, perhaps in prayer, then put his arms out stiff and straight in front of him. Gannoway placed the baby on top of his thick arms, expecting him to curl them toward his chest and cradle the baby, but the priest walked out of the room with arms like boards stuck out in front of him.

Gannoway turned his attentions then to Gerda. She coughed now, but the bleeding had stopped. He cupped her feet in his hands, searching for tinges of blue or black, before beginning stitches. In the shadowy room he couldn't be certain, but his heart filled with sadness as he stroked the instep of her darkening foot. He was alone with her in the dim light. Through a space in the curtains he could see the sun was shining; it was past noon.

Outside this room, the house was quiet. Gannoway could hear someone moving about and he knew Margaret had sent another neighbor to replace her. The goodness of these people stung his eyes. He sewed carefully, talking softly to Gerda though he knew she couldn't hear him.

"You've a beautiful baby girl, Gerda," he told her. "She has lots of dark hair and her eyes are almond shaped, just like yours. They're blue now, but dark as midnight. I'll wager they turn brown."

Gerda moaned, trying to speak. "Priest" she said.

"Yes," he answered. "Yes, the priest came." Gerda quieted then and Gannoway noted the change. She knows, he thought, while I struggle to learn. He recalled her previous deliveries, how now would be the time she returned to herself and they would be doctor and patient again. He felt a sense of urgency to say something to her. He wanted to tell her about his baby. He wanted to tell her about his ritual that brought her back to him. He wanted to tell her that she, Gerda, had helped him let his baby go.

"I've never told anyone this," he said. His voice was a soft murmur that Gerda could hear even through the fever and pain. She could not understand the words, but his voice was like a trail of light through the darkness. It became the tether she clung to as she drifted away.

Kaup and Jungels argued for a moment about whether they should take the priest's car or the doctor's buggy, and then they argued about who should drive. Jungels had wanted to give up neither the driver's seat nor the baby, and Kaup was too tired to argue long with him. He finally stood back and let the priest make up his mind.

"I can drive the car. I can handle the buggy. And I can even take care of that there baby you're holding like it's something you don't want to touch." Kaup said testily. "Doc put you in charge, but he didn't tell you to do everything yourself."

Jungels turned in circles in the yard, first facing the car, then the buggy, then John. His black cassock fluttered in the breeze and twisted around his legs.

"My car," he said at last. "It's warmer. You say you know how to drive?" Kaup nodded, though it wasn't completely true. He had ridden with his brother several times and he'd watched carefully. Perhaps it was a result of his limp, the handicap that slowed his walking, but something in him had made things-that-go a specialty of John's. A moment's glance and he knew what to do and how to do it.

"Let's go then." The priest's bottom lip stuck out like a child's. Kaup held the passenger door open for him and waited for him to get settled before cranking the engine. The priest never guessed that this would be John's first time in the driver's seat. He drove carefully, afraid that any sudden stops would send the baby off Father Jungels's arms into the windshield, but he handled the car with assurance as well. He struggled more with his conscience than the vehicle, but the hours ahead would erase that worry.

The speed with which they traversed the two miles to town exhilarated John. It seemed to him that they had just left the Vogels' house and then they were stopping in front of Mrs. Gaines's small white bungalow. He'd had no time to worry about whether or not the widow would take the baby. He was simply doing his job and he was doing it well. He thought about his wife, about telling her about his wild ride into town. He was smiling when he stopped the car. "You wait, and I'll run up and let her know what we've got," John said to Jungels.

Perhaps if he had presented the idea more slowly, instilled in her the direness of the circumstances, the woman would not have shut the door in John's face so abruptly. As it was, he said "flu" and she said "no," and John was standing alone on the porch with a cold wind at his back.

Could he blame her? She'd known Lloyd Paulson, the first man to die of this sickness, since he was a baby. She hadn't known he was sick until she heard he was dead. She had lived in Stuart for forty years, had taught piano for twenty of those years. She knew each of those who had died in the last month by name and many by some individual quirk of their nature—this one insisted on sitting sideways on the piano bench, that one had a tin ear. They'd all been healthy. She'd played bridge with three friends one afternoon and the next day one of them was dead and another was so close to it that she'd never fully recover. Yes, Mrs. Gaines was afraid, more afraid of this flu than she had been afraid of anything in her entire life. That wasn't a baby in Father Jungels's arms, that was a plague, and she'd have no part of it.

John Kaup walked slowly back to the car and stood looking down at the bundle in Jungels's arms. Father Jungels's face went white when John told him what had happened.

"What are we going to do?" John asked.

Jungles stared out the windshield for a moment, then said, "You've got a wife, John. Let's go to her."

John stepped away from the car as if Jungels had pushed him. He shook his head. "Oh no, we can't do that," he said. "My Christina's a good woman, you bet your life, but she don't want any part of this flu." He thought about his cot in the shed back of his own house. He could see his children waving at him through the glass above the kitchen table as he left each day. They had pressed their lips to the glass and he had pressed his to the other side and that was as close as Christina would let him come to his children until he quit this dangerous job.

"No, not Christina," he said again. He didn't want to share any of those memories with the priest, at least not outside the confession box where he would have to look him in the eye when he said the words. He placed his hand on the roof of the car and looked first up the street, then down it.

"There's a new widow in town," he said. "I mean, she's not a new widow." He blushed at his mistake. There was more than one new widow in town. "I mean she's new in town. She works over at Kroger's."

"Mrs. Davies!" Jungels said. "Yes, the woman who used to live in the back of Kroger's store! She's living in that little saltbox the other side of the church. Yes, Mrs. Davies will help us." John rushed to the driver's seat to start again.

It was a bleached blue October day, mercifully warm, and the two men drove through it with hope-laced fear. Nearly an hour old and the baby had not eaten. John looked at it out of the corner of his eye, frightfully aware they could have in their possession a homeless orphan, or a tiny corpse. Why wasn't she crying? he wondered.

This time when he got out of the car he took time to straighten his clothes and smooth his hair. He felt his chin and wished he'd had time to shave that morning. Before he knocked on the door he tried on expressions, hoping one would bring out the sympathy in the woman.

Emily Davies opened the door before he had finished knocking. She must have been standing on the other side of it waiting for him to knock. She wore a navy blue dress of heavy wool that buttoned high on her neck and was cinched tight at the waist. Her eyes were softened at the outer edge with a soft downturn of the eyelids, which should have made them appear kind but instead made them look curtained in some way. John took his hat off and held it to his chest when he spoke. He learned quickly and he wasn't going to make the same mistake twice. He explained the situation carefully from beginning to end, mentioning even that this was the first time he'd ever driven an automobile. He hoped to impress upon her the rarity and urgency of the situation. When he finally stopped talking his mouth was dry and he swallowed audibly.

"So you see," he said, "we need your help."

Emily Davies had watched his face carefully as he talked. When he finished she looked out toward the car where Jungels nodded toward her encouragingly.

"Whose baby did you say that was?" she asked.

"The Vogels' baby, Fritz and Gerda Vogel," he said, nodding his head in agreement with his answer. "You no doubt know them, they trade there at Kroger's. Fritz is a big man." He held his hand up to show how much taller Fritz was than himself. "And Gerda's a lovely woman, dark hair? Got three or four kids already, I forget how many, but she's a good mom to 'em." He kept nodding, hoping the affirmative movement would help her find the answer he needed to hear.

She took a deep breath and crossed her arms low across her chest. Then she smiled, a strange smile. "You say you got a German baby out there that needs somebody to take care of it?"

John felt a chill go through him then and he tried to remember what he'd heard about Emily Davies. She was new to town, but she had relatives here, didn't she? He was not one to listen to gossip and he regretted that now. He looked back to where Jungels waited in the car and wondered if the priest should have been the one to come to the door; someone who knew people better should have this job.

"Well, yes ma'am," he said slowly. "I guess the Vogels are German, no denying that, and they're good folk." He put his hat back on and then took it off again. Emily Davies seemed to be chewing on the inside of her mouth, looking toward the car where the priest and the baby waited. "I'll tell you what," she said as she took a step out onto the stoop, forcing John to step backward. "You take that Hun baby off my property right now. I don't want the germs in my house." She let the outer door slap closed as she stepped back inside. She locked the door from the inside.

John stood staring at the closed door, not sure what to do next. It had been a long day already, he hadn't had a full night's sleep in weeks, there was that baby needing help, and he was tired and scared. Good heavens, was it tears he felt burning his eyes? The thought made him angry and he turned and walked quickly back to the car, his limp pronounced but not slowing him down.

Christina said no, as John knew she would. She had her own family to protect.

"How can you ask this of me, John?" She whispered to keep her own children from hearing what she knew she had to say. Their faces were pressed to the window, trying to see what John held in his arms. It was a bundle of flannel that moved.

"We took it to Mrs. Gaines," he said. "But she said no, she was afraid. And then we took it to Mrs. Davies." He didn't know how to say what had happened on that porch, what he had seen in that woman's face. "What am I supposed to do, Christina? I can't throw this baby into the street, can I?"

Christina looked at him, and then at the baby in his arms. She didn't move closer, but she seemed to soften. John saw it first in the way her shoulders dropped, and then her lips loosened from the straight line she'd held them in, just a little, just enough for John to know, yes, she would help them. He stepped toward her. She put her hand up. "Wait," she said. "Just—wait." She turned away from him and walked to the edge of the porch and with her back to him she bowed her head. When she turned around she reached toward the baby with no reservation in her eyes. "Go," she said, "the doctor needs you."

Her prayers were private. Not even John knew the true nature of her plea then, but the story, the one that was told and told again over the years, was that in the moment of decision, she didn't so much *pray* to the Mother of Jesus, she *bargained* with her. One can imagine her face set like that of a willful daughter. "Protect mine, and I will care for this one," she said, so the story goes. "I will take this baby from a flu house and I will care for it as my own, but save *us*, Mother of Mercy, save *us*."

How could they know that time to bargain was in itself a kind of miracle? The Vogels, Baums, Kaups, and Gannoways did not know, and perhaps never learned, that this deadly virus attacked one out of every five people in the world in the autumn of 1918. The speed and virulence of the illness unsettled even the most hardened veteran of the sick room. Some victims fell sick in the morning and were dead by evening. Others lingered for days in a fevered and painful state while their lungs filled with fluid or their kidneys failed. Despite all efforts of medicine and religion, Death snapped shut its jaws more than 50 million times in service to this Devil Flu, rendering the number of combat casualties in the war that had so frightened them a wan cousin of its horror.

The virus, though they'd welcomed a baby from a house filled with sickness, never sickened the Kaups. They lost neighbors and friends to it. Mrs. Kaup's cousin died in a matter of hours after coming down with a fever. Standing on his own front porch, John could look up and down the street and not see a house that hadn't been infected. The Kaups welcomed the baby and loved her, and when the time came to give her back, they dressed her in a white gown of blue dotted Swiss and carried her, triumphant between them, back to the Vogel farm.

No one knows the exact date the baby came home, but if you take the template of family stories and lay it across a history of the world, you'll be startled by the light of hope that shines through. How the presence of miracles can become a legacy.

"Armistice Declared!" the headlines read the week the family was reunited. After nearly four years, the world had grown not only tired of the brutality of war but also incapable of continuing. The Devil Virus roared throughout the world along a path of troop movement. In America, virtually every army camp was under quarantine. The flu, as much as anything else, had brought the warring nations, at least temporarily, to their knees.

CHAPTER TWENTY

Gerda wakes in a dark place. A pinprick of light wavers in the distance. She remembers a boat ride. Memory returns as she comes ashore at last, but it is a shoreline of bereavement, and she fights her return, refuses to disembark on dry land again.

Her father left her behind. She knows this even though the room is dark and all sound muffled and far away. The rocking motion of the water lulls her back into sleep even as her fear of being abandoned pulls her upward into consciousness like a string attached deep in her chest. Against her will she rises toward light and sound and tries to call out. Her tongue is thick and leaden in her mouth. He'll come back for me, she tells herself, but even as her mind forms the words, she knows it isn't true. Her father left her behind on this boat crossing this unknown river and she is, unequivocally, alone. Heavy coins weigh her eyelids and sadness closes her throat. She begins to cough. Her body fights for air even as her heart splinters into shards of light. Pain. The pain is so great, so encompassing, she knows nothing else, has never been anything other than this body of heat and agony. She twists and struggles to get away from this Now, this beast that is ripping her apart. There is nowhere to go. Every moment, each new movement crushes her.

When next she rises toward the light, she is lying beneath Elizabeth's bed. She recognizes the smell of the birthing room, though she can see nothing. Those screams, Elizabeth's screams, how could she have thought she could forget them? The piercing keen of pain and sorrow would always be with her. This time, though, she would reach Elizabeth. She would say the whole prayer Elizabeth had tried to teach her. She would shout the prayers. This time the Blessed Mother would hear her. Gerda would become Elizabeth and this time Gerda and the prayers would save her. Gerda says the prayers bearing down, says them again breathing in, breathing out. "Oh most gracious . . . ," she murmurs, "was left unaided."

Gerda says the prayers like blood flowing from the body. Just this prayer. Just Gerda. This baby, they would save.

Too late. Too late, pounded the pain in her lungs, her head, her every muscle.

When the baby leaves her, Gerda sleeps, too weak even to reach toward this new creation. The rocking motion of the boat too strong, she can't fight it. She lets the darkness take her.

Sometime later—hours? Days? It doesn't matter, it's all the same—she hears a man's voice, the rise and fall of spoken words, but she knows that can't be true. In death there is only silence. She feels herself drifting closer to the sound, as if his voice is a tether between one world and the next, and though she cannot understand his words, she knows he is talking about loss. She knows there is sadness in his words, and as she comes closer to the shore of this Now, she remembers the baby. The baby died, the voice is telling her, and the pain of grief is so great she pushes herself away again. No, she will not disembark in that land of sorrow. She drifts, but now the rocking motion is that of a moving train. The man in the black homburg hat is sitting beside her and she wants to tell him something. She is reaching for his arm even as he rolls down the long embankment, red blood on white snow.

Dr. Gannoway's voice wakes her. His face is so close to hers, his warm breath fans her cheek. She smells the sweet odor of apples. She opens her eyes and he smiles at her.

"You come back to us, Gerda," he says quietly. "You are strong beyond measure, you come back to us." He slips his arm beneath her shoulders to help her sit up. "You must swallow some of this broth to help you get your strength back."

She closes her eyes and does not open her mouth to the warm moistness he holds to her lips. Such things are for the living and she has no use for this fragile life. So much death. She has always known she would not survive the loss of a child; that particular grief would wear a black robe and carry a scimitar and it would take her to another world. She, like Elizabeth, would not live in this world where her baby did not. Tears slip hotly from the corners of her eyes and the rocking movement pulls her backward into darkness.

Now Fritz's voice brings her back again. It is his voice, but is in some ways a stranger's as well. He is a feeble man who speaks as though each word, each breath comes at great cost. "Gerda," he says softly. "Mrs. Kaup says the baby is getting stronger ever day. Says she hardly ever cries."

Dear Fritz, she thinks sadly. He doesn't know about the baby. He is strong, though, much stronger than she is, and he will survive this loss. It isn't the same for him. She knows he loves his children, but he is always moving forward. He is of the outside world, not really living for the babies. She believes this without rancor, seeing it only as the difference between them. He would find someone to care for the children; perhaps he would make new babies with another woman. As for Gerda, she will not live at all. Her time in this world a part of some past that now belongs to someone else.

She drifts away again, the boat her father had set her in rocks more gently now, its movements not so painful. She feels only a dull ache and a fever that burns less brightly.

She doesn't know how long she's been asleep when she awakes with a start. The room is again dark, but she can see the glow of lamplight in the kitchen. The aromas of dark coffee and frying bacon fill the room. She is so thirsty she can't remember the taste of water. Her lips so dry and cracked they feel scarred.

She closes her eyes and immediately begins to wash the beautiful body of her sister with a lavender-scented cloth. The decades-old blood comes off slowly but reveals the young woman Gerda had loved with her whole heart. She slips a white linen dress over Elizabeth's head, drapes her hair across her shoulders, and picks up her cold, cold hand. The *S*-shaped scar shines white against the redness of her palm and when Gerda touches it Elizabeth whispers, "Gerda. Gerda. Shelter. Shelter."

She is so tired. She wants to rest, and so she turns toward the promise of shelter, but when she opens her eyes again she is staring into the mirror at the foot of the bed. The eyes staring back at her are dark brown. Elizabeth's were gray, deep gray, like Father's.

Gerda. Shelter.

There's a knock on the outside door and then quick light footsteps run toward it. She hears Katie talking and then the boys start to chatter. Each high voice is so different from the other, so alike, so familiar. Gerda is too weak to cry, but that's what she wants to do. She wants to cry with relief knowing the children are alive and well. Her baby is gone, but her older children are still with her. She presses her palms to her eyes and the effort to keep from crying makes her cough. Dr. Gannoway is beside her.

"Look at you, Mrs. Vogel! You're awake." He pulls instruments from his big black bag and watches her face. "We're going to beat this thing, Gerda. You and I are going to win this battle." He talks softly, as one would to a frightened animal. Gerda struggles to sit up.

"Fritz?" Her lip splits when she says his name and it begins to bleed. The sting waters her eyes and she is afraid to say more. What if she had been wrong when she heard him talking? Maybe he too had died. Looking around the room, she begins to recognize the life she had been living. She remembers now the stories that the sickness had taken so many. The whole town had been infected. They had closed the schools, the churches, and businesses too. That all seems so long ago, as if it had been in a different life, lived by someone else.

What if she has lost Fritz too?

"He's strong as an ox," Dr. Gannoway says. "Somewhat of a sick ox, but an ox nonetheless. He had a touch of pneumonia and I almost had to tie him down to get him to take care of himself. Your good neighbors have kept the farm in order. Dan Liable and his hired man even got the potatoes in." Gerda remembers seeing Fritz and the children walking toward her beside the wagon filled with potatoes. The milking, she wonders, who had finished the milking? Gannoway rambles on about who did what for how long. He tells her how often he's been to see her since the baby came. "I thought this flu was going to get you," he says softly. He listens to her breathing, pressing the stethoscope cone to her back. "But I see color in those cheeks of yours that gives me hope."

"The baby," Gerda whispers. She takes a deep shuddering breath. She wants to know if Jungels had gotten here in time to baptize her little one. She wants to know where they had buried it, but that question will not form in her mouth. "The baby," she whispers again, "did the baby get baptized?"

"Oh yes, Jungels came just as he'd promised." Gannoway recalled the priest's actions the day the baby was born. How Father Jungels had kept his gaze so assiduously on the ceiling, not on the woman to whom he rendered the sacrament, and the memory made the doctor laugh. They would never be friends, but they had learned to fight Death side by side. "Don't know what we'd have done without him that day." He pauses, uncertain if he meant to refer to the sacrament or the priest's actions. He holds the memory in his mind, and considers the mysteries it holds. They are his to keep. "You know," he says at last, "I do believe the Kaup family has fallen in love with that little one of yours. Mrs. Kaup told me this morning she was the best baby she'd ever cared for. She said if all babies were that good, she'd have a dozen of them. Never fusses and hardly cries even when she's hungry. She just looks around with those big eyes of hers—did I tell you how much she looks like you?"

Gannoway is repacking his bag as he talks. There are still more patients to see, though the summit of this horror seems to have been reached, and now the world is moving back toward stasis.

Gerda coughs and struggles for breath. She isn't sure she understands him. "The baby's alive? My baby?" She tries to stand, but her legs are made of rubber. Gannoway stops and looks at her, his mouth agape.

"You didn't know?" He sits down beside her. "Oh my dear Gerda."

Knowing what she does about grief, she would have thought his words would heal the hole in her heart. There is joy, yes, and relief, but something else too. She touches the scar in the palm of her hand and the scent of lavender lingers in the room.

She thinks about the prayers she had said like breathing. She remembers the boat ride, her father's back, the wide river she had crossed in pain and sorrow, and even though she hears herself now laughing and crying and asking when she can see the baby, when can she hold her little one, she feels as if some part of her is standing on the other side of that river, looking back at herself, at her family, viewing their joys and their sorrows from a distance. Some part of her now lives in a world she cannot revisit until this body, this mother's this lover's this woman's body, lies down for the last time. The scars of grief blossom at last into a language she can only now bear to understand.

On the wall above her bed hangs a cross, on the floor lies a rag-braided rug, a white cup sits on the table beside her, outside a horse whinnies, the sound of a train curls across the short-grass prairie, a motorcar passes on a road that will become a highway, and the roots of a tree lengthen alongside the leg bones of her sister.

Of what, of what, of what, they all ask, *of what had she been so afraid?*

Dedicated to my mother

Christina Margaretha Vogel Gettert
October 14, 1918–May 8, 2011

BIOGRAPHICAL NOTE

Karen Gettert Shoemaker is the author of *Night Sounds and Other Stories*. Awards for her writing include a Nebraska Press Association Award for Feature Writing, two Independent Artist Fellowship Awards from the Nebraska Arts Council, and a Nebraska Book Award for Short Fiction. Her work has been published in a variety of newspapers and journals, including *The London Independent*, *Prairie Schooner*, *Kalliope* and *The South Dakota Review*, and anthologized in *A Different Plain: Contemporary Nebraska Fiction Writers*, *Times of Sorrow/Times of Grace*, *An Untidy Season*, and *Nebraska Presence: An Anthology of Poetry*.